Download

J. Y. Morgan

Yellow Rose Books

Nederland, Texas

ISBN 978-1-932300-88-8
1-932300-88-0

First Printing 2007

9 8 7 6 5 4 3 2 1

Cover design by Donna Pawlowski

Published by:

Regal Crest Enterprises, LLC
4700 Highway 365, Suite A, PMB 210
Port Arthur, Texas 77642

Find us on the World Wide Web at
http://www.regalcrest.biz

Printed in the United States of America

Acknowledgements:

I would like to thank the Academy of Bards and Midget for hosting my stories online for so many years. Special thanks go to the MerwolfPack, which is a special corner of the Internet emailing world and the place where I met my partner seven years ago. This meeting was the inspiration for the story line.

My gratitude goes to the Regal Crest Enterprises team for publishing this book and for believing in me. Thanks to Donna Pawlowski for a wonderful front cover. I especially want to express my thanks to Jane Vollbrecht for her tireless support, advice, skill, and patience during the editing process. Her words were always welcome and uplifting. Additional thanks are extended to Brenda Adcock for her copy editing skills and helpful opinions. Immense thanks go to Pam Salerno, who jumped in and answered my prayers when I needed an eagle eye and honest advice.

Many thanks are extended to all my friends who supported me when *Learning to Trust* was published and for urging me to pursue the publication of *Download*. I want to thank my friends in England for always being there when I return home and for not forgetting me. To all the hockey players and close friends who have become my American family, I appreciate all the support, love, and laughter you provide my partner and me. I love you all.

Finally, thanks go to my partner and our animals. They allowed me to neglect my chores and sacrifice valuable time with them while I toiled away on the manuscript. Leslie, the support you have given me while I pursue my dream has been wonderful. I love you with all my heart.

To Lester Mary:

My heart and home will always be wherever you,
the hounds, and da boyz are.
Always and forever...

Your Boo xxxx

Chapter One

CORY TURNED THE car radio louder and let the music surround her, soothing frazzled nerves. She reviewed the frustrating day she'd had at the school where she taught—a day that started on a low note and ended up going from bad to worse. It hadn't been the kids' fault really; the job was beginning to get to her—the job, the paperwork...basically everything. Her life, in a nutshell, was boring. Day one of the new school semester was over, and the Christmas holidays seemed now a distant memory.

Cory was jolted back to reality by the sounding of car horns. She moved through the intersection and resumed her commute home. Thirty minutes later, she finally pulled into her driveway, exhausted. As she opened the door to her house, she was welcomed as always by the three cats, hungry for food and company. She patted each one on the head and opened the cupboard, searching for the food that would quiet Mungo, the large tomcat. He demanded his food and cried mercilessly until he received it. The way he mewed, she worried the neighbors would think she never fed him. Cory was thankful Sam had taken their long-haired German shepherd, Holly, to work with him. At least she didn't have to fit an evening walk into her plans.

When the cats were fed and purring their satisfaction, Cory turned her attention to her needs. She made a mental note of all the jobs she needed to do that night. She had to cook, do the laundry, mark the newest pile of English and maths books, and read her e-mail. After making herself a cup of tea, she settled in the living room. She turned on the television for background noise, placed her laptop on the coffee table, and hunkered down for a bit of quality 'Cory' time.

The computer slowly downloaded the e-mails. Many were about a story set in an ancient civilization on an author's fan list. Cory had recently joined the list. While the author was taking a break in writing, the members of the list had begun a role-playing skit. Currently, the skit involved searching for the story's main characters' young daughter who was lost in the woods. Some of the list members had joined forces to pretend to look for the child. The exchanges had turned comical, with people battling the bad guys with chocolate bombs and candy bars. Cory's eyes drifted over the e-mails, a smile beginning to curl on her lips as she read the ongoing activities of the skit. Cory was desperate to join the fun. The people on the e-mail list appeared friendly, but Cory lacked the nerve to reply to any she read. She felt intimidated by other people's boldness. She scanned farther down, and an e-mail caught her eye. The humor of the e-mail jumped out at her, and she realized she had a goofy grin on her face.

```
From: Dylan Matthews

    Please let me join in the search, I will leave no
stone unturned in my search for the little one...
```

The rest of the e-mail was a blur. Cory knew this was her opportunity to join in the game. She quickly composed a return e-mail.

```
From: Cory Williams

    I, too, would like to join the search. Wouldn't
four eyes be better than two? Dylan and I could start
our own team or jump in with another group. Looking
forward to playing with you all,
Cory
```

Hurriedly, she pressed the send button before she chickened out. *Move one made...I hope they let me play.* She read the remaining e-mails in her inbox. Weary from the day's toil, she leaned back into the sofa, turned her attention to the television, and struggled to keep her eyes open.

She was in a field full of poppies. The smell was fresh, and the view ahead was the color of blood. Into this vision walked a tall, dark-haired woman, a conflict of emotions warring over her face. She appeared to be tormented or angry. Cory leaned toward the woman and touched her hand. Her presence seemed to appease the taller woman. Cory felt the peace; the woman's anger soothed. The woman turned, and sapphire eyes smiled down. Cory felt like she was drowning...

The sound of loud purring nudged Cory out of her slumber. She opened bleary eyes, only to be confronted with another pair—not as wonderful as the image she'd just experienced and the breath not so sweet. "Hey, Mungo, come for your evening cuddle, have you?" She stroked the soft coat of her dominant, black and white long-haired cat. The cat, undeterred, continued to nudge and claw his way up her chest. "Oh boy, not now, honey. Mum's got to work."

Cory sat up, a little disoriented from her unexpected sleep. She wiped stray cat hairs from her mouth and tried to place the irrepressible cat on the seat beside her. "Daddy will be home soon. I know you want some fuss, but if I don't correct these books tonight, I'll never get it done." With a few more strokes, Mungo got comfortable and settled into the cushion, resting his head on Cory's lap.

Cory checked the time on the DVD player. She'd been asleep for an hour. Disappointed, she glanced at the floor; thirty-four creative writing books still to check. It was going to be one hell of a long evening.

"BLOODY TRAFFIC. WHY they have to work on the roads in the middle of rush hour is beyond my logic! The fucking motorway was packed bumper-to-bumper. I'm starving. What's for dinner, Cor?"

Cory blanched. She'd become so engrossed with her work that she'd lost track of time. "I'm sorry, Sam. I got caught up in my marking," replied Cory, knowing she was about to get a lecture.

"For Christ's sake, Cor. You and your school work." He looked disdainfully at the computer. "I see you found time to download and read your e-mails. I guess I come pretty low on your priorities now. The one day I ask you to do something around the house, and you forget." He slammed the door, and Cory heard his footsteps bang on the stairs.

Cory put her work back into her school box. She'd have to go in early the next day and complete the remaining books. She entered the kitchen and was nearly toppled over by Holly's enthusiastic greeting. Cory knelt down and let the dog lick her face a few times. She stroked the long fur, calming the excited dog with quiet murmurs. Once the dog had settled, Cory rummaged around in the kitchen junk drawer for the Indian takeout number. She knew her husband well, and she could easily pacify him with a curry and a few beers.

To Cory's surprise, when Sam came downstairs an hour later, his mood appeared brighter. "Hey," she said.

Sam flipped the dial on the television, smiled at her, and picked up the dinner tray from the coffee table. "Hey, yourself."

Cory watched a few moments of the rugby game Sam had switched to. She waited until he finished eating. "I'm sorry about earlier, Sam. You know how it gets at the beginning of a new term. I was so exhausted, I fell asleep. I think I'm still trying to recover from New Year's Eve." She cuddled up to him and pulled his arm around her waist.

Sam kissed her lightly on her head. "It's alright. I miss you sometimes."

Cory rested her head on his chest. "That's an odd comment. We just spent two weeks together." She waited for Sam to reply, replaying his comment in her mind. It was ironic in a way, as she thought they spent too much time together. *We're in each other's pockets.*

"We were in the same house, but you spent all the time on that computer. I barely spoke to you," Sam said bitterly, never taking his eyes off the television.

Cory straightened up, removing Sam's hand from her abdomen. "That's not fair. You were working upstairs. I tried to make plans with you, but you were busy."

"I'm sorry, Cor. I didn't mean to hurt you," Sam said. "I think that came out harsher than it was supposed to. You do understand that I have to work when I'm home, love..."

"But you were on holiday," Cory interjected. "I get lonely on the holidays, and you were busy. Why shouldn't I find some friendship groups of my own?"

Sam patted Cory's leg. "Maybe we should make some sort of New Year's resolution to spend more time together. Then you wouldn't need to spend time online with imaginary friends."

Cory stood up, offended. "They're not imaginary. They're very much alive." Pausing she counted silently to ten, trying to calm the anger that churned in her. "I miss having friends around, Sam."

Sam held his hand up to Cory. "You have friends, love. I thought you were happy. You used to love spending time with me."

Cory squeezed Sam's hand reassuringly and sat back down. "I do enjoy time with you. However, I realized last summer how few friends we have who live near us. I wish I could see my old college friends more, but we're scattered all over the country. The Internet keeps us connected. I get to chat to them daily, and it doesn't cost much. I get to see the kids grow when they share photos."

"But you still see them."

"I know, but not often." Cory jumped in, cutting him off before he could continue. They had been through this conversation before.

"You have Rachel," Sam added.

Cory sighed. Sam didn't understand her social needs. "It's not the same. We're colleagues and friends. We see each other all day and talk about work. We meet at the gym or down the pub, and we still talk about work, the students, or life...with you."

Sam pulled his hand away. "What's wrong with talking about us?"

Cory blew out a frustrated breath. "There's nothing wrong with talking about us. I just want to be seen as an individual sometimes. I want people to be interested in me and my interests, not always us. That's why I like meeting new people online. These people are my friends. They don't view me as part of a couple. I'm an individual in their minds. I get excited at the thought of finding out new things about people. I love the new social aspect the Internet offers." As she thought about these new friends, her mind drifted back to her new contact that she'd mailed earlier in the evening.

"I still don't get it, Cor. We have each other and the animals. Most people would give their right arm for that. You always want more. We're fine as we are. We don't need more people in our lives."

Cory rubbed Sam's arm reassuringly. "I know." *You're never going to see my side. Your needs are so different.* "I have more work to do, so I'm going upstairs to the office where I hope I can knock off a chunk of it before bed."

Chapter
Two

THE FOLLOWING MORNING, Cory was delighted to see an e-mail from Dylan on the group list. She nervously opened it.

```
Dylan Matthews
Subject: Chocolate War

Hi Cory,
    I'm so excited to have you on board. We're going
to be team mates. Let me know how you want to play
the next move.
    Looking forward to having some fun,
Dylan
```

With that thought in her head, Cory trudged off to another day at school.

CORY GLANCED AT her watch. It would be another two hours before she could get home and download her e-mails. *You're becoming obsessed. Focus on your lessons and the kids. It's just a stupid game.* The weather was lousy, a typical winter's day in England, but for once, she was pleased that it was raining hard. Due to the torrential downpour, she cancelled her after school netball club and got an early get-away.

As soon as she got home that evening, Cory scanned down her ever-growing e-mail list. The day had been a busy one for traffic on her list. Her heart began to pound when she saw a private e-mail from Dylan Matthews. *Calm down. It's just an e-mail. Anybody would think the Queen had sent it.* She opened the e-mail.

```
Dylan Matthews
Subject: The Search

Hi Cory,
    I hope you don't mind the private mail, but we
keep missing each other on the group mail. I thought
maybe if we got together and did a joint report in
```

regards to the "Chocolate War," we'd be able to come
up with some good ideas and possibly get a good
response from other players. I've been reading the
posts you've sent to the list since you joined the
skit. Your writing style is very good—much better
than mine—I struggle to express my ideas in words.
What do you think? If you'd rather work on your own
reports, I understand. I hope you don't mind me doing
this off list.
Dylan

Cory read the rest of the posts concerning the role-play and then
went back to Dylan's e-mail. She read it twice before hitting the reply
button.

Cory Williams
Re: The Search

Hey Dylan,
    Thanks for the e-mail. I was going to e-mail you
privately tonight, so you beat me to it. Great minds
think alike. I think it's a good idea to work
together. You can translate some of these American
sayings, as I'm in the UK, and there are some words
which I have no idea what they mean (vbg), and I'll
do the writing.
    One question I've been dying to ask: what is in
the bar of chocolate that everyone is going on about?
Hershey's, I think they're called. We don't have them
over here. I have to admit, I'm not really one for
chocolate, but we'll keep that a secret between ourselves (g).
    Keep sending me ideas, and I'll put them into
sentences. I like your humour. It made me laugh. It
was one of the reasons I joined the role-playing. So
what do you want to do next?
Cory

Cory reread the e-mail before hitting the send button. She checked
her watch and knew there'd be no point in waiting for a reply because
of the time difference between the UK and the States. She had no idea
what Dylan did for a living or where he or she lived in the United
States. She cleared out her inbox and then did some schoolwork.

CORY PLACED THE tray of dinner and a beer in front of Sam. She
tried making polite conversation, but he was too engrossed in the latest
Premiership Football match. She settled onto the other small sofa. While
drinking her glass of Guinness, she found her mind drifting back to the
e-mail, or to be precise, the e-mail sender, Dylan. It was kind of mysteri-

ous. She didn't even know if her new contact was a male or female. She found herself wondering whether she wanted Dylan to be a man or woman. *What does it matter? You can never have too many friends.*

She watched the game, and then tried to get into the shoot 'em up film, *Reservoir Dogs*, that Sam had flicked to on the Sky Network. After an hour, she couldn't stomach the sheer violence and death that seemed to appear in every scene. "I'm going to bed," she stated.

"It's early. Why don't you come over here and have a cuddle? You've hardly said two words to me tonight," Sam grumbled.

Cory stood up and stretched. "It takes two to have a conversation." She smiled at him to show she was joking, but in her heart she knew she wasn't. Their nights recently had been just this: the television and cans of beer. "I'm beat, and this film's not my cup of tea. I'm going to read. Take your time." She bent over his reclined body on the sofa and kissed his cheek.

"Night, love. I'll be up soon."

"Sure." Cory wiggled her fingers at him in a goodbye gesture, but Sam's eyes never left the television.

Cory climbed the stairs, and on her way past the office, she collected her laptop from her desk. *One more download. What's the harm in that?* On her way upstairs, she'd decided to check her e-mail in bed where she could relax without Sam making comments. Within five minutes, she was comfortable, and her inbox began to fill with thirty-five messages. Her eyes scanned down the list, and the penultimate name was the one she'd been searching for: *Dylan Matthews*. She anxiously double-clicked on the title.

```
Dylan Matthews
Re: The Search

Hey Cory,
     How's it going? Thanks for the reply. I was a
little worried about sending you a private e-mail,
but I was pleased that you agreed. In regards to our
battle plan, how about we go further out and do a
wider search of the forest. We'll pack lots of sup-
plies and stuff. You're good at writing, so if you
can write a couple of descriptive paragraphs outlin-
ing our plans, we'll be good to go. What do you
think?
     As for the chocolate, I'll keep that between the
two of us (vbg). How can you not know about Her-
shey's?
     I thought I'd introduce myself. I'm 32, female,
and work as a computer technician at a corporate
sports apparel company. How about yourself?
     Hope to speak to you later,
Dylan
```

Cory hit the reply icon without a moment's hesitation, but then she paused, unsure of what to write. She had a lot of questions she wanted to ask, but didn't want to scare Dylan off by being too nosy.

```
Cory Williams
Re: The Search

Dylan,
     Great ideas. I'll think some of them over and put
some thoughts down in an e-mail. As for me, my days
are hectic at the moment. It is heading towards a
busy time at work. I'm a primary school teacher, so
real life and kids keep getting in the way. Don't
they know there's a chocolate war on (g)?
     About myself. I'm 29, but not for long. My birth-
day is right around the corner. I'm about 5' 5",
blondish, short hair, and green eyes. My partner's
name is Sam. How about yourself?
Cory
```

She glanced at her watch. Ten-thirty p.m. Not much chance of any return e-mail. She picked up her book to read. She knew it wouldn't be long before she'd fall asleep, and the next day was her regular Friday session at the gym after school, so she needed the rest.

Chapter
Three

FRIDAY'S LESSONS FLEW by. For the most part, Cory had enjoyed her day; however, she'd found herself distracted at times. She'd had memories of a recurring dream that she couldn't shake: images of bright blue eyes gazing into hers and of the smell of brass and leather. If she closed her eyes, she could picture a fur rug and hear the sounds of birds chattering on a spring morning, but she had no idea why these images kept recurring. For the past three nights, she'd had the same dream, and she'd been reluctant to get out of bed in the mornings.

Cory looked in the gym mirror. She traced the faint outline of definition across her stomach. As she dressed, she thought about the brief message in her inbox that morning from Dylan stating that her evening had been busy, but she'd promised Cory a more detailed e-mail when she arrived at work. Cory's pulse was racing. *I must have pushed myself too hard. I hope I'm not coming down with something.*

Sam was waiting for her as she stepped outside the gym. The cool winter's night air was bracing, and she found herself wishing she'd put her track pants back on. She jumped into the passenger seat. "Hey, honey, how was work?" She leaned over to kiss him, but he turned his head to check for cars behind him.

After negotiating the other cars that were entering and leaving the crowded gym parking lot, Sam answered her question. "It was okay. Business is picking up."

"That's good, isn't it?" Cory queried.

Sam shrugged his shoulders. "Depends how you see it. On the one hand, I'll be working loads of overtime, but on the other hand, it'll cut into our time together." Sam was a salesperson for a large company that sold bricks and blocks to building corporations. While he could do the majority of his job at home using the phone and computer, he still had to check in on work sites and meet with clients. These meetings often took him away from home.

Cory ran her fingers gently across the graying flecks at the side of his dark brown hair. "You'll manage. It's why you're so good at your job. You know how busy I get this term at work. We've always managed before." With no reply forthcoming, Cory settled into an awkward silence with thoughts of the past year running through her mind. *We're stuck in a rut. When did life become so boring?*

At the house, Sam parked his car next to Cory's. She rarely drove to school any more, as Sam dropped her off and picked her up.

"I'm going to walk Holly. The dinner's all prepared; just try to remember to turn on the oven before you get engrossed in your e-mail."

Cory thought she detected a hint of sarcasm in his voice, but he'd gone into the house to collect the rambunctious dog. Pushing the comment aside, she entered the house.

Her e-mail downloaded while she put the lasagna in the oven. She walked over to the kitchen table and stared intently at the screen. An e-mail from Dylan was in the list. She noted the time. It had been sent only five minutes before.

```
Dylan Matthews
Subject: About me

Hey Cory,
     What can I tell you about me that won't put you
back to sleep? As I told you, I'm 32 (an older
woman!) I'm an only child, spoiled, as any only child
should be. My life is very settled at the moment. I
have a partner; her name is Sarah. We live near Bos-
ton, in Massachusetts, in a small but cozy ranch
house.
     I once lived in Germany for three years. I never
got to go to England. I've lived in Houston, Texas,
and also California. I moved back home to be with my
father after my mother died.
     Sarah and I bought this house a few years ago.
We've been lucky in that the things we do to the
house are because we want to do them not because we
have to. I'm in the middle of redecorating and fur-
nishing the computer room. Picture me sitting in my
guest bedroom filled with piles of junk. My monitor
is on a plastic file cabinet, and I'm sitting cross-
legged with the keyboard on my lap. Not very comfort-
able, I might add. My butt is numb.
     I grew up in a small town, and I went to college
for four years at Providence College. I love sports.
I played softball (baseball for women) and ice
hockey. I love ice hockey. I did try soccer, but I
wasn't that great at it.
     We don't have any pets; Sarah is allergic to the
fur. We have been together for five years. We are
kind of opposites.
     I hope that my relationship with Sarah doesn't
bother you. I didn't want to lie. That's not the way
friendships are made. This is always hard for me, not
knowing if somebody will dislike me because of my
lifestyle. I mean, if they don't like me because they
```

think I'm a jerk, that's okay. That I can handle. Homophobia I have an issue with!

Thanks for posting a report this morning. You write well, but then again, you're a teacher, and you're supposed to know these things.

If you write down what to do about the "war," we can work out a report and then maybe we can chat over the weekend. Saturday would probably be a good day. Let me know what you think.

Okay, time for me to ask a question. You said you had a partner called Sam, and I'm assuming you're a female, although Cory could be a name for a boy or a girl. Is Sam male or female?

Hope to hear from you soon,

Dylan

Cory read the e-mail slowly, digesting the information, and then she hit the reply button.

Cory Williams
Re: About me

Dylan,

Have to say I like the name Dylan. As for your partner, why would I have a problem with it? We met on a list that features stories and topics about het-ero and same-sex relationships. Personally, I believe that there is little love in the world as it is, and so if you find it, you should go for it. Doesn't mat-ter what their colour or gender or what language they speak. Love is rare, so you ought to treasure it.

Sam is my husband; we've been together five years. I noticed it's the same amount of time you've been with Sarah. (It must have been a good year for relationships). He's my best friend, and we get on great most of the time.

I've been teaching for seven years, and love it. I live in the middle of England, and although the weather drives me crazy at times, I like it.

That's enough about me. I'm about to take a bath and relax. I'm absolutely shattered; I've been to the gym. I ran well, and my figure is slowly getting back into shape.

I'm around all evening and weekend if you want to chat.

Take care.

Cory

In the bathroom, Cory lowered her tired body slowly into the small tub. She closed her eyes, and it didn't take long for her to relax into a light sleep.

She felt someone hugging her from behind; a head rested lightly on her shoulder. She could feel the breath of the person gently caressing her ear. She breathed in deeply, and although the smell was familiar, it wasn't Sam's. It was a sweet, mildly floral smell, like baby's talcum powder. The arms, although strong, were longer than Sam's and much softer; she felt safe. The arms around her suddenly tightened, and she felt herself warm to the touch of the body pressed against hers. Silky lips started nibbling her ear...

Cory awoke with a start, a mixture of emotions coursing through her body. One unmistakable feeling was that of arousal. *It's been too long since you've had any action. Now you're having erotic dreams.* She shook her head to try to dispel the feelings. When that didn't work, she ducked her head under the water. Finally, she took her body wash and gently scrubbed the sweat off her body. Once finished, she stepped out of the bath and dried herself quickly, grabbing her bathrobe as she left the bathroom. She stopped on the landing for a few moments contemplating her next move. The urge to do one more download of e-mail before she settled downstairs for the evening was irresistible.

There weren't many e-mails, but that didn't matter. The name she'd hoped to see appeared on screen.

```
Dylan Matthews
Subject: Friday

Hi Cory,
    Good evening, well, it's still afternoon my time,
but you must be halfway through your evening. This
time difference thing is kind of weird.
    A quick question. Does "shattered" mean "really
tired," because in the States it usually means
"drunk," which I think you use the term "pissed" for,
which means "really mad" here. I think I might need
to employ a translator soon (vbg). This friendship
should be entertaining at least, and a learning expe-
rience, too.
    I'm still at work, so I'd better go and look
busy. By the time I get home, you'll be tucked in
bed, having sweet dreams (I hope). I guess since
tomorrow is Saturday, we should be able to meet up
and swap e-mails about midday onwards. I'm not too
busy this weekend.
    The weather over here is amazing. The snow is
coming down thick and fast. What's the weather like
on your end?
    Hope your evening goes well,
Dylan
```

Cory smirked when she read the line about being shattered. *Imagine the old ladies at the gym if I'd been drinking before working out.* She had so many questions she wanted to ask Dylan. So many things she wanted to tell Dylan. *Would Dylan be interested? Would Dylan understand her past choices?*

```
Dear Dylan,
    I guess I should tell you more about myself.
```

Unsure of how to begin such a personal e-mail, Cory shut down the computer and chose to wait for the morning and a fresher mind. She headed downstairs to a mundane evening with Sam.

A CAT SHIFTED against Cory's legs. Cory lifted her tired head off the pillow and opened sore, gritty eyes. She took a few moments to focus on her alarm clock. *Typical. It takes a sledgehammer to wake me on a school day, and on weekends, a pin could drop, and I'd know about it.* She laid her head back on the pillow, turning it slightly to see if Sam was still asleep. He slept very lightly, and every sound or move usually woke him. After a few more minutes, she could feel her bladder pressing against her stomach. She gently lifted the duvet off her and tried to quietly shift her body out of the bed.

"What's up?" asked Sam, groggily. "You alright?"

"I tried not to disturb you." Cory slipped her feet into the pair of slippers tucked neatly beside the bed. Despite the central heating, she could feel the winter chill of morning.

"You fidgeted a lot last night. Bad dreams?" Sam turned over to regard his wife, concern edging his voice.

"I don't know what's wrong. Maybe it was something I ate. My stomach feels sickly." Cory leaned over and kissed his rough, unshaven cheek. "Go back to sleep. I'll sort the animals out. No need for us both to suffer."

"Come back to bed. I'll rub your tummy if you want," offered Sam.

"No, I'll only move around, and you look tired. How about I make a cup of tea?"

Sam muttered a reply under his breath, but Cory couldn't hear it.

She got out of bed, and a waiting menagerie of animals followed her into the bathroom and then downstairs, where the cats sat patiently on the kitchen counter and Holly danced at the door. After making sure each cat had its own bowl and letting the dog out into the garden, Cory switched the kettle on and took two mugs off the mug tree. She placed a teabag and spoon of sugar into each mug. She took a pint of milk out of the refrigerator and poured a small amount in the mugs.

A deep bark caused Cory to glance up from her task. She could see Holly's face pressed against the patio door. She opened the door and placed Holly's food on the floor. Then she poured boiled water into the

mugs and stirred each one. She placed their mugs of tea on a tray and
headed back upstairs.

Cory deposited Sam's tea on the bedside table beside his slumbering body and went across the hall to their office. She scanned her e-
mails. A sense of disappointment descended when she noticed that
there were none from Dylan. *Cut it out, you idiot. You owe her an e-mail.*
After a review of Dylan's e-mail from the day before, Cory set about
writing her response.

```
Cory Williams
Subject: A little history

Hi Dylan,
    I had trouble sleeping for some reason. I keep
getting these dreams, and they wake me up. I usually
remember my dreams, but for some reason, I can't
quite piece this one together.
    I guess it'd be good to give you some background
about me.
    I lived and went to school in the small town of
Warwick, which is the next town to Stratford—upon-
Avon (where William Shakespeare was born and lived).
    As for college, I always knew I wanted to teach.
However, I was unsure which subject to study. I even-
tually talked to one of my teachers, and she sug-
gested I study Physical Education. She reminded me
how short of an attention span I have, and she
thought P.E. would keep me interested. It did, and I
survived the four years of study. I've been teaching
in the same school for nearly eight years.
    Sam and I met on New Year's Eve five years ago.
I'd gone down to visit friends in Wales and got
drunk. I met Sam that night. We have lots in common,
although we are complete opposites. He's a very
quiet, solitary person who likes his own company. Me,
well, I can talk for England. He doesn't speak to any
of his family, except his father, and I'm from a very
close family. You can't go a week without phoning
home, or else they send out a search party. This
infuriates the hell out of Sam, as everyone knows
everyone else's business, but at least I know I'm
loved. So how did you and Sarah meet?
    I am a middle child and suffer from the middle
child syndrome, never the first to do anything and no
longer the baby of the family. My sister, Kerry, is
my full sister; my mum has been married twice. My
real father left when I was one, and I haven't seen
him since. My mum married a wonderful man three years
later, and he has been great. It's nice to know he
chose us and knew what he was getting. They've just
```

celebrated their 25 years together. They fight like cats and dogs, but they do love each other. My brother, Mike, is five years younger than me.

When my mum and biological dad split up, we went to live with my grandparents, and they kind of brought us up. We would spend every weekend with them. My granddad is my hero. When we were younger, my sister would spend hours helping my nan (grandmother to you, I'm sure) in the house with the cooking. It's probably why she went into the catering business. As for me, I was always out with my granddad doing deals and scams. I love both Granddad and Nan dearly. Unfortunately, my nan has passed away, and it hurts so much that Granddad is now very ill. He has terminal cancer of the stomach.

Enough about my history for the moment. I'm planning on having a lazy day, but whenever I plan these, something always crops up.

Oh yeah, excuse my ignorance, but what states surround Massachusetts? I never spell this correctly. The spell checker always picks it up. And I call myself a teacher!

I must stop rambling or this will never get sent.

What do you think we ought to do next with our reports? You're the older, so you decide. (vbg)

You said it was snowing in your last e-mail so I hope the snow's not too deep. It's quite a nice looking but cold day here. I'll speak to you later.
Cory

PS: I missed hearing from you in my morning mail. In the future, I'll have to make sure I e-mail you before I go to bed.

Chapter
Four

THE REST OF the weekend went by in a blur for Cory. By Sunday evening, she'd become frustrated with her lack of time on the computer and eagerly seized her first available moment to read her e-mails. She opened Dylan's.

```
Dylan Matthews
Re: A little history

Hey there,
     I'm sorry about the lack of e-mails. I played ice
hockey on Friday evening and got taken out in a
vicious attack. Nothing too serious—a bang to the
head, which made me sick, and a bruised hand. Still,
that's the price I pay for playing such a physical
game. You should see the other girl. The doctor sug-
gested I rest the hand, so typing was out.
     I haven't had a lazy day in a long time. Good for
you. Did you get to do nothing, or did real life take
over? As for rambling, I'm not one for idle conversa-
tion, but with you it seems very natural. I've always
been told I'm very hard to get to know—that I keep
too much to myself. What I like about our e-mails is
the fact that we're part of the skit, but also we're
getting to know each other. It is a little more per-
sonal.
     As for family, my mother was diagnosed with a
tumor on her kidney about seven years ago. That's the
renal cell area. She had it removed. I was living in
Germany at the time; luckily I had planned a vacation
(holiday) for six weeks at the same time. The doctors
told us they got all of the tumor and cancer. Four
and a half years later, they found it was growing
back. In the meantime, I was back in the States, but
living in Texas. To make matters worse, I was think-
ing about moving to California. I asked my mother
what she thought I should do. She said to go. I saw
her the Christmas before she died, but by then, she
was in the hospital and not doing well. I left to go
```

back to California, and two weeks later, my father called to tell me to come home. I didn't get to see her before she died. She died on January 10. I moved back home in April. I will never leave my family again. I never realized how important my family is to me, and I never want to miss any of it. I hope that makes sense. Sarah was very close to my mother, and she was so upset. I was in such shock I don't really remember any of it. I knew I had to be strong for my father. It took me almost a year before it sank in, and I let myself really cry.

I don't speak to my friends from college that much, but my friends from elementary school I do. I've known them for 25 years. So if this friendship thing between us works out for us (looks good so far), you might be stuck with me as a friend for a long time. You still have time to back out.

As for our search section of the "war," I have no idea what to do next. Give me some time to think about it. Do you have any ideas? Just because I am the elder doesn't mean I always know what is best.

In answer to your question, Massachusetts is in the Northeast, also known as the New England states. We are on the east coast. The beach is 20 minutes from my house. We are near New Hampshire, Vermont, New York, Rhode Island, Connecticut, and Maine.

The snow isn't too bad, but it's very cold outside. There has been a warning for frostbite.

My computer room won't paint itself, so I need to tear myself away from the computer and do it. I'm going to hit the gym later. While I'm there, I may come up with some more ideas for our report to the list. I hope I am not too shattered afterwards. (Using my new favorite word).

Have a great evening, Cory. Talk you later today—probably tonight for you.
Dylan

Cory reread the e-mail. When she got to the third paragraph, she felt a lump form in her throat. The e-mail had touched her heart, and she desperately wanted to give Dylan a hug. *I must be getting my period. I hardly know the woman.* However, the honesty and openness in their e-mails were comforting. She hit the reply button:

Cory Williams
Subject: Bored across the pond

Hi,
    Sorry to hear about your accident. I haven't had a chance to check my e-mails until now. No lazy day

for me. I did manage to finally clean the house, and
we desperately needed to tile the utility room. Our
dog, Holly, is a longhaired German Shepherd. When it
rains, she gets very wet and muddy when she goes
through the farmer's fields on her walks. When she
comes through the back door, she rubs against the
cream walls and leaves dirty marks on them. It was a
pretty easy tiling job. Sam and I worked together
like a well-oiled machine. It's a shame we don't do
other things as easily. I did spend plenty of time
with my granddad, and then went out with a few mates
for some drinks.

I also went to the gym. I went through a stage
when I first met Sam where I spent a lot of time com-
muting to his house. This meant my gym and sport time
decreased. Sam and I got into a comfortable life
together, and the weight crept on. Fortunately, I
have caught the fitness bug again and now go to the
gym regularly throughout the week. I have to say, I'm
beginning to notice the difference in my body. I'm
very impressed you play ice hockey. I used to watch a
little bit when I stayed at my grandparents' house.
What position do you play?

Your last e-mail touched me when you spoke about
your mother. My nan passed away a month after your
mother. I'm still having a hard time dealing with it.
I feel bad that I didn't go to see her body at the
funeral home. It hurt too much. Now we're reliving
the pain with my granddad's illness. One day I hope
we can talk about it face-to-face, as I haven't
talked much about my nan's death. I think you'd
understand my feelings.

However, today I feel like we need to lighten the
mood, and I am one very bored person over here. UK
television is not fantastic on a Sunday night. Even
Sky Satellite is crap.

So you drew the short straw, as I figured I'd
waffle on a bit more.

What are your musical tastes? My musical tastes
include pretty much anything. Here are some of my
favourites: Cher, Annie Lennox, The Beautiful South,
Robbie Williams, Celine Dion (but I'm only admitting
that to you), Dolly Parton, Bette Midler, Pink, and
Texas, to name but a few.

I have too many films to name a favourite. I like
romances and action/adventures. I like movies that
have strong female role models. I do enjoy science
fiction movies, too.

I love watching and listening to comedians. My
favourites are Billy Connolly, Alan Davis, Victoria
Wood, and Jasper Carrot. All British-based ones. Have

you heard of any of them?

My ultimate favourite TV show was *Cagney and Lacey*. I loved it! (I was in Sharon Gless's fan club, yet another secret I'm revealing.) I like science fiction shows, particularly *Star Trek—Next Gen* and *Voyager*, *Stargate SG-1*, and *Battlestar Galactica*. However, I'm not on any online stuff. I enjoy watching soap operas, especially *Eastenders* and *Emmerdale*. They're UK shows, and you wouldn't know them. I like them as they make my life seem wonderful because every character is usually going through a crisis.

Anyway, I hope I haven't sent you to sleep. I am enjoying getting to know you. You said you were redoing your office. How's the refurbishment going?

Have a good evening. Mail you tomorrow. I might send some pictures of me (be scared—be very scared).
Cory

"Are you listening to me? Earth to Cory."

Sam's voice jolted Cory back to reality. "Sorry, what did you say?" She focused her attention on Sam, who was stretched out on the three-person sofa. She settled farther back into the other two-seater, but her movement was halted because Holly was sleeping behind her. The dog's quiet snores reverberated against Cory's back.

"I said do you want to watch *Silent Witness*? It's the new series. You were miles away. What are you doing?" Sam said in an irritated tone.

"You know I told you about that role-playing in the group I've joined in. Anyway, I met someone on there, and we've joined forces." Cory caught the smirk on Sam's face. "Don't laugh. I'm having fun, and she seems really nice. Her name's Dylan."

"She could be a guy for all you know."

"No, she's definitely female and lives with her partner, Sarah, in America." Cory said the last part rather quickly.

Sam coughed a little. "You mean she's a lesbian?"

"That's usually what it's called when two women live together. Why are you pulling that face?"

"It's not natural, Cor. Gives me the willies."

"At least it's you getting the willies. They certainly don't want them." She grinned at him and decided it was time to change the subject. She looked at her watch. It was too early to go up to bed, but too late to really do anything productive.

Cory closed the top of the laptop and stretched her arms above her head. She moved over to Sam's sofa and lay down beside Sam. She waited for him to reposition his body to accommodate her slightly smaller frame. Then she snuggled up against him and watched *Silent Witness*.

An hour later, she was yawning and very comfortable. She wasn't actually cuddling with Sam. It was more like she was using him as a pillow. His arm was around her, but there was no pressure, and he hadn't shown any interest in stroking her hands—or anything else. It was comfortable—like an old friend. This worried her. If she'd wanted just friendship, she'd have married her best friend, Angela. She slid onto the floor and crawled to the laptop.

"Where're you going?" Sam demanded.

"I'm going to check my e-mail one more time. I have a feeling Dylan might have mailed me."

"You're always on that bloody thing. We never spend time together."

"We've just spent an hour watching the television. What do you want us to do?"

"Nothing, but it'd be nice if you paid me as much attention as you do your e-mail mates."

"Here's the deal. I'll check my e-mail, and then we'll have an early night. You feeling amorous?" She watched as he suddenly found the remote control interesting and began surfing the channels.

"Look, the golf's still on. You check your e-mails; don't worry about me."

Cory shrugged. It worked every time. All she had to do was mention the prospect of sex, and Sam suddenly found something else to do. It usually depressed her, but at this moment, she was focused on one thing: an e-mail from Dylan. *I know there's a mail there. I just know it!* She downloaded and didn't have to wait too long.

```
Dylan Matthews
Re: Bored across the pond

Hey there,
    I am glad you decided to write. The office make-
over is going well. I did some painting, and it's
looking pretty good. I have to do a second coat next
weekend. I was going to write tonight and send you my
favorites list. Great minds think alike. Without fur-
ther ado:
    My musical tastes vary like yours. My favorites
are Elton John, Melissa Etheridge, Taylor Dayne, KC &
the Sunshine Band, and anything from the 80's.
    Some of my favorite films are The Other Sister
(with Juliette Lewis), The Santa Clause movies, Bird-
cage, and Too Wong Foo, Thanks for Everything, Julie
Newmar.
    I like various shows and enjoy buying the series
on DVD so I can watch them at my leisure. Some of the
shows I like are Buffy the Vampire Slayer, Party of
Five, Le Femme Nikita, and my soap opera, Days of our
Lives. I tape it daily, but don't tell anyone. It'll
ruin my image.
    And your e-mail didn't put me to sleep.
```

More about myself: You asked me about Sarah. We both moved home after break-ups. We worked for the same company. I played hard to get, because I was so unsure of another relationship. That was over five years ago. We are both so opposite that sometimes I wonder how we stay together. We have a great time together, so that must be it. Sarah doesn't like computers, so she's not into e-mailing lists. She likes cop shows and real life trauma in the E.R. shows. My stomach can't stand those shows.

My friends from college know me as a different person because I wasn't 'out' in college. I am, at most, only an hour away from my best friends from elementary school. When I came out to them, and to myself, they understood and stood by me. My friend Nancy (who has seen me at my worst) lives two streets over. My friend Katy lives ten minutes away; my friend Ellen also lives ten minutes away, but in the other direction. My friend Patsy (who is gay, too) lives about forty minutes away. Finally, my friend Faye lives about an hour away. My other good friends are Helen and her partner, Jo. Helen is on my ice hockey team. Speaking of which, I play a defense position on the first line.

I think I have written plenty for this e-mail. Remind me, and I'll tell you about my job in the next e-mail.

I hope you had a good day (if you are reading this in the evening) or will have a good day if this is morning.

Take it easy, Cory.
Dylan

Cory checked the time; it was getting late. She toyed with the idea of responding but knew Dylan wasn't expecting one until the morning. She shut down the computer, collected her things, kissed a slumbering Sam on the cheek, and climbed the stairs to bed. The weekends never seemed long enough, and she knew she had another grueling week ahead at work.

Chapter
Five

CORY READ DYLAN'S latest e-mail.

Dear Cory,
  I've been thinking about other things to ask you.
I know a lot about your likes and dislikes. How would
you describe your personality? I'll go first and tell
you how I see myself and my values.
  I believe in my friends, and once I make a
friend, they're a friend for life. I can be very
self-centered. I like to think the best of others,
and it gets me into trouble sometimes. I find it hard
to focus on jobs at times and am a terrible procras-
tinator. I hate failing at things, and I despise
being wrong. I think about 'what ifs' a lot. I have
trouble sometimes saying what I want to say. I've
never been one for words. I'm much better at writing
it down (believe it or not). I can be selfish, but
then, I am an only child. I'm also moody (Gemini is
my sign), especially when I have PMS. Lucky for you,
you're not in the States. I am very self-confident.
I'm also a good verbal fighter, but I usually give
the silent treatment when I argue with people. Sarah
can't stand that. I can be stubborn, but my cousin
says that I have a good heart. I will do anything for
the people I care about. I do hate losing, but I'm a
good team player when I play sports. However, when
things don't go my way, I can sulk.
  Speaking of sulking, Sarah and I aren't talking
at the moment. I thought I'd surprise her and do the
dusting and vacuuming yesterday. Apparently, I didn't
do a good job, and she bitched about the fact that I
didn't move or lift items of furniture to clean
underneath. I told her she should do it herself next
time, because all she ever does is criticize how I do
things. She called me a slob. I called her a neat
freak. Anyway, the argument escalated from there.
When we fight, it's so stupid. She's so picky sometimes, and sometimes, I feel like a two-year-old.

Maybe I act like one, too. It sucks to be in the house right now. I wish we weren't so alike at times, because neither one of us will admit we're wrong.

Needless to say, I slept in the guestroom. It was the best night's sleep I've had in a while. I realized the mattress in there is better for my back.

Thanks for being there. This time difference is a pain in the ass, though. I don't know how the people who have fallen in love over the Internet conduct romances if there's a big time difference. I wish you lived right down the street so I could drop by and we could really chat. But then I think, what would I do if you didn't like me?

Have a good one,

Dylan

PS: I have a friend whose birthday is coming up soon. We're getting to know each other, and I want to make a CD of songs for her birthday. Do you know of any music she really hates? I was wondering if you could speak to her for me because I'll have to make it very soon. She lives overseas in the UK (vbg). Oh yeah, keep it a secret from her. I don't want her to know.

Cory tried to focus on the details of Dylan's e-mail, but her mind kept reviewing her most recent dream; it had felt so real she'd woken very aroused. She pieced together her memories of the dream.

She had been by a lake watching the ripples on the water. They were circular, as if the water had been disturbed and was now resettling. She had watched the circles decreasing in size. Something was missing...or someone. Her heart was pounding; she felt scared, worried. Her eyes scanned the circles, but they'd almost disappeared. She had returned to the fire near the lake. She could feel her body shaking with fear while she steadily stirred the embers of the fire. She needed to get some more wood. She knew she would need the heat of the fire for later. She went to the edge of the tree line and bent down, collecting thin sticks for kindling wood and thicker sticks for the fire's fuel. As she straightened, she felt arms encircle her waist, and she gasped, dropping the wood as she did so. The arms were wet, and drops of water were falling on her shoulders from the wet, black hair that was draped over her.

The owner of the arms began to kiss her ears, and Cory had turned in the hold and gazed up into the bluest, brightest eyes she'd ever seen. She had watched the pupils of the eyes dilate with desire, and it warmed her heart to know she was the reason behind this lust. She hoped the same was reflected in her eyes. She stared a moment longer, willing her partner to drown in her own gaze, to see the desire she hoped was now evident on her face. She closed her eyes and as lips met lips she had felt herself melting, falling...

Cory's attention returned to the e-mail in front of her. She needed to either write something or get ready for her day at work. She checked the time.

Cory Williams
T.G.I.F.!!!!!!!!

Hey there, Dylan
    I've decided you're bad for my workload (vbg). This week, I've written more e-mails to you than I think I have in a lifetime. (That's a compliment by the way). I decided today you're like my "Dear Diary." Writing to you is like journaling, only it's interactive, because my journal replies to me (with such compassion, might I add).
    You asked me to describe my personality. Having read your description, I'd say we're very similar, in many ways. I would describe myself as caring, and I like to think the best of others. However, I can be very pigheaded at times. I consider friendship the most important thing in the world. Both you and I hate failing, which is a good thing. I think we're a pair of "go-getters."
    Unlike you, I'm not a procrastinator. I have to get things done. I can get into "zones" where all I focus on is a project or work. It drives people crazy, but these projects don't last long. I consider myself to be honest and truthful—well, 99 percent of the time. I'm not sure anyone can be 100 percent of the time. It does depend who I am talking to. I wouldn't want to be honest and truthful if it was going to hurt someone's feelings.
    I am very shy when I first meet people and get tongue-tied, but once I know them, I can chew the hind leg off a donkey. I see you're more the strong, silent type, huh? (vbg). I do wish I had your relaxed attitude about life. As much as I could talk for my country, I can also worry for it. To quote Sam: "I worry about not having anything to worry about." Of course, I just reread this, and I think I ought to be put in an asylum.
    Thanks for saying I write well. I do want to write a book one day. I do write poetry. I haven't shown it to anyone, but I want to post some online, and I need a volunteer to read it. Any volunteers? I do love to read. If I have some down time, I'll read a book. In the winter, I like to lie in front of the fire with a book, and in the summer, on my hammock. Either way, I love escaping into a world created by someone else.
    I was sorry to hear you and Sarah had an argu-

ment. You made me giggle when you said you had a better night's sleep in the spare room than in your
usual bed. Have you made up? I'm not much into housework, either. Who'd have thought you actually have to
move furniture when you clean? We obviously went to
the same school of cleaning.

If it's any consolation, I haven't seen much of
Sam this week, either. When I did see him, he stated
that he thinks my computer time is becoming an addic-
tion and I should focus more on him. So I tried. Once
I mentioned discussing his feelings, he couldn't get
out of the room fast enough. In our house, I'm usually the one who starts the sulks or moods. Sam hates
it when he's wrong, and he will turn an issue into my
fault. Sam and I rarely engage in fights. He refuses
to argue, which gets my goat. I love a good row. But
he's also very caring and supportive of my fads and
crazes. He puts up with my selfishness and my obses-
sions. He doesn't moan when the house is untidy. He
does all the housework and a majority of the cooking.
He enjoys the chores, and he's home a lot of the time
in the day.

Anyway, I added you into my Messenger account, so
we should be able to instant message later on this
weekend. We'll have to pick a time when we're both
online. I agree with you, this time difference sucks
(to use my new terminology learned from your last e-
mail). It should be fun to chat at the same time. I
always seem to have a quirky grin when I'm e-mailing
you.

Your postscript made me laugh out loud. So you
want to make me a CD of songs for my birthday? I
would like to listen to more of the artists you like,
so surprise me. I do like strong female singers.

Well, I am running very late for work now, but it
is Friday, and I don't have to prepare much today.

I especially like this point in my e-mails as I
know I'll get a reply soon, and then I get to ramble
all over again. Looking forward to catching up with
you over the weekend.
Your friend,
Cory

Cory checked the e-mail through. The fact that Dylan had acknowl-
edged her birthday was enough, but wanting to make a gift for her
warmed Cory's heart. After sending the e-mail, Cory ran into the bathroom attached to the bedroom, waking Sam as she did so when Holly
jumped off the bed to greet her.

"Where's the fire?" he said.

Cory poked her head around the ensuite door. "I'm late. I didn't notice the time. I have to shower and find some track bottoms. You couldn't go downstairs and sort me some out could you?"

"What have you been doing? You've been up a while." Sam sat up in bed, rubbing the sleep out of his eyes.

"I was reading my e-mails, and I decided to reply to a few." She looked up at Sam and saw the look of disinterest sweep across his face. "Please, can you find me some track bottoms?" she implored.

"ARE YOU SURE you want to do one more set?" Cory asked as she struggled to lift the last set of leg presses. "I'm not in the mood for this."

"I thought you were slacking off during this workout. What's wrong? Had a bad day? You seemed okay. I didn't hear you murdering any of the cherubs through the wall of your classroom." Rachel grinned.

Cory released the weights and got off the machine. "No, it was a pretty good day, really. I feel like I'm making progress with the kids. I'm thinking about tonight."

"You going anywhere special?" asked Rachel, as they walked over to the stretching mat.

"No, we never go out. It'd take a nationwide emergency to get Sam off the sofa tonight. I'll probably just watch the television or surf the Internet, check my e-mails or something."

"Made any new friends?" enquired Rachel, as she settled on the stomach cruncher.

Cory paused and then replied. "Yeah, I've made a friend in America. Her name is Dylan. I'll tell you about her over a bottle of water."

After their cool down, the two friends made their way out to the entrance and purchased some flavoured water. Rachel leaned against the wall and looked at Cory. "Come on then, spill the beans."

"What?" asked Cory, puzzled.

"Your new mate, why all the mystery?"

"No mystery. I've met someone who I can talk to. She seems nice. We have the same interests. We're getting on well," Cory answered, fiddling with her laces. "She lives with her partner on the east coast, near Boston."

"Male or female?" asked Rachel.

"Male or female what?"

"The partner, is it a male or female?"

"Er...female," Cory replied, finally looking at Rachel. When she didn't see any sign of disgust on her friend's face she continued. "Sam doesn't know why I can be so relaxed about it. He has this thing about homosexuality being wrong and unnatural. What do you think?"

"Personally, I think it's a man thing. I mean women are more comfortable around each other. We're used to hugging and telling each other how we feel. I think men get threatened that we—women—might actually survive without them."

"I know what you mean. It's like when I went down with the college crowd for that hen weekend. Sam asked how we'd all fit in such a small farmhouse. When I told him I'd shared the bed with Angela, he acted really freaked out. He couldn't believe we shared a bed," Cory said, laughing as she remembered the look on Sam's face when she'd told him. "I had to tell him so many times that nothing had happened. He kept saying, 'but what if you'd woken up hugging her?'"

Rachel giggled. "What did you say to that?"

"I told him she'd have probably hugged me back and then pushed me out of bed to make the tea."

"Too funny." Rachel studied Cory for a few moments. "Personally, I need the physical contact with my friends. I'm not into this macho British stiff upper lip and no touching. I hug and I kiss my mates. I also tell them my inner most secrets."

"Me, too," Cory responded.

Rachel continued, "If you ask me, I think most women are one small step away from being gay. I've had friends who I've been so close to that there was a thin line between friends and being involved." She glanced at Cory, "However, when I think of getting physical with a woman and getting physical with a man, I just know guys do it for me. I can see why some women choose women. I haven't met anyone yet who hasn't had a crush on another woman at some time in her life. What do you think?" She looked directly at Cory.

Cory could feel her face reddening. It had begun when Rachel mentioned the word "gay." She broke eye contact with Rachel and turned her attention back to her shoe laces. She remembered back to all her school and college crushes. *Speak, idiot. Say something before she puts two and two together.* "I guess so. I do think people should be with whoever makes them happy, regardless of gender. I wish Sam would be more tolerant."

"You seem a little nervous. What's troubling you?"

Cory sighed and finally lifted her head. "I like Dylan, and one day I hope to meet her. When that happens, I don't want to hear Sam's wisecracks or sarcastic comments anymore." *Ask her what's on your mind. Just say it. She'll be okay.* "So gay people don't bother you?"

"Cory, people are who they are. If someone's a nice, caring person and they want to be my friend, I don't care what color, religion, gender or sexual inclination they have. I'll still be their mate. It's what they're like inside that matters the most." At this, Rachel leaned over and gave Cory a squeeze. "If you've got more on your mind, I'll listen, without judgment."

Cory let out a slow breath. "It's refreshing to talk to someone with such liberal views. Sam and most of my family rarely see past the differences in people. Thanks for the offer to chat. I might just take you up on that sometime."

CORY PEEKED into the living room and found Sam asleep on the sofa. She didn't have the heart to wake him. Closing the door quietly, she crept upstairs and showered. Then she slipped on her jogging bottoms and sweatshirt. Unwilling to wake Sam until she had checked her e-mail, Cory entered the office and booted up her computer. She twiddled with a pen distractedly while she waited.

```
Dylan Matthews
Re: T.G.I.F.!!!!!!!
```

Hi Cory,
    It may be the weekend for you; however, some of us are still working. Take pity on me (vbg). I'm answering some of your questions from yesterday and today, and then I have some for you.
    I understand why you didn't go to see your nan when she was lying in rest. It's hard to remember who they were when you see them that way. I did see my mother in the casket, and unfortunately, a lot of times that's all I can picture when I think of her. I think you were smart not to go, despite the pressure from your family. Now you get to remember the woman from your childhood and not a lifeless figure.
    In regards to workouts, I love running. I usually run three miles and then bike. Every other night, I lift weights. Then, as I've mentioned, I play hockey, usually only once a weekend. But I do go to tournaments when they're scheduled.
    I have so many things I want to ask you. Sometimes I feel like I've known you for ages, and then I realize it's only been a little while. I've decided I need to write down questions that I want to ask you when I think of them so it'll jog my memory. In response to your query, ask any question you like. I usually don't have a problem with answering.
    You don't need to thank me for making you a birthday gift, but it's good to be described as "wonderful." I want to say that my new friend is pretty cool, too.
    Today was a much better travel day then yesterday. I usually have a long commute to work, but yesterday was the worst. I may ask the boss to shift my time a little bit so I'm not hitting all the traffic. I drive a pickup truck—a Toyota Tundra. It is great. Three years old. It's green.
    By the way, thanks for the photographs. Holly is a beautiful dog. The cats looked very cute. Do they have names?
    I've just reread this, and I think I have waffled enough (I love these new English phrases). I was

going to throw another topic at you, but I have forgotten what I was going to say. Oh yeah, I remember:
what do you think about soul mates? What's your idea
of a soul mate, and do they have to be romantically
involved?

I hope you have had a great day. Let me know if
the attachment came through.

Take it easy.

D

Cory grinned. She couldn't help it. Dylan's personality on the computer screen made her smile. She spent some time going over e-mails she had saved from Dylan. She reviewed what she knew about Dylan and then stopped on the last few questions. *What do I think of soul mates?*

Cory Williams
More about me

WARNING: HUGE E-MAIL. YOU MAY NEED CAFFEINE TO
KEEP YOU AWAKE!

Time to tell you more about myself, I guess, so
let me jump right in at the deep end. I guess I have
been in love three times in my life. Not to be too
cocky, but I've been out with stacks of people. However, only three people have held my attention for
longer than two weeks.

The first one was a guy at college, named Darren
Jones. He was wonderful, and it was like in the movies—there were sparks between us, and my heart pit-
ter-pattered when he was near. We went out for about
nine months, and I was totally smitten. We got on ace
until an old flame of his who he'd always fancied
came back on the scene. You can figure the rest. He
broke my heart, and it took years for me to trust and
give away my heart again. In a way, I don't think I
ever have, properly. It was fragile and tattered for
ages.

Then, I met someone else at college, and we got
on well, and we were together for a little over a
year. We went everywhere together and practically
lived together, but I couldn't give the relationship
what it needed, and we finished when I left college.
I regret the fact that it was my fault we finished.

A couple of years after leaving college, I met
Sam, and he gave me the attention I'd been missing.
We only got to see each other at weekends, so we
would go out a lot and stay at each other's. We get
on very well most of the time. It's not the heart-
beating, knee-quaking romance that I had previously,
but, he's there for me...and we have an okay life.

On the subject of soul mates, I'm divided. I'd

like to think there was someone out there who made me
feel complete, but then it would mean that Sam isn't
mine. In my opinion, a soul mate is someone you can
open your heart and soul to. I think, maybe, they're
someone who you feel comfortable with and want to be
with forever, even if you can't be with them right
now. Maybe someone you think about constantly and
can't get their image from your mind. In my definition, this person has the same likes and dislikes,
most of the time. They bring a smile to your face
even when they're discussing everyday life. You feel
a connection to them even though you may never have
met them or are likely to. I'm not sure they have to
be involved. Maybe they should be involved, but time
and place prevent it. I don't know. I don't think
it's exactly like you read in romance novels—sometimes, that's way up in the clouds. I mean, the
chances of meeting someone who knows what you're
thinking and can feel what you're feeling is a bit
unbelievable. So I don't know. I guess I don't want
to believe in them because that would mean mine was
out there without me. However, I am a firm believer
in fate and that things happen for a reason.

        As for a car, I have a Ford Fiesta, about ten
years old. I rarely use it, as I get lifts everywhere
and car-share, trying to do my bit for the environment. The cats are called Mary, Mungo, and Midge. I
have always had a cat. Sam is the dog person. I like
the fact that cats are more independent, and they
come and go as they please. A dog takes a lot of
looking after.

        So how about you? You said I could ask you any
questions, so here goes:

        What about your love life? You've told me a lit-
tle about you and Sarah, but how did you meet her?
When did you know you were gay? Did you come straight
out or hide it? How did your parents react? Are you a
big believer of love at first sight and soul mates?

        These questions are pretty personal so ignore any
you don't want to answer.
Cheers,
Cory

Cory sat back and read through her e-mail before sending. She
stopped to ponder her soul mate reply. *It's exactly how I feel about Dylan.
I wonder if Dylan feels the same. Maybe I'll pluck up the courage one day and
ask her.*

        She reread her comments about love. *Well, I haven't lied there. I may
have omitted a few facts.*

        "What's for dinner?"

Cory cringed when she heard the words. *Oh shit, dinner's not cooked!* She hurriedly pressed the send button, and ran downstairs, bracing herself for the show down.

"Hi, did you sleep well?" asked Cory, desperately trying to work out what kind of mood Sam was in.

Sam closed the fridge door. "I can't believe I went out like a light. It's unusual for me to sleep in the day."

"You need to come to bed earlier. It's all those movies you watch late into the night."

"Actually, it's your fault I'm tired. You've been so restless in your sleep."

"I've always moved about," Cory retorted, defensively.

"No, this is more than usual," Sam fired back. "You keep tossing and turning. You even murmur things. I didn't mean to make you angry. Is something worrying you?"

Cory pulled out a stool and sat at the kitchen counter. She rested her head in her hands and rubbed her forehead. She didn't know how to answer the question. "I guess I'm stressed. Next week's schedule after school is busy. I have a cross country meet with the kids next Thursday. Can you help marshal it?"

"I'm on a business trip Thursday night. You've forgotten all about it, haven't you?" Sam chopped the mushrooms he'd taken from the fridge as he spoke.

"Shit, it'd slipped my mind. I guess I'll be brave and spend the night on my own. It won't kill me. But we'll have to ask Mum and Dad to look after Holly. I'll never get myself organized enough to walk her, and she'll be home all day alone."

"I'll call your parents later. However, knowing you as I know you, you'll panic now for the next five nights about staying on your own. Phone Rachel and ask her to stay over. You can go to the gym together and get some of the planning you've been moaning about out of the way. Go on. She'll jump at the chance to have a night away from the kids." Sam handed her the portable house phone, which was never very far from him.

Chapter
Six

THE LIGHT CREEPING through a crack in the bedroom curtains woke Cory. It appeared to be a lovely, fresh Sunday morning. It was the end of January, and the weather was reasonably mild for the time of year. Cory stretched and felt the muscles ripple in her back. She groaned slightly as she felt a pull in the over-worked muscles of her abdominals.

"Morning, sleepy head. Holly and I have been down the field, and she's worn out. Here's your tea. I'm off to play a round of golf. What are your plans for the day?"

"I thought I'd check my e-mails, do some correcting, write my plans. You know, the same ole, same ole."

"Want to come play golf?" Sam asked, grinning.

Cory pulled a face and slid under the covers. "No way. I'd rather mark a thousand books than follow you over a golf course." Cory's voice was muffled under the duvet. "And, don't even pretend to be hurt. You only asked because you knew what my answer would be."

"I'll call you when I'm heading home."

Cory surfaced and glanced at the clock: 9:00 A.M. Cory did the math. It was 4 A.M. in the States, but there was bound to be a morning message off Dylan. She grabbed her cup of tea, put on her bathrobe, and made her way into the office.

Holly settled herself at the door of the office, while Cory sank into the large leather chair. She glanced at the piles of paperwork that were scattered around the room. She made a mental note to talk to Sam about putting up shelves. She peered at the computer screen, her heart beating slightly faster and her hands trembling.

```
Dylan Matthews
Re: More about me

Dear Cory,
     Here's my return e-mail, and it's just as big as
yours was. It's lucky you have no limit on your e-
mail size.
     I don't know about love at first sight as much
as, "Ooh, this person is special, and I want to get
```

to know them better." As for soul mates—I think I define it as people who are supposed to be together and they fit. I think my parents were soul mates. They were perfect together (unbiased opinion, of course). I also don't think it happens as often in real life as it does in books. In most of the books I've read, the two main characters fall in love instantaneously. It's like the characters have known each other for years. At least that's how it is in some lesbian romance novels I've read. I'm not sure about straight fiction. (I'd rather poke my eyes out than read about some guy's throbbing member). I do believe in fate, whether for the good or bad.

I've been in love four times. The first time was a woman I really liked and couldn't stop thinking about. I almost got kicked out of my house for her. She dumped me after a month or so. For her, it was a conquest of being the first woman I was ever with. We only got as far as kissing (but it was good kissing). Her name was Kelly. Losing her was hard, but I survived.

The second was Tina. We lasted over two years. Sometimes when I'd look at her, my stomach would flip. We broke up when we were living in Germany. It's a long story that I'll make very short. She left me for a man—a man who ended being friends with her so he could get to know me. Go figure.

The next was Michelle, who was older and attached. We became friends through work. We used to flirt, and she would call me a tease (which I guess I was). I met her while I was with Tina. Anyway, I came home from Germany and was at her house. She grabbed me, and it sent shocks through my arm. From then on, I began to look at her very differently. I really thought about being with her, and I tried to become her mistress. I really hate myself for that. The long and the short was she stayed with her girlfriend, and I met Sarah about a year later.

Here is my how I met Sarah story. Try to stay awake.

I came back to the States from Germany and started working in a local grocery store. Sarah came home from Ohio (a different state, farther west than Massachusetts). She had recently broken up with her girlfriend. Sarah started working in the same store about a month after I did. She says she fell in love with me the first time she saw me. I was afraid of her. She was this tough girl with slicked—back hair. She also smoked and drank a lot. She stopped smoking when she found out I wouldn't be with anybody who smoked. She stopped drinking about a year or so ago.

I used to drink, but I was afraid it was becoming a problem and stopped. Now I have an occasional beer, but nothing to excess. (My father used to drink a lot, but he hasn't had a drink in 25 years).

Anyway, Sarah and I went walking on the beach one night, and I stepped into a hole. I almost couldn't get my leg out. She helped me, and we sort of went from there. She did all the chasing, and I let her. I like to go to the movies and play putt-putt golf (miniature golf). This bores her to tears, but in the early days, she did it to please me. Once I got to see there was a great person under all Sarah's bravado, I let my guard down. I was also afraid to commit, but I did. The only scary thing is that I know that Sarah loves me so much more than I love her. My love is growing, but for me, it wasn't love at first sight.

WAKE UP! I'VE FINISHED!

You asked in one of your e-mails what my accent was like. There's a movie, *Good Will Hunting,* that was set near here. I sound like the actors in that.

You asked when I knew I was gay. I finally admitted and accepted myself when I was 22. I get jealous when I hear of young people, like when they're in high school, who know they're gay and come out. I wish I'd had the guts to do that. I was so confused back then. How could I be something that my parents told me never to become? I struggled with my sexuality. I didn't have anyone to talk to or any support groups.

At first, my parents didn't take it very well. I didn't tell my mother. She asked me, and I knew I couldn't lie. She cried and told me, "Daddy won't be happy." As it happens, my father didn't talk to me for a while. Then my mother got sick, and she begged my father to accept me.

Would you mind if I asked you some questions? I'm of two minds whether to ask you now. Actually, I am almost afraid to ask. I don't want to upset you or make you mad. Then again, you've asked me some personal ones, so here goes. In your last e-mail, you said you'd been in love three times, but only named two of them. I'm curious why you didn't name the third one. Was the second person a woman?

I'm still at work, so I should go and check on some computers. I hope this e-mail finds you well and rested after a good night's sleep.

Take it easy, kiddo.

Dylan

Cory read the last section of the e-mail; she'd known what the question was going to be before she'd read it. She'd wanted to write the answer in her original e-mail, but she hadn't had the guts to actually put it into written words. *How do I tell her about my past? Should I tell her my big secret? I haven't told a soul. Now it's haunting me.*

The doorbell rang. Holly jumped up barking, instantly on guard dog patrol. Cory looked out of the window but couldn't tell who was at the door. She tightened the belt on her robe and went to answer the door.

She peered through the glass and then opened the door.

"Morning, Cory, I'm not interrupting something, am I?" her neighbor, Craig, asked.

"No, Craig. I'm just being lazy. It is Sunday, you know." She flashed a grin at him. They'd been neighbors for over a year and yet they'd spoken only a few times—the odd occasion when they had been gardening out the front and on New Year's Eve when they'd had a street party with all the neighbors.

"I wanted to ask if you fancied going out next week, as we share a birthday."

Cory looked blankly at Craig. She had no idea he even knew her birthday was this month. "We share a birthday?"

"Yeah, you told me at New Year. Only I have five more years of experience on this earth than you. Do you fancy it? My brother and his wife are going to be here."

"It should be okay. I'll have to check with Sam, but we have no set plans for the weekend. Can I invite my sister if she's around?"

"Sure, the more the merrier. I'll talk to you about a date in the week. We still have to sort a babysitter out." He smiled at Cory.

Cory rubbed her goose-bumped arms. "I'll pop over tomorrow and we can firm the details up."

"You'd better go in before you freeze. It looks a nice warm day until you get outside."

"I know. I'm beginning to realize that. Thanks for the invite." Cory closed the door and went upstairs to e-mail her sister an invite. Her mind returned to Dylan's e-mail. She was in turmoil.

```
Cory Williams
It's me

Good Morning, Dylan,
     I figured out your question before I read it. The
second love of my life was Deb. We went out for over
a year at college and kept it very quiet. We were
best friends and lovers. She wanted to tell everyone
about us, but I wanted the secrecy. I think my house-
mates suspected, but they didn't say anything. I'd
had many boyfriends and had managed to get myself
quite a reputation as a man-eater (not by choice or
```

action). People figured I was still hurting from Darren and that was why I didn't have a boyfriend. The fact that Deb stayed every other night didn't seem to register with them (and they had to go through my room to get to the bathroom).

I'm only just coming to terms with this really, and Sam doesn't know. When I left college, I thought that side of my life was over (very naïve of me).

Since getting involved with this e-mail list and reading all the lesbian novels, I'm now feeling more secure about my relationship with Deb and what it meant in my life. I've denied it for so long. You're the first person I've told. I want to tell my friend, Angela, but I'm worried about how she'll react. I'm scared of losing her friendship.

So you now know more about me than my best friend, and it's good to have someone to talk to. However, now I'm worried that Sam will read one of my e-mails, and it'll all come out. Did I tell you I was a worrier?

I do want to talk to you about it one day. Who knows? Maybe we'll talk on the phone.

There, I've bared my soul. I hope you don't think less of me now for my cowardliness.

I want to write more, but I'm scared of losing your friendship, which is ironic, as I think this will actually make our friendship stronger. Hopefully, after telling you, I'll be brave enough to tell Angela. I don't like carrying this secret around.

I really do feel like I could tell you anything.
Take care, Dylan.
Cory

Cory sent the e-mail and felt the weight of the world shift off her shoulders. She took a deep breath and felt at peace with herself. *Is Dylan my soul mate? What if she is? Do I tell her?*

AFTER THIRTY MINUTES of monotonous shirts and pants, Cory whooped with delight as she folded the last piece of ironed clothing onto the finished pile. She dropped onto the sofa next to Sam and snuggled up. He pushed her away. She turned hurt eyes his way. "What's wrong?" she asked.

"Nothing's wrong. Why do things have to be wrong?"

"Usually when a wife hugs her husband, he's supposed to hug her back." Cory answered angrily.

"Says who?" replied Sam.

"The books...in movies...real life. For god's sake, Sam, it's not like I jumped your bones. I only wanted a cuddle. It's not like I'm going to get anything else. You've made that pretty clear." Cory stood and went to the other sofa.

"Look, I'm tired. I have a lot on my mind right now. I didn't mean anything by it. So do you want a cuddle?" Sam opened his arms, but Cory just glared at him.

"No, I think I'll go find something to do that won't interrupt your evening activities. I didn't realize I was an inconvenience." When she reached the door, she held Sam's stare. "If you're not careful, I may find somebody who's willing to let me in and be with them. Then I'll be gone in a flash. I'm tired of this, Sam. I'm fed up of being ignored, and I hate feeling like I'm not a woman." She held onto the door for support as she delivered her final statement. "So make up your mind. Either you're in this marriage, or you're not. Either way, I need to know." She left the living room and went upstairs to the office. She sank into the cold, leather chair and let the tears stream down her cheeks.

Cory tried to keep the negative thoughts out, but she lost the battle. *Maybe he's getting it from other places. Maybe he's having an affair.* She shivered at the thought. *He has someone else.* Her hands shook and her breathing was ragged. She needed to feel connected to someone – anyone. She checked her e-mail. She glanced down the screen, pleased to see there were two e-mails from Dylan. She opened the earlier one.

```
Dylan Matthews
Re: It's me

Hey Cory,
    I had already guessed that the answer would be a
woman since you never gave a name. I don't judge any-
one, and I'm pleased you felt you could trust me with
your secrets. I'll try never to break this confi-
dence. I'll always be here to answer any questions
and support you through any decisions or be a shoul-
der to cry on, if you need one.
    I thought that you might need a bit of light
relief after baring your soul, so I have some more
survey questions. We still have so many things that
we don't know about each other.
    I was thinking of some things and thought I would
write them down. Hold on tight because there's quite
a list.
    Favorite snack? Mine is M&M's
    Favorite sport? Ice hockey
    Favorite perfume? CK 1 and Eternity for men
    Pepsi or Coke? Pepsi
    Favorite Spice Girl? Mel G (I'm still heartbroken
they broke up).
    Favorite body part (male or female)? I like legs,
butts, hands, and breasts (not necessarily in that
order).
```

What do you look at first in a person? I like
their eyes and smile.
    Do you sleep with or without pajamas? I sleep
with but would prefer without. However, I won't be
the only one in the bed naked.
    Do you like jeans (or pants) tight on the butt or
loose? I like 'em slightly loose, not baggy like lots
of teenagers wear them.
    Wine or Beer? I like either, although I don't
drink to excess. My favorite drink is water.
    Can you whistle with your fingers in your mouth?
I can't, but I am learning. (See how tough my day
is?) A colleague is teaching me while I write this e-
mail. Hey, I just learned to whistle, and now I am
light headed (vbg).
    Do you like sneakers, boots, or shoes? I wrote
mine in order of preference.
    Do you prefer a shower or bath? I like a nice hot
shower.
    Are your favorite undies cotton or silk? (If this
is too personal, pass). I prefer cotton.
    That should keep you busy and out of trouble.
See? Now I'm finding things for you to think about so
you won't get bored.
    You said you were a bit of a poet. Any chance of
my getting to read some of them? By the way, I enjoy
your e-mails and finding out about you and your day.
I haven't met anybody else on the Internet and become
friends. I think it is great. Talk about fate. It was
meant to be that you read my e-mail and became part
of the chocolate war.
Your friend,
Dylan

Cory wiped the tears away as she smiled at Dylan's remarks. She
minimized the e-mail and opened the second e-mail. She noted that it
had been sent only ten minutes earlier.

Dylan Matthews
Hey...

Cory,
    Okay, you're going to think I'm crazy, but are
you okay? A few minutes ago, I got this almighty
feeling in my chest—kind of a crushing sensation. I
couldn't get you out of my mind. I had this urgent
feeling that I should contact you. Don't ask me why I
felt like this. Anyway, I'm worried about you. I'll
check later to see if I've scared you away or if you
want to hang out with me, like forever. I feel a connection between us. Do you feel the same? Have I

freaked you out?
　　Your crazy (needs to go visit the shrink) American friend,
Dylan

Cory read the text over and over. *She felt my pain. No way. But why else would she be e-mailing? Does she really feel a connection? Do I feel it?* She maximized the first e-mail, looked at the questions, and then hit the reply button.

Cory Williams
Re: It's me

Hi Dylan,
　　I'm fine, but thanks for worrying. I think there definitely must be a connection, as Sam and I have just had a row. We seem to be having more of them recently. I'm not really in the mood to go into details, but I will later. You haven't freaked me out, and it's nice to know you care. I'm going to answer the lighthearted questions you asked as my head feels like mush. I think I've cried myself out.
　　My favourite snack has to be crisps. I think you call these chips. I'm a sucker for anything with a savory taste. Chocolates and sweets are okay, but they make me feel sick after a few.
　　My favourite sport is rugby. I love watching England play. I've watched them play Wales live, and the atmosphere is brilliant. There isn't the hooliganism in rugby fans as there can be, and has been, when watching football (your soccer).
　　My favourite perfume is FCUK (French Connection). I like Tommy Hilfiger, too.
　　As for Pepsi or Coke, I'm not really a pop person. I kind of like banana milkshakes, and I love a good cup of tea. I think I'd buy Coke if there was a choice at the store.
　　As for my favourite Spice Girl—I'd opt for a dead one (vbg). They kind of give us Brits a bad name. Just kidding. They're okay in small doses. Now they're no longer together, the music world is a better place, in my opinion.
　　My favourite body parts are eyes. I love eyes. You can tell a lot about a person's personality from their eyes. Mine are green, but I'm partial to blue-eyed people. People can try to disguise all their emotions, but their eyes give them away. When I first meet a person, I look for what kind of person they are inside. I focus on their personality and if they can make me laugh.
　　I don't wear any pyjamas (notice I use the cor-

rect spelling (g)). I like the feel of fresh linen on my skin and the unrestricted movement. I am a wriggler in my sleep, so I get tangled in the clothing when I do wear it.

As for drinking, my theory is if it's got an alcohol content, I'll drink it—not that I have a drinking problem. I drink when I want to relax occasionally. Give me a few glasses of wine, and I'm anybody's.

I can whistle using my fingers. You definitely need a more exciting job if this is what you get up to in your work time. Actually, I'm kind of jealous that you get time to lark around. My day is usually non-stop.

I prefer cotton underwear. However, if I'm wearing trousers or jeans I always wear a thong as I can't stand underwear lines, and it's comfier. When I'm wearing track bottoms, then I go with your everyday briefs, but definitely cotton. Have we just crossed a border?

I will think of other questions to ask you later. I guess I should go downstairs and face the music. I told you at the beginning of the e-mail that Sam and I had a fight. It was over his lack of affection. Sam and I are having difficulties when it comes to romance and the intimacy part of our relationship. To totally embarrass myself, I'd like some sex and he won't give me any. Now I've gotten myself worked up and paranoid that he's having an affair. I'm going crazy. Any advice?

Take care, and once again thanks for thinking about me,
Cory

Cory checked the e-mail and sent it. She glanced at the clock on the computer. *The evening is almost over, and, as always, I've spent it all alone. Yet again, I'm going to have to be the one to hold out the fucking olive branch.*

She went heavy-hearted into the bathroom and poured herself a hot, bubbly bath. The aroma of the oils instantly relaxed her raw nerves, and she sank into the foam. Her eyelids were heavy, but she resisted the temptation to sleep. *How do I feel about Sam? What do I want from our relationship? Do I really have a connection with Dylan? She's three thousand miles away. I need to talk to Sam, but what should I say?*

AS BEDTIME DREW nearer, Cory knew she needed to clear the air with Sam. She hated going to bed not speaking to him. She went down to the living room and pushed the door open. Sam was lying on the sofa; he sat up as she entered the room.

"Fancy a cup of tea or a glass of milk?" Cory asked quietly.

"Glass of milk, thanks, unless you're going to pour it over my head," Sam said, sheepishly.

"You might deserve it at times, but think of the cost of carpet cleaning." Cory ruffled his hair and smiled. He seemed responsive. *Do I risk another fight or let sleeping dogs lie?*

She went into the kitchen. Cory poured two glasses of milk and returned to the living room.

"I'm off to bed. I'm knackered. Are you coming or staying here?"

"I'm coming up. I'm pretty tired myself." Sam wrapped his arms around Cory's waist and waited for her to look at him. "Cor, I'm sorry about earlier. I...umm...I didn't mean for you to take it the wrong way. I'm tired, and I'm sorry I upset you. I should have come up to check on you...but.... I'm not good at this emotional stuff."

Cory listened as Sam struggled to find the words. "I know, but once in a while I'd like to be the one who's apologized to. You're lucky my mum gave me the advice about never going to bed on an argument. Otherwise, you'd still be here feeling sorry for yourself."

"I know. Come on." Sam held his hand out to Cory. They walked upstairs together.

The couple undressed in silence and slid under the covers. Sam leaned over and pecked Cory on the forehead.

"Night, love."

"Night, Sam," Cory closed her eyes. One sentence kept replaying over and over in her head. *Do you feel a connection?*

Chapter
Seven

IT WAS THE eve of Cory's big day. She had managed to get her workload cleared and was taking a well-earned rest. The television was on, but it was more background noise than entertainment. She couldn't focus anyway. Her mind kept returning to the photo Dylan had sent that morning. It was the first picture of Dylan she'd received, and it had been a pleasant surprise. However, she hadn't expected the jolt of familiarity when she'd looked into the bright, sapphire eyes that smiled at her from the photo. They were the same eyes that were in her dreams, and they were beautiful. The only word she could think of when she looked at Dylan was "gorgeous." Her focus returned when she heard the ping of her mailbox. She glanced to her inbox, surprised to see another e-mail from Dylan.

```
Dylan Matthews
Pre-Birthday Mail
```

Okay, I know it's technically your turn to send a message, but nothing's going on over here, and I figured I could annoy you. I also forgot to say in my earlier e-mail that I was glad you and Sam sorted out your differences and have been getting along. I'm impressed that you made the first move and haven't held a grudge. You're a bigger person than I am. Remember, I chose the spare room.

So what did you think of little ole me? Okay, not so little since I'm almost six feet tall, but you can't really tell from the picture. I know it's long overdue, but I had problems connecting the scanner while the office was being refurbished. The scanner is now fitting in very nicely with my new office furniture, so expect plenty more pictures where those came from.

I finally put myself on "no mail" from my other e-mail lists. To quote this morning's message from my new UK friend, "a certain somebody a thousand or so miles away has my undivided attention." So between taking twenty to thirty minutes to reread her e-mails and trying to make sure I answer them, there's no time for the other e-mails. Do you know who the person might be?

I know you're going to be very busy over the next few evenings, so your time for e-mail will be less, but I have a few questions for you. If nothing else, it'll keep you occupied for a few minutes, anyway.

What would be your ideal date night? I'd have to say mine is a dinner and then a movie. After the movie, I'd like to come home and slow dance in the middle of the living room, then make our way to the bedroom and...take it from there.

How would you spend a lazy Sunday afternoon? Mine would be, especially if it's snowing, to stay in bed. I'd like to make love all day, only getting up to go to the bathroom and get something to eat. Someday, I'll get that dream. These days, I'm up at the crack of dawn and doing chores most of the time or playing hockey.

Enjoy your last evening of being 29. Think of it this way: I'll always be four years older than you. Oh, how did your cross-country meet go? And one more thing. This has been on my mind recently. Do you think someone can be in love with two people?
Your friend,
Dylan

Cory read the last question over repeatedly. *Could I love someone else and still be in love with Sam?*

Cory Williams
Re: Pre-Birthday Mail

Hey mate,
The cross-country meet was a huge success. Many of the other schools' coaches gave positive comments, so I got lots of praise off the boss. I am the "bees-knees" of the moment. It never hurts to keep the boss sweet.

I will answer the questions in reverse order. Can you be in love with two people at the same time? My answer would be no. Here's why I think this. You can love many people in many different ways at the same time but can only be IN love with one. That person holds your entire heart, and if you were in love with two people, it wouldn't be true love. I think you can fall in love with someone new, but at the same time, you'd be falling out of love with the other person. Plus, to be in love with two people would mean cheating on both of them. Just my opinion, feel free to ignore it.

As for my perfect date, I liked what you wrote. That would be my perfect date, too. See? We are so in tune with each other. It's probably why we get on so well. I have to add that my date would also involve strawberries and melted chocolate. I also liked your perfect lazy Sunday.

I'm not going to be around much the next three nights, but how about meeting up for an online chat next week? I'm off to visit my friend Angela and her fiancé, Dave, next weekend. I think I'm going to tell her about Deb. I've hated keeping this secret, and she's supposed to be my best friend. I have a week off after next weekend. I can't believe the February half-term break is right around the corner. It's a pity you can't come over and visit. I have nothing to do that week. I can only dream that one day we'll meet up.

I'd better be going as I'm not getting any younger (vbg).

Your kindred spirit (I loved the series, *Anne of Green Gables*).

Cory

PS: I hope you don't mind me saying you are very good looking. If it wasn't for Sam and Sarah, I'd be knocking at your door (vbeg).

Cory paused after writing the postscript. *Don't delete it. You know it's true. You do find her attractive. Too bad we're both involved. I've made my bed – it's just a pity my husband doesn't like to lie in it.* With bitter thoughts in her head, Cory pressed the send button.

CORY BLINKED OPEN her eyes and sniffed the air. A wonderful aroma enveloped her. *Ahh...fresh coffee – now I know it's my birthday.* She wiped the remnants of drool away from the corner of her mouth and looked to her bedside table. There rested a card against a mug of coffee. She opened the card.

Cor,
Happy Birthday
Love, Sam

It wasn't exactly gushing with sentiment, but the thought was there. On cue, Sam entered the bedroom, carrying a tray with more cards tucked under his arm.

"Happy birthday, sweetheart, I hope you slept well. The post arrived early. It makes a nice change. At least you get to open your cards before work. There's also a parcel from America. The postman was trying to shove it through the letterbox so I rescued it from him."

Cory felt the butterflies in her stomach. "Does it have a sender's name on it?" She crossed her fingers hoping it was from Dylan and not from her American aunt.

"It's off your new mate, I think." He placed the tray on the bed. "Look, I have a few calls to make to the business office. I'm going to hop into the shower first." He gave her a quick peck on the cheek and disappeared into his bathroom.

Cory flicked through the cards, recognizing the senders by their handwriting and postmark. She picked up the parcel; the handwriting was clear and bold. She tore the tape and opened the manila envelope. Inside were two wrapped presents and a card. She carefully opened the card. It read:

```
To, Cory
    I hope you have a very happy birthday. Thinking
of you, and I hope you like the presents. The CD is a
"Cory Special." The t-shirt is my size because I
didn't know what would fit you. It's from the place I
work.
Take care,
Dylan
```

She carefully unwrapped the smaller gift. Inside was a home made CD labeled "Cory's Birthday Mix." She scanned the contents and found there were many artists by whom she'd asked to hear songs.

Each title captivated her, and she needed to hear the words of the songs. She slipped from the covers and placed the CD into the stereo. Noticing the time, she quickly opened the other present. It was a purple t-shirt. She tried it on, and it drowned her. She hugged the shirt to her. It had a hint of fragrance—a scent that was familiar to her, but she couldn't remember where from. It reminded her of her dreams.

"Cory, you're going to be late if you don't hit the shower."

"I'll be fine; don't nag." She wished she had time to listen to the whole CD and e-mail Dylan.

As she dressed, she listened to the first song. The lyrics stirred images and emotions Cory hadn't felt in a long time. They made her think of Dylan. *You're dreaming. She only sent you a CD of her favorites. There's no deeper meaning behind the lyrics. Cut the crap and focus on your current relationship. You're lonely and frustrated. She's three thousand miles away, she's living with someone, and you're fucking married. Get your head out of the clouds.*

After dressing, she went into the office. Sam was typing at his desktop computer. He looked up. "So what did you get?"

"A CD of songs by artists who aren't well-known over here and a t-shirt."

"You're not sulking because I haven't given you a present, are you?" Sam asked.

Cory shook her head. "No way. The deal was you got me a laptop for Christmas, and it would be my birthday present, too." She kissed his head. "I'm not sulking, honest."

"In case you were..." he grinned and pointed to his desk drawer. "Look inside there."

Cory opened the drawer and picked up a small present. She tore at the wrapping paper and revealed two more CDs: the latest Mariah Carey and Texas albums. "Sam, you didn't have to. We made a deal, but thanks, I've wanted these for ages."

She gave him a hug, and then pulled him up out of the chair. "Come on, I have to get to work. The world won't stop because I have a birthday."

"I HAVE A few minutes to talk. I wanted to check you got home okay."

"Yeah. Jean didn't mind giving me a lift." Cory nestled the phone into her neck so she could boot up her computer.

"I'm sorry I couldn't pick you up. The boss called an emergency meeting. I'm hoping to be out of here in an hour. I have to do a few follow-up calls before I can leave."

"Take your time. I understand. Thanks for the flowers. They're beautiful, as always. Everyone at work was jealous, and the kids giggled when they got delivered to the classroom."

"Good. Anyway, the quicker I get these calls done, the sooner I get home. See you later."

Cory listened to the dial tone. *No "I love you" or anything.* She placed the phone on the coffee table and watched as her e-mail downloaded. She smiled when she saw Dylan's name.

```
Dylan Matthews
Happy Birthday to You

Happy Birthday, Cory!
    Since there was no e-mail from you this morning,
I take it that you were a very busy girl, opening
tons of presents. Did you get anything special in the
mail?
    My day has only really begun, but I'm hoping
yours was stress-free.
    Thank you for the compliment about my looks. It
was a boost for my ego. You're very good looking
yourself, so we'd make a good pair (if it weren't for
our respective partners).
    Anyway, I'm making this short because I know
you'll be busy the next few days. As it happens,
coincidentally, my hockey team has an away tournament
so I'll be busy, too. I'll e-mail later and tell you
```

how we played.
    Enjoy yourself tonight. Think of me skating my
socks off.
Love, Dylan

It was the closing sentiment that Cory noticed; it was the first e-mail from Dylan that had been sent with love as the parting gesture.

Cory Williams
RE: Happy Birthday to You

Hey Dylan,
    Thank you so much for the CD. I haven't had a
chance to listen to all of it yet. I'm going to put
it on after I send this e-mail. The t-shirt was very
baggy on me, but it will make a good nightshirt for
when we have visitors.
    Tonight, Sam and I are going over to my parents'
house. Hopefully, he'll be home soon. He got called
to a meeting. Mum's cooking a family meal, and I want
to spend my actual birthday with my granddad. It
could be the last one with him.
    On the bright side, I am looking forward to going
out this weekend with the neighbors and my sister. It
should be fun.
    I'll miss your e-mails this weekend, but I hope
you have fun skating. You'll have to let me know how
you did and who you played when you get back.
    Thanks again for the gift. It really did brighten
my day.
Love, Cory

Chapter
Eight

"I WISH WE were going to the restaurant before we drink," Cory whispered to Sam, as they huddled together on the bus ride into town. "I'd have eaten a snack or something."

"Same here."

"I hate drinking on an empty stomach." Cory patted her abdomen for emphasis.

"If Kerry and Pete had turned up on time, we'd maybe have made the earlier reservation. Typical of your sister, though. Let's try and go with the flow. I get the feeling Craig likes to be in control."

TWO HOURS LATER, and with more alcohol inside her than originally planned, Cory felt very mellow. They'd visited three pubs and were currently drinking in the tavern next to the Indian restaurant. The pub was packed. There was limited seating space, and the group had separated slightly. Cory had found a space by the wall to lean against and a shelf to rest her empty beer glass on. She smiled as she watched her sister wrestle her way through the crowd that mobbed the bar.

"How're you doing, little sister?"

Cory took the offered beer. "Fine."

"Really?" Kerry nodded over to the corner of the pub. "The way you're glaring at Sam, you could have me fooled. What's he done now?"

Cory looked over at Sam, who had spent a majority of the evening monopolizing Pete's company. She noticed he was a little unsteady on his feet. "Nothing."

"Yeah, and I'm the Queen of England. I think we should go and interrupt those two before they drink anymore. They look like they've had a skin full."

Cory followed her sister through the crowded pub and sidled over to Sam. "How're you doing?"

"Not bad. Pete and I were discussing football and stuff." He placed his arm roughly around Cory's neck, trying to steady himself. "Cor, I'm starving. Do you think you can ask Craig if we can go next door? If I don't eat now, I'm going to regret it."

The restaurant was beginning to empty after a busy first seating.

Cory was relieved when they were seated quickly. The group placed their orders without too much delay. They were all seasoned Indian eaters, and everyone seemed to have a favorite curry preference.

Cory turned her attention from the story her sister was relating to check a fact with Sam. She hadn't noticed, however, that he had left the table. "Hey, Pete, where did my other half disappear to?"

Pete shook his head. "Last I knew, he was going to the Gents." He looked toward the restroom door. "I should go and see if he's okay. He wasn't feeling too good."

Cory pinned her eyes on the restroom door, concerned that Sam hadn't let her know how he was feeling. "Thanks, Pete, I'd appreciate it."

Five minutes later, Pete arrived back. "I'm sorry, Sam isn't doing well at all."

Cory looked over Pete's shoulder. "Where is he?"

"He was too embarrassed to come out through the restaurant door. He went through the bar entrance and said he was walking himself home. I tried to convince him to come back in here. He told me to tell you he was sorry."

Cory chewed her bottom lip, trying desperately to curtail the tears that threatened to fall. There had been no goodbye or checking in with her. Sam had made his decision and shut her out once again. She felt her sister nudge her arm.

"Hey, you okay?" Kerry asked as she put her arm around her baby sister.

"Yeah, a little bit tipsy," Cory lied. "I guess I'm worried about Sam."

"He's a big boy. He'll be okay. I have to say, I'm a bit surprised. Are you sure everything is okay with you guys? You're usually inseparable, but you've hardly said two words to each other tonight."

"No. I can't believe he's left me in town. He left me with no money, and on my birthday, no less. I guess the pressures of work and stuff are getting to us," Cory whispered. "I'm so embarrassed. This is our first time out with Craig and Karen. What are they going to think of us?"

"They were fine with Pete's explanation. Don't overthink this. Anyway, Craig and Karen are enjoying spending time with their family, and they've had a fair bit to drink, too. They'll probably not even give it a second thought tomorrow."

"I know. Do you think I should go and look for Sam?"

"No, then I'd worry about you. Let's try to enjoy the meal and we'll go straight back to your place afterwards." Kerry rubbed her sister's shoulders comfortingly. "And don't worry about the money. Pete and I are paying for your meal — our treat."

BACK AT THE house, Cory, Pete, and Kerry went in search of Sam. All were relieved when they found him passed out in the bedroom.

Cory checked his pulse and made sure he was breathing okay. Then she said her goodbyes to her sister and brother-in-law.

Cory crept back into the bedroom. She quietly took off her clothes, put on the t-shirt Dylan had sent her, and went into the office. Exhausted and upset, she sank down against the warm radiator and cried. When the tears dried up, Cory downloaded her e-mail, desperate to feel needed. She was disappointed when she didn't see the now-familiar name. *Idiot, she's out of town. Kind of hard to e-mail when you're playing a game of hockey.* Cory opened a new e-mail, feeling the need to pour out her feelings and take a chance.

```
Cory Williams
Depressed Person

Hi Dylan,
    What a crap evening (and birthday celebration)
I've had. It started out really good but disinte-
grated into a mess. Sam got drunk and abandoned me in
town. He left me on my own with the others, no good-
bye or anything.
    I feel so lonely. I know I have to face up to the
fact that maybe my marriage is not the fairy tale
romance I dreamed of, but that's hard to do.
    Dylan, you asked the other week if I felt a con-
nection to you, and yes, I do. I feel like I've known
you forever, and the songs you sent hit home in so
many ways. I think that in another time or place,
maybe we were meant to be together. I like you a lot.
I think we might be soul mates after all.
    Anyway I wanted you to know your friendship means
the world to me. I'm off to sleep off my alcoholic
state.
    Love,
Cory
```

Cory closed the laptop. *I hope I don't scare her away.* She went into the spare room and lay down on the bed. She stared up at the ceiling, dreaming about another time and another love.

She could smell the morning dew on the grass all around her. She snuggled up. The arms that were wrapped around her were strong, and they made her feel secure. She pulled closer at the body and felt the warmth transfer from it to hers. She could feel the muscle against her softer body. Her hands began a bold wander up the strong back, and she felt the muscle ripple, and then a giggle. Her head lifted and she looked straight into the azure gaze of the woman she loved.

Cory opened her eyes. She was covered in sweat. A heat pulsed to her core. The throbbing in her groin was a mixture of pain and pleasure. Her legs trembled. She shifted slightly under the cover and felt the moisture touch the inside of her legs. For the first time in her life, not stimulated by another human hand, Cory felt desire. She'd never felt the urge before. Never needed to take care of her own needs. The images in her mind were strong and clear: blue eyes, black hair, and a lazy smile. Her hands began to wander over her breasts. She left one hand on her breast and settled the other between her legs. The liquid there was warm and slick. She dipped her fingers in it and slowly stroked her center. Her body tingled. She spread the juice over her swollen clitoris. She intensified the pressure and speed while her mind replayed images of her dreams. One name repeated over and over in her fantasy: *Dylan, Dylan, Dylan.* Her muffled sounds of passion were soon replaced by gentle sobs as she realized she was beginning to fall in love with someone she could never have.

CORY LAY ON her side. She hadn't slept much, and the tears stung the back of her tired eyes. She didn't want to cry anymore. There was a tentative knock at the bedroom door. She ignored it, burying herself further under the covers.

Sam poked his head around the door. "You talking to me?"

"No. Go away, but leave the tea on the table." Cory wanted to stay angry with him, but she didn't have the energy. "And get me some headache tablets. They're in the bathroom."

Sam retrieved the pills quickly and sat on the edge of the bed. "Cory, I'm sorry. I shouldn't have mixed my drinks."

"No shit, Sherlock."

"I felt sick and knew I needed a bed. I guess I should have said goodbye to you first."

"You guess?" Cory said. "It's okay, Sam. You can quit groveling. I'm not mad, just disappointed."

"Why'd you sleep in the spare bed?"

"You were sound asleep and snoring like a wart hog," she lied. She felt Sam bend down for a kiss. She turned her head to the side.

"Hey, you are mad."

"No. I'm very tired, and you smell of beer. I need some time on my own today. I promise I'm not mad. A bit unhappy. We'll talk later, okay?"

Sam stood up. "In that case, I'm off to the driving range. We'll go out later, if you want. Just let me know." He didn't even attempt to kiss her again.

Cory stared at the ceiling again. She practically knew the plaster patterns by heart, she'd studied it for long enough. *A fine mess you've gotten yourself into this time, Williams.*

FOCUS ON YOUR work. Quit staring at the computer. One day without contact with Dylan, and Cory was miserable. She finally gave up. She was getting nowhere with her work.

She missed the e-mail on her first check. As she rescanned, she spotted Dylan's name, under a different e-mail address. With fear, and a lot of curiosity, she opened it.

```
DYLAN@free-mail.com
```

```
Hey there,
     Surprise! How did the birthday celebrations go?
     I can't get to my usual e-mail right now, and I
wanted to send a quick one to say hello and let you
know I'll be away a few more days. The tournament
teams have asked us to participate in some training
sessions in addition to the games. The coach hinted a
few weeks ago that this might happen. We were waiting
for the arena to let us know about ice availability.
I took her warnings and booked vacation time off
work. There are only a few of the players who have
commitments at home. If I'm honest, a little bit of
time away from Sarah at the moment is very welcome.
     We're not getting along. Things have changed
between us, and I can't explain it to her. I don't
understand it myself. Anyway, I need some time to
think, and this trip is the ideal opportunity. I've
borrowed a friend's laptop, so that's why the new
address for a while. I can't promise regular e-mails
because she's going back to town tonight, but I'll
try.
     I have the next week off, too. I am trying to
decide where to go and what to do. I have money saved
and might take a trip overseas. I was thinking about
visiting England. I know it's short notice, but you
did say you were on break, too? I should be able to
get a last minute flight. What do you think? Should
we meet? I leave the choice to you.
     I have to go and practice. E-mail me at this
address. I won't be home until later this week.
     I'm getting excited, and I don't even have your
answer,
Love, Dylan
```

Cory gulped. "Oh, my God, she wants to visit," she said aloud. "Shit, this could really happen." *Breathe, and put your brain into gear.* "She's just a friend...just a friend."

Cory hit the reply button and typed the only answer her fingers would allow.

```
Dear Dylan,
     Wow. I'd love to have you visit. We're obviously
living parallel lives, as Sam and I are going through
a difficult patch, too. I'm excited to think you
```

might be coming over. Let me know if you can get a flight out. Next weekend, I'm at Angela's, which is close to Heathrow airport. We could pick you up on Sunday when we leave.

I'm so excited. Looking forward to hearing from you.

Take care,

Cory

Chapter
Nine

CORY OPENED THE front door to Sam. She was pleased to see he had managed to get home early from his monthly sales meeting. "Let me help you carry some of the groceries."

"I'm okay. I just needed the door opened. Did you get all the packing and chores completed?"

"Yes. I left school right on the bell. Thanks to you, there wasn't a lot of tidying up to do. Are you sure Mum was okay about having Holly over the weekend?" Cory asked.

"Your mum said she'll be good company for Granddad."

"How was he?" Cory followed Sam into the house and helped him.

"He looks a bit pale. Your mum thinks he's tired and a little depressed. I promised him you'd go over when we get back from Angela's Sunday, or maybe Monday. I told them you had a friend coming to stay. You know what your mum's like. She can't wait to meet her."

"Speaking of Dylan, she's definitely arriving Sunday evening. I said we'd pick her up. Is that okay?"

"Of course we'll get her," he said, frowning. "There's no way I'd let her wander around a strange country all alone. I may not take much of an interest at times, but I'm not a monster at heart." He checked his watch. "Are you packed and ready to go? We need to hit the road. I'm hoping the traffic will have died down by now so we won't get stuck."

THE JOURNEY DOWN to the coast took longer than expected. The Friday commuter traffic didn't help, and they'd idled for ages on the M25 road that circled London. They finally arrived two hours later and parked outside Angela's tiny terraced house. Cory excitedly hugged her friends and followed them indoors.

CORY WATCHED AS Angela checked the roast beef cooking in the oven.

"How's it going?" Angela asked.

"Not bad. It's hectic at school, but it always is this time of year. You know that." She grinned at her friend, who was also a teacher, but in a different year group. "Listen to those two in there. I didn't realize Chelsea was playing Aston Villa tonight. I hope the two rivals will be talking after the match."

"Me, too. How are you and Sam getting along? Any chance you might be pregnant, yet?" Angela asked.

"Fat chance," Cory said, pretending to count on her fingers. "When did we last see each other? Just before Christmas, wasn't it?" Cory sighed; the joking was over. "I hate to admit this, but we haven't been intimate since before then." Embarrassed she turned her eyes away from Angela's sympathetic stare. "I haven't even brought up the subject of trying for a baby since last year. He's always stated he's never going to be a father, and I guess he really means it. He's not interested, Angela. I keep telling you this. I know it's a hard concept to take in, but I guess I'm not pretty or sexy enough."

"Rubbish, and you know it," Angela retorted. "Any guy would love to have you in his life and bed. Have you talked to him?"

"I've tried a million times." Dejectedy, Cory shook her head. "To be honest, I'm not bothered any more. I'm so sick and tired of the rejection."

"Why the sudden change of tune? This isn't like you. You're usually such a fighter. I could kill him for what he's done to your self-esteem. You and Sam usually get on so well."

Cory caught Angela's worried expression. "That's the problem. He's more my best friend than my lover. I can count on one hand the amount of times we've made love over the past two years. That's hard to accept, and although we get on great, I think I deserve more. We deserve more."

"You do, but do you think you're placing too much emphasis on the sexual side? I mean, no one else has ever held your attention for longer than two weeks, except Darren, and he didn't know a good thing when he met it."

Tell her. The timing couldn't be better. She's given you the perfect lead in. Cory opened her mouth to spill her secret when the guys walked in, searching for food and beers.

Cory whispered, "To be continued."

CORY WOKE, DISTURBED that Sam was leaning over her, holding her arms by her head.

"Hey, baby, calm down. Shush. It was only a nightmare. No one's leaving you, stop worrying."

Cory looked at him, confused. *What's going on? Where am I?* Slowly, she returned to the present. "Wha...what did you say?"

"Shush, go back to sleep."

Cory pulled her arms out of Sam's light grip. "I'm too wired to sleep at the moment. What did you mean by 'nobody's leaving me?'"

Sam smothered a yawn and repositioned his pillow under his head. He placed his hand over Cory's stomach and lightly rubbed. "You were crying out in your sleep and waving your arms about like a possessed person. You kept saying 'don't leave me...please take me with you.' Were you dreaming about your real father again? I thought we got all that sorted."

"No, I don't think I was." Cory rubbed her sore eyes. She took a few relaxing breaths and tried to remember what had caused her so much pain. She couldn't. "I haven't a clue what just happened. I'm all right now." She kissed Sam lightly on his cheek. "Go back to sleep. You've got an early tee off in the morning. I'll wake you, if I need you."

Cory lay staring into the darkness. *Did I dream about my biological father?* She'd had dreams like this before, but she always remembered them. This one was different. Her mind wandered to Dylan. *Maybe I'm nervous. What if she doesn't like me? What if she rejects me? What if she's nothing like I expect? What if there's no friendship?* Questions tumbled around and around. She reviewed Dylan's last e-mail in her mind.

```
Hey Cory,
    I'm excited about the flight and a little ner-
vous. Life here sucks, so I'm relieved to be getting
away for a while. I finally got up the courage to
tell Sarah I was going away. She was furious. She
actually threw a mug at me. It's a good thing I have
quick reflexes from hockey. She's so pissed with me
that she's spent the past few nights with her mother.
I haven't told her where I'm going yet. I don't know
how to explain it to her. I think she thinks I'm
going up to my friends' house in New Hampshire.
    My flight leaves here Sunday morning, and I
arrive early evening. I'll send you the exact time
when I have the itinerary in front of me. I should
have the flight number, as well. Hopefully, we can
catch up sometime over the weekend. I've got your
cell phone number, and I'll call you if we don't tag
up on the computer.
Love,
D
```

Cory couldn't get the image of someone throwing a mug at Dylan out of her mind. She was concerned that Sarah would get physically violent. *Will she hurt Dylan?* Cory felt nauseous, but there was nothing she could do about Dylan's circumstance. She rolled over and tried to get comfortable on the air mattress bed. She closed her eyes, settling on the image of Dylan in her latest photo. Slowly, her breathing evened out, and she fell into a deep slumber.

"MORNING, SLEEPYHEAD. DID you sleep well?" Angela asked as she passed Cory a steaming cup of tea.

"Like a log," answered Cory. *There's no need to tell the world that I had a silly dream.* She glanced up as Sam came into the dining area.

"That's a joke, isn't it?" he said.

"Sam, not here," Cory implored.

Ignoring his wife's plea, Sam turned to Dave. "She spent the whole night tossing, kicking, and yelling. I'm surprised you and Angela didn't come in to see what was going on. She sounded like someone was attacking her. If my game's poor today, it's because I'm knackered."

"Are you okay, Cory?" Angela rubbed Cory's shoulders.

"I'm fine. Honestly, one bad dream and he thinks I'm crazy. Must have been the cheese we had at dinner. Now, can we forget about it?" Cory tapped Angela's hand and gently removed it from her shoulders. "Angela, would it be okay if I checked my e-mail?"

"Sure," Angela replied.

"Cory, we're not at home now. Can't you leave the damn computer alone for five minutes?" Sam picked up his toast and coffee and headed out the back door.

Dave looked to his fiancée and then at the back of his golf partner. "I guess we're leaving. We'll meet you in town later. Enjoy yourselves." Dave kissed and hugged Angela goodbye.

Cory watched her friends' displays of affection for each other. *I want that. What a contrast. My husband storms out the door without a parting sentiment.* Unable to bear the loving gestures between Angela and Dave, Cory went into the living room and hooked her laptop up to the phone line.

After closing the door behind Dave, Angela went to sit near Cory. "Are you really okay? You'd tell me if something was wrong, wouldn't you?"

Cory looked at her best friend. "I'm fine, really. I'm worried about my granddad. I want to check my e-mail and make sure he's okay. Mum said she'd send me an update." *Now you're lying to her. This has got to stop, Williams. Today you have to confront your past, or you'll never be able to face the future.* "Let me do this and then I'm yours for the rest of the day. Deal?"

Angela nodded. "Deal. I'll go and clear up the breakfast dishes."

Cory glanced down at the contents of her mailbox. There were over two hundred messages, but they were meaningless to Cory. She was looking for one special name, and it didn't take her long to find it.

```
Dylan Matthews
Getting ready to travel

Hiya,
    I'm assuming you made it safely to your friend's
house. I hope so. I missed your evening e-mail.
```

My day went okay. I didn't do much after work. As for Sarah and me, I'll tell you more when I see you tomorrow. That has such a nice sound to it.

"What are my plans for the weekend?" I hear you ask. I have packing to do, and then a long, scary plane ride.

I did read your e-mail from last week, and I'm sorry your birthday weekend sucked. I should have replied the other night when I got home from the tournament. I didn't because I wasn't sure what to say. However, we'll meet tomorrow, and I don't want it to be left between us like an elephant in the room. I've also been thinking about how well we get along in our e-mails. Who knows? Maybe in another time and place, we would have made a fantastic couple. No one really knows what fate has in store for them. What I do know is that I consider you to be an important part of my life. I enjoy getting up in the morning because there's usually a perky good morning e-mail waiting for me. I also enjoy going to work for the same reason. I know that whenever I check my e-mail, there's usually a note or two from you. I can't wait to meet you this weekend.

E-mail me when you can. Let me know how it went with Angela. Are you really going to tell her about Deb? You've got guts.

Like I said before, I missed hearing from you last night.

Your friend,

Dylan

Chapter
Ten

CORY STARED OUT at the English Channel. She listened as the waves crashed time and time again over the rocky shore. Cory took a deep breath. She loved breathing in the moist, salt air. Her home was miles from the seaside, and she always felt like a child when she got any chance, no matter how cold the weather, to stand on the edge of the land. She turned to face Angela. "I'm so jealous that you get to see this everyday."

"It's not all it's cracked up to be. Packed with tourists in the summer and freezing winds in the winter. I guess I take it for granted. You look rather melancholy. Are you sure you don't want to share what's on your mind?"

"I do," Cory finally admitted, "but I'm not sure you're going to like what I have to say." She summoned up the courage to tell Angela everything. *It's now or never.*

"Why do you say that?" Angela asked.

"Because you love Sam, and you want Sam and me to be happy." Cory allowed herself to be steered to a nearby bench. It gave her chance to collect her thoughts.

"Yeah, but if I'm honest, I want the best for you. Ultimately, you're my best friend, and I love you more. So start talking, Williams, or I'll have to torture you."

"I don't know where to start." Cory fiddled with the zip on her fleece jacket.

Angela placed her hand over Cory's. "Let me help you out. Last night, I was saying you were getting twitchy because you've been with the same person for so long. I mean, before Sam, as I remember it, your longest relationship lasted nine months."

Cory felt the pressure above her hand, stilling her twitching fingers. "No, it didn't," Cory interrupted and took a deep breath.

Angela let go of Cory's fingers and waved her hands in the air. "Hold on. I've known you twelve years."

Cory nodded in agreement.

"I swear you said Darren was your longest relationship. You always told me you hadn't had a long term boyfriend before college."

Cory nodded again. "That's true."

"And Sam is the only serious fellow you've been with since college, isn't he?"

Cory nodded for the third time. "Yes, he is the only serious relationship I've had since college." Cory braced for the next question, knowing what it was going to be.

"So, how can there have been anyone else? I don't understand what you're trying to say. I think I'd have noticed someone hanging around a lot. I mean for God's sake, back at college, we had to go through your bedroom to get to the bathroom. There was hardly ever a guy in there." Angela continued to gesticulate wildly. "The only other people in your bed a lot were Deb and me..." Angela stopped abruptly.

Cory felt the blush creep up her cheeks. She waited for the penny to drop. She could practically hear the clang. She watched Angela's expression change from confusion to alarm. *Shit, what do I say now? Admit the truth, idiot. Make a joke about it. Say something.* "I guess I don't need to tell you who it was or when it was." Cory shuffled in her seat. She'd never experienced Angela speechless before. *She has a right to be. Not only do you announce that you dated a woman, but that you've hidden it from her, too.* Cory swallowed a lump of nervousness. She hadn't thought about how her silence for so many years would affect their friendship. "Say something, please. Anything."

Angela stood up and took a few steps away from Cory. "Want to walk? I need to move. I'm cold...and shocked."

"Sure. Let's walk to the nearest pub. I could do with a drink. Confessions of the soul tend to make me parched."

After a few minutes of silence, Angela spoke. "I knew you and Deb were close. There'd even been gossip about you two spread around college."

"Really? I never heard any."

"That's because Carol, Frankie, and I dismissed them as rumors and backed up your honor."

"Thanks. You're good mates."

"Not good enough, though," Angela bit back. "Didn't you trust us? I thought we told each other everything. I need a bloody stiff drink." Angela pointed to a pub across the main road. They walked toward it in silence.

Cory reviewed various statements of friendship that she could offer Angela, but none of them sounded sincere. *You didn't trust them. It's the truth. You didn't tell them because you didn't think they'd understand. Admit it to yourself, and then admit it to your best friend.* A nervous panic gripped her chest like a vice. Cory felt out of control.

They ordered their beers at the small bar and settled into a quiet corner. The pub was relatively quiet, given the time of day. Cory was clueless as to what to say, so she waited for Angela to take the lead. It didn't take long.

"So, are you going to let me in on this big secret or keep it from me for another six years?" The sarcasm dripped from Angela's lips.

Cory hadn't seen Angela this angry in a long time, and never had it been directed toward her. She knew the bitterness was justified. If the tables were turned, she'd feel just as betrayed. "I was scared. I wanted to tell you, I swear. In fact I did tell you, a few years ago." She saw Angela raise an eyebrow. "Remember when we went out for that meal and ended up drinking those four bottles of wine. We got so drunk." She waited for the acknowledging nod. "I admitted it then, but you never remembered the next morning."

"So remind me now. How long were you and Deb an item? It couldn't have been that serious. I'd have picked up on it. I'd have known. You can't care for someone that much and not tell your friends. Live a lie like that and not have us know."

Cory took a large sip of her Guinness, more for courage than to quench a thirst. "We began dating at the start of the fourth year, and it lasted until a few months after college. It just happened." Cory stopped. Angela's piercing stare made her edgy. She could see the hurt and disappointment in Angela's eyes. It hurt to feel the distance growing between them. "I was scared you wouldn't understand. I didn't want to lose your friendship."

"I'm never going to stop being your friend. Yes, I'm shocked, and yes, I'm upset. But not about whom you slept with, but because you kept it from me. You didn't trust me."

"I wanted to. Deb wanted me to. So many times I've tried to tell you, especially back when it was happening, but I was so scared, so confused."

"Scared and confused about what?"

"I was confused about who I was. I've known all my life that I like both sexes. I know that men find me attractive, and I tried so hard back then to fit in and be normal. When Deb came along, she opened feelings in me that I'd never felt before, not even with Darren. We were friends and lovers." Cory watched Angela's eyes widen and her jaw drop slightly.

"Oh come on, Angela. She practically lived with us. You said yourself you had to go through my bedroom to get to the bathroom. You're telling me you never thought about why she spent so many nights at our place?"

"I thought she was having a pretty rough time where she lived, and that because you two got on so well, it was a place for her to take refuge. I put it down to the fact that, whilst everyone else in the group had long term boyfriends, you'd sworn off them. I guess I must have been a laughing stock to you and Deb."

"Never!" Cory slammed her free hand down on the wooden table top. "Not once did we ever think that. I went through hell trying to be one person for Deb and a different person to you guys. I didn't know what I wanted. I loved Deb, but even then I couldn't admit it to myself, let alone others."

"We'd have understood."

Cory shook her head. A lone tear tracked down her left cheek. "You say that now, but back then, I heard your comments about the couples we had in the ladies' football team."

"That was different. They weren't my best friend."

"It's easy to say now. We're older and wiser."

"I know," Angela said. "We'll never really know what would have happened. I'm curious, why did you break up? I mean, if it was so good, why?"

Cory shrugged, wiping the tears away surreptitiously. "I left college and got involved in my new job. I moved back home. Meanwhile, Deb was still at college, and I guess my unwillingness to admit the relationship and the distance tore us apart. She wanted me to make a commitment, and I wasn't ready. In the end, she got bored and found someone else." Cory couldn't hide the tears anymore, and she dropped her head into her arms.

"Oh, my god, you went through all that alone." Angela rubbed Cory's back, soothingly. "You could have talked to me. I would have listened and tried to understand. I'm shocked. I had no idea you liked girls, I thought it'd always been guys for you. I mean, you sure went through your fair share."

Cory lifted her head and caught the teasing smirk. "I had my doubts in secondary school. I had the biggest crush on my P.E. teacher. She was the reason I went to college. At first I thought I was bisexual, but as the years have gone on, I'm confused." Cory downed the rest of her pint and held up her glass, indicating to Angela that she wanted another one.

"I can understand why. Going from thinking you're gay, to bisexual, and now being straight. It's enough to make anyone have doubts. Let me go and get another set of beers, and we'll talk some more. What a bombshell. Still, I bet you feel better. At least there's nothing else hidden in the closet, no pun intended."

Cory laughed uneasily and watched Angela saunter toward the bar. *Good one, Williams. Now she thinks you're straight. You were supposed to tell her that you're not sure any more.*

Cory took the offered glass out of Angela's hand. "Cheers." Cory held up her glass and clinked it with Angela's.

"Here's to no more secrets." Angela took a large swig of beer.

"Angela, I have another secret to tell you."

Angela spluttered and choked on the mouthful. "Bloody hell. What can you possibly have to tell me now? You said you weren't pregnant. You promised me you'd be my bridesmaid in July. I swear if you're not there beside me on that day, I'll never speak to you again."

Cory snorted. "Which part of our conversation haven't you been listening to? It'd have to be the bloody Immaculate Conception for me to be pregnant. No, I am not, and I'm not likely to be." She paused long enough to summon up the strength to admit her feelings for Dylan. "I've met someone."

At this statement, Angela did choke. It took a few moments of vigorous coughing and back patting before she regained her composure. "You're not joking are you?"

"No, I'm very serious."

"How long have you known him?"

Apprehensively, Cory began ripping off small sections of the cardboard beer mats. She tried to smile and make a joke of her friend's assumptions. "You definitely have not been paying attention today, my friend. After our last bit of conversation, you still assume it's a guy."

"Oh shit, it's a woman?"

Cory took a deep breath. *Here goes nothing.* "Yes, it's a woman."

"Fuck. How many secrets can one person keep? I can't believe you've kept all this to yourself. Christ, now you're telling me you're having an affair." Angela said.

"I'm not having an affair, and can you shout a bit louder? I don't think they heard you over the other side of the bar," Cory retorted.

"But you just said you'd met someone."

"Yes, the term was 'met' someone, not slept with them. Look, this is going to sound somewhat weird, so stay with me." Cory took a sip of her beer, "And let me finish before you bulldoze your way in, okay?"

"Okay, but I'm beginning to worry already."

"Remember I recommended a book to you at Christmas?"

"Yes."

"I wanted to read more, so I joined a mailing list on the Internet. Anyway, the mailing list began a writing skit, and through this I met Dylan. And, well, things have gone from there."

"What do you mean 'things have gone from there?' Details, Williams, I need details. Who is she? Where is she? And more importantly, what have you done with her? Fess up. I need to know what mess you've got yourself in now."

Cory felt Angela's arm touch her shoulder and moved away instinctively, hurt by the accusations.

"I'm kidding, pal. Take your time, but I want all the details."

"I think she's my soul mate—my missing link."

"You're serious, aren't you?"

"Yes. I never went looking for this. It just happened, and I don't know what to do."

"So, you're a couple?"

"Not even close. She lives three thousand miles away, and is with another woman. It's really all in my mind."

"Three thousand miles? So, I take it she's not the lady next door?"

Cory smiled at the comment. "God, no, I wish she were. It'd make things much easier. She lives in America, near Boston. She's...wonderful." Cory's voice wavered on the last section. She picked up her pint and drank the remnants. "I know it sounds bizarre, but I feel like I've come home."

"I hate to be the person to rain on your parade, but I'm going to give you the facts as I see them. Number one, you've never laid eyes on this person. She could be anyone. She could be an axe murderer for all you know. Number two, you said she had a girlfriend, and I hate to remind you, but you're married." Angela counted off with her fingers as she stated the facts. "Let me see, reason three is you live in two totally different countries. Oh wait, continents would be more precise. Reason four, you both have homes, families, and jobs. Finally, do you even know if she feels the same way?"

Cory considered Angela's list. "Okay, when it's put like that, it sounds stupid. I swear I can't explain it, but she makes me feel so happy and safe. All your points are valid, but I know there'd be solutions if she was interested. Things happen for a reason. I can't get her out of my head. Did I tell you she's gorgeous, too?" Cory sighed and put her head in her hands. She knew it sounded absurd, especially now she'd said it out loud.

"In my opinion, you're lonely and feeling undervalued. Where does Sam fit in this equation? Do I have to remind you of the vows you made? You're really thinking about throwing it all away on someone you've never met, are probably never going to meet, and who may never return your affections? Cory, wake up and smell the coffee. Life isn't like it is in the movies. She's not going to drop everything and come to your rescue. You chose your life, and now you have to live it."

Cory wiped fiercely at the angry tears falling down her cheeks. "You're wrong."

"Wrong about what?" Angela asked. "Which bit am I wrong about?"

"All of it, some of it. I am going to meet her, and very soon. She's...she's flying over tomorrow."

"She's the friend you're meeting tomorrow? You could have said."

"I was going to, but your mouth just ran away. At least I know how you feel." Cory looked at her empty glass. Where was a drink when she needed one?

"Hey, cut me some slack. I've just found out that my best friend is bisexual, has kept it a secret from me, and is now head over heels in love with some girl she's never met and whom she's meeting tomorrow. Did I miss anything?" Angela passed her empty glass to Cory. "God, I need another drink. You're going to be the death of me."

Cory left the table and five minutes later, returned with her hands full. "I thought we might need some sustenance to soak up the alcohol. All they had were crisps and sandwiches, so I got us a mixture. I have to go back and fetch my drink."

"Good thinking. I was about to send out a search party for you."

They ate in silence. Cory turned her attention from her sandwich every now and then to observe Angela pushing her lunch about on the plate. She desperately wanted to talk more about Dylan, but Angela's facial expression wasn't giving much away.

"So, you don't know how she feels about you?"

Cory's eyes widened at the abrupt question and the tone in which it was asked. "I'm not sure. My heart and soul tell me she likes me — more than likes me. But my mind keeps telling me to be serious." She chewed thoughtfully on a piece of meat, trying to determine what to say. "She really is the whole package. She has long black hair, a deep tan, beautiful blue eyes, and she says she's tall. What would someone like that see in little old me?"

Angela coughed slightly. "Have you looked in the mirror recently? You're beautiful, even if I say so myself. Who wouldn't fancy you? I could throttle Sam for what he's doing to your confidence and self-esteem. You used to be so confident and were the first to boost your own ego. Now you doubt yourself so much. Speaking of Sam, have you told him?"

"No, I wouldn't know where to start. It's not a conversation you can have over the dinner table. Can you imagine the scene? 'Pass the salt, honey, and by the way, I'm gay and in love with someone else.' It would kind of give him indigestion or a heart attack."

"But if you're serious about Dylan you have to tell him. It's not fair."

"I told you my feelings for Dylan are probably in my head. I have figured out one thing, though. Sam and I aren't working. I'm going to enjoy my week getting to know Dylan. Then I'll sort my life out."

"Just promise me you won't jump into the unknown."

"I promise. Now, this conversation is officially closed. Thanks for listening. I feel like a great weight has been lifted off my shoulder."

"No problem. That's what old friends are for."

LATER AT THE house, the guys settled down to watch another football match.

"Are you two going to watch the game?" Dave asked Angela and Cory as he tossed a beer to Sam, who had settled himself down on the two-seater sofa.

"No, I'm feeling a little tired, love. I think Cory and I need an afternoon nap. We might surf some sites for more wedding ideas, as well," Angela said.

Cory looked blankly at Angela. She didn't recall having a conversation with Angela about websites. "Is that okay with you, Sam?"

"Makes a change from downloading and sending e-mails, I suppose." Sam replied without turning his head from the television screen.

Angela and Cory made their way up the narrow stairs. When they got to the top, Cory turned to Angela. "I have no idea what you're up to, but, thanks I needed some space."

"I figured as much. I thought you might want to check your e-mail. Maybe there'll be one from Dylan. Which reminds me, have you two ever spoken over the phone?"

"No, we kept meaning to, but we could never find a time when we were both around. I have downloaded Messenger as I've been told you can chat that way for free. I haven't gotten 'round to buying a microphone and headset. Why'd you ask?" Cory settled herself on Angela's bed.

"I guess I'm curious about Dylan. She seems to have captivated you. I don't think I've ever seen you so caught up with someone. You have a twinkle in your eyes when you talk about her. I want to know what she's like." Angela pulled Cory into a hug and whispered, "I'll always be here for you, no matter what happens." After releasing her, Angela settled down and yawned. "I'm going to take a nap. The phone socket is behind the table. Take your time, and say 'hi' to Dylan for me. Tell her to pack a few sweaters. I heard the weather forecast, and it's going to be cold this week."

"I will." Cory stood up and found a comfortable spot in the corner of the bedroom near the phone socket. She hooked up the laptop and waited the few seconds it took to boot up.

There weren't many e-mails and, more surprisingly, there wasn't one from Dylan. Disappointed, she decided to surf some education websites. After a while, her eyes were drawn to a flashing icon in the corner of the screen. She clicked on the little blue man. *"Dylan Matthews is now online."* Those simple five words made Cory's heart miss a beat. She clicked on the message box.

```
Cory Williams: Hey there.
```

A few moments later, Dylan replied.

```
Dylan Matthews: Hey, there yourself. How you doing?
Cory Williams: Okay, I guess. You got time for a
chat?
```

Cory crossed and uncrossed her fingers hoping that Dylan would have a few minutes to spare. Contact with Dylan was exactly what she needed.

```
Dylan Matthews: For you, I always have time.
```

The sentiment in the line made Cory feel very warm all over. Her heart rate increased slightly with anticipation—this was her first present time chat with Dylan.

Dylan Matthews: You okay? You seem a bit down. I can
always tell. How's the visit going?
Cory Williams: The visit is going better than
expected. I told Angela about college, Deb, and other
stuff.
Dylan Matthews: Wow. So how did she take your myste-
rious past?
Cory Williams: Okay. Better than okay, really. She
was very supportive. A little bit upset that I hadn't
told her, but understanding in her own way. She said
she loved me and didn't care about my past.
Dylan Matthews: Good. I don't want to have to come
over there and beat her butt around the block. So, do
you feel better?
Cory Williams: Yeah, it feels good to finally have it
off my chest. Enough about me. How are the holiday
plans going?
Dylan Matthews: The VACATION (sorry, I couldn't
resist that) plans are finally taken care of. I was
in the middle of sending you an e-mail. My flight
leaves very early tomorrow morning, about 6 A.M., so
I'll be getting in around 5 P.M., your time.
Cory Williams: How long is the flight?
Dylan Matthews: About 6-7 hours. Have you got a pen
and a piece of paper handy? I have the flight details
here, if you want them.
Cory Williams: Hold on.

Cory looked around the room. She didn't want to disturb Angela's
nap. She spotted a pile of schoolbooks tucked in the corner. She got up
and picked up Angela's jotter and a pen, tore out a page, and resettled
herself in front of the computer.

Cory Williams: Sorry, I had to find a pen.
Dylan Matthews: Ok, I'm flying American Airlines,
flight number AA281. That's all I know, except its
Heathrow, London. Are you sure this is okay, Cory?
You're not just being nice and secretly dreading a
loud American arriving on your doorstep?
Cory Williams: Hey, I'm positive. I had nothing
planned, and Sam is away one of the nights, so I can
do the tourist bit with you. How long are you stay-
ing?
Dylan Matthews: I leave next Saturday. Sarah isn't
happy, and we've had another fight. I need to get
away and clear my mind.
Cory Williams: Is it that bad?
Dylan Matthews: Yeah. I'll fill you in tomorrow. I
can't believe we will be meeting in about 24 hours.
How are you feeling?
Cory Williams: Truthfully, I'm a bag of nerves, kind

of excited, and a little bit scared—all rolled into one. I think my biggest worry is the great friendship we have built up won't translate in real life. Does that make sense?

Dylan Matthews: Definitely. It's exactly how I am feeling, too. So where are you now?

Cory Williams: In Angela's bedroom. She's sleeping, and I was checking my e-mail. Then I thought I'd join her. We spent some time drinking this lunchtime, and that always makes me tired. I guess I'd better let you go and do some packing. I'm looking forward to meeting you, Dylan. I'll be at the arrival gate to meet you. Take care. Love, Cory.

Dylan Matthews: Yeah, I have tons to do. Take care yourself, and I'll see you tomorrow. Love, Dylan.

Chapter
Eleven

DYLAN CHECKED HER luggage at the American Airlines desk. Afterwards, she found a seat in the quiet terminal. It was very early in the morning and the airport was understandably empty. Dylan had decided to take the earliest available flight for two reasons: it had turned out to be the cheapest option, and she had needed to get out of the house. Sarah had gone crazy when Dylan had told her she was going on vacation alone. She sat contemplating the few hours she'd spent at home packing and Sarah's early arrival home from staying with her parents.

"Where are you going? You just got back from that hockey tournament. I thought you were spending your vacation painting the bathroom. I came home so we could talk."

"I need my space, Sarah. I need to think things through. Who am I kidding? We need some space." Dylan said slowly, summoning up the courage to face Sarah. She continued packing her case, avoiding Sarah's eyes.

"So where are you going? To the house in New Hampshire?" Sarah asked.

Dylan paused in her movements. She hadn't thought about what she'd tell Sarah. She'd hoped to go away and leave a note. She really didn't want to get into a conversation about Cory and England. She turned and saw Sarah looking at her passport lying on the bed next to her wallet.

"Unless I'm stupid and they've changed the rules on state-to-state travel, I'm guessing you're leaving the country."

Dylan met Sarah's stare. "Er...yeah...I decided to go and see what England is like." She saw the disbelief in Sarah's expression.

"You're going to fucking England! Don't you think that's a bit drastic? What happened to talking things through? Where are you going to stay? Who are you going to stay with? What about money?" Sarah advanced toward Dylan.

"Sarah, calm down. Jesus, I'm taking a vacation on my own. It's not a crime."

"I'd have taken time off to go with you. We could have spent some time talking."

Dylan threw a pair of socks in her suitcase. "I've tried talking to you, but you won't listen. It's either your way or no way."

"That's not true. Will you stop moving around for five minutes and explain where you're going?"

Dylan placed the rest of her socks into her suitcase, closed the lid, and stood in front of Sarah. "Okay. I'm going to stay with a friend."

"What friend? Oh, wait a minute, not that girl you've been e-mailing. You said it was just a friendship."

"It *is* just a friendship."

"No...no...I knew something was going on when she sent that card to you." Sarah slammed her hand onto Dylan's suitcase.

Dylan saw the pain in Sarah's frantic eyes. "Sarah, I said it when you asked before and I'm saying it again, there is nothing going on between Cory and me. We're friends. She's married. The card was a thank you card for sending her a birthday gift." She turned back to her personal items beside the case and carefully placed each one into her hand luggage. She hadn't lied. There was nothing going on between Cory and her, unless her dreams counted.

"Remind me how you two met again?" Sarah asked.

"How many times do I need to explain this to you? We met on a mailing list, and we teamed up together. We share the same interests, and she listens to me. End of story. I am allowed to have friends. This is supposed to be a relationship not a fucking prison sentence." Dylan zipped up her backpack.

"So what happens to us?" Sarah asked.

"Nothing. Maybe we should use this opportunity to find a solution to our constant fighting. I hope we can take this week to think. I mean really think. We need to look at what has happened between us lately and see what the future holds, if anything, for us."

"I don't understand. What do you mean by 'anything?'"

Dylan heard the pain in Sarah's voice. She could hardly bear to watch, knowing the words she was going to utter would break Sarah's heart, but she did. "I think the spark has died, Sarah. To be honest...I don't think I love you anymore."

Dylan stood silently, unable to go to Sarah, unable to stop Sarah as she collapsed against the bed and sank down to the floor. *I'm so sorry. But you're not the one. I've finally found the one.*

"You know I don't like being by myself in the house."

Dylan threw her hands in the air. "I just told you I don't love you anymore, and all you can think about is being on your own in the house. I think we just found the answer to all our questions."

"I didn't mean it to come out like that. Dylan, don't go. Please, give me five minutes. I promise I'll listen. This isn't like you."

"I know. I do care for you, but we're not good together anymore. We're so opposite." Dylan passed Sarah a tissue and waited impatiently as Sarah wiped her eyes and blew her nose.

"Opposites attract."

"Not anymore. We barely agree on anything. We can't even watch the same TV shows. We're rarely in the same room. You watch your shows upstairs, and I watch mine in the bedroom."

"Don't go blaming me for not spending time together. You're always at fucking hockey."

"I know. You said you wanted to talk, not have a pissing contest. I'm not trying to lay blame. I'm trying to tell you how I feel. I'm trying to explain what I think is wrong in our relationship."

"Stay, Dylan, stay. I'm begging you. We can work through this. We could go to a counselor."

"Maybe." Dylan checked her watch and picked up her luggage. She walked over to the door. "Look, go and stay at your parents' house. You're always there anyway, or have somebody come stay in the guest room. You had your chance to talk to me this week and try to work things out, but you chose to hide away and sulk. Now it's my turn." Dylan felt heartless. She wished she could stay and resolve their issues, but she had a flight to catch. Heart-to-hearts weren't her strong point. She knew she'd become more sarcastic if Sarah riled her defenses any more.

"Please..."

Dylan placed her luggage at the doorway and went over to Sarah. Her tears melted some of the steel in her heart. Dylan knelt down and hugged her. "I'm sorry, so sorry. Use this time to think, please. We'll talk when I get back, I promise. I'll call when I get there." She gently placed a kiss on Sarah's head, gathered her things, and left the house, silent tears tracking down her face.

THE ANNOUNCEMENT OF her flight interrupted Dylan's thoughts. Her stomach churned. This was it, no turning back. At the end of the flight, she'd be meeting the woman she felt was the one — the only one for her. *What do I do when I meet her? Do I appear cool and aloof? Should I shake her hand? Maybe I could hug her.* A small smile glimmered on Dylan's face and her pulse quickened. If this is what one thought did, what would meeting the real person do? Dylan hoped she wouldn't faint.

SAM TURNED THE car into the pick-up lane at the arrival terminal. "You run in. We're late, that accident and tail back held us up. Dylan should be through passport control by now. I'll circle 'round the building."

Cory looked up to the roof of the car and said a silent thank you to whoever had listened to her wishes. She had desperately wanted her first meeting with Dylan to be just the two of them. She opened the car door and proceeded through the entrance of the terminal. The airport was humming with activity. She glanced up at the arrivals monitor and saw Dylan's flight number; the plane had landed. She was actually here. Cory felt a wave of nervous nausea. She stood with the growing crowd waiting to welcome weary travelers to the country.

EXHAUSTEDLY, DYLAN WATCHED as all the various pieces of luggage slid on to the carousel. She was relieved when she saw her suitcase drop down. She grabbed hold of the handle and checked the label. Then she walked through the 'Nothing to Declare' door of customs and handed in her customs form. She turned the corner and walked through the double doors. She instantly spotted Cory. Dylan cockily winked at her and headed over to where she stood. Dylan stopped in front of Cory, a huge grin plastered to her face. She had no idea what to say.

"Hi, Dylan, how was the flight?" Cory's heart was beating double time. She knew her hands were shaking but she had to do something as Dylan seemed to be frozen to the spot.

Dylan found her voice. "It was okay — long, boring, but smooth. No complaints. Any flight that lands on the ground is a good flight to me." Dylan held out her right hand to shake Cory's, at the same time, as Cory stepped toward her, and they ended up in an awkward hug.

Cory wrapped her arms around Dylan, one arm around the top of her shoulder and the other around her waist. She pulled Dylan into a more comfortable hold. "Welcome to England. I've been looking forward to this." She gave Dylan a squeeze and then let her go.

Dylan had to remind herself to breathe. Her body was on fire. She could feel Cory's hand on her waist, and it seemed to be burning a hole in her side. She heard the words, but they made no sense. All she knew was how wonderful it felt to hold Cory, and she didn't want to let go. She felt Cory pull away, and she reluctantly released her.

"Hi, yourself. How you doing?" Dylan asked, giving Cory a killer smile.

Cory stared, mesmerized. *Williams, you are in so much trouble.*

After the formal welcoming, Cory waited with Dylan's bags while she went to the restroom. She used the time to call Sam.

"I'm coming into the pick-up zone. Where are you?" Sam asked, rather brusquely.

"We're using the ladies, but we have to do it one at a time because of the luggage. We're five minutes away. Just pull in and wait. We won't be long."

"So, what's she like? Has she got two heads? I bet she's been beaten by the ugly stick, and you can't wait to get back to the car."

Cory heard Sam's chuckle. "Well, she's definitely very noticeable, Sam. I'll say that about her. You would most certainly stare if you saw her in a crowd. See you in five." She closed her cell phone and waited patiently.

Cory and Dylan stepped out into the chilly, night air. Cory spotted Sam parked in the nearby pick-up zone. "Dylan, about Sam, he's not a man of many words. I don't want you to feel bad if he doesn't talk much."

"You don't have to apologize for him. I'm not one for small talk, myself. I don't think we need to worry with you around. I imagine people struggle to get a word in edgewise." Dylan faked an injury as she felt Cory's elbow nudge her side.

"You're such a fool. Let's get out of here." Cory linked arms with Dylan and led her over to the car.

Sam got out of the car. Cory could see by the look on his face that he was astonished by Dylan's looks.

"Sam, I'd like you to meet Dylan." As Cory went past Sam to open the passenger door, she whispered, "Pull your jaw up, love, you're drooling."

Sam shook Dylan's hand and then immediately set about putting the luggage in the trunk of the car while Dylan and Cory argued light-heartedly about who should have the passenger seat.

"Dylan, you have the longer legs. Since it's got better leg room, take the front seat."

"You take it. It has all your stuff by it. I'll be fine in the back, I promise," Dylan said, as she headed toward the rear of the car.

"When you two ladies have quite finished, I'd like to get home before Christmas," Sam cut in sarcastically.

The journey back north was quiet. Cory felt she ought to do something to ease the atmosphere in the car. She turned to ask Dylan a question, and saw that she was sleeping. Dylan's face was relaxed. She looked stunning. All Cory wanted to do was drink in the beauty of this woman before she awoke. Cory turned back and pulled down the sun visor to look in the mirror on the backside. Feigning something in her eye, she fiddled for a bit, and then leaned back in her seat, "forgetting" to put the visor back up. Perfect. She had an excellent view of Dylan. She noted the long, ebony hair, tied loosely into a ponytail, the twitch in the corner of her mouth, and the tanned skin. The woman was flawless, no marks, no spots. She looked amazing. Cory trailed her eyes from the face down the broad shoulders; they looked muscular and firm. She licked her lips. *What are you doing? You're practically salivating over a woman, and your husband is sitting next to you. Snap out of it! Focus, Williams, before you get out of your depth.* She shook her head trying to rid the voice of conscience taunting her.

"Are you okay?" Sam asked.

"Pardon?" Cory turned to Sam, the spell broken.

"You seem distracted. You've been staring into space for the past ten minutes. What are you thinking about?" Sam met Cory's eyes and then returned his gaze to the road.

"I was making plans for the week ahead. I was going to take Dylan to Warwick Castle tomorrow. Will you come with us?" Cory asked, silently praying he'd say no.

"No, I'm too busy. I'm sorry you're going to be doing the hosting on your own for most of the week. It's my busiest time. You know, the building business is picking up and I've got clients to see. It's only two months until bonus time. I still need a few more orders to meet my target."

"Okay."

"You seem upset. If you really want me to, I could change my timetable around."

"No. It really is okay. I understand." Cory tried to keep the smile from appearing on her face. "I figured we'd go to the castle, then pop in and introduce Dylan to Mum and Granddad, as we'll be in the area. That's if Dylan is up to it—you never know how jetlag can affect people." Cory glanced into the visor mirror. Her gaze was met by a dazzling smile. She blushed at being caught looking. She turned and adjusted the seat belt. "Speak of the devil, how are you feeling?" she asked.

Dylan stretched and yawned, "I've been better, but a few more hours shut eye and I'll be good to go. I didn't sleep on the plane at all. My body is still on US time. All I need is something to eat and I'll be livelier in no time."

DYLAN EXAMINED SAM as he drove. For a guy, he seemed cute enough, but he looked older than his years, with the gray speckled throughout his dark brown hair. She watched his interactions with Cory to see how affectionate he was. She knew quite a bit from the e-mails. So far, she'd seen nothing in the couple's interaction to tell they were a couple. They acted like brother and sister.

AN HOUR AND a half after leaving the airport, the sedan pulled up in front of a decent-sized house. Dylan got out of the car and looked at the brick design on the front of the house. She glanced at the dimly lit front yard. It looked tidy from what she could see. She heard a deep bark emanating from inside.

"You do like dogs, don't you?" Sam asked.

This was the first direct conversation Dylan had received from Sam. She followed Sam to the front door of the house. "Never owned one, but they don't bother me. She's a German Shepherd, isn't she?"

Sam's face lit up as he opened the door and a huge fluffy bundle of fur leaped his way. "Yep, she is and the biggest softy in England. She has a tendency to get over excited and will probably lick you to death.

Holly get down," Sam shouted as the eager dog bounded over to Dylan and stood full height trying to lick her new toy.

Dylan bent down and stroked Holly. The longhaired fur was soft to touch. "Has she been here alone all weekend?" Dylan inquired.

"No, my parents had her. Dad dropped her off earlier," Cory answered.

Dylan let Holly smell her and she stroked the side of her face as the dog calmed down. Dylan turned to Sam, who was taking the bags out of the trunk of the car. "She's beautiful and really friendly." Dylan giggled as the dog poked her nose into Cory's bag, and while doing so almost knocked Cory over.

"She's the best looking dog for miles," answered Sam, as he led them into the house.

"He adores her. She gets more attention than I do. You're on to a winner if you like his dog," Cory said as she headed toward the kitchen.

Dylan smiled at the comment and followed Cory, while Sam went upstairs with her suitcase and their bags. Holly followed him. Dylan knew who she'd prefer if she had to choose. She couldn't believe the change in Sam as he interacted with the dog.

Dylan stepped into the room with Cory. "Obviously, this is the kitchen. Let me check the cats got fed, and then I'll give you a tour."

"Sure. Where are the cats?"

Cory did a quick look around the kitchen. "They're either sleeping somewhere warm or roaming down the fields looking for voles. The river runs through the farmer's field at the end of our road. I had the neighbors feed the cats for us while we were away. The tins of cat food have been moved, so they definitely got fed. Let me show you the house."

Dylan followed Cory out of the kitchen, back down the short hallway, and into the room nearest the front door.

"This is the living room and through those double doors is the dining room."

"Which we rarely use, except for holidays and special occasions," Sam interjected as he walked in. "Dylan, I put your case in the guest bedroom."

"Thanks." Dylan looked around the room. Cory hadn't lied when she'd said she liked blue. The carpet was dark blue. The sofas were slightly lighter, but still blue, and the curtains were blue and cream. The walls were magnolia, and framed pictures dotted various places. Dylan looked at them. There were a few of Holly, some of Cory and Sam's wedding, a photo of Cory when she graduated, and one of an older lady, who she decided was probably Cory's grandmother. Above the fireplace, there was a large family photo. It was evident from the smiling faces that there was a strong resemblance running through the family. "It's very spacious."

"Ready to go upstairs?"

"Sure." Dylan took in her surroundings: the hallway, the telephone table, Cory's butt. She tripped on the first step and held onto the banister for support. *Concentrate. You could have fallen down and broken your neck, and it would have been your own fault.*

Cory continued with her tour. "This is Sam's domain," she said, as she opened a door on her left and led Dylan inside. They were in the office. Dylan saw a desktop computer and piles of paperwork strewn on the floor and shelves. "As you can see, filing isn't his forte." Cory grinned at Dylan. "Not that I'm any better." They both chuckled and walked back onto the landing.

"This next room is our third bedroom, or Granddad's room. It's the room he stays in at Christmas or when he and Sam do the wine run to France." She turned wistfully to the bed, her mind on the happier times when her grandfather had been full of life. She felt a hand on her shoulder.

"I'm here for you, Cory, if you want to talk. I know it's going to be hard, but you've told me so much about him in your e-mails. I was hoping we'd be able to sit down one day and talk face-to-face about grief." Dylan was stunned. She'd heard the words, and they sounded like her voice, but surely she wasn't volunteering to have a heart-to-heart.

Cory felt the hand tighten on her shoulder. "Thanks. It means a lot that you offered." She turned and headed to another door.

"This is your room. This door here goes into the bathroom. It's all yours. We have our own toilet and shower in our room. Just make sure you lock the door leading to the landing, as Sam uses this bathroom to do his pondering." She pointed at the various golf and men's health magazines stacked on the counter. "I've warned him it's out of bounds to him until you leave."

Dylan placed her backpack next to her case. "Thanks for the advice."

Cory walked out of the guest room and into a much bigger room. "This is the master suite."

Dylan scanned the room and saw the pine bureaus, bed side tables, and large queen-sized bed. "You have a lovely house. I'm looking forward to this week."

THE THREESOME SETTLED for the remaining few hours of the evening in the living room. Sam and Cory sat on one sofa, and Dylan and her new found friend, Holly, sat on the other. They'd had cheese and crackers for supper and a few bottles of beers. As the time ticked on, Cory noticed Dylan's increased yawning and fidgeting. "Hey there, sleepyhead, want to call it a night?"

Dylan grinned as she saw the concerned look on Cory's face. "I'm busted, big time, and here I was thinking I was looking perky."

Sam got up, muttered something Dylan didn't catch, and left the room. Dylan raised a quizzical eyebrow in Cory's direction. "Something

I said?"

"No, he's taking Holly out. Mum and Dad tend to feed her too many treats, and it upsets her tummy. He's taken her down to the field, more as a precaution. We don't want a surprise parcel on the floor in the morning." Cory got to her feet. "So, are you ready to hit the sack?"

"Yep, I hear I'm going castle visiting tomorrow, so I should get some rest." Dylan followed Cory up the stairs.

Cory turned as she got to her bedroom door. She caught Dylan's eyes. "I've had a good evening. I was a little nervous about meeting you but...well...we seem comfortable around each other." *Yeah, so comfortable you're bumbling like a fool.* She paused; she wanted to say much more but common sense kicked in. "'Night then, if you need anything, I'm in here." She opened the door to her room.

"I think I'll be out like a light. See you tomorrow, and Cory, I had a good night, too. It feels like we've been friends for longer than we have." Dylan turned and headed for her room.

Cory shut her bedroom door and flopped onto the bed. How was she going to keep her hands off Dylan? She'd been so close to falling into her arms. She'd found it distracting having Dylan in the same room all evening and not being able to stare. Cory began to undress. Her mind was a mess. She had known that there was something special about Dylan, but she'd never imagined it would be so intense. *She's involved with someone else. You're a married woman.* She repeated the mantra as she finished preparing for bed. She settled under the covers, and turned to greet Sam as he entered the room. "Hey."

"So that's Dylan, huh?" he asked. "She seems nice, but a little quiet for my liking."

Cory snorted. "That's the pot calling the kettle black."

"What do you mean? I talked tonight," Sam replied, defensively.

"You only ever speak when you want to, and then it's short and to the point. The only time you have verbal diarrhea is when you've had a beer or two, and then we can't bloody shut you up."

Sam changed into his night clothes. "Are you sure she's gay?"

"Yes. I can't believe you asked that question."

"Well, she's a bit of a stunner. I thought it was a waste of a woman her being gay and all."

Cory moved into a sitting position, momentarily stunned into silence by his comment. She found her voice, "Are you trying to say that she can't be gay if she's so good looking?"

"She's hardly your stereotypical lesbian, is she?" Sam replied.

"I hate it when people assume others are something they aren't by their looks. What exactly does a lesbian look like?"

"You know, shaved hair, pierced noses, kind of butch, that sort of thing. What? You're looking at me like I have two heads."

"You are so narrow-minded, it scares me. I can't believe you just said that. There's no typical lesbian; they come in all shapes, sizes, and looks. That's like saying every straight person looks like Mum or Dad. You shouldn't assume things." She lay back down, turned over, and pulled the sheets to cover her shoulders.

Sam climbed into his side of the bed, "You mad at me?"

"A little. You don't see the person for who they are. You see them for what you think they are. Remember the saying, 'Don't judge a book by its cover.' Maybe you should try that; some people aren't whom they appear to be. She's here for a week, and if you can't get past the fact that she prefers women, I suggest you stay away from her. She looks like she could do you some serious physical damage if she got angry."

"Ouch...low blow, Cor."

"It's true, Sam. She stood at least three inches above you. She also looks like she's truly muscular. Did I tell you she was an ice-hockey player?"

"Whatever. I suggest you don't get too close to her. You never know — she might try to seduce you."

"For fuck's sake, Sam, she's practically married. Just because she's gay doesn't mean she's going to jump the bones of every woman she sees. If you can't say something nice, then don't open your mouth at all."

"See? I can't win. If I don't talk, I get moaned at. If I do talk, I get moaned at."

Cory felt Sam pull her into a hug, but she resisted. "You need to fil-ter what comes out of your mouth." She relented and let him hold her a little.

"I promise that when Dylan is around, I'll be as nice as pie. All I ask is that you think about what I've said."

Sam kissed her on the back of her neck and rolled over. She was relieved the conversation had stopped there. She closed her eyes and let images of the day ahead lull her into sleep.

ACROSS THE HALLWAY, Dylan was having trouble sleeping. When she closed her eyes, visions of Cory came into her head: vivid, clear, and very real. She'd watched Cory all evening. She liked her gig-gle; it was cute and quite infectious. Throughout the evening she'd pur-posely made comments that would provoke Cory to laugh. She'd also watched the couple's interaction closely. They had sat on the same sofa, but had kept their distance from each other.

Dylan lay in the bed listening to the sounds around her. She could hear the slight buzz of the alarm clock on the bedside table. From the next room, she could hear a conversation; she couldn't hear the words, just muffled voices. Dylan wondered what Sam and Cory were talking about. She was jealous. She wished she was in the bed with Cory, and if she had any choice, they wouldn't be talking. The week was going to be torture. *You're playing with fire. She's straight and married — a path you've wandered down before.* Memories of the past haunted her. As she lay awake in a foreign country, remembering a time long ago, tears flowed. *Are you willing to risk your heart again? Will she hurt you like Tina?* She had no idea what to think, all she knew was her feelings for Cory were getting stronger and harder to ignore. Dylan snuggled her body deeper under the covers and shut her eyes; sleep finally over came her and she surrendered to her dreams.

Chapter
Twelve

CORY COULD HEAR Sam snoring lightly. She nudged him gently at first; there was no movement from him, so without mercy, she elbowed him.

"Oww, what'd you do that for? I was awake," Sam grumbled.

"You were not, you lying toad. I heard the snores. The alarm's gone off. You need to get up."

"Five more minutes won't hurt. I'm comfy and I want a cuddle." Sam moved closer toward Cory.

Cory felt Sam's arm snake around her middle. She tightened her muscles. It didn't feel right. For months, she'd wanted him to touch her, show her how much she meant to him. Now with her feelings for him changing, she didn't want this closeness. He moved closer, nuzzling her ear. "Sam, I need the loo desperately. Let me out." Cory moved toward the edge of the bed, but Sam held on tighter.

"Oh, come on, Cory. We never cuddle any more."

Cory felt his lips move down her neck. Instead of desire, Cory felt panic. She didn't want this. She didn't want Sam, especially with Dylan in the next room. She wriggled out of his grasp and forcefully removed his arm. "Sam, I need to wee, and if you don't let go, you'll be lying in a puddle. We don't have time. Holly needs her walk, the cats need feeding, and you have a meeting," Cory said, clambering to her feet.

"I can't win. I try to be amorous, and I get pushed away. When I'm not, I get nagged. You need to make up your mind."

"That's not fair. I hate doing *it* when I wake up. I'm not a morning person," Cory answered from the adjoining bathroom. "You know that. Plus, we have a guest. I wouldn't feel comfortable." She heard the bed creak and the footfalls on the carpeted floor. She washed her hands and turned around to see Sam leaning against the bathroom door.

"The guest thing never stopped you before." He unhooked his bathrobe from the back of the door. "I'm off to make some tea. Shall I pour a cup for Dylan?"

"I don't think she drinks tea. Maybe a cup of coffee. What time is it anyway?"

"Coming up to a quarter past seven. Maybe it's a bit early to be waking her. I'll get the coffee pot ready, and you can start it up when she wakes."

Cory followed Sam out of the bathroom and got back into bed. She pulled the covers around her. The room was somewhat chilly, and a slight frost clung to the bedroom window. She prayed it would be a nice day. She didn't mind the cold, but she hoped it didn't rain. She put the radio on and closed her eyes, listening to song after song. Her thoughts wandered from Dylan to her grandfather. She would visit him after the castle trip.

Her muses were interrupted by Holly bounding on to the bed, followed by Sam bringing a cup of tea.

"Hey, lazybones, I thought you had plans today." Sam said as he placed the tea on the bedside table.

"I do, but I thought Dylan might need a lie in."

"No, I think she's up. I heard movement from above when I was in the kitchen, which reminds me, I need to fix those floorboards. Anyhow, I'm going for a shower."

Cory waited for Sam to get into the shower. Then she got out of bed and put on her robe. She opened the door to the bedroom and walked the short way to the spare bedroom. Her heart was pounding and her tummy churning. She tapped gently on the door.

"Come in. I'm awake."

Cory opened the door slowly and peeked around it. Her stomach somersaulted at the sight of her guest. Dylan lay curled on her side, one arm tucked under her head. Her hair was loose and draped over her shoulder. She greeted Cory with a smile.

"Good morning. Did you sleep well?" Cory asked as she stepped farther into the room, restraining herself from leaping onto the bed. Cory realized Dylan's gaze was lingering on her exposed neck line. Self-consciously, she drew her robe more tightly around her. She couldn't help but notice the look of disappointment on Dylan's face.

Dylan moved up toward the head of the bed and stretched. "I slept great, and the bed is really comfortable. Come and sit down. You don't have to stand on ceremony." She patted the bed in front of her.

Cory watched with uncertainty as Dylan's hand patted the bed. *She's gorgeous. How am I going to sit next to her and not pounce on her? Don't be stupid. You'd end up making a fool of yourself, and she's forbidden fruit. Friends are all you are.* Hesitantly, Cory sat down on a spot a little farther away than Dylan had indicated.

Dylan yawned lazily. "What great adventures have you planned for today?"

"I thought we'd shower, have a little breakfast, and then drive over to Warwick before the holiday rush arrives. It's half term for the kids over here, so there will be lots of tourists, even for February." Cory paused slightly and then continued, "After that, I'd like to visit with my granddad, if it's okay with you."

"That's a great idea. I'd love to meet your grandfather. He sounds like a very special person. You've told me so much about him, and I want to meet your mum, too." Dylan's eyes moved to the firm thigh that had escaped from beneath the terrycloth robe.

Cory watched as Dylan scanned her thighs. "I have to wait for Sam to finish in our shower, and then I'll do the same. Do you want a drink? I'm going downstairs to prepare breakfast." Cory rose from the bed. She couldn't help but notice that Dylan was having trouble meeting her eyes.

"Yeah, I'll have whatever you're making. I need to pee. I'll meet you downstairs when I'm done, okay?" Dylan threw the covers off her body and scurried into the bathroom.

Cory stared at the closed door. Feeling uneasy and worried that Dylan didn't like being in her presence, Cory went back to her room. Sam was out of the shower and half dressed.

"How was sleeping beauty?" Sam asked.

"Okay. She looked okay to me."

"I'm going to iron this shirt, and then I'll be off. I don't know when I'll be back, but I'll ring your mobile if it's going to be late. You have a good day." Sam pecked Cory on the cheek as he passed. "The cash card is on the countertop in the kitchen."

ACROSS THE HALLWAY, in the bathroom, Dylan was battling with her conscience. *She's married...she's married...and she's straight. She has no interest in you except as a very good friend. Get your mind out of the gutter, Dylan, and accept it as it is. She is not attracted to you, and she is not in love with you. She's your friend. Don't blow that on your stupid libido. Now take a nice cold shower, and get your butt downstairs.*

Dylan's thoughts settled on Cory's legs—the image of the soft smooth skin on the very toned thigh muscles. She became aroused when she imagined her hands roaming higher up the legs. *Fuck. I haven't had sex in months, and the sight of a pair of firm thighs has me acting like a teenager.* After checking the bathroom doors were definitely locked, she sat down on the edge of the tub. She spread her legs wide apart and moved her right hand down her body. When she reached the mass of dark curly hair, she felt the slick liquid that signaled her desire. Her hand moved lower. She rubbed her fingers over her swollen clitoris. The wetness increased with her fingers' slow movement. She knew what she needed and where she liked to be touched. She'd been her only satisfaction for months. With her eyes closed and her focus on the woman who captured her waking dreams (as well as sleeping ones), she increased the tempo. She placed a finger inside her vagina and whispered Cory's name over and over. She continued to apply pressure and came quickly, spasms rocking her body. After the last tremor, she slid down the edge of the tub to the floor. She sat panting slightly. She could feel the perspiration on her forehead and behind her knees. Dizzily, she breathed deeply, filling her nostrils with the scent of her arousal. After a few minutes, she stood on shaky legs and stepped into the bath, ready to take a belated cold shower.

"HAS SAM LEFT already?" Dylan asked as she entered the kitchen and stared at the vast array of food laid out on the table in front of her.

"Yeah, he has a meeting down south, but he could be down at the golf range, for all I know. He tends to keep his own schedule in the week, sometimes working and sometimes playing golf." Cory pulled out a chair and gestured at Dylan. "Sit here and dig in. You'll need a hearty breakfast, as we have a lot of walking and steps to climb at the castle today."

"There's enough food here to sink a battleship."

"I didn't know what you liked, so I prepared you a full English breakfast: bacon, sausage, mushrooms, scrambled eggs, baked beans, toast, butter, jam, and coffee." Cory passed a plate to Dylan.

"Do you guys eat this food every morning?" Dylan inquired, heaping a little of everything onto her plate.

"You have to be kidding me. If I ate this stuff every morning, I'd be a prime candidate for a heart attack. Plus, I never have time before work. We usually only make a big breakfast when we have visitors staying or on the occasional weekend."

Dylan tasted each item on her plate. The taste was very different from the same food items in America. "This is great, much better than what..." Dylan swallowed her bite quickly. "Oh shit! I haven't called Sarah, and I left in such a crappy mood. I can't believe I haven't thought to call her. I'm sure she's freaked by now."

"Calm down and backtrack here. Why were you in such a bad mood?"

"It's a long story, Cory. I'll explain on the way to Warwick. Can I use your phone? I'll leave money for the call."

"Of course you can. You don't have to ask. It's on the sideboard over there." Cory pointed to the kitchen countertop. "Do you want me to leave you alone? You do realize it's four in the morning there."

"If I don't call her now, I won't get a chance because of the time difference. She'll be at work and nowhere near a phone. You can stay in the room. I don't have any secrets from you. I'll make it quick." Dylan got up and grabbed the cordless phone.

"Did you eat enough breakfast?"

"Yeah. It was great. Thank you."

"No worries. I'll stack the dishes in the washer while you make your call."

"Sure. What's the international code from here?"

"001 before the main number," Cory answered.

Dylan pressed the numbers, her stomach churning. She hadn't even given Sarah a second thought. *There's your answer to all your questions. You don't care about Sarah.* Guilt settled in the pit of her stomach as she waited for the call to connect.

"Hi, it's me," Dylan said, but it was all she could say as the barrage of sarcasm flowed through the phone line. She held the phone away from her ear until she heard silence. Then she spoke. "Calm down. I'm fine. I'm sorry. It was a long flight and then a long drive. My brain was mush by the time I got here. The time difference threw me." She listened to Sarah's ranting and tried to interrupt, but Sarah was on a mission. Dylan lifted her eyes and caught Cory staring at her. Dylan smiled and rolled her eyes at the phone.

So preoccupied with making Cory laugh, Dylan missed her cue to speak. She turned her back to Cory and walked back at the table. She lowered her voice. "Sarah, there's nothing I can say or do. I've apologized. I didn't mean to worry you. I'm sorry for the way I walked off. It hurts me, too, but we need time apart. I wasn't being mean when I left; I was being truthful. We need to think things through. We need to really consider where this relationship is going, or not going, to be more accurate."

Cory watched the slumped form of her friend. She walked over, knelt down, and put her hand on the small of Dylan's back. She began to rub in tiny circles.

Dylan leaned into the touch, pleased that Cory continued her ministrations as she spoke to Sarah. "Please stop crying and listen. I'll be back in a week. We'll sit down and talk then. All I ask is that you spend some time reviewing the past year. Are you happy? Are you sure I'm making you happy? Are we happy as a couple? Personally, I don't think we are. There's something missing, and you must feel there is, too." There was a pause in the conversation as Dylan listened to Sarah's reply. Dylan's muscles tightened and her body jerked upright. Her upper torso tensed and she didn't care that Cory could feel her visceral anger.

"Slow down. If you think that I could do that, you don't know me at all. If that's how you see this, then we're obviously over. I can't believe what you just said." Dylan paused, listening to more abuse. Finally, she replied, "If that's what you want, then there's no need to discuss us anymore, because there is no us." Dylan listened to Sarah's rants and raves. "Look, this is an expensive argument. You've made your point. It's over. We'll sort out the living arrangements when I get back."

Dylan pressed the disconnect button and took a deep breath. She turned to Cory. "I'm sorry you had to hear that."

"I gather she's not happy, huh?"

"There's an understatement if ever I heard one." Dylan hung her head and ran her fingers through her bangs. Sarah's comments had been too close to home. *She called you at your own game. She said you were only interested in Cory. You finished the relationship because she knew what was really on your mind. You're a shit, Dylan Matthews, a shit.* Dylan felt Cory's arms encircle her waist and pull her toward her. She didn't resist, she needed the comfort.

Conflicting emotions ran through Dylan's head. Part of her wanted to turn and grasp the lips that were lightly touching her neck and the other part of her psyche was screaming at her to let go. She went on instinct and tightened her hold on Cory. She felt the moisture of her tears run down her face and heard the wracking sob that left her mouth. Embarrassed, she moved away slightly and looked into the saddest, greenest eyes that she'd ever encountered. They tore at her heart. Unable to hold the glance, Dylan turned her head away.

"Want to tell me what's going on?" Cory whispered into Dylan's ear, which was right by her mouth.

Dylan shook her head, but in the next breath she replied, "Not right now. Maybe later. I wouldn't even know where to begin, except I'm a single woman again."

"I'm sorry. I didn't know things were that bad between you."

Dylan wiped at her eyes. "Neither did I, until recently." She ran her fingers over the wet spot she had left on Cory's shoulder. "I...I need to go and clean up before we leave. I didn't mean to make a mess of your top."

Cory put her hand over Dylan's fingers, stilling their movement. "It's just water. It'll dry. I'm more concerned about you. Take as much time as you need upstairs. I'll be here when you're ready."

Dylan stood up and pushed her chair under the table, steadying herself with her hand on the chair back. She moved her hand to Cory's shoulder and squeezed lightly. "Thanks. I won't be long."

Chapter
Thirteen

THE JOURNEY TO Warwick was quick. Dylan soon forgot her troubles and marveled instead at the fields filled with sheep and different varieties of cows. She loved traveling down the winding country roads. Neither spoke about the phone call. Dylan spent the drive pointing out things of interest to her and listening attentively as Cory explained what they were or the history behind the buildings.

They entered the town of Warwick. "I want to drive you the long way around so I can show you my hometown. The main road has a variety of black and white Elizabethan buildings and a variety of old brick buildings that I hope you'll find interesting."

"How old is that building?" Dylan asked.

"I can't remember the exact dates," Cory admitted. "I know a lot of the buildings date from the 1400's, but we did have the great fire of Warwick. It wasn't on the same scale as the great fire of London, but it did burn down a lot of the town's houses."

"Wow. Why is that building so twisted and lopsided? It looks like it's going to fall into the road."

Cory looked at the Lord Leycester Hospital. "It's about six hundred years old. They made the houses out of wattle and daub back then. Over the years, the wood has warped, giving the building its tilted look."

"I'm amazed at the history of the town already."

They drove around the main square of the town. It was very quiet — almost deserted.

"Is it always this quiet?" Dylan asked.

"It depends on the time of year and week. On a Saturday, we have market day, so the town is usually busy. It's hell to park your car. In the summer, we have a lot of tourists, mostly Americans, Japanese, and Europeans, so the streets are full, and the castle gets so crowded it's not funny. It's going to be busy today, but nothing like the summer time."

They drove down West Street, and Cory pointed out The Tudor House Inn. Then they turned left into the castle driveway. The driveway was a beautiful wooded, winding pathway, which couldn't be seen from the roadside. Cory glanced to her left to see a look of total amazement on Dylan's face.

"Are you okay?" Cory asked, touching Dylan's leg reassuringly.

"Yeah. This kind of natural beauty takes my breath away. It's like fall at home. The trees look so wonderful with all the reds, yellows, oranges, and browns that I wish they could stay that way forever. I hate it when the leaves fall off and the trees are barren, but many of these trees must be evergreens because they're still green."

"Yes, I know exactly what you mean. I love autumn time, too. It is nature at her most radiant, but spring is good because it brings new life." A loud screech interrupted Cory's thoughts.

"What the hell was that?" Dylan cried, looking around for signs of children or women being attacked.

"That would be the residents," Cory said, grinning.

"The residents? I thought the castle was uninhabited."

"Oh, it is. These are the residents of the grounds." Cory slowed the car to a halt and pointed up into one of the yew trees.

Dylan followed Cory's finger and gazed at the tall tree. After a few seconds, she spotted a peacock perched very proudly on a branch. He screeched again as if to prove a point and then flew down to the next branch.

"I've never seen a peacock before. Are there many of them around?"

"Yep, and also peahens, but it always makes me wonder why, in the bird world, the females look so dull and dowdy and the males have all the beauty and looks. It's unlike the human world where the female is considered the more beautiful of the species," Cory said, as she pulled into a parking spot.

"Amen to that. I thank God everyday for beautiful women like you to ogle." Dylan felt the blush rising in her cheeks. *I can't believe you said that out loud, you fool. You might as well tell her how much you like her and totally make an idiot of yourself.* She fumbled around on the floor pretending to look for something. She could feel Cory's eyes on her.

"Why thank you, ma'am, for the compliment," Cory drawled out in her best southern American accent. "You're quite the looker yourself."

"Now you're embarrassing me."

Cory touched Dylan's arm. "Can we help it if we happen to be the two best looking chicks in the neighborhood?"

Dylan grinned and exited the car. She opened the rear door and collected her backpack from the seat. She waited patiently while Cory put her fleece coat on and picked up her smaller backpack.

They made their way on foot a little farther up the castle drive. From the town of Warwick, it was easy for people to forget that the castle was built on a hill until they began the walk up to the entrance; even the fittest people noticed the incline.

Given the number of cars already in the parking lot, it was no surprise a number of people were already ahead of Cory and Dylan in the line for tickets. "Dylan, this is my treat, no arguments. I get to play the host today, okay?"

"Sure, but remember that when you're whining about my paying your way when you visit Massachusetts," Dylan replied.

"I'll remember. So, I get to visit you one day?"

"For sure."

Cory paid the ticket price. When she finished, she linked her arm through Dylan's.

Dylan shot Cory a puzzled, questioning look.

"What?" Cory asked.

"Nothing. You're okay walking like this?" Dylan indicated their joined arms.

Cory looked at Dylan. "I have no idea what you're on about. Why wouldn't I be comfortable? I'm the one who linked your arm, aren't I? You don't mind, do you? It's a little chilly, and you're very warm. I'm like a leech on anyone who's radiating heat."

"I'm sorry. I didn't want people to stare at you and assume we were a couple. I thought it might make you uncomfortable."

"Ms. Matthews, you think too much. I doubt people will even notice. It's quite common for women to hold hands and link arms here. It must be the European in us, and it wouldn't bother me if they did consider us a couple. We make a pretty cute couple."

Dylan watched the rise and fall of Cory's comical eyebrow wiggle. She swallowed her nerves. Her heart was taken and she knew she was in big trouble. *To hell with it I'll deal with the feelings later. Today, I get to enjoy myself.*

DYLAN'S FIRST VIEW of the castle was magnificent. It stood on a colossal mound of earth, all proud despite its weather-beaten appearance. It was magnificent, and Dylan stared at the fifteen hundred years of history before her.

Cory moved closer. "It's wonderful, isn't it?"

"Breathtaking. You're so lucky to have this amount of history on your doorstep."

"I know, but I never appreciated it as a child. It was only when I left to go to college that I realized what a quaint town it is. I love coming to the castle and thinking about centuries gone by."

After admiring the view, they meandered slowly past the rose gardens.

"I love roses," Dylan said, as she read the sign on the gate.

Cory glanced into the enclosure. "There's nothing to see this time of year. You'll have to come back in the summer when the aroma and colors are brilliant."

They continued their walk up the slight hill and stopped on the old moat bridge, before the large iron gates of the castle. Cory took her camera from her pocket.

"This would make a lovely picture with the castle behind you. Can

I take one?"

As Cory held the camera up, a passerby asked if Cory wanted him to take a picture of the two of them. Cory and Dylan looked at each other and nodded. Cory gave the man a quick demonstration of how the camera worked. Cory walked over to Dylan and placed her arm around Dylan's waist.

Dylan responded by putting her arm around Cory's shoulders and pulling Cory closer to her.

"You two make a sweet couple. Enjoy your day," the man said as he passed the camera back to Cory.

"Thanks." She turned to Dylan. "See? I said we made a cute couple."

Dylan grinned and linked her arm through Cory's as they passed under the huge gates.

"I think we should walk around the castle systematically. We'll leave the ramparts and towers until later."

"Lead on. I'm following you."

Cory began the tour in the armory. They toured the room and looked at the various uniforms the British armies had worn.

Dylan pointed at one garish design. "Drag queens must have designed some of these older costumes."

Cory glanced up at the pictures and models in their frilly uniforms. "It was the Stuart period of time."

"Who were the Stuarts?"

"The monarchy of that time period. Anyway, all the rich men wore make-up and long curly hair."

"I rest my case — the first transvestites."

At another display case, Dylan began giggling. "I've figured out why the British lost a lot of wars."

"We have not lost a lot of wars. We used to rule an empire."

"The important word in that sentence was *used* to rule an empire. Don't forget, you lost the Revolutionary War against us, and I know why."

"No doubt because you Americans had such great battle plans and better soldiers."

"No, it was because your guys wore red uniforms and battled in straight lines."

"You're an idiot sometimes." Cory nudged her friend, but laughed at the joke and common sense reason Dylan had given.

"I'm serious. Nothing like showing up on a battlefield wearing red. Not that the blue that the United States wore was any better, but red just announces you right away. How long do you think it took armies to discover camouflage?"

"Good question. The British could have done with some bright spark in that war."

They continued on their tour and studied the various swords.

"Look at the size of these swords. They're huge," Dylan said.

"I know. They have some demonstration ones in these boxes here. Try picking one up."

Dylan followed Cory's example and lifted a couple of the swords. "The soldiers must have had biceps of steel. Have you felt the weight of this one? I'm amazed soldiers could carry them, let alone fight with them."

Cory took the sword out of Dylan's hand. She had to use two hands to hold the sword off the ground. "Too heavy for me. They have some other weapons in the corner. How are you at shooting a long bow?"

They walked to the far corner of the armory and waited to talk to the tour guide who was standing by one display model.

"Want to see whether the Kingmaker would have wanted you in his army?" the guide asked.

Cory nodded. "Sure I'm game for anything. I might learn something I can use in my classroom."

"Here, hold onto this piece of wood and pull the string back as far as you can. Then let go. The arrow will rise, indicating the distance the longbow arrow would have traveled had it been a proper shot. Overall, it measures how powerful your shot is." The guide demonstrated the action.

Cory took over. She struggled to pull the string only an inch or two before letting go. The arrow rose pitifully.

"Oh, you'd have never made it into the army. You'd have been in the kitchen probably. What about you ma'am? You look like a strapping woman. Now he'd have had you."

"Not likely," Cory said.

Dylan caught Cory's innuendo and smiled. She changed places with Cory and shifted her stance until she was comfortable. She pulled the string back until it was level with her face. Her bicep muscles drew taut, and she gritted her teeth. Dylan put all her strength into the pull, and then she released it. The power indicator rose significantly.

The tour guide let out a whistle. "You'd have made a fine longbow man. Unfortunately for King Richard, you're the wrong gender, but I'm sure he'd have found a good use for a strong girl like you." He raised his eyebrows suggestively.

Cory leaned over, took Dylan by the arm, and looked directly at the guide. "And I repeat my previous statement of not likely."

The guide began to chuckle, and he bid them farewell.

"You are so bad sometimes. That poor man was dying of embarrassment." Dylan was still smiling at Cory's defense of her honor.

"He shouldn't be so suggestive."

They left the armory and headed for the dungeons. There was a small line as they reached the dungeon entrance.

"What's everyone waiting for?" Dylan asked, as they joined the end of the line.

"The stairs down to the dungeon are only wide enough for one person to go either down or up at a time, and the dungeons aren't that big. That man over there in costume makes us queue up and sends down a new group when another has comes up."

"He makes us do what?" Dylan watched as Cory's interest focused on the entertainer's codpiece.

"Huh?"

"Quit staring at his manhood and answer the question." Dylan nudged Cory's attention back to her. *She must be straight. She can't keep her eyes off that man's groin.*

"I wasn't staring," Cory answered. "Okay, I might have been, but purely out of curiosity, not desire. I was wondering if his appendage actually reached the end of his codpiece or if it was just for show. What was the question?"

"You said the guy will make us 'queue.' What's a queue?"

"You're kidding me, right? To queue is to stand in a line. It's the great British tradition: see a line and stand in it. It might not be going anywhere, but we're too polite to barge our way in, so we queue." Cory saw the line in front of her move forward. "We're on the move. It's quite dark and smelly down there. You're not afraid of small places, are you? You've gone a little pale." Cory teasingly nudged Dylan.

Shit, shit, shit. There's no way I'm admitting to being scared. Deep breaths. I can do this. How hard can it be? It's just a little dungeon. So what if it's dark, dank, and underground? Be brave, Dylan. If she can do it, so can you. She repeated this mantra until they got to the tiny entrance. Her knees began to buckle, but there was no way she was going to let this beat her. She grabbed at Cory's hand, aware that her nerves had made her own hands clammier than usual.

"You okay?" Cory asked, holding more securely onto Dylan's hand.

"I'm fine. I didn't want you to slip. The steps look kind of wet. You don't mind, do you?"

"Of course not. Thanks for looking after me. Down we go. Take a deep breath. It's the last fresh one for a while."

They walked down about twenty steps and then turned right into a narrow entrance. The dungeon smelled putrid and was very cold.

"I feel like if I close my eyes, I'll be transported back. I can feel the pain and anguish that was suffered in these chambers by my countrymen hundreds, or even over a thousand years ago."

Instinctively, Dylan nestled closer to Cory for warmth and security. The place was forebodingly eerie. "I hear you," Dylan said.

While Cory read all the writings on the wall, Dylan battled with her senses. The walls seemed to be closing in on her, and panic was slowly seeping through her body. She tightened her grip on Cory's hand, afraid to let go of her anchor to normality.

Cory looked up and then leaned into Dylan, and whispered in her ear, "I can't believe how dark your eyes look. Are you sure you're okay?"

Dylan smiled meekly back. "Uh...is now a good time to tell you I suffer a little from claustrophobia?"

"You're kidding me." Cory put her arm around Dylan's waist. "You're shaking. You're deadly serious, aren't you?"

Dylan nodded.

"No worries. We can go straight back up, if you want."

"Thanks, but it was my decision to come down here, trying to be brave and not look stupid. I should have told you when you asked. I can do this, but do you mind holding my hand? I feel safer with you near me. Maybe you could tell me a bit about the place. It might take my mind off my fears." Dylan felt Cory's hand squeeze hers.

"We can hold hands, and I'm going to keep my arm right here." Cory tightened her arm around Dylan's waist. "Okay, the thing hanging from the ceiling was a torture rack. They would put prisoners in there and hang them from the ceiling. The channel running along the floor was an early drainage system, and over in that tiny opening is a toilet. It's only a hole in a piece of stone, and you can see right down to the River Avon flowing below it. Want to take a look? I promise to look with you."

Dylan nodded. "Sure, but don't let go of me."

They went into the tiny enclosure and peered down the hole. As they leaned over to look, their heads met, and as if drawn by a magnet, Dylan turned to study Cory. In the dim light, she saw Cory's tiny nose wrinkle up at the smell. She observed Cory's eyes crinkle as she peered down the hole. She was too spell-bound to look away. A small cough brought her back to the present. A group of people was waiting to enter the small opening. Cory and Dylan both apologized and exited out of the tiny space.

Dylan smiled at Cory. "It's kind of scary down here, all isolated and barren. I'd have hated to have been down here on my own for years at a time. It makes you want to be near those whom you care about, makes you realize how much you need the company of others. Do you know what I mean?"

"Totally." Cory pointed to an inscription on the wall. "Behind that board are the markings made by a prisoner hundreds of years ago. He was in here for years until he died a slow painful death. I think he felt like what you just described. It must have been awful to have been down here. Let's get out of here. It's pretty depressing."

The two of them walked slowly toward the exit and waited patiently for the people ahead to walk up the steps. Even though they were exiting, Dylan didn't release her hold on Cory. She clung to her hand and followed Cory to freedom.

When they reached the fresh air, they took very deep breaths. Dylan pulled Cory into a hug. "Thank you. That's the second time today you've comforted me. It's so different from when I'm with Sarah."

"How come?"

"With her, I have to be the strong one. I always do the protecting. I don't know what it is about you, but my barriers come crumbling down, and I let you see the real me. No walls, no lies, just me, and I'm not as strong as I seem."

Cory returned the hug. "I understand. It felt good to support you. I rarely get to do that with Sam. I always have to be the little woman, and he gets to be the hero – the one in control."

With their hands linked, they walked toward the rooms that housed the torture chamber relics. They had to separate to move through the narrow doorway. They entered a small room, which had two display cases. Dylan went over to look at one of them. It was filled with ancient instruments of torture.

"They were barbaric, weren't they?" Dylan said, as she looked at a particular set of gruesome thumbscrews. "How were these used, exactly?"

"Like the name suggests, they put them on prisoner's thumbs and then screwed the nut 'round until it crushed the thumbs. Many prisoners would confess their army's secrets. It was excruciatingly painful." Cory pinched Dylan's thumb to make her point more clear.

"Ouch. I get the idea." She looked around a bit more. "So what's this scold's bridle?"

"That would have been something I'd have definitely been tortured with." Cory laughed aloud.

Dylan gave Cory a quizzical look. "Why?"

"It's for gossiping women. The gossips of the town had this put over their head. The piece of metal on the inside of the mask would fit on top of the tongue so the woman couldn't talk any more. Husbands would use them on their wives when they talked too much – or so legends say. Read the writing above each one, as it'll give you a more accurate account. Cory pointed to the notices attached on the wall.

Dylan shook her head. "No, you explain it in a more interesting way, and your explanations are more fun. I could listen to your accent for days. So what else did the poor wives have done to them?"

"Remember the inn I pointed out to you on the road into the castle?"

"Yeah, The Tudor House was its name. What about it?"

"They have a chastity belt on display. It's shaped like a pair of knickers made out of metal. It has a lock on it and a hole in it. Before they went to battle or on journeys, husbands would put it on their wives to make sure they couldn't sleep around."

"Now that is barbaric. How'd they pee or poop?"

"I have no idea, and I don't even want to go there, thank you. Can you imagine trying to sit down in metal underwear?"

They made their way through the displays to the stretching rack. Dylan ran her hand over the wood. "Okay, this one is self-explanatory."

"I know. Look at those pictures. They used the rack as a tool to extract confessions out of prisoners. Then there were different kinds of stocks used as punishment for mild crimes, such as being drunk and disorderly or theft."

"I've seen some of these in historical films and shows." Dylan went over to a pair of stocks. She examined the picture of a prisoner in the stocks and listened to Cory explain more history.

"The stocks were blocks of wood with ankle and wrist holes cut out. When prisoners were in the stocks, the local villagers would throw rotten food at them. Sometimes they were put in the stocks for a day or more.

Dylan listened, fascinated by the endless knowledge Cory possessed and her cute accent, which got broader when she was excited. Dylan especially enjoyed the way Cory gesticulated to animate her stories. Dylan found herself falling further under the spell of this charming woman. She knew that she could easily love Cory more than life itself, and that was a very sobering thought.

After the torture chamber, they meandered through the Kingmaker display. It consisted mainly of Madame Taussaud's wax models. Dylan took note of the intricate detail of the costumes and models. She thought they looked so lifelike.

Their wanderings found them in the main hall and into more modern times with the Royal Party of the early 20th century. Cory pointed out who was who in the royal family and how they were related to Queen Elizabeth II.

As they left the main hall, they walked toward the first tower, the Ghost Tower. Cory fumbled for Dylan's hand.

Dylan looked at her questioningly. "Is there something I should worry about inside here? You don't seriously believe it's haunted, do you?"

Cory shrugged. "Who knows, it's so dark and creepy. Scares the shit out of me. Once on a television show called 'Jim'll Fix It,' two girls asked if they could spend the night in the Ghost Tower. They looked petrified when they came out the next night. They were so brave in my eyes. I get scared of my own shadow." Cory looked at the Ghost Tower door. A man with his face painted silver was dressed in rags and appeared to be standing guard in front of the door. "He's new. They never had a guide up here before."

Dylan pulled Cory into a side hug and left her arm around Cory's shoulder. "Fear not, my princess. I will protect you." Dylan squeezed Cory gently, thankful that she had another legitimate reason to hold her close.

They walked toward the man and stood in the small line of waiting tourists. The guide welcomed them and pushed the creaking door inward. Cory and Dylan walked slowly into the darkened room. When everyone had entered, an eerie voice began its monotone dialogue about the history of the castle. Even Dylan had to admit it was spooky as an involuntary shiver walked its way up her spine. She looked at Cory and smiled when she saw an 'I told you so' look on her face.

They paused to listen to the story about the demise of the inhabitant of the tower and proceeded to walk up the wooden stairs to the deceased man's bedroom chamber.

The room was dim, with only the light from a candle illuminating the room. It gave the room a supernatural presence, with shadows dancing across the room. The tape recording played again as the story of a ghastly murder was further revealed. A model stood in the middle of the room.

"It looks so human," Dylan commented as she observed another visitor put her hand out to touch the model. The lady screamed as the model jumped to life, scaring the unsuspecting visitor.

Cory leaped toward Dylan and clung tightly to her hand. "If I wasn't scared before, I am now."

After the yells and squeals died down, the visitors were allowed a few minutes to investigate the room. Dylan and Cory stood in front of a wide, but extremely short bed. Cory gazed at the bed, and then at Dylan beside her. She began to giggle.

"I thought you were supposed to be frightened," Dylan said. "What can you possibly find amusing in such a scary room?"

"I'm still scared. However, I was just imagining you in that bed."

Dylan's eyebrow rose in a questioning stare. "And you would be imagining me in that bed because?"

"Because it's so short and you're so tall. If you were alive in those days, your legs would be dangling off the end. You'd have to sleep diagonally to get all of you in. They must have been midgets in those days. Have you noticed how low the doors are around here?"

"Have I noticed? Stupid question. I've nearly knocked myself out a few times. It's okay for you vertically-challenged people. But yeah, could you imagine me in there?" Even in the low light, Dylan caught the embarrassed side glances from Cory. *I'd love to know what images are going through her head.*

After the Ghost Tower, Dylan and Cory had the ramparts and two big towers left to explore. They walked along the edge of the grass. The weather was mild for February. It wasn't warm, but neither was it too chilly.

Cory glanced up at the cloudy sky. "I'm pleased the rain has held off, as we can still eat beside the river. I know a nice little spot that is sheltered by trees and has a bench. While you were upstairs back at the house, I packed a little lunch in my rucksack and made a flask of hot coffee."

"That sounds like a good plan to me." Dylan gazed up at the battlements and the soaring towers.

They began the climb up the parapet. As they walked the walls, Cory peered through an arrow slot. "I couldn't hit any target through these little holes."

"I'm with you there. Do you know why they made them so small?"

"I do. The holes had to be tiny to prevent someone on the other side hitting the shooter."

"Makes sense."

Dylan walked over a metal grid. "What are these metal sections for?"

"They're grill holes for boiling oil. The soldiers would wait for the enemy to come underneath and then tip scolding hot oil over them." She glanced around surveying the area. "Although, I have no idea how they got the boiling oil up the ramparts. My guess is they did it very carefully."

"True. It must have been a horrible death to be doused in burning oil." Dylan shuddered. "I'm so happy I was born in the twentieth century. The medieval times are a time I most certainly do not want to visit, not that I'm ever likely to get a chance. I can only imagine what they would have done to card carrying lesbians."

"Ouch. That doesn't bear thinking about."

They entered the first tower, Guy's Tower. Cory went first and Dylan climbed behind holding onto Cory's fleece coat for added support. They climbed steadily going 'round and 'round on the narrow stairway. After about a hundred and eighty steps, they were both breathing harder. Cory paused for a moment and then continued with the ascent. They stepped out, and the wind caught them unawares. They both ducked down for cover. Cory led them to the edge of the tower. They spent a few minutes taking in the tranquility and view.

They were the only ones at the top of the tower, and Dylan took full advantage of this. She put her arm around Cory's shoulder. When she felt no resistance, she gently pulled Cory nearer to her until her arms were wrapped around her. Dylan felt Cory's hands entwine around her waist and squeeze.

Cory pulled slightly away and looked at Dylan. "That's a cheesy looking grin you're wearing. Are you having fun?"

"I wanted to say thank you. It's been wonderful so far. In fact, I wanted to say thank you for coming into my life." Dylan squeezed Cory tighter as she said the last few words.

"It's me who should be thanking you. You've opened up a side of me I never knew I had. You've offered me friendship with no strings attached, and you know the real me, but you haven't run away. You know all my secrets, and you accept me for me. For that gift, Dylan, I'll never forget you." She looked up into Dylan's eyes.

Dylan looked down as Cory looked up. The temptation to kiss Cory was tremendous. She bent down lower and rested her forehead on Cory's. *God, I want to kiss her. No, we're just friends. Move away before you blow that, too.* Dylan broke the hold and walked over to the turrets to take in the view. She felt her throat dry up and her legs weaken slightly.

She leaned on the wall for support; her whole body seemed to be mutinying against her will.

"Want to see my senior school?" Cory asked. She walked along the edge of the tower, pulling Dylan along.

They walked around the circular tower top. Cory pointed out significant landmarks and Dylan listened attentively. They both agreed that the view was magnificent. At photo opportunities, Dylan borrowed Cory's camera and took some shots of sights she wanted to remember. They descended from the tower and walked along the stockades and onto Caesar's Tower. They spent time climbing the smaller tower that had recently been renovated and could now hold tourists. It gave a splendid view of the River Avon and the small waterfall that sent water crashing down to the water wheel where the eel run used to be.

After the towers, they ambled out of the main castle grounds and headed down toward the River Avon. They crossed the bridge and walked along the edge of the river until they arrived at the old boathouse. It was sheltered away from the wind, and Cory settled on the bench. Dylan joined her.

"Thanks for making the lunch. The warmth of this coffee feels great. I don't think words can describe how wonderful this morning has been."

"No words are needed. I can see it in your face. It's nice to be able to share one of my favorite places with you."

After eating, they relaxed against the back of the bench with their feet up against the wall of the boathouse.

"Want to tell me about Sarah? You guys didn't sound too happy on the phone this morning."

Dylan twiddled her thumbs. She wanted to tell Cory everything, but she was in a conundrum. If she told the truth, it would mean expressing her feelings for Cory. *Keep it brief; state the facts.* "Yesterday, as I was leaving to come here, we had a huge argument. I basically told Sarah our relationship wasn't working. She got mad when I told her I was coming here to visit you. She thinks that I have feelings for you and that maybe there's something going on between us." She paused, trying to assess Cory's reaction to Sarah's accusations. "I told her to think about where we're heading, because I think we've drifted too far apart. We want different things out of life, and I told her we'd talk about it when I got back."

"But this morning in the phone call, you ended it?"

"She was being unreasonable and saying really mean things about you. I finally gave in to my real feelings and told her what I thought."

"So, it's definitely over between you and Sarah?"

"We haven't been getting along well. We are so different that it is difficult at times — hell, most of the time. We hardly talk to each other, and our sex life is non-existent. I can't remember the last time we were intimate. It feels like we're together out of habit, and I think it's time to admit it isn't working and move on. It's hard to explain, really. I did tell her that I wasn't in love with her anymore."

Cory reached over and took Dylan's hand. "Dylan, I understand, and you know it. I'm having the same thoughts about Sam and me. At least you've talked it through with Sarah. Out of curiosity, what did you say when she asked about us?"

Dylan met Cory's eyes. "I lied and told her she was wrong."

Dylan watched Cory's eyes widen in surprise and then confusion.

"Cory, I asked you the other day if you felt a connection and you said you did."

"I do."

"I have to admit that the reason I asked was because you're con-stantly on my mind. I think—no, I know—you're my pebble on the beach. Ironic, really. I find the girl of my dreams, and she ends up mar-ried and three thousand miles away from me." She stopped speaking when Cory broke their eye contact. *You've scared her away. You couldn't keep it to yourself, idiot.* "Shit, I'm sorry, Cory, I know it's one-sided, and I promised myself I wouldn't say anything, but today has been so good I got carried away. Please look at me." She touched Cory's chin and moved her head to face hers. She noticed tears trailing down Cory's cheeks. "Talk to me, please."

Cory opened her mouth, but no words came out. She leaned for-ward and closer to Dylan.

"Are you sure?" Dylan whispered.

Cory nodded her head and smiled slightly.

Dylan moved forward and met Cory's forehead. Her lips mere mil-limeters away from Cory's. The shrill sound of Cory's mobile phone broke the spell.

Cory turned toward her backpack.

You were going to kiss her? You were fucking going to kiss her. Dylan shook her head and then watched as Cory rummaged around inside her bag.

Cory pulled out her phone as the ringing ceased. She checked the caller ID. "Fantastic bloody timing as usual, Mum." She glanced at Dylan, who was studying the ground. "You okay?"

Dylan nodded and forced a smile as her answer.

"I need to check what she wants. She rarely calls my mobile, as it costs too much money. I'm worried there may be a problem with Grand-dad."

"Make the call. It's important." Dylan stretched her arms above her head. Her body was tight with tension, and she needed to release some of it. She thought about going for a short walk, but she wanted to be near Cory in case she got bad news.

Cory dialed her mother's number and waited for her to pick up. "Mum, it's Cory. Anything wrong?"

"Your granddad wasn't feeling well this morning. The doctor just finished his visit. He wasn't too optimistic and said we should prepare ourselves. I thought you might want to come and spend some time with him while he's still got the energy. You're on holiday this week, aren't you?"

Cory moved the phone away from her ear and cleared her throat. She took a deep breath as the tears formed. "I'm actually at the castle at the moment. I have a friend staying. I was going to visit afterwards. What did the doctor actually say, Mum, word-for-word. You do have a tendency to over exaggerate."

"The change in your granddad over the past few days has been dramatic. He's very jaundiced and his breathing is labored. The doctor says the cancer has spread to his lungs and liver. They want to take him into the hospice, but he's refusing to go."

"Did they give him something for the pain?" Cory questioned. The tears dropped freely now.

"They've put him on heavier doses of morphine. The doctor said a week, maybe two at the most. I want you to come over, but I needed to prepare you for the change. He's been asking for you."

"I'll be there in half an hour. Do you want me to get any groceries?"

Dylan watched the changing emotions displayed so clearly on Cory's face. Gone were the laughter lines, replaced by a frown and worry lines. Dylan placed her arm around Cory's shoulders and rubbed them gently. This gained her a thankful smile, and she continued the light massage.

Cory ended the call and placed her hand over Dylan's. "I'm sorry. I've got to go over to Mum's. Do you want to stay and look around the castle more or come with me?"

"That's a no-brainer. I'm going with you. How's your grandfather?" She moved her arm fully around Cory's shoulders and leaned her head on Cory's. "It's okay to cry. It really is. It's better to let it out now than later." She felt the body beside her stiffen. Cory sat up and moved slightly away. Dylan tried not to show the hurt she felt at the growing distance. *You had to try and push it. God, you nearly kissed her. Can you pile any more worry on her plate? Be her friend, and nothing more.*

"Not good. The doctor says it's not going to be long now. Let's walk. I'll fill you in as we go." Cory wiped the wet from her face with her sleeve.

Chapter
Fourteen

WITH GROCERY BAGS in hand, Dylan followed Cory up a tiny driveway. She waited patiently as Cory unlocked the back gate and went through it. She knocked on the window of the back door, which was immediately on her right. They were greeted by a woman of similar height but much stockier in build than Cory.

"Hi, Mum. This is my American friend, Dylan. Dylan, this is my mum, Rita Jackson." Cory pointed to each woman in turn and then moved aside.

"Hello, Mrs. Jackson. Cory's told me so much about you." Dylan held out her hand, and Rita shook it briefly.

"Nice to meet you, Dylan, and if my daughter's told you things, I should be worried." She laughed and patted Cory on the back. "Cup of tea?" She moved away from the door and toward the kettle on the counter top. Cory and Dylan followed Rita into the kitchen.

"Yes please, but I think Dylan might prefer some coffee or pop. I haven't managed to convert her into a tea drinker yet, but there's still time. Dylan, would you like pop or a hot drink?" Cory asked.

"Would pop be soda?"

"Yes, dear," Rita said.

"I'll have some Pepsi, if you have it."

"I think there's a bottle in the shed, Cory. Go outside and check for me."

Cory's childhood home was a post-World War II house. The enclosed passageway down the side of the house still had the old coal shed, which was now a larder, and next to it, an outside toilet. Cory went to look in the larder. After a few minutes of searching and moving wine bottles, she found a liter bottle of Pepsi. She carried it back inside and poured Dylan a glass.

"Is Granddad awake?" Cory asked.

"He's sitting in the lounge. He's perked up since I told him you were coming," Rita said as she placed Chocolate Digestive cookies on a plate in front of Dylan.

Dylan spoke to Cory. "You go in and spend some time alone with your granddad. I'm going to get the scoop from your mother about what kind of child and teenager you were."

"Thanks. I think I will," Cory said and then turned to her mum. "Behave, and no baby photos under any circumstances."

CORY OPENED THE door and entered the main living room, commonly referred to as the lounge. "Hello, Granddad. I see you've got your feet up. No rest for the wicked, huh?" She surveyed the physical changes since her last visit. He was pitifully thin and his skin had a yellow tinge.

"They've let you out of that madhouse, then? You never seem to work. Not another holiday?" He smiled at her.

Cory leaned down and kissed him on the cheek. "I'll have you know they reward us teachers with time off. It's half term. I was actually touring the castle with a friend."

"You practically live at that castle. I don't understand the fascination. Once you've seen it, what else is there to see?"

"You heathen. It's British ancestry at its greatest."

"Where's your mum?"

"She's making a cup of tea and talking to my friend." Cory watched her grandfather's chest rise and fall heavily. She could hear a rattling sound as he inhaled. He'd always had a weak chest, suffering badly from asthma, but this was much more pronounced. He wore sweat bottoms and a t-shirt, which showed the bones of his chest. She studied his face. His cheeks were sunken, but his eyes held the familiar twinkle.

"Friend? Anyone I know?"

"No, she's American. She's over for a week, and she's come to see the Kingdom." Cory paused, waiting for the third degree.

"A Yank? Don't tell me you met her through that computer thing you're always playing on."

Cory grinned and nodded. "As a matter of fact, I did meet her through the Internet, and I don't think she'd appreciate being referred to in that manner. Please, Granddad, be on your best behavior. You can tell her all about your trips to Las Vegas. I'm sure she's been there." As if on cue, Dylan walked into the living room with mugs of hot tea and cookies on a tray.

"My, you're a big girl, aren't you?"

Dylan smirked at the old man's comment and put the tray on the coffee table. "Yes sir. My parents fed me well. My name's Dylan." She held out her hand and shook his.

"I'm Arthur. Dylan? What bloody name's that for a girl?"

"Granddad, don't be so rude." Cory nudged him gently. "Be nice, or no whiskey."

"Cory, he's on medication. He can't have any alcohol," Rita said as she entered the room. She shot a warning glance over to her daughter. "Don't stir things up."

"Leave the poor girl alone, Rita. I'm eighty years old," Arthur rasped. "I can drink what I want. What's it going to do? Kill me?" He laughed at his own joke, the laugh turning into a cough.

"You're a sick old codger," Cory said with a chuckle, but her stomach was churning. She'd always thought her granddad was strong enough to survive anything, but looking at him now, she knew he'd met his match.

"Where's Sam? Out working or playing golf?" Arthur asked as he repositioned himself on the chair.

"Doing both, I think. He's entertaining some clients today by taking them around the golf course. He's got a busy schedule this week. He's away tomorrow night and possibly Wednesday, too. If I didn't have Dylan staying, I would have brought Holly with me and come over for the nights."

Cory watched as Dylan charmed Arthur with stories of America and her exploits playing ice hockey. They all traded stories of places they'd visited, but he soon tired. At the sound of his deep, grating snores, Rita, Cory, and Dylan left the room.

"What do you think?" Rita asked as they stood in the kitchen.

"I think the doctor was right, Mum. I hope when it happens, he doesn't suffer and he knows how much he's loved. Is he going to the hospice?"

Rita shook her head. "He's made me promise not to send him. He wants to be with family. I want him here, and he'd give up if we sent him there. The nurses visit every day, and he has his medicine."

Cory nodded and put her arm round her mum. "I'll be over every day, okay? If you need anything, phone me."

CORY PLACED HER car keys on the hook and deposited her bag on the small sofa near the window. When she turned back, she saw the flashing light on the answering machine. She pressed the play button.

> Cor, it's me. I'm on my way home. Want to go out
> for a meal? Talk it over with Dylan and let me know.
> I hope your day was better than mine.

Cory looked over her shoulder at Dylan hovering awkwardly by the doorway. Cory's mood had darkened on the journey back to the house. Emotions swirled through her. She didn't know how to handle the news that her grandfather's death was imminent or what she could do to help her mum. "I should have called Sam earlier and told him about Granddad. He loves him as if he were his own grandfather." Cory took her coat off and draped it over the stair banister.

Dylan copied Cory's actions and followed her to the kitchen where Holly greeted them with her usual enthusiasm. Cory fussed over the dog, and then hugged her fiercely. Releasing the dog, Cory looked up at Dylan. "She's named after my nan."

"Who is?"

"Holly. She's named after my nan. Granddad and Nan were married for fifty years. We got Holly the weekend that Nan died. Granddad has never been able to bring himself to call her 'Holly.' He calls her 'Tiger,' instead." She continued to stroke Holly. A lonely tear rolled slowly down Cory's cheek.

Dylan leaned down and wiped the tear away tenderly with her thumb. She heard the front door opening. She stroked Cory's cheek for a final moment and then moved away to a stool behind the breakfast bar.

Cory stood up and moved to the far side of the kitchen. She switched the kettle on.

Sam walked into the kitchen. He nodded briefly at Dylan and bent to stroke Holly. He glanced from one woman to the other. "You two look grim. Who died?"

Cory dropped the mug she was holding, burst into tears, and ran out of the room.

Sam stared open-mouthed at Dylan. "What'd I say? Oh, shit, not Arthur? No, she would have called me."

Sam looked devastated. Dylan continued to lock eyes with him. "No, he didn't die. We just got back from there, though, and the news isn't good. Cory wanted to tell you face-to-face. The doctor hasn't given him long—a few days—maybe a week." Dylan walked over to where Cory had been, crouched, and began picking up the broken mug.

Sam watched her movements. In a moment, he spoke. "I'd better go up and see her and apologize for my stupid comment. I didn't think. I should have been more sensitive."

Dylan rose and deposited the bits of china on the counter. "She just needs a few moments alone. She hasn't said much since we saw him. It's probably shock. As for Arthur, I don't know him, but he seemed in good spirits, although he did appear to tire easily."

Sam went to the mug tree and removed two more mugs. "I'll make her a drink and take it up. I know how she shuts herself off from the world when she's hurting. She did it when her nan died, and she's been building walls around herself for ages now. At least she has you here with her this week. I have to go away for the next two days. I can't cancel it unless in a dire emergency. The business deal needs closing. You'll keep your eye on her for me, won't you?"

"For sure. That's what I'm here for. I'll keep a very close eye on her."

"Thanks." He filled a mug with tea. "I'll just take this up to her."

CORY LAY ON the bed, with her face buried in a pillow soaked with her endless tears. She knew Sam hadn't meant anything by the comment. It was more bad timing on his part. However, the comment had hit home hard, and she'd run—run away from life and from her anchor in it all: Dylan. Her mind went over the day's events—the castle,

the near-kiss, her dying grandfather. Her mind lingered on Dylan's dec-
laration of her feelings. She shuddered. *Would I have cheated on Sam?
Would I have tasted forbidden fruit?* She'd wanted to so much, and then
the phone call from her mum had led to the pain she felt now.

She held the pillow tightly to her face. In her mind, she could picture her granddad: his sallow cheeks and yellow complexion, his frailty,
and his age. When had that happened? He'd always been so strong.
He'd always seemed so young to her, so fit. A sob caught in her throat,
and she felt hands rubbing her back. She rolled over and met Sam's sad,
puppy dog brown eyes.

"Hey, sweetie, I brought you up a cup of tea. I'm so sorry." Sam
spoke softly as he stroked her back and ran his fingers up through her
hair. Strands of wet hair lay plastered to the edge of her face. He
stroked them behind her ear.

Cory cleared her throat. "It's okay," she said, hoarsely. "I know you
didn't mean it. It was a stupid joke, and in a different situation, I'd have
probably said something similar." She began to sob. "It's really going to
happen, Sam. He's really going to die."

Sam lifted her up in his arms and cradled her. He held her tightly
and let her cry.

DOWNSTAIRS, DYLAN ROCKED lightly on the stool while her
fingers tapped with frustration on the wooden counter top. She wanted
to be the one comforting Cory. *I know her better than Sam does. I know how
she's feeling. I've been there. I want to be the one holding her and kissing the
pain away. The poor girl's heart is breaking, and all I feel is jealousy. When are
you going to understand that you can never be with her, you fool?* Dylan
thought back to the moment on the bench. *She does feel something for me.
She does want to be with me.* Dylan stood up and stretched. Her back
ached, and she was restless. The moral dilemma nagged at her. She
needed to exercise and get rid of the antsy, frustrated feeling. She
walked up the stairs toward her room. When she reached the landing,
she nearly collided with Sam.

"How is she?" Dylan asked, anxiously.

"Sleeping," Sam whispered. "Do you want me to get you anything?
Would you like to go anywhere? She'd kill me if I didn't play host to
you."

Dylan grinned as she heard the words. In her mind, she held an
image of a little blonde whirlwind knocking the hell out of him. "I was
just about to change into my running gear. I haven't run in two days,
and I need to get rid of the cobwebs."

"I don't think that's too wise, not that you can't stand up for yourself, but it's dark outside. You don't know the area at all, and as I just
said, Cory would kill me if anything happened to you. I could take you
down to the gym, if you want. I could do with a small workout myself."

"Sure."

"Okay. I'll meet you downstairs in ten minutes." Sam opened the airing cupboard and took out two hand towels. He tossed one in Dylan's direction.

Dylan caught it deftly. "Thanks."

CORY WOKE UP feeling stiff, uncomfortable, and with a rumbling stomach that ached. Disoriented, and with stinging, dry eyes, she tried to ascertain the time: 8 P.M. She rubbed her eyes and ran her fingers through her disheveled hair. She slowly lifted her body up onto her arms. Her head was pounding. She stood up just as slowly, rearranging her clothes that had tangled around her body. She switched on the main bedroom light, wincing as her pupils contracted in the bright light. *I feel like a juggernaut ran over my body.* Her body was sore from where her clothing had dug in. She pulled off her sweater and dropped it on the floor. Then she unhooked her bra and picked up her lounging clothes beside the bed. She pulled the old t-shirt over her head. Then she took off her pants and exchanged them for some looser flannel ones. She went into the bathroom and rinsed her tear-stained face with cold, refreshing water.

She opened the bedroom door and was greeted by Holly, who had been guarding the door. The house was silent. She walked down the stairs and into the lounge, but there was no sign of life. She continued down the hall to the kitchen, turning on the light as she entered. On the counter top was a bright yellow post-it note, written in Sam's clear print.

```
Cory,
    We've gone to the gym.
    We'll collect a take away on our way back. Call
my mobile if you need anything,
Love, Sam
```

Cory read the note and a small pang of jealousy surfaced. Dylan and Sam were together without her. She didn't want Sam to befriend Dylan. She wanted sole friendship rights. *Behave yourself, Williams. She's an adult and can go where and with whom she wants.* She poured a glass of wine and took the bottle into the lounge. Bored, she flicked on the television and watched the Monday night edition of *Eastenders*. As the closing credits rolled onto the screen, she heard the familiar sound of the car's diesel engine. A key turned in the door, and soon chattering filled the hallway.

Sam peeked his head around the door. "How you feeling?" He entered the room and stood in front of her.

When Dylan mimicked his actions, Cory felt like a little child being checked on by her parents.

"I'm fine," she snapped, and then wished she'd kept her ire in check as she saw the glance go from one to the other. She stood up. "Honestly, I'm fine. Now the shock has worn off, I'm feeling better. I'll take that food off your hands and dish it up." Cory put her hand out to take the bag out of Dylan's hand, but Dylan pulled her arm away. Cory was hurt and confused.

"I was going to help you serve the food, if you want me to, that is." Dylan held on tightly to the bag.

Cory smiled sheepishly and nodded her head.

Sam sat down on the sofa opposite to Cory. "If you two are doing that, you don't need me. I'm knackered. Dylan can sure run, Cor." He grinned at Dylan. "I think I ran more today than I have all year, and it was mostly trying to keep my pride. I nearly fell asleep in the gym shower. I was exhausted. I'm going to ache in the morning. You wouldn't mind bringing an old man a beer, would you? My legs won't function."

"That'll teach you to show off." Cory headed toward the kitchen, followed closely by Dylan.

For a few seconds, an awkward silence filled the kitchen. Then they both began to speak at the same time.

"How..."

"I shouldn't..."

"I'm sorry. You go first," Cory said as she reached up to get the plates out of the cupboard. Dylan came up behind her and helped her lift them down.

"Are you sure you're feeling better?" Dylan asked as she kept her hand on Cory's, tenderly stroking her thumb. "You had me worried there for a while."

Cory met Dylan's questioning eyes with her own. "I'm sorry. I'm usually pretty good at expressing my feelings, but this was too raw to deal with." She reluctantly removed her hand from Dylan's tender ministrations and moved over to the breakfast bar, where she placed the plates on separate trays. *Even in your darkest moments, she can affect you.*

Dylan closed the cupboard door and went to help take the Chinese cartons out of the bag. "I understand; I really do. I always have a hard time talking about my feelings...unless I'm around you, and then I find myself opening up," she admitted, quietly. "I've told you more in my e-mails than I've ever told anyone else. I thought it was just because we were e-mailing. I guess what I'm trying to say is that in an e-mail, you can write what you want and then just press the send button. You don't have to see the look on the other person's face, but now that I'm face-to-face with you, I find myself wanting to tell you all about me."

Cory smiled encouragingly. "I know."

Dylan's voice cracked. "I know the hurt of losing someone you love. It has been over two years since my mother died. I still hurt, and I miss her so much. I still haven't come to terms with it, and I don't know if I ever will." An errant tear tracked down the stoic features.

Cory reached up to wipe the tear away, but Dylan leaned back, avoiding the contact. Cory made a connection by firmly ensconcing Dylan's hand in hers.

Dylan took a few calming breaths and squeezed Cory's hand. "I just wanted to tell you that I'll always be here for you, as your friend."

"Thanks, and I'm here for you, too." Feeling a need to lighten the atmosphere, Cory added, "So, how was the gym? Sam certainly looks like he had a good workout. I was a little surprised to see you'd gone to the gym together."

"I bet. I was all ready to run around the streets, but Sam said you'd kill him if I went out on my own in the dark."

"Now there is something he does know about me. I would have been mad. It's way too dark and cold for you to be running around the streets. I don't care how tough you are, Matthews."

"Anyway, Sam offered to take me to the gym instead. It's a well-equipped gym, and I was able to get a good run in, which is what I wanted."

"I'm glad you listened to him," Cory said as she spooned the various Chinese dishes onto the plates.

"I didn't do it for Sam, I did it for you," Dylan replied as she opened the fridge and took out a beer for Sam, placing it on his tray. "I'd do anything for you," she whispered, barely audible.

AT ELEVEN O'CLOCK, Sam rose up and yawned. "I've got an early start in the morning. I'm off to bed. You coming, Cor?"

Cory shook her head. "No, I'm a little wired. I think my unexpected sleep this afternoon recharged my batteries too much. I'd only toss and turn." She moved her attention to Dylan. "Are you willing to stay up and keep me company?"

Dylan wasn't about to miss the opportunity to spend some time with Cory. Despite the aching muscles and tiredness behind her eyes, Dylan nodded. She was willing to glue her eyes open if it meant spending time alone with this woman.

Sam bent down, kissed Cory on the cheek, bid them both a good night, and closed the door on his way out.

Cory surfed the television channels and settled on the movie, *Beaches,* which was being shown on the terrestrial Channel 4.

Dylan watched the first ten minutes of the film but couldn't focus. She looked over to the other sofa and watched as Cory shifted her position regularly. Dylan looked down at her feet that were dangling over the edge of the longer sofa. "You okay?" Dylan asked. "You're fidgeting."

"You noticed?"

"Kind of hard not to, the way you're rocking around."

Cory sat up and moved her feet to the floor. "I can't get comfy."

"Do you want to stretch out? We can switch sofas."

"No. You don't fit fully on the one you're on."

"If you'd like, I could rub your shoulders for you. You look wound up tighter than a drum," Dylan said. She scooted up the sofa and patted the space she'd cleared.

Cory jumped up from her sofa and moved quickly to the larger one. She settled between Dylan's outspread legs.

Dylan rested her hands on Cory's shoulders. Her breath was near Cory's neck. She began to firmly massage along the top of Cory's shoulders.

"God...that feels great."

When she heard Cory groan in pleasure, Dylan increased the pressure. "This okay?" She murmured into Cory's ear.

"Perfect," Cory answered.

Dylan felt Cory relax under her touch. Even though she was barely paying attention to the movie, she watched as the friendship between the two women developed. Dylan continued to rub Cory until she leaned too close, preventing Dylan access to comfortably stroke Cory's muscles any more. Dylan rested her hands on Cory's shoulders, content to have contact with her. After a while, she moved her arms in front of Cory and folded them across her body.

Cory rested her head on Dylan's chest. She gestured briefly to the television. "I love their friendship. I always wanted to have a friend like CeeCee."

Dylan tried to focus her attention on the screen and not on Cory's hand that was rubbing the top of her knees. The rubbing was sending tickling sensations up her leg. "I think everybody wants that." Dylan's voice broke slightly. *Oh dear, Lord, she's trying to kill me. Move her hand. No, don't move it. We're just friends. Dear, sweet libido, please calm down. Can she feel my heart racing? She must surely be able to hear it.* Relief came when Cory moved her hands to pull Dylan's arm more firmly around her.

"This part is so sad. Why did she have to die?"

"I don't know. At least they got to spend time together beforehand."

"I always cry when she does."

Dylan tightened her arms even more snugly around Cory. She bent her head slightly and smelled the skin behind Cory's ears. Her blood felt like it was on fire. She closed her eyes. She wanted to kiss Cory desperately. *Just one kiss. What harm can it do?*

Dylan focused on Cory as she wriggled and moved slightly away from her. She looked down and watched Cory twist around so she was facing her. She felt Cory's hand gently press against her heart.

"What's going on in there?"

Dylan swallowed hard. *Tell her she's the most beautiful person you've ever met. No, keep your distance. She's off limits. You only live once, Dylan.*

Tell her how you feel. Dylan looked away from the hand and to the pattern on the sofa.

Cory moved her hand to under Dylan's chin and tilted her head so she could look into Dylan's eyes.

Dylan closed her eyes. She shook her head slightly. *So different. They do say timing is everything.* Earlier in the day, she hadn't had a second thought about kissing Cory. However, now, she'd seen a different side to Sam. *I can't do this to him. I can't do this to us. The guilt will crush Cory. I can't do this to Sarah. I owe her more than that.* Dylan kept her eyes shut. She felt the sting of tears on her eyes. She took a steadying breath, and opened her eyes. Her resolve was teetering on the brink, all it would take was for her to move forward an inch at the most, and those luscious lips would be hers to savor, hers to devour.

Dylan broke her hold on Cory. She placed her hands on either side of her body and pushed herself up. She steadied herself on the arm of the sofa. Then she lifted her legs up and around Cory, and placed them on the floor. She stood up. "I'm going to bed. I think jet lag finally hit me. See you in the morning." She touched Cory lightly on the shoulder and left the room. *You coward. You could have explained how you felt.* But that would have required words, and Dylan didn't possess any.

Chapter
Fifteen

CORY AWOKE TO a gentle shaking of her body. She opened sore, puffy eyes to see Sam in front of her. "Hey there. You didn't come to bed last night. Why did you sleep on the sofa? I thought you'd lost your way, or that Dylan had worked her charm on you."

"I couldn't sleep," Cory said. Her throat hurt, and she was having trouble focusing. "Dylan and I watched a movie. She went to bed when it finished, but I stayed down here. I wanted time to think about Granddad. I knew it was coming, but it's still a kick in the gut when it arrives."

"I know, Cory, but it's for the best if he's suffering." Sam turned to collect the remnants of the previous night's meal.

"I know, but it's hard facing the truth. I'm going to see him today."

"Don't forget to walk Holly tonight. I'm down in Leighton Buzzard overnight. It's an important deal, but in an emergency, I want you to call me. I'll pop over to see Granddad on Thursday."

"He'll appreciate seeing you. He always asks after you." Cory removed the blanket she had covered herself with.

"I've already walked the dog and fed the cats. It's only just turned six. Why don't you go to bed? You look exhausted." He bent down, kissed her on the forehead, and then helped her up off the sofa. "Go on. I'll call you later." He pointed her toward the stairs.

Cory climbed the stairs. She paused when she saw Dylan's closed door. *What happened to make her run away from me? Am I reading mixed signals?* Cory used the bathroom and then settled into bed. It felt wonderful after a night on the couch. Soon she drifted off to sleep.

FOR THE SECOND time that day, Cory was awakened by a gentle shaking of the shoulder. She opened bleary eyes and took a few seconds to focus on Dylan.

"Hi. I brought you a cup of tea. I hope it tastes okay. I've never made tea before." Dylan placed the steaming cup on the bedside table. "Feeling any better?"

"I wasn't aware I was ill."

Shit, you've got your work cut out here, Dylan. Take it easy. Don't make her madder. Think before you speak. Dylan tried again. "I was up early this morning and went running. I saw Sam before he left, and I asked him how you were this morning. He said you slept on the sofa. He asked me to keep a close eye on you. He said you weren't feeling a hundred percent. So I let you sleep in, and thought I'd bring you something to drink. I should have let you sleep. I'm sorry."

"No, I'm the one who should be sorry. I didn't mean to snap. It was good of you to bring the drink. How late is it?" Cory sat up, rearranging her shirt as she did so. She puffed the pillows up behind her head and leaned back, bringing her knees up to her chest.

"It's heading toward midday," Dylan answered. "Can I sit down?"

"Sure." Cory indicated to the space below her legs. "Shit, I'm a lousy host. You must be starving. Let me get you some food." Cory made a move to get out of the bed, but a powerful arm held her back. She resettled against the pillows.

"Where's the fire? Slow down. It may have escaped your notice, but I'm a full-grown adult. I know how to make toast and coffee," Dylan said and stuck out her tongue, trying to alleviate the tension. "I'm fine. I enjoyed my run this morning. The countryside around here is great. I liked watching the sun rise and the countryside come awake."

"I can't believe you went out so early."

"I had trouble sleeping. Anyway, I read some of my new book and watched some of the morning TV shows. Some of them made me laugh. I liked watching some of the British talk shows. I also found the perfect show for me. I think it was called *'Can't Cook; Won't Cook.'* I couldn't decide which contestant I would be. I mean I can't cook, but I also won't cook." Dylan realized she was rambling and stopped talking. *Do I mention last night? Do I just forget it happened and pretend I have amnesia?* Dylan decided the latter was the best option. "Do you have any plans for the day?"

"I thought I'd take you over to Stratford-upon-Avon. It's where a certain Mr. William Shakespeare was born and bred. If it was summer, we could take a rowing boat down the river. However, it's too cold for that, but we can feed the ducks instead. Then, on the way back, we can visit and see how my granddad is doing, if you don't mind."

"We can do that. Take all the time you want with your grandfather. We've got a lifetime to get to know each other, and I can come and visit again. Your grandfather's time is limited. I can amuse myself. I might take a walk into the town and give you some time alone with him."

Cory moved forward and knelt to the side of Dylan. She put her arms around Dylan and hugged her tightly. "Has anyone ever told you how wonderful you are?"

Cory thought Dylan seemed surprised at this spontaneous action. She wrapped her arms around Cory's waist and pulled her into the biggest hug she could muster.

Cory broke the hug. "At the rate we're going, we'll never get anything done today."

"Okay. Go and shower. I'll make you a sandwich, and don't forget to drink your tea." Dylan stood up, placed the mug in Cory's hand, and sauntered out of the room.

DYLAN STARED AT the black and white buildings. "I'm still amazed at these old buildings. There are more here than in Warwick. They all look like they're pubs. I think it's true what I heard about Britain."

"What did you hear?"

"That there really is a pub on every corner. Here there seems to be two or three to a street."

"Yeah, Stratford was a great place to come and drink as a student—lots of pubs. The college clubs would put on a coach trip every summer. I even played a golf drinking game around Stratford."

"Golf? I'm confused. What do you mean?"

"Drinking golf. Do you know the rules of golf?"

"Yeah."

"Okay, in the drinking game, each pub is designated as either a pint or a half-pint pub. You have to order the designated size drink in each pub. The pub also has a par. So say each pub is par four. That means you have to drink the beer in that many mouthfuls. If it takes more than four gulps, then you're over par. If you do it in fewer, you're under par. If we were really desperate to make our score better, we sometimes downed a drink in one."

"I'd have lost track."

"We often did. Some people were good at organizing the games and made play cards so you could keep score."

"I'd have passed out on the third hole."

"We did a nine hole game once at Stratford. I got so sick." Cory pretended to vomit. "Bad memories."

They made their way slowly up and down the streets. They looked at souvenir shops, perused some of the clothes stores, and studied the various styles of buildings. They took photos of Shakespeare's birthplace and wandered down to the river. The weather wasn't that bad for the time of year. It wasn't warm, but neither was it freezing. They had their coats on, and it was warm enough to sit on the bench and watch the ducks. There seemed to be hundreds of them milling around.

Cory sat a little closer to Dylan. "You always seem to be so warm. I can feel it from here." She pointed to the ducks. "Isn't it sweet?"

"Isn't what sweet?"

"The pairings of the ducks." Cory took a package out of her bag. She opened it and took out the slices of bread she had packed. "Did you know mallards mate for life?"

"No. I didn't. How the hell do you think they recognize their mate?

They all look the same to me."

"True." Cory broke off some of the bread. "I wonder how they keep their relationships strong. I never seem to be able to commit to anything."

"You committed yourself to Sam."

"I know, but I'm not sure we're going to be for life. These birds have a life-bond." A very loud female mallard began to quack loudly. Cory's giggled at the determined bird. "I bet she's giving her other half a really good telling off. What do you think he did?"

"Either he stayed out all night or forgot the groceries." Dylan chuckled as she watched the interaction. "It's good to see you smile. You love animals, don't you?"

"I adore them. I could animal watch all day. They fascinate me with their use of instinct. I sometimes wonder if they really can speak to each other. Wouldn't you like to know what they thought of you?" Cory passed some bread to Dylan. They threw pieces of bread to the ducks, who soon gathered around their feet.

"To be honest, I've never really thought about it." She looked at the different species of ducks that had collected near them. She fed the birds that came close to her.

"Would you like to play my favorite duck-watching game?"

"Sure. How do I play?"

"We watch the ducks and then name them after friends, family, and famous people, depending on their personality."

CORY PULLED ONTO the driveway and caught sight of a shadow at the front bay window of the house. "Shit. Poor Holly. She must be crossing her legs. It's gone six." Cory fumbled frantically with the key, finally turning it and opening the door. She took a deep breath. There didn't seem to be a smell. Holly came bounding out of the living room.

"I'm going to put my backpack in my room." Dylan ran up the stairs.

"Good girl, Holly. Go and fetch your lead. We're going walkies." At the sound of the "W-word," Holly went mad, barking and running back and forth to the kitchen. On her third attempt, the German Shepherd came back with the lead in her mouth. Cory placed it in her pocket. "Dylan, I'm off down the field would you like to come or stay?"

"Are you crazy? It's pitch black out there. I'm not letting you go on your own. Sam would kill me if anything happened to you. In fact, I'd kill me if anything happened to you," Dylan yelled from the guestroom. She ran down the stairs and met Cory at the front door.

The temperature had dropped significantly, and both women shivered as they walked around the open landscape by the River Avon. Each breath came out in a fog of steam.

Cory saw Dylan shaking in the chilly air.

"You wimp. You're not cold, are you? I thought you came from a place so cold it makes your snot freeze in the back of your nose." Cory jokingly nudged Dylan and received a sheepish grin.

"So, I'm a weenie. It's a different kind of cold here. It's a kind of damp that goes through to the bone. At home, the winds can freeze you. Plus, look how many layers of clothing you have on. I noticed yesterday and today how many people were wearing fleece. I swear you've probably got fleece panties on."

"You never know." Cory smiled. She moved closer to Dylan and slipped her arm through the crook of Dylan's elbow. They walked a lap of the field and then headed back toward the house.

When they got back, Cory fed the animals and ordered a pizza. She observed Dylan from the corner of her eye. She'd offered the washing machine to Dylan and watched as she sorted her gym clothing and regular clothes in tidy piles. She noticed the stretch of Dylan's legs and the taut muscles as she bent over to put the clothes into the machine. The woman was a goddess and didn't look to have an ounce of fat on her.

After Dylan had finished in the laundry room and the pizza had been delivered, they went into the living room. Cory moved the two beanbag chairs stored in the corner of the room and placed them on the floor in front of the television. They ate the pizza lounging on them rather than the sofas. Cory was showing Dylan the latest music that was top of the charts in the UK.

"It's good to see you cheerful again. I enjoyed today."

"So did I. Thank you for helping me entertain Granddad. He really got a kick when you taught him how to play poker."

Dylan smiled. "I don't think I taught him. I think he knew exactly how to play. I'm pretty sure he was hustling us."

"No wonder he beat us hands down. It's a good job we were only playing with tooth picks."

"True. But your mom managed to get her chores done while we were there, and the time away from looking after your granddad was a nice break for her."

Cory watched as Dylan touched her shin and winced. "Do you need a cushion? Look at us sitting on these bags when we have two comfy sofas." Cory made a move to get up but stopped when she felt Dylan's hand on her arm.

"I guess I over did it last night at the gym. Sam and I were lifting weights, and I may have been showing off. My back and legs are stiffening up. I have a cramp in my shin. I don't think the damp air helped earlier. Maybe a warm bath would loosen them up."

Cory hesitated and then said quietly, "I could give you a massage if you want."

"Sure. If you don't mind, I'll have a quick shower and slip into something more comfortable."

HALF AN HOUR later, both women were back in the living room. They had showered and changed into comfortable sleeping shorts and tops.

Cory placed a large towel from the bathroom flat on the floor. "Are you ready for the torture?" Cory asked as she wiggled a bottle of massage mousse in front of Dylan's face.

"Yeah, I'm game."

"I should mention that Sam thinks I massage like Monica on *Friends*. He says I'm too rough."

"I'll let you know afterwards. A second opinion never hurts."

Dylan rolled over onto her stomach and the towel. She placed her arms under her head.

Cory looked at the long body waiting for her. "Er...Dylan, I can't massage you with your...uh...top still on," she stuttered, regretting her offer of a massage. "You're going to have to take it off." Cory was flustered. This was so different than the massages she had performed on her other friends. *Couldn't let her stick to the warm bath, could you? No backing out now.*

Dylan wriggled about, pulled off her t-shirt, and settled back onto the towel.

Cory took in the sight beside her. Dylan's back was tanned and firm. The muscles in her arms and back were defined. Cory's eyes traveled from Dylan's back down to the narrowing of her waist and halted at the waistband to Dylan's shorts. She rubbed some vanilla and lavender mousse between her hands and began her slow rubdown. The skin was soft, like velvet. Her hands ran up and down Dylan's spine slowly, savoring the experience. Cory moved up toward the top of Dylan's shoulders and began to knead the flesh beneath her fingers.

"This feels awesome. Sam is so wrong."

Dylan's words spurred Cory on. She poured more mousse onto Dylan's back and began another trip over the shoulder blades and down the spine. She felt every inch of Dylan's back, taking in every little mark, stroking every blemish and wanting desperately to kiss where her hands had traveled. She didn't think it wise to linger on the sight of Dylan's pert ass and went straight for the back of the thighs, taking in the muscles and rubbing the tight hamstrings.

Having thoroughly massaged the back of Dylan's body, she decided the legs would be easier to do if Dylan faced her. She tapped Dylan's shoulder but received no response. She peered down and became aware of the contented smile on Dylan's face. Her breathing was slow and steady. She was asleep. The massage had worked. Dylan looked totally relaxed, completely calm and at peace with the world. *Do I leave her to sleep half-naked or wake her up? What a dilemma, Williams. Do you stare at the naked form of your desire or cover her up?* Her morals won out, and Cory gently covered Dylan's back with a blanket. It would protect her modesty should she wake suddenly or turn over in her sleep.

Cory leaned against the sofa, her body scant inches from Dylan. She ran her fingers slowly and gently through the ends of Dylan's drying hair. The texture was smooth and very soft. Cory stopped after a couple of minutes, not wanting to catch one of the little tangles of knots that had developed while drying. All Cory wanted to do was join her — creep under the cover and wrap around her body. At that moment, she knew she was in too deep. Her whole life was changing, and she needed to face it head on. *I am in love with Dylan, one hundred percent. But what about Sam? What about my marriage? Does Dylan care for me? How can we even be together? She lives three thousand fucking miles away.* So many questions revolved in her head. There was no doubt she'd ever felt as she did when Dylan innocently touched her. The touches seemed to burn a path on her skin. When Cory closed her eyes, she could remember everything about Dylan: her skin, her smile, her smell, and those eyes, so open, so blue, and so honest.

Cory wasn't aware of the time. Dylan's consistent deep breaths had kept her mesmerized. Suddenly, she was shaken out of her thoughts by heavy rain lashing at the window. She shuddered and shifted closer to Dylan. She glanced out of the window and saw the shadow of the tiny tree in the garden shaking violently. She hadn't noticed the wind picking up, but now she was very aware of it. Rain ran off the house and hail stones thudded against the window panes.

DYLAN STRETCHED, REMEMBERING at the last moment that she was topless. She felt around and grabbed her top. She put it over her head, pulled it down, turned over, and lastly, removed the blanket.

Cory looked down. "Are your muscles feeling better?"

"Thanks for the cover, and yes, I feel lots better. The massage was awesome. It's been a long time since I allowed myself to totally relax like that." Her voice was husky from sleep. "I've never fallen asleep during a massage before, not even with Sarah. If Sam thinks your massages are too hard, he has no idea what a good massage feels like. I thought you did a wonderful job."

"I was going to ask you to flip over, so I could massage your calves, but you'd fallen asleep. There's a storm developing outside. I hope it doesn't go on all night. I hate the clatter and whistle of the gale force winds. Sam usually makes me feel somewhat safer, although he's never sympathetic."

Dylan saw Cory tremble. "I'll keep you company."

"Thanks. I'm going to make some hot chocolate. Would you like some?"

Dylan nodded eagerly. "That sounds like a great idea. I'd offer to help, but I'm feeling decadent, and I'm going to slouch here."

"No worries. I'll be back in a few minutes."

Cory wandered back into the lounge as Dylan was stretching and yawning. "You perhaps should go up to bed instead of having hot choc-olate with me. You're obviously tired."

"A little. I'm usually full of energy, but the past few days, my body clock has been shot to shit. Tomorrow it should straighten itself out, and then in a few days I have to go home. Then it'll have to adjust again." Dylan took the mug of hot chocolate Cory offered her. "So what plans have you made for us tomorrow?" Dylan held the mug between her hands. She felt warm and toasty inside, and it wasn't the hot chocolate. One look from those emerald eyes and she was lost.

Cory sat on the floor next to Dylan. "It's funny you should ask, as I have made plans for the rest of the week. Some you're going to like and others, well, you have the choice not to join me."

"What have you planned? You have that mischievous twinkle in your eyes."

"Me, mischievous? Never. I actually need your help, if you're will-ing. The painters have been in school this week, and I need to go in there."

"What needs doing?" Dylan blew lightly on her hot chocolate and tentatively took a sip.

"I have to put up new wall displays and restock the bookshelves before Monday. We tore stuff down on Friday, and it's all over the desks. I can't do it with the kids in class, as there'd be too much chaos. So I figured if I went in and did that tomorrow morning and got it out of the way, afterwards, I could go over to check on my granddad. Then on Thursday and Friday, I want to give you a tour of the capital as pay-ment for your services." She brought her mug back up to her lips and took a slow, lingering sip.

"You're taking me to London?"

Cory nodded. "Yes. Granddad looked pretty good today, so I thought we'd head down to London on Thursday and stay until Satur-day."

Dylan stood up slowly, never letting her gaze leave Cory's. "I'd love to see it. If you're sure it's all right to spend two nights away, then cool, we can do the thing at your school. I'm interested to see where you spend your days. Will I need to raise my hand tomorrow if I need to go to the bathroom?"

"You are a big kid." Cory stood up, too. "No you won't have to, but if you carry on teasing, I may have to reprimand you."

"Promises, promises." Dylan felt retreat was her only option for fear that Cory would make her expand on that statement. "I'm going to bed now. I hope the storm doesn't bother you. If it does, you know where I am."

"Thanks, Dylan, and thanks for the offer." Cory switched off the lights and followed Dylan's ass up the stairs, with Holly trailing behind.

THE NEXT MORNING, the storm was replaced by a bright morning sun. Cory crept down the stairs on her way to walk Holly. When she reached the bottom step, she could hear Dylan's voice coming from the living room. She walked to the door and peered through the crack. She saw Dylan pacing back and forth, her hands running constantly through her black mane. Cory listened as Dylan spoke into the phone.

"Sarah, if that's how you feel then go ahead. I won't stop you. You were the one who sent the text. You were the one begging me to call. Now, I'm calling, and you won't listen. All you want to do is shout, scream, and demand things. I'll be back on Saturday."

Dylan paused. "Whatever. If you move out before then, that's your decision. You're blowing everything out of proportion and laying blame at the wrong door. I have to go — this isn't my dime. Think about what I've said. I'll see you Saturday, maybe." There was a brief pause and then the door flung open. Dylan hurled out of the room. She ran straight into Cory.

"Oh shit...sorry...this isn't what it looks like," stammered Cory, picking herself up off the floor, the force of the collision having knocked her down. "I'm so embarrassed."

Dylan shook her head and felt her jaw. "I'm sorry. I had no idea you were there."

"I was...I wasn't here for long, and I wasn't really listening. I was surprised you were up. I wanted to say good morning. I didn't want to disturb you, but you sounded angry." Her rambling was halted by a hand over her mouth.

"Whoa, slow down there, motor mouth. Come up for some air. It's your house, and I should have asked first to use the phone. I promise to leave the money."

Dylan rubbed her jaw again. "God, your head is solid. Shit, my jaw's killing me. How's your head?" Dylan placed her hands on the Cory's head.

Cory felt Dylan's fingers probing her skull. "Quit that." Cory waved away Dylan's hands, smiling to express she wasn't annoyed. "What are you doing?"

"Let me be. I'm checking for a lump. Your head must have one hell of a bruise on it." Dylan walked toward the kitchen and headed for the freezer. "Where's your ice maker?"

"My what? Oh, ice maker. We don't have one, and there aren't any ice cubes, either. There's no real need for them in this weather."

"What do you use on bruises to reduce the swelling?" Dylan asked.

"Bag of peas or carrots...anything frozen. I've been known to put a frozen piece of steak on a bruise or two." Cory walked into the kitchen to find Dylan searching in the freezer. "Dylan, relax. I'm fine. I promise." Cory turned to switch the kettle on and make a cup of tea. Her heart was beating fast. *She can sure move when she needs to, and silently, at that.* "As for using the phone, I've already told you it's no problem. I was just surprised you were using it this early in the morning. I thought everyone in America would be asleep."

Dylan closed the freezer door, walked over to the counter, and pulled out one of the breakfast bar stools. She sat down and leaned on the counter top. She watched Cory prepare her tea. "Usually they are, but Sarah works the graveyard shift every four weeks. She sent me a text message earlier and asked me to call her. I didn't really want to speak to her, but curiosity got the better of me."

"Whatever was said, she definitely riled your feathers. Would you like to try some tea, or would you rather stick with coffee?"

"Coffee, thanks. Yeah, she pissed me off. She's all for moving out. I told her to wait until Saturday. We can split the joint belongings fairly. She did say she's still going to contribute toward the house. Anyway, either we sell it, or I buy her out."

"It seems very sudden. She's not even prepared to talk it through with you." Cory moved round the counter, passed Dylan a mug of coffee, and rubbed her briefly on the shoulder. "I'm sorry. I knew you guys were having difficulties. I know yesterday you said you were a single person again, but I guess I didn't realize it was final. I figured you'd patch things up when you got back."

Dylan took the coffee mug that Cory offered her. "It's been bad for a while. We just didn't want to face it. Ultimately, we make each other miserable. We fight and do things to hurt each other. I knew she wasn't the one for me, but the relationship was 'safe.' It's what I needed after Tina. It's just hard that it ended this way — over the phone."

"Do you want to stay here for the day? It would give you time to gather your thoughts."

"No, I want to go with you. We made plans, and I do want to see the school. It will take my mind off things. I'm sure you have a list of things a mile long for me to do." She patted Cory's hand. "What dirty jobs have you got lined up for me?"

Cory gave her an innocent look. "Me?" She pointed a finger at her own chest. "Me, plan jobs for you to do? Me, work you like a slave? As if I would. I'm hurt at the suggestion." She placed her hand over her eyes, feigning an insult. However, her attempt failed miserably as she caught Dylan's eye, and burst out laughing. "Okay, honestly, I have a few things that I need you to help me with. Also, the school's computer server has been playing up. It'll be a few weeks before the technician visits. I thought you could use your magic hands on it, if we have the time."

THE SMALL CAR pulled up to the school a matter of minutes after leaving the house.

"This might sound crazy, but I'm excited to see where you work." *Who am I kidding? Anything and everything about Cory gets you excited. Get over it, already. She's straight and married.* Dylan shook her head slightly. She furtively glanced at Cory, as she concentrated on parallel parking outside the tiny building. Dylan gazed admiringly at Cory's profile—a profile she decided she could look at forever.

"I hate trying to get into these parking spots. The car park is closed for resurfacing. I thought most of the residents would have left for work by now." Cory put the car in gear, pulled the hand brake, and turned off the engine.

"I see you weren't lying when you said you had a quick commute to work," Dylan said. "I'm jealous. Mine can take anywhere from one to two hours, depending on traffic. The thought of a seven minute drive would be heaven. Did the car even warm up?" She saw Cory wince. "Did I say something wrong?"

"No. The short journeys are hurting the car. It never gets a chance to warm up. I've already replaced one exhaust pipe because of it. The exhaust fumes never get hot enough to evaporate. Therefore, the water lies in the exhaust and rusts it away."

"Could you walk to school or ride a bike?"

Cory shook her head and pointed out of the window. "Walking is out of the question. All the pathways run through farmer's fields, country lanes, and hills. It'd take me thirty minutes or more. I could bicycle, but the weather is so unpredictable. I also carry boxes of school books."

"I guess I touched a raw subject, huh?" Dylan shrugged apologetically.

"No problem."

They got out of the car, opened the school gate, and walked up to the large front door. Cory used a key to unlock the door, and they entered the school. Dylan followed Cory's lead through a hall and down a corridor, until they stopped at a door labeled "WILLIAMS 6."

Dylan peered into the classroom. The desks, chairs, and coat racks were sized for children aged eleven and under. She wondered what it would be like to see Cory in action. She could picture Cory helping the students with questions and getting lost in the crowd when she sat at a desk to help. Dylan waited for Cory to unlock the classroom door. Then she picked up a box that Cory indicated needed to come into the classroom with them.

The classroom was small, smaller than it looked in the pictures Cory had sent in one of her e-mails. She took in every last detail, from the furnishings to the bare display boards to the boxes of classroom books. Dylan's investigations were interrupted by Cory's instructions for the first task.

"Okay, the first thing we have to do is put up the backing paper on all these display boards. Then we'll go around and add the borders. It's tricky to do on your own. However, I did it myself last year."

"I'm impressed. How the hell did you do that? These boards are huge." Dylan stared at all the boards. She hoped they could accomplish the tasks by the deadline of two o'clock that they'd discussed on their way to the school. She prayed that they wouldn't end up arguing like Sarah and she usually did when they attempted projects together.

"Don't ask. It took forever, and involved measuring tapes and knives. Having a second pair of hands really is a bonus."

"Oh—now I find out my true worth. I'm only a pair of hands to you," Dylan said teasingly. She received a playful whack to her tummy.

"Suck it up, girl. Your charm and blue eyes may have fooled others. Me, I just see a decent-sized pair of hands that can hold this backing paper. Plus, you have the height I need, so I won't have to get the step ladders."

FOR TWENTY MINUTES, they harmoniously toiled away, covering the boards with brightly colored paper. Dylan held the paper in place while Cory stapled it to the board. They added contrasting borders. After that, Cory brought in the theme boxes and maps. They decorated two of the boards with a history theme of Victorian Britain. On the third display board, they placed a large map of the world—a place for the students to record the countries they had studied in their time at the school.

"Can you do me a favor?" Cory asked.

"Sure. What do you need?"

"If I write on the chalk board the areas we've studied, could you type and print them out?"

"Sure. No problem. But I suggest you write clearer than you did in that card you sent me. It took me three or four rereads to decipher all the words."

"I will, so long as you remember to add the extra 'u' in some of the words. I know how you Americans like to leave them out," Cory joked.

The rest of the time in the school went quickly. Dylan thought they worked extremely well together. She was surprised, but happy, that they complemented each other in so many actions. The displays were finished in no time. By mid-afternoon they were on their way to Cory's parents' house.

Chapter
Sixteen

"CORY, I DON'T think we should go to London. Your grandfather looked very sick," Dylan said.

Cory tapped the steering wheel lightly. She had been debating the upcoming trip since leaving her mother's house. She had been surprised at how frail her grandfather had become in only a few days. "I've thought about it, and I'd still like to take you. You spent so much money coming over here. I'd like you to leave with memories of more than this car and my mother's house."

"Okay, it's your call. But I think you should visit him on our way to London."

"That's a deal," Cory said, a little brighter, "and if the worse case scenario happens, I'll only be an hour away."

"And I'll be closer to the airport."

CORY AND DYLAN took Holly on a walk when they returned home. Then Cory fed the animals while Dylan chopped and diced vegetables and some chicken for a stir-fry.

Cory placed the chicken in the pan and then added the vegetables. After a few minutes, she put some previously-cooked rice into the pan. She stirred the food together. The ringing of the phone interrupted her actions. "Can you watch this for me? It needs to boil before we set it on simmer."

"Sure." Dylan took the wooden spoon from Cory.

Cory followed the jingle of the phone. She found the cordless receiver on the coffee table in the lounge. She came back a few minutes later.

"Sorry about that. The food smells yummy. I hope it tastes as good. That was Sam on the phone. He says hello. He has to stay overnight again. The deal is closed, but the architects took them around the golf course. Of course, they stayed in the nineteenth hole a little longer than intended. I told him about our trip to London and Granddad. He said he might meet us there tomorrow or drive straight home. He's going to decide in the morning."

"Was he okay about us going to London?"

"Yes. He suggested I ring the Travel Lodge hotel to book us in. Remind me to do that after dinner." Cory tried to sneak a quick taste of the food, but her hand was smacked away by Dylan.

They opened a bottle of wine and settled on the sofas in the lounge.

"This is delicious. Will you write down the recipe?"

Cory shrugged nonchalantly. "I'll send it in an e-mail. Then you'll have it when you get home."

"What are the plans for this evening?"

"It's quiz night at the local pub. They hold one every month. It lasts about an hour. The questions are based on a variety of general knowledge categories. We could go, if you want?"

"All right, but you might have to be the brains behind our duo."

"I'm sure you'll do fine. It's quite a nice little pub, and they have a huge fire."

THE PUB WAS a five-minute drive away from the house. Cory and Dylan were soon established in a corner of the one-roomed building. They had chosen a seat near the fire.

Dylan sipped her pint of beer. She surveyed the pub. It was small and cozy. It had a homey air to it. She swirled the beer in her mouth. "You were right about the beer. It's very strong." Dylan decided to limit herself to one pint. She needed to keep her wits about her when she was so close to Cory.

Dylan found the pub quiz fun. The pub had filled with many competing teams. She had been impressed by Cory's general knowledge. However, she also held her own and showed that there was more than air between her ears. At the end of the quiz, they had won second place and received a bottle of wine each. Dylan had kept her deal with herself and had drunk only one pint. Then she had switched to soft drinks. Cory, on the other hand, had drunk four pints of Guinness. In Dylan's judgment, Cory was a little drunk.

The last order bell rang loud throughout the pub.

"Do you want another drink?" Cory asked.

Dylan shook her head. "I'm all set, if you want to leave."

"Okay, let's head home." Cory stood up and picked up the empty glasses. She deposited them onto the bar. "Thank you. I'll see you next time," she said to the owner and exited out of the pub. The air was cold. Cory put her arm through Dylan's as they walked to the car.

"Did you have fun, D?" Cory whispered.

Dylan liked the shortening of her name. She felt Cory relax into her. "I had an excellent time." She watched as Cory tried to put the key in the lock of the driver's door. "I think I should drive."

"But it's the other side of the road," Cory protested.

Dylan looked up and down the country lane. There wasn't a car in sight. "You're house is one road away. I'm used to a stick shift, and I'm pretty sure I can remember to keep to the left."

Cory swallowed a tiny hiccup. She passed her keys to Dylan. "Thanks. I should have been more careful and not drunk so much."

"Don't worry. I'll just add this to one of my British experiences."

WHEN THEY ARRIVED at the house, Dylan helped Cory upstairs.

"I want to stay up and chat with you."

"Go to bed. No arguments. You fell asleep in the car, and it was only a five minute trip. The sleep will do you good." Dylan walked Cory to her bedroom door. "Will you be okay?"

"Yes. Thank you for looking after me." Cory stood on tiptoe and kissed Dylan briefly on a cheek. "Goodnight. Thank you for a wonderful day. You're a star."

Dylan was too dumbstruck to do anything but smile. She opened the bedroom door and watched as Cory walked to the bathroom area. She closed the door behind Cory and headed downstairs to let Holly into the yard. She was wide awake and very frustrated.

CORY AWOKE WITH a start. She remembered the pub and the quiz. She remembered getting into the car, but past that, her mind was blank. *Stupid, stupid, stupid. You had to drink more than you could handle. God only knows what you did or said last night.* She glanced at the clock: 1 A.M. She needed the toilet. She'd been dreaming of her granddad in his coffin waving at her and saying goodbye. It had disturbed her. She was cold. She didn't want to be alone. *You can't go and visit Dylan. It's the middle of the bloody night.* She used the bathroom. Unwilling to go back to sleep for fear of having the same dream, Cory walked to Dylan's door. She knocked lightly. There was no answer. She rapped a little louder and heard a muffled sound. She opened the door slightly. "Dylan, you awake?" she whispered.

"I am now. What's the matter?"

Cory walked into the room. Holly followed her. "I had a nightmare. I'm too scared to sleep on my own. I wondered if you'd let me bunk down with you. Help me chase the demons away." Cory stood by the bed. She fiddled with the hem of her t-shirt.

Dylan lifted the duvet. "Come here. You must be freezing."

Cory settled into the bed. She faced Dylan and moved into Dylan's welcoming arms. Dylan pulled her nearer, and she went willingly.

"You *are* cold. Let me warm you up," Dylan said.

Dylan was like a furnace. Cory felt extremely safe and secure. She enjoyed the comfort of Dylan's hands soothingly stroking her back and placed an arm over her side to return the hug. After a few minutes, Cory felt Dylan release her hold. She moved back a little, relieved that the extra space allowed her to rearrange her body. She could make out

Dylan's profile as she examined her in the moonlight.

Cory felt Dylan's fingers touch her face. They moved slowly down her cheek and paused briefly at her mouth, before following the outline of her lips. Cory opened her mouth slightly and moistened her lips. Her tongue touched the fingers. She licked Dylan's index finger, gently at first, and then with increasing pressure. Seductively, she pulled the digit into her mouth. After a few seconds, Cory released the finger and slowly replaced it with another. One by one she sucked and licked them all.

The electricity between the pair was fully charged. Cory could feel the moisture between her legs. She was swollen and knew what she needed. She moved closer to Dylan and kissed her neck. In return, Dylan pulled her closer into a hug and nibbled the soft skin of her neck. Cory moved higher up the bed, catching Dylan's gaze. Then she lowered her head toward Dylan's mouth.

"This can't happen. You're drunk." Dylan placed her hand over Cory's mouth. She leaned forward touching her forehead to Cory's, her hand still between their mouths. "Cory, as much as I want you, and I do, you're not mine to have." She blew out a slow breath and removed her hand. "I'm sorry." She kissed Cory on the forehead and then pulled her into a hug.

"Do you want me to leave?" Cory asked.

"No. Stay. Let's sleep. We'll talk tomorrow."

Cory cuddled closer, resting her head on Dylan's shoulder. She closed her eyes and was asleep in no time.

SAM LOOKED ON from the bedroom door. He'd arrived home to what appeared a deserted house. No barking dog and no wife in his bed. He'd noticed Dylan's door ajar and had pushed the door slightly open. The light filtering through a gap in the curtain, settled on two bodies, so closely wrapped together they looked like one. Cory's blonde hair contrasted with the black of Dylan's. The morning sun danced over Dylan's tanned arm as it held the body beneath it. He noted how Dylan's body spooned Cory's. Both women slept peacefully.

He continued to stare at Cory's face. She was so beautiful, so young. Jealousy stirred in the pit of his stomach. However, two things prevented him from waking them. One, he trusted his wife, and the other was they were fully clothed.

He opened the door wider and signaled to Holly. The dog got up and walked out of the room. Sam glanced one more time at the bed. Then he closed the door quietly behind him, and set off for a morning run.

DYLAN STIRRED AND opened bleary eyes. She peered at the head on the pillow in front of her. After a few moments, she remembered

Cory's early morning visit. She continued to look at Cory. She knew she'd done the honorable thing. However, it didn't stop her holding the woman tightly. She inhaled the faint smell of mint shampoo and the fragrance of Cory's skin. She wished things were different. She wished the woman in her arms were single, but fate wasn't being kind. *Stay strong and keep the faith. If it's meant to be, it will be.*

Dylan lay alone with her thoughts until she felt the tension return to Cory's body. She slowly released her hold and moved across to her side of the bed. However, she was prevented from going too far by an arm snaking its way round her body.

"No. Stay. Where do you think you're going?" Cory said.

Flustered, Dylan had no answer. She'd expected it to be awkward. Mornings after the night before usually were. Even though they hadn't made love, something physical had happened. They had definitely crossed a line and opened a chasm.

Cory rolled over to face Dylan. Dylan smiled shyly at her. "I was just...er...just going to the bathroom. I have to pee."

"Oh. I was enjoying being held. I thought we could talk a little, but only if you want to."

"I'd love to stay cuddled up to you all day, but my bladder is full. Plus, I was promised a trip to the big, bad city." She saw the sides of Cory's mouth turn up and she relaxed more. *We're going to be okay. That's all that matters. Focus on the friendship.*

"You're right. A trip to the city it is. I have to walk the dog anyways." Cory sat up and looked around the room.

Dylan watched her eyes dart around the room. "What's wrong?"

"Holly's not here. I swear I left the door open." Cory peered over the side of the bed.

"Maybe she went downstairs. She probably got bored waiting and went to walk herself. She's a smart dog."

"She's clever, but she has yet to work out how to close the door by pulling on the handle." Cory signaled to the door with her head.

"Shit. Do you think it was Sam?" Dylan asked.

"Well, if it wasn't we have some bloody polite burglars roaming the area," Cory remarked.

Dylan walked around the bed and placed a hand on Cory's arm. "Calm down. Sam obviously didn't think too much about it because he didn't wake us. All he would have seen was us sleeping."

"Dylan, how close were we sleeping when you woke up?"

Dylan blushed at the memory of how close Cory's body had been to hers, where their bare skin had touched, and how it had felt to hold Cory in her arms. "Okay, point taken. We were close. How about we go and check before we jump to conclusions?"

"But..."

"Nothing happened. Remember that if he asks what's going on — nothing happened." *Keep telling yourself that. You're so full of bullshit.*

Cory got out of the bed. "Thanks to you. Imagine what he would have walked in on had you not been so strong."

"Let's not even go there," Dylan said, bitterly.

With that comment, Cory went in search of Sam, while Dylan slipped quietly into the bathroom, deciding a low profile was the best way to start the day.

CORY PAUSED OUTSIDE the closed bedroom door. She took a few calming breaths before opening the door. She saw Sam's overnight bag on the floor next to the bed. It confirmed what she already knew: he'd come home early. She let out a slow breath. *Nothing happened — nothing happened.* Cory repeated Dylan's mantra, but she knew it was a lie. Everything had happened. Deciding to play it cool, she stepped into the shower and let the water trickle down her face. She changed the dial on the faucet and the water pounded against her. She stood under the water, thinking about what she'd nearly done with Dylan. She knew in her heart she'd have gone all the way had Dylan not stopped them. She'd have been powerless to resist any advances Dylan might have made. Thankfully, Dylan hadn't made any.

Cory took longer in the shower than usual. She attempted to get a check on her feelings. She thought of what she would say to Sam. As she stepped out of the shower and grabbed a towel, she heard the bedroom door open. She walked out of the ensuite naked, except for the towel in her right hand. She casually toweled the water from her hair. Inside, she was shaking like a leaf. She greeted Sam. "Hi, I didn't realize you'd come home. How was work?" She continued to wipe the water off her body trying to disguise her nervousness. She felt Sam's eyes on her body.

"There were hardly any cars on the road, so I was earlier than anticipated. Your mum phoned my mobile last night and asked me if I'd spend the day with your granddad. She needs to go out, and your dad's busy. She thought your granddad might want another man around, should he need help changing or toileting."

"Sounds like a good idea."

"Yeah, so I thought I'd grab some comfortable clothes. I was kind of surprised you were in the other room when I got back."

Cory gave a nervous laugh. "I was being a baby. I got all upset about Granddad, and I began to have nightmares about his death. Dylan offered me comfort, and I guess I fell asleep."

"And that's all that happened?"

"What are you implying?" Cory began to get dressed. She avoided any eye contact with Sam. She was afraid he would see the truth.

"Look at it from my point of view. I come home and find my wife in the arms of a lesbian, who's drop dead gorgeous." Sam began to peel off his clothes.

Cory took a deep breath. *He has a point. Don't lose your temper.* Nevertheless, the guilt she felt fueled her anger. She could feel months of rejection surface. It filled her with bitterness. She couldn't stop the words from flowing. "For God's sake, my grandfather's dying and I needed some support. I spent yesterday trying to be strong for Mum and Granddad, but inside, my heart was breaking. I needed to be held. I needed the pain to go away, and you weren't here. You were playing golf."

"That's below the belt. I was working."

"Dylan comforted me. Would you be asking me this if it had been Angie or Rachel who'd been comforting me?" Cory said. "Just because she's gay doesn't mean she fancies me. She has a girlfriend, and she has some morals." *More than I do.*

Cory continued to dress. She glanced occasionally at Sam. She could tell by his stance and quietness that she had hurt him with her words. When she had finished dressing, she walked over to him and placed her hands on his shoulders. "I'm sorry. I didn't mean to have a go at you. I know you have to work. This is so hard for me. I never thought he'd die. I never thought I'd have to face his death. He always seemed indestructible. He's never been ill, and he's always been there for me. I don't know what I'm going to do."

Sam took Cory in his arms. "Babe, he's had a good life. He's a wonderful bloke, but it's time to say goodbye. You can't let it eat at you. Why didn't you call me last night?"

"I wasn't sure you'd understand. You're not close to your family. You don't need them. You're often unemotional."

"I could have tried."

"Sam, how do I say goodbye to my hero? He's the only man who has always been there for me." As she said the words, she knew she'd struck a blow to Sam's pride. She felt him physically recoil and release her. She might as well have hit him with her own hand.

"Thanks for the vote of confidence," Sam replied.

"I didn't mean it like that. He's been there for me my whole life. He brought me up when my biological father left. He's always supported my choices. He's been my guiding light." Cory chewed on her bottom lip. "When I get back from London, I think we need to sit down and talk...about us."

"What about us?"

"Not now. Dylan's here. She's probably heard the whole conversation."

Sam picked up his wash bag and headed toward the shower. "God forbid, we upset bloody Dylan."

Cory followed him and stood at threshold of the bathroom. "What is your problem? We have a guest. I will not have this discussion at the moment. Dylan's flight is early Saturday morning. After I've seen Granddad, we need to talk, whether you like it or not."

Sam turned and glared at Cory. "What do we have to talk about? Life is okay. We're doing fine."

"Sam, if you really believe this, then you obviously haven't listened to a word I've said these past six months. We never make love. You never talk about your feelings."

"You always bring this up. It always comes back to that. It's my problem, and I will solve it." He closed the bathroom door. Cory stood staring at the wooden door.

CORY WAITED WHILE Dylan positioned her suitcase in the trunk of the car. When Dylan moved aside, she squeezed her bag next to it. "Do you have everything?"

"Yeah. I double checked after breakfast." Dylan got into the passenger side of the car and waited for Cory to sit beside her. "Sam seemed okay over breakfast. Did he say anything to you?"

Cory started the engine. She looked in the rear view mirror and guided the car off the driveway. "Yes. He thought you might have seduced me."

"What did you tell him?"

"The truth. I told him I was scared and you comforted me. Nothing more — nothing less."

"Cory..."

"Dylan, I'm feeling a little raw at the moment. Sam was quite angry, and I'm embarrassed about my behavior last night. I was drunk, and I shouldn't have put you in a compromising position. I need to focus on the road. Can we talk about this later?"

"Sure, but can I say that you have nothing to feel embarrassed about?"

Chapter
Seventeen

THE RECEPTIONIST AT the hotel greeted them with a smile. "How can I help you?"

Cory placed her bag on the ground, opened her wallet, and passed her credit card to the clerk. "I have a room booked under the name of Cory Williams for two nights." She tapped her fingers on the desktop as she waited for the confirmation.

"Mrs. Williams, a queen room, checking out Saturday morning."

Cory looked at the receptionist and then Dylan. "I think there may be a mix up. I ordered a room with two twin beds." Cory caught Dylan's quirked eyebrow. She seemed to be enjoying her predicament.

The receptionist searched the database again. "I'm sorry. It's definitely a queen, but I think we may have a twin on the second floor. We're quite full at the moment. If you don't mind waiting, I may be able to locate one."

Cory whispered to Dylan, "Are you okay with a queen?"

"It's fine with me. I think I've proved to you I can behave."

Cory blushed crimson. "We'll take the queen." Cory filled in the required paperwork and waited for the keycard to the room. When the receptionist handed her the key, she turned back to Dylan.

"Room 119."

Dylan scanned the signs on either side of the foyer. "We need to go down that corridor."

Cory picked up her bag and followed Dylan along several long hallways.

"This is us," Dylan said.

"Okay. We'll drop off the bags and then head out to see a little bit of London," Cory suggested.

CORY CHECKED her map of central London. "We need to cross this road."

"Are you sure?" Dylan asked, frustrated. "We seem to be going in circles."

It took them several minutes to get across the busy road. When they reached the other side, they paused in front of a very high wall. "I think you're right." Cory consulted the map again. "I'm pretty certain that the palace is in this direction." She indicated with her right arm. "I think this is the palace wall." Cory pointed to the area that was surrounded by a tall brick wall. "After this walk, I hope Auntie Liz is waiting for me with a cup of tea."

"Auntie Liz. Too funny, but I bet it wouldn't be if the Queen could hear you call her that."

"I know. I'd have been court-martialed in the medieval times."

Dylan walked along with Cory. She was enjoying listening to Cory's interpretation of the buildings and their history. They turned a corner and stopped in front of a large, golden statue. With the palace gates in sight, Dylan came face-to-face with a mass of other tourists. She gazed at the crowd. "For some reason, I thought I'd be the only person here." She stared at the palace. It was beautiful and ornate. "It takes my breath away." She looked at the gates. "I've seen these gates on TV. It was when the news broke about the death of Princess Diana. I never dreamed I'd be standing in front of them."

"Now, that was a sad day for England."

Dylan scanned the crowd again. "I can't believe the crowd is five deep. Are those the Queen's guards?" Dylan pointed at the guards, who stood as straight and still as statues. They were dressed in thick grey coats and black, bearskin hats.

"They're not allowed to move a muscle or acknowledge anyone," Cory whispered in Dylan's ear. "I have no idea how they manage it. I'd go crazy after five minutes."

Dylan giggled. "You wouldn't even make that. You even fidget in your sleep. Close your mouth. You know it's true."

"You're right. Sam says it's like sleeping with a snake."

"The palace is beautiful. Can I borrow your camera? I want to take a photo of you in front of the gates."

"Sure."

They had to wait several minutes before they could get a clear shot. Dylan played with the camera's zoom lens while she waited for people to clear. She spent the time staring through the lens at Cory. She was beautiful. Her eyes gazed straight at the camera. She wore an open, trusting expression on her face. Dylan's thoughts began to think about the next day. It would be their last full day together. *You only have two days to work up your courage and talk to her. Open your heart.*

AFTER THE PALACE, they walked up toward Pall Mall, and onto the main streets. They spent the rest of the day catching the Tube back and forth. They spent a long time on Oxford Street, browsing and buying souvenirs for Dylan to take home. Their last port of call was Big Ben and the surrounding sights.

They climbed the stairs out of the Tube station and into the darkness of early evening. Big Ben and the Houses of Parliament were lit up. The clock tower loomed over them. Its height astounded Dylan.

"It's huge."

"I always forget how big this building is. I've seen Big Ben lots of times on the evening news, but I've never really considered how beautiful it is." Cory laughed. She watched Dylan bend down with the camera pointed at the clock tower.

"I hear you, and will you quit giggling at me. I know I can get the whole building in this frame if I just crouch a little lower. I want a photo of Big Ben."

"Actually, Big Ben is the bell inside the tower. However, over time, the building has just come to be called Big Ben."

"Don't be such a smart alec and help me out. I know I can angle the camera to get the shot."

With the photo successfully taken, they wandered up to the bridge over the Thames.

"Wow," Dylan said. "This is even more magnificent. What's it called?" She stared at the gigantic wheel all lit up in neon blue. It rose above the river, slowly turning, taking its passengers on their journey over London.

"It's the London Eye, but many people know it as the Millennium Wheel."

"Can we take a trip on it tomorrow?"

"Sure. I've never been on it, so it'll be a new adventure for the both of us."

"The reflection of the lights on the water gives it an air of tranquility. It looks like it's floating above the river. This is the perfect end to our adventures today."

"I know. It's been fun but exhausting."

"Tell me about it. My feet are killing me. I'm not sure I want to spend the time finding a restaurant. I was hoping we could eat at the hotel tonight."

"Are you sure? I thought you wanted to try and get tickets for a West End show."

"I know. Maybe tomorrow we can get tickets to see *Cats* or *Les Misèrables* and eat in China Town. Tonight, I just need food and a bed."

"Okay. Remind me to pick up a leaflet for the theater booking office at the Tube station. I'll call when we get back."

THEY SHOWERED AND dressed casually for dinner, both choosing black jeans and sweaters. Cory's was an emerald green top, which emphasized the color of her eyes, while Dylan wore a red turtleneck. The menu was simple, yet the food was excellent.

As Dylan ate, her thoughts centered on her feelings for Cory. She thought back to their brief interaction in bed that morning. Casually, she said, "Can I ask you a question?"

"Of course. What's on your mind?"

"I'm curious. If I hadn't put my hand over your mouth this morning, would you have kissed me?"

"Yes." Cory held Dylan's gaze. "But you didn't want to kiss me."

Dylan paled. *She's been thinking that all day?* "You're wrong, Cory. I desperately wanted to kiss you. I still do."

"Then why didn't you?" Cory asked.

"Because I didn't want you to hate me."

Cory stretched her hand across the table. "I could never hate you. It isn't possible."

Dylan squeezed Cory's hand reassuringly and then released it. "Think about it. You have a husband and a settled life. You're not mine to kiss."

"I know that, but my life's not settled. All I know is when you're around, I feel so alive. I feel things I've never experienced before emotionally and...sexually," she whispered.

"But what about Sam? Do you love him?" Dylan saw Cory's attention move down to her plate of food. She watched as Cory used her fork to push the French fries around aimlessly.

"Not as much as I should."

"How come?"

"If I really loved Sam, then I wouldn't be having these thoughts about you."

"True. Do you want to talk about these thoughts?" Dylan watched as Cory shrugged. She waited patiently for Cory to look at her. After a few moments of silence, Cory made eye contact with her. "You're not alone in your feelings. Talk to me," Dylan implored.

"I wanted to kiss you. In fact, I've been desperate to kiss you since I saw you in the airport. I have all these exciting feelings when I'm with you. You make me smile. You know what I'm feeling before I speak. I get goose bumps when you're near me. I...think...I've fallen in love with you."

"You love me?" Dylan asked.

"I tried to fight it. I thought it was displaced. I knew we had a connection in our e-mails. You said so yourself."

"That's because I feel the connection, too."

"I didn't want this to happen. My world's turned upside down, and I don't know what I should do."

"You're not alone, Cory. I feel the same. It makes me so sad. The thought of leaving here after a great week together is tearing me apart." Dylan reached across the table and linked her fingers with Cory's other hand. She rubbed Cory's fingers with her thumb. She steeled herself for the words she didn't want to say. "I wish in my heart we could be together. In reality, it'd never work. We live in two different worlds."

"Two worlds that came together this week," Cory implored.

"I know. I wish things were different. I wish you weren't married. My feelings for you are one of the reasons Sarah and I broke up."

"They are?"

Dylan nodded. "I would have settled for a life with Sarah. Then I met you. Something in your e-mails called to me. I don't know what it was, but I couldn't get you out of my mind. It seems so surreal. If someone had told me two months ago that I'd be sitting in a restaurant, three thousand miles from home, pouring my heart out to a woman I met online, I'd tell that person they were crazy. But here I am, and I don't have a solution."

"I'm dreading Saturday. I don't want you to leave."

Dylan examined Cory's features. She wanted to keep this moment in her mind forever. "We still have a day together, and I'm looking forward to spending it with you. I'm putting off thinking about anything past Saturday. Let's enjoy the time we have left. Finish your meal. There's still time to watch a movie in the room."

THE NEXT DAY, Dylan looked at the view over the city. "I'd love to come back to visit again. Your country is beautiful."

Cory joined Dylan at the window. The London Eye rose above the River Thames. They had spent the morning visiting Trafalgar Square and Covent Garden. "I'm glad you like it. I'm hoping you'll get to see more of it." She looked over her shoulder at the family and other couples that were in their capsule traveling the Eye with them. All attention was on the sights of London and not on them. She placed her hand over Dylan's. "It felt good to talk last night."

"It did," Dylan answered.

"I'm scared." Cory moved her body to lean against the capsule window. She wanted more privacy.

"It'll be okay. I promise. Things happen for a reason. We entered each other's lives for a reason. Fate must have things planned for us." Dylan pointed up to the sky. "Neither one of us has any answers. We just have feelings and a shit load of confusion. You're married, and I have a huge mess waiting for me back home. I'm not sure I have anything to offer you."

Cory moved her arm around Dylan's waist. "No more talk about things we can't control. Let's enjoy the rest of the day and evening. Tomorrow we can talk before you leave."

"Deal."

Cory pulled Dylan closer. She turned to look out of the window as their capsule reached its highest point over the ancient city.

Chapter
Eighteen

DYLAN AND CORY arrived at the airport with time to spare, found the American Airline's International desk, and joined the line with the few other passengers ahead of them. Cory stood with Dylan until only those with tickets could proceed to the desk. She stood watching Dylan, who appeared to be working her charm on the American Airline's clerk.

Five minutes later, Dylan sauntered toward Cory, her backpack slung casually over her shoulder. "That was easy," Dylan said, cockily.

"Could your head get any bigger? I saw you chatting up the lady. I can't take you anywhere." Cory linked arms with Dylan, and they walked up the stairs toward the departure area and food court. Cory felt the tightening of her chest when she thought about Dylan leaving. Quelling the fear, she continued with the conversation, "What did you get for your trouble?"

"Extra leg room. I was cramped on the way over because I booked at the last minute. Today's flight is emptier. She said she'd make sure my wishes were accommodated."

"I bet she did," Cory answered. "I'm sure if she'd had her way she'd have personally made sure *all* your wishes were granted."

"Don't tell me you're jealous. It was a little bit of harmless flirting to get something. How about some breakfast?" Dylan said, pointing to the breakfast bar. "We have about an hour before I have to go through to the gate."

DYLAN PUSHED HER scrambled egg around her plate. "What are your plans for today? Mine are to sit on a plane for seven hours, arrive home, and see what Sarah has left for me."

What am I going to do today? Break up with my husband...leave my heart at the airport. Cory swallowed down the pain. "I guess the first thing is to pick myself up after you leave and find the car. Then make my way to see Granddad. After that, I'm going home to speak with Sam."

"You're going to talk to him today?"

Cory placed her knife and fork on her plate. She rested her elbows on the table and placed her face in her hands. She rubbed her eyes, and then looked at Dylan. "If I had a choice, I'd just curl up into a ball and cry."

"Do you have any idea what you'll do after talking to Sam?"

"Not really."

"When you think of the future, what do you dream about?"

Cory shrugged her shoulders. "I haven't really thought too much about the future. I've really been living day-to-day. I guess if I could have a dream come true, it would be to make a life with you."

"How?"

"I have no idea."

"What are you going to say to your family when they ask what went wrong between you and Sam?"

"What is this, twenty questions?" Cory saw the hurt expression cross Dylan's face. "I'm sorry. I didn't mean to jump down your throat." She tapped her fingers on the table top. "I'm going to let them know that Sam and I aren't compatible. I'm going to explain that I want more out of a relationship."

"Have you given any thought to telling your family about your feelings for me?"

"No. I'm just coming to terms with my feelings. Nobody else needs to know." Cory saw the change in Dylan's appearance. The hurt was replaced by a frown.

"They do at some point. I'm gay, Cory. I would love to think we could have a future together. I don't want to live my life in a closet. I'm out and proud to be who I am. How are you going to handle that? You can't even admit your sexuality to yourself."

"Why does it matter whether I'm gay, straight, or bi? Why do I need a label? I just know how I feel about you."

"But it's not just about feelings. This is a whole life change," Dylan said. "I don't mean to push, but this is difficult for both of us. I care for you so much, and it hurts me to see you so unhappy. But realistically, what future do we have together?"

Cory's eyes brightened. "Whatever future we want, if we're both willing to try."

"You say that now, but are you really willing to give it all up for me? I need to know. I need to know that I'm not going to be a passing phase, that I'm not just an experiment, or a bored housewife's five-minute fling. I've been with a straight woman before. It broke my heart."

"I'd never do that to you." Cory pushed her tray to the far side of the table and moved to sit on the same side of the booth as Dylan. She placed her hand on Dylan's.

"The problem is if you did leave, I'm not sure I'd survive," Dylan said.

"Where does that leave us?"

"With hope." Cory allowed Dylan to put her other arm around her shoulder. The closeness helped ground her. It gave her some belief, despite Dylan's words. Dylan continued. "Nothing is going to happen between us until we're both ready, and free to live our lives the way we both need to."

Cory smiled sadly. "You're right." Thankful for the privacy the booth afforded them, she held Dylan's hand tightly. "I do need to sort my shit out before I do anything else, and I will. Can you be patient with me?"

"Take as long as you need. No matter where I am, you hold my heart."

Cory felt Dylan lightly kiss her head. "I'm going to miss you so much. I never thought we'd connect as much as we have."

"We'll be okay." Dylan checked her watch. "I really should be heading toward the gate."

There was a short line when they arrived at the security checkpoint. They stood to the side. "I guess this is the moment we've been dreading, huh?" Cory said.

Dylan placed her bag on the floor and opened her arms. "Definitely."

Cory walked into the hug. She felt Dylan squeeze her firmly. She buried her head into Dylan's chest. "I love you, Dylan. I couldn't help myself." Cory felt the body against her tremble. She held Dylan tighter and heard a stifled sob. Cory took a small step back and moved her hands to Dylan's face. What she saw tore at her heart. Tears welled in Dylan's eyes. "No tears. Where's my brave warrior?" Cory didn't know where she found the strength to hold back her own tears. "Think about this. Next vacation, I'll come and visit you. We'll spend Easter together, even if I have to swim the ocean to be there. Would that be okay?"

Dylan nodded. "I'd like that. I'm sorry. I didn't know it would hurt this much. I've just found you, and now, I have to let you go." Dylan took Cory's face between her hands.

The tender kiss on her forehead settled Cory's racing heart. It sealed in her mind what she knew in her heart. "You okay?" Cory asked.

"Yeah, I promise I am. Let the count down begin. I'll call you when I get home, or send you an e-mail, if it's too late to call."

"How about you do both? Call my mobile, and if it's switched off leave a message. That way I get to hear your voice. I'll miss you." She pulled Dylan in for one last hug. "Now scoot."

Dylan released Cory. She turned and walked toward the checkpoint line. She turned and blew a kiss.

Cory pretended to catch the kiss and play acted by putting her hand in her pocket. She took out her hand and patted the pouch closed. She gave Dylan a smile.

CORY WATCHED DYLAN walk around the checkpoint wall. She couldn't stop the tears anymore. She turned away and followed the signs to the parking lot. Her mind was moving faster than her brain could handle. She had so many decisions to make and questions to answer. She had a hard time focusing on the simple task of finding her car. She wandered aimlessly through the concrete multi-story parking lot, staring at unfamiliar cars. Frustrated, she leaned against a wall and blinked several times to clear the tears. She couldn't believe the step she was about to take. *You can do this. You can do this.* She took a deep breath. She needed to find her car before anything could be sorted out. She remembered Dylan's voice and how she had laughed when Cory parked the car. *Remember B for breasts and butts*, Dylan had said. She'd left the car in zone B. She walked down the ramp toward the correct zone level.

After paying the parking fee at the ticket machine, she easily found her car. When she opened the door, the musky scent reminded her of Dylan. She sank into the seat. All resolutions of toughness were gone. She knew she had to move. The ticket would only last another ten minutes, and then she'd have to pay the fee over again. She started the engine and reversed out of the space.

THE TRAFFIC WAS light. With no weekday commuters on the road, her journey back north went quickly. As she pulled into her parents' road and crested the hill, she noticed too many familiar cars parked outside her parent's house. Sam's, Kerry's, Mike's, and even her uncle's. Her heart began to pound, her blood ran cold, and she knew what she'd find when she entered the house.

She checked her phone. She'd turned it off the previous night to save the battery, but she'd never switched it back on. Her only focus had been Dylan. She hadn't given the phone a second thought.

She parked behind Sam's car and turned on her phone. Instantly, it beeped, alerting her to a missed call. She checked the screen. There had been two missed calls: one from her mother and one from Sam. She opened the car door and saw Sam coming out of the front door.

"I'm too late, aren't I?" She leaned against the car. She saw tears in Sam's eyes.

"We tried to call you this morning. Your mum has been going frantic. She kept getting your voice message."

"When...when did...when did he pass away?"

"It happened at six thirty. I tried the hotel, but you'd checked out already. We didn't leave any voice messages. We didn't want you to be upset on your drive back."

Dazed, Cory felt Sam place his arms around her shoulders. She rested her head on his shoulder and sobbed. When she was steady enough to walk, he helped her up the pathway and into the house.

"Is he still here?" she asked.

"Yes," Sam said, "the undertakers won't be able to get here until later. He wanted to be cremated and scattered at the same site as your grandmother. It means they have to come from Birmingham. Your mum has laid him out upstairs for people to pay their last respects to him."

Cory looked around. She saw her siblings sitting on the bottom step of the stairs. "I can't believe it happened."

Kerry and Mike both stood up and kissed Cory's cheek. Kerry took Cory away from Sam's hold and hugged her tightly.

"Shush, he doesn't hurt any more. He's with Nan now."

"I should have been here for him."

"None of us were here, except Mum and Dad. He didn't die alone. Mum rocked him to sleep and stayed with him. It was too early in the morning. Don't beat yourself up."

Cory stayed in Kerry's embrace. The words soothed her. "I should have been here yesterday, even last night. Instead, I was watching a show in the West End."

"No, you shouldn't have. I saw him yesterday morning, and he told me all about your friend. He liked meeting her. He was glad you were taking a few days away. He said you deserved to have fun on your holiday."

Cory allowed her sister to comfort her. The closeness anchored her. She thought over the words. "He really said that?"

"Of course he did. He knew he didn't have much time. We all knew. He enjoyed his last few days. He told me so. I promise."

Cory released her hold on Kerry. "Where's Mum?"

Kerry pointed upstairs. "She's sitting with Granddad. You should go up and see her. She's been frantic with worry."

"I can't go in there. I can't." Cory collapsed on the stairs, pulling her legs to her chest. She rocked back and forth. "I can't go and see him."

As she cried, Rita came out onto the landing. She walked down the stairs and pulled her middle daughter into her arms. "Hey, my baby, it's over now. He's not in pain anymore. He's at peace and with your nan."

Cory let her mother rock her like she had so many years ago as a baby. She looked at her mother through tear-stained eyes. "Nan's probably busting his chops for making her wait two years."

Rita chuckled. "You're probably right." She wiped a tear from her eye. "She never did like waiting for things. Are you going to go up and see him? He looks peaceful. I've dressed him in his best suit, and he's wearing the buttonhole from your wedding. I've put his favorite socks on like he asked me to. You made him very proud, Cory. He loved you dearly."

Cory peered through the banisters. Now that the door to the bedroom was open, she could see the very edge of her grandfather's feet. She knew what word was written along the bottom of the sock. She could see half the letters of the word 'Granddad.' Cory burst into tears again. She'd bought him those socks for Christmas.

After more tears and hugs, Cory felt her mum pull away.

"I have to go. The nurse is here. She's going to collect the morphine and other medical supplies."

Kerry claimed the place Rita had vacated. She handed Cory some tissues.

"How're you holding up?"

"Not good. Nothing can prepare you for this. No amount of pre-knowledge can really take the pain away." Cory blew her nose and wiped her tears.

"I know. You really should think about going in there to say your goodbyes. I know you didn't when Nan died, but maybe this would help. I heard somewhere that the dead can hear our thoughts and words."

"I don't know. I've never seen a dead body. I'm scared."

"It's Granddad. There's nothing to be scared about. How about if I come in with you, will that help?"

"Maybe." She did have things she needed to say, and if it was true, maybe he'd hear her thoughts. She could tell him goodbye and that she loved him. She let Kerry lead her up the stairs.

Cory stopped at the bedroom door. "I think I want to do this alone."

"I'm proud of you." Kerry kissed Cory on the cheek and left.

On shaky legs, Cory entered the bedroom. She stared at the body — a shell, not the grandfather she loved so much. He was thin, frail, cold, and tinged yellow from the liver cancer. She knew her grandfather's soul had left the body. She bent down and kissed his bristled cheek. "I love you, Granddad, and I always will. Thank you for always being there." Cory hoped Kerry was right, and that he could hear her words. She shivered and left the room. She sat on the top stair, leaning against the wall. She thought of the one person she wished were there, holding her. She looked to her side as Sam came and sat on the step below her. He took her hand and squeezed it gently. "How are you feeling?"

Cory studied him. For the first time, she saw how crushed he was. "I'm okay. How are you?"

"Shocked, I guess. Your dad's more cut up than he'll admit. What do you want to do?"

Cory found it difficult to talk. Her mind wouldn't stay on one thought for long. She was exhausted and wanted to sleep. She wanted to close her eyes and let the pain go away.

Sam tapped her hand lightly to bring her back to the present. "There's nothing more we can do here. How about we go home?"

"Where are Mike and Kerry?"

"Mike's helping your dad settle your mum down. I told them we'd probably leave soon. Kerry left with Pete. She was going to come back over later. We can come back, too, if you feel up to it. We'll leave your car." Sam helped Cory up. He led Cory into the kitchen and out to the car.

WHEN THE CAR bumped over the edge of their driveway, Cory awoke, her heart pounding. She was drained. Her head hurt, and her eyes stung. "We home?"

"Yes. You were out like a spark. I think you should go and lie down in bed. Later, I'll call your dad and check on your mum. Hopefully, the funeral home will have given them a date and picked up the body, I mean Arthur."

Cory listened to an odd word here and there. She just wanted to take some headache pills and sleep. She swayed on her feet, and Sam put his arm around her.

"To bed with you."

Cory went up the stairs, supported by Sam. She sat down on the bed. Sam helped her undress and get into bed. She then relaxed against the pillows. Sam covered her with the duvet.

"Can you find me some headache pills? My head's about to split in half."

"I'll be up in a minute with some water and tablets. I'll leave Holly here for company." Sam kissed Cory on the forehead and left the room.

Alone, Cory reviewed the past several hours. She felt like she was grieving for two people. *Dylan — I should let Dylan know.* She didn't have the strength to get to the office, and she didn't know Dylan's phone number to leave a message. She glanced at the clock; it was midday. She wondered how far across the ocean Dylan was.

Sam entered the room, and Cory lifted her head. "Here you go. Two tablets and a glass of water. I'll come and check on you later." He closed the bedroom door. She patted the bed, and Holly jumped up next to her.

"Granddad's gone, Holly, really gone. What am I going to do?" The dog licked the salty tears that were flowing silently down Cory's cheeks. Cory stroked Holly's coat. "You haven't got a clue what's going on, have you? But you're here for me." Cory cuddled up to Holly. She cried until she was too exhausted to cry any more. Then she slept.

DYLAN CLIMBED ABOARD the shuttle bus. The weather outside was crisp. She loved the New England climate. It was always changing, and each day brought a surprise. It was definitely a nice change to see the blue sky. She'd missed it the past week. England had been beautiful, but overcast.

Dylan claimed her truck from long term parking and headed for the house. Thirty minutes later, she was pulling into her driveway. There was no sign of Sarah's SUV. *Thank God — I didn't have the strength to face her today.* She wanted to get into the house, check her e-mail, and call Cory. She checked the time: 3.45 P.M.

The house had a distinct chill to it, and it wasn't just the cold air. Several pieces of furniture were missing. She walked toward the bed-room. As she entered the room, she stopped in her tracks. The king-size bed no longer took up the majority of space in the room. The closet doors were wide open, and her clothes were scattered on the floor. There was a note pinned to the bureau mirror.

```
Dylan,
    Welcome home. I took what I felt I deserved.
There's still more I want, but thought it was only
fair for you to be here.
    I hope it was worth it.
Sarah
```

Dylan didn't have the energy to move furniture around. She went into the spare room and placed her bags on the bed. She reread Sarah's note. *Was the trip worthwhile? You know it was—even if nothing develops, you felt love again.* Her thoughts settled on Cory. *I miss her laughter. I miss those dreamy, emerald eyes and stunning body. Damn it—I miss her, period.* She needed to keep busy, otherwise, she'd crawl under the covers and not resurface until Easter.

Dylan loaded the washing machine, and then went into the spare bedroom. She looked up Cory's number, but only reached her voice-mail.

She went into her office and downloaded her e-mail. She was disap-pointed when she saw there was no e-mail from Cory. She went to an e-card website and chose a card of a dancing bear that turned into a red rose. Under the bear, she wrote a simple note.

```
Dear Cory,
    Thank you for a wonderful visit. Good luck with
all you have to face. I'm always at the end of a
phone (hopefully, you still have my number) or com-
puter. Until next time...I'll miss you.
D
```

She pressed the send button. She'd procrastinated long enough. The rest of the chores needed to be completed.

EVERY HOUR ON the dot, Dylan checked her e-mail. Several hours had passed, but there was still no message from Cory. She began to pre-pare her meals for the week. The phone ringing interrupted her actions. Hoping it was Cory, she pressed the connect button. "Hello."

"You sound bright and breezy."

"Oh, Helen, how goes it?" Helen played on her ice hockey team. She was an athletic trainer at a local college.

"I take that back. You sound miserable."

"I'm sorry. I was hoping you were someone else." Dylan settled onto the sofa in her office.

"Should I hang up?" Helen asked.

"No, it's good to hear from you. I just have a lot on my mind."

"You must be exhausted."

"A little."

"I won't keep you long. I was calling to see if you were available to play tomorrow. It's your turn to drive."

"I'm playing," Dylan said. The thought of spending the evening alone made her sad. "What you up to?"

"Nothing much. Jo's away on business, so I'm trying to amuse myself. What's going on your end?"

"Same ole—same ole. I've got a few beers in the fridge, if you're interested." Dylan and Helen had dated briefly, but they'd agreed that they weren't suited as a romantic couple. A friendship had grown through their love of ice hockey and of each other as people.

"Sure. I'll be over in about an hour. Have a cold one ready for me."

CORY WOKE UP as her arm hit Sam's back. She lifted her body and opened her swollen eyes. She felt Sam move beside her. "Sorry, I didn't mean to wake you. What time is it?"

"Just past six a.m."

"It's morning already."

"You've been asleep since we got back from your parents' house." Sam climbed out of bed and put on his sweat pants and sweater. "You must be starving."

Cory swallowed. Her throat hurt. "So, it wasn't some bad dream. He's really gone?" The tears began forming again.

Sam nodded. "I'm afraid so. I'll be back in a minute. Holly's whimpering to go out."

Cory lay staring at the ceiling. Her thoughts drifted back to the previous day. *I need to let Dylan know what's happened.* She peered around the room for her backpack. It was on the floor by the bed. She leaned over the edge, a pain shooting through her head. She put her hand into the side pocket of her bag and pulled out her mobile phone. The phone indicated she had a voice message.

```
     Hi, Cory, it's me. I landed safe and sound. I
just wanted to say thank you very much for an enjoy-
able week. I'll e-mail you and maybe call tomorrow. I
miss you.
```

A sad smile tugged at Cory's lips. Dylan was home.

Cory deleted the message and swung her legs over the side of the bed. She needed to e-mail Dylan and let her know what had happened. As she sat upright, the pain in her head increased, and she collapsed back onto the bed. She knew if she moved too much she'd throw up. She closed her eyes. She heard Sam enter the room.

Sam placed a cup of tea on Cory's bedside table. "Here, take these pills. From the look of you, I'm guessing you have a migraine."

"A killer." Cory let Sam place the tablets in her mouth and held a glass for her to drink from. "Thanks. Any news from Mum or Dad?"

"Your dad called last night. The funeral is set for Thursday."

Cory placed her arm over her eyes to block out the faint morning light. "Can you call dad and let him know we'll be over later. I'm just going to rest quietly and hope it passes quickly."

"Sure. Anything else?" Sam pulled the phone cord out of the wall. "Sleep. I'll make sure nothing disturbs you." He kissed her on the forehead and closed the door.

Chapter
Nineteen

"YOU ARE A piece of work."

"Good morning, Sarah. How sweet of you to come by and welcome me home." Dylan heard the rustling of sheets from the other side of the bed.

Sarah grabbed the comforter off the bed, revealing Dylan and Helen together.

"I knew there was something more to you two. I've always had my suspicions. It's not enough you leave me for an English whore, you have to sleep with this one, too."

"Sticks and stones will break my bones," Helen said.

"Please, Helen, don't taunt her. She enjoys it too much." Dylan felt like she was trapped in a trashy television talk show. "Sarah, in case you've forgotten, you took our bed and left me with nothing but the guest bed. Where else was Helen going to sleep? Do you think we'd be dressed in our winter pajamas if we'd had sex? And, for your information, Cory is *not* a whore." She grabbed her robe from the edge of the bed and ushered Sarah out of the room. "I don't think we need to have yet another scene in front of Helen." She leaned back around the bedroom door. "Helen, I'm sorry you got caught in this. I'll go and put the coffee on."

Dylan walked through the living room to the kitchen, where Sarah stood waiting for her. She could tell by Sarah's stance that she was furious. "I'm brewing some coffee. Do you want some?"

"How could you? How can you do this to me? You always swore there was nothing going on between you and Helen."

"Sarah, I promise on my mother's grave that there's nothing going on between Helen and me, and if I hear you making trouble for her with Jo, you'll regret it." Dylan waited for Sarah to stop pacing. "Do you believe me?"

"Yeah. But look at it from my point of view. I come home to find my ex-girlfriend snuggling in bed with another woman."

"Excuse me." Dylan clenched her fists together, struggling to control her anger. "I think you've got your facts incorrect. We were not snuggling. When I woke up, Helen was way over on her side of the bed, and you know it. Anyway, why should it matter to you? You're the one who ended our relationship, or have I got it wrong?"

"I...I was angry. I wanted you to call and beg me to stay."

"I guess that plan backfired. To what do I owe the pleasure of your company this early in the morning?" Dylan held out one arm and waved it around the room. "Was the bed not enough? Do you need to take more stuff from the house?"

"We do need to split the furniture. Half of what's in the house is mine."

"You know what? Take what the hell you like," Dylan yelled, giving way to the frustration she felt. Her blood was pumping, and it took all her strength not to physically lash out at Sarah. She'd never hit another woman in her life–technically; ice hockey didn't count. "I'm going to be out of here by lunch time. I suggest you come back later if you want to remain in one piece." It was just words. She'd never lift a hand to Sarah.

"Whatever," Sarah said, heading toward the door, "I'll be back for the sofa and chairs. Michelle and I need them for our place."

Dylan stared at her. "And you called me a piece of work. Who the fuck is Michelle? Remember who paid for that furniture in the first place." Dylan followed Sarah out of the house. "Oh, to hell with you. If that's what it takes to get you out of my life, take them. Just leave me the fittings and the entertainment system." She looked past Sarah and noticed the truck. A woman was leaning against it, a cigarette in her mouth. She extinguished it as Sarah got nearer.

"It didn't take you long to meet someone new. For all I know, you could have been cheating on me this entire time," said Dylan.

"Don't turn this on me. You're the one who wanted someone else. Michelle was there when I needed a shoulder to cry on. You were too busy chasing someone else."

"I'm done with this conversation. Do what you like later, just make sure I'm not around."

Dylan closed the front door and turned to find Helen waving a white pair of panties. "Is it safe to come out?"

"She's gone. I'm sorry. Did you hear some of the conversation? I mean, we were hardly quiet." Dylan walked back into the kitchen and poured the coffee.

"Yeah, I heard a little. Wow, last night when you said you guys were through, I didn't quite believe it. Now I know. I can't believe you're going to let her take the furniture. You paid for it."

Dylan shrugged her shoulders. "If it's what will keep her happy and out of my way, then she's welcome to it. Plus, I do feel a little guilty. My actions did cause the break up, although, I'm not sure where this Michelle fits into the equation."

"Why guilty? And, who the hell is Cory? Sarah didn't have a high opinion of her. I think you left out a few major details last night."

Dylan passed Helen a cup of coffee. She'd hoped not to have to reveal too much, until she knew whether there would be a future with Cory. "Cory's a woman I met online. I went to England to meet her."

"You went all the way across the pond to meet a woman you barely know? Oh, my God, it must be love."

"I guess it happens to us all someday. I don't know. I never went looking for it. I tried so hard not to, and then I fell so hard it hurts."

"Does she love you back?"

Dylan lifted her head and looked straight at Helen. "She says she does. I mean, I know she does."

"You don't sound too convinced."

Dylan remembered her last image of Cory—the look of hurt on Cory's face and the love in her eyes. "She loves me, but it's complicated."

"In what way?"

"For starters, she lives a whole continent away." *Stop beating around the bush and tell her everything.* "She's...she's...married," Dylan said, realizing how bad it sounded. She closed her eyes waiting for the fall out. *One...two...three...*

"Married. No, not another straight woman. Dylan, when will you ever learn? It wasn't enough that Tina stole your heart, promised you the world, and then dumped you for a guy. What is it with you and straight women?"

"I don't know. I can fill you in on all the details later. Go home and get changed for the game. I need to check my e-mail. I haven't heard from Cory since I left, and I'm kinda worried."

AFTER HELEN LEFT, Dylan checked her e-mail. There were none from Cory. She checked the clock and counted forward five hours. It was past midday there. Paranoid, she focused her attention on the phone. *She lied. You're nothing to her. She's too scared to leave her cozy life and be with you. It was all a sad dream—she played you.* Unable to believe the taunts in her head, Dylan dialed Cory's home number.

"Hello?"

"Hi, Sam. It's Dylan. Is Cory around?"

"No. We had some bad news. Arthur died yesterday morning, and Cory's gutted. She's asleep, but I'll let her know you called."

"Okay, tell her I'm sorry."

"I will."

Her heart crumbled when she thought of Cory's grief.

CORY TOOK A shower to help her aching head; Sam waited in the bedroom for her.

"You feeling better?"

Cory felt weird. She'd been with Sam for years, but here he was looking at her naked body. She didn't know what to do. She relaxed and began to dry her body. "Better. Did you call Dad? How's Mum doing?"

"Not too good. Your dad said they had to sedate her last night. I promised your dad we'd go over."

"We can head over after I check my e-mail. I need to let people know what's happened."

"Cor, do you really think now is a time to do that? Your priorities lie with your family. E-mails can wait. I mean, if you hadn't been playing with your e-mail buddy these past few days, you'd have been there with him. You'd have been able to say goodbye."

Cory wiped at a tear and nodded her head dejectedly. The guilt that had been eating at her suddenly blossomed. "You're right. Family comes first."

DYLAN TOOK OUT her frustration by shooting hoops in the driveway. She dribbled around the tiny driveway and turned to shoot at the hoop. "Hey, Matthews, you ready for the game?" The unexpected sound of Helen's voice made her jump, and like her life, her aim went off track. The ball sailed over the backboard. "I'm ready. My equipment's in the truck. We should hustle, or we'll miss the face off." Dylan placed the ball on the ground and picked up her truck keys. "The truck's open."

"Did you call Cory?"

"Yeah." Dylan pulled out of the driveway.

"And."

Dylan shook her head. She had no words to describe the nightmare she was living. All her hopes and dreams were crashing around her head.

"Come on, Dylan, give me a break. I'm trying to help you here, but a conversation requires two people. How about I ask the questions and you answer?"

"I'm sorry. I called her house and Sam, her husband, answered. Cory's grandfather died yesterday."

"Was it sudden?"

"No. He's been sick for a while, but we had hoped he'd survive longer. I don't know if Cory was there when it happened. Sam told me Cory wasn't taking it very well, and that was all he said."

"Did he hang up on you?"

"It was a brief conversation. Now I'm worried about Cory. She loved her grandfather so much. I met him while I was there. He was quite a character. She spent the last two days of his life away from him, with me. Knowing Cory, she must be guilt-ridden. What if she blames me?"

Helen placed her hand on Dylan's arm. "Stop thinking like that. It's not your fault, and even if she feels bad about not being there, it's not likely she'll blame you. She knew it was coming, and she made the choice to be with you. She knew the consequences. Call her tomorrow before work. Get the truth before you jump to conclusions."

CORY SETTLED INTO the rocking chair and rested her feet on the radiator. She had called work and told them of the death. Her boss had expressed his sympathy and arranged for her to take the week off. Sam hadn't been as lucky. He had deals that needed his direct attention, and clients that wouldn't wait. Cory plugged the phone line into the laptop's modem. She hadn't checked her e-mail since leaving for London. She listened to the modem as it attempted to make a connection. She'd missed the squawking noise. The system connected, and she pressed the receive button. Her inbox was full. She was excited to see two e-mails from Dylan. She opened the first one and pressed on the web link. She watched the greeting on her screen. It made her throat contract and her eyes water. She'd cried so much over the weekend and was surprised she had any tears left. She opened the second e-mail.

```
Dylan Matthews
Call Me

Dear Cory,
     I called yesterday, and Sam gave me the bad news.
I'm so sorry. If I could be there with you, I would.
So here I am, miles away from you, and I feel use-
less.
     Please call me when you get this, if you can or
want to, that is. It doesn't matter what time of day—
I need to hear your voice. I want to know you're
okay, but most of all, I need to connect with you.
I'm going crazy.
D (CALL ME)
```

Cory cried even more. Sam hadn't told her about Dylan's phone call. She disconnected her modem line and called Dylan. She waited nervously, to hear Dylan's voice. The phone rang, once, twice, and then she heard a clatter, followed by a dull thud.

"Hello," Cory said, hesitantly, worried that Sarah may have answered.

"Huh?"

"Dylan, is that you?"

"Yeah. I'm sorry, I banged my head. The phone scared me awake."

"I'm sorry. I didn't even think about the time difference."

"God, don't think about that. I'm happy you called. When I phoned yesterday, Sam said you weren't too good. I've been worried about you," Dylan said. "I'm sorry about your grandfather. Give me a second to take a sip of water, my mouth feels like it's full of cotton balls."

Cory took a deep breath, trying to keep her composure. "I'm devastated about Granddad. I didn't get your message, Sam didn't tell me you'd called."

"That figures. Cory, I was sorry to hear he'd died. I know what a special man he was. Were you able to be with him?"

"No. He passed away while I was at the airport."

"Shit. I feel bad. I kept you from him."

"Don't think like that. It's bad enough that I've been on a huge guilt-trip. It was going to happen. If I hadn't been with you, I could have been at work, or somewhere else. Now the shock is wearing off, I'm beginning to see things more rationally."

"You sound more upbeat than I expected."

Cory relaxed against the cushions on the rocker. She pressed her feet against the radiator and rocked the chair slightly. "Occasionally, I feel like it's all a dream. Then, I realize it's not. Waking up is hard, as it suddenly hits me that I'll never see the sparkle in his eyes or his smile again."

"I know. I had those same feelings when my mother passed away. I didn't get to see her, either. It is good to hear your voice. If you hadn't called today, I was seriously thinking of catching a plane back over. You had me scared."

"I wish I could have spoken to you sooner. This is really the first opportunity I've had. How are things your end? Did you see Sarah?"

"I'm doing okay. Sarah wasn't here when I got back. But she took the king-size bed, and then came back to take more stuff."

"No way."

"Oh, yeah, she's shown her true colors. I need to do some math and see what I can afford to replace. We didn't get a chance to discuss the actual house. She was way too angry, but it looks like she's got a new girlfriend."

"Bloody hell, already? She only finished with you on Wednesday."

"Sarah was never one for being on her own. From the rumors I've heard, she's always needed a bed buddy. At some point this week, I need to look into the house situation, but I'm waiting for Sarah to make the first move. She's still paying her half of the mortgage, so it's no skin off my nose. Any news when the wake and funeral will be?"

"Thursday morning's the funeral. The entourage is going to leave from Granddad's house. We're having the wake afterwards at a local pub."

"You're having it afterwards. We usually have the wake a day before the burial. We go and pay our respects, view the body, and show our support."

"I've heard of Catholic families doing that here. Our tradition has been to have it after the funeral service. It's either at someone's house or at a pub or restaurant. There's usually a lot of food and alcohol. It's more like a party for the deceased, a celebration of their life, where everyone gathers to help the family remember the good times." Cory didn't want to think about the funeral any more. "I miss you."

"I miss you, too. I want to be there. I wish I could be the one holding you and wiping the tears, but I know I can't. Even if I could, it would cause you problems. How's Sam been?"

"He's been very thoughtful. He's hurting, too. I'm pissed off with him, though, because he never mentioned your call yesterday."

"It probably slipped his mind."

"This doesn't change anything. I've made my decision. I'm going to talk to Sam after the funeral. I'm going to tell him it's over. I haven't had a chance to think beyond that."

"Take your time. I'm not going anywhere. When you feel the time is right, you'll talk to Sam. I know how you feel about me, and I trust you. I know that now. For a few moments, when I hadn't heard from you, I got worried that you didn't really care about me."

"No way! I swear, Dylan, I wanted you by my side. It's at these times that I realize what a pain in the neck the long distance really is."

"The miles between us do suck, but remember, we both have a lot to deal with. Apart, we can focus on the issues without distractions. There's no rush. Let's take it one day at a time."

"One day at a time sounds good."

"I hate to cut this conversation short, but I have to get up to go to the gym and then to work. I wish I could stay here and talk to you all morning."

"I could call you later. I'm going to visit Mum today. I could call you before I go to bed."

"I have another game tonight against a team from New Hampshire. I'm leaving work early, and I'm not coming home."

"Did you play yesterday?"

"Yes, I did. Today, I feel like a bus hit me. I played my butt off. I might have taken my frustrations out on the opposition. My body clock is messed up, too."

"It doesn't help that you have a crazy Brit calling you early in the morning. Don't worry, I'll send you an e-mail later."

"I'll look for it. It'll probably be the highlight to my day. Thanks for the call. I feel so much better knowing you're okay. Have a good one."

"Good luck tonight. I hope you win." Cory felt distanced by the phone call. The words that she wanted to express to Dylan faltered on her lips.

"Me, too. Bye."

Cory stared at the phone. Her heart ached. She missed Dylan so much. She closed her eyes. If she concentrated hard enough, she was sure she could smell Dylan's scent, picture her blue eyes. Easter was going to be a long time coming.

Chapter
Twenty

THURSDAY WAS COLD and bleak. Cory pulled back from the window and drew the curtains closed. At least the weather matched the occasion and her mood. She picked her black suit trousers off the bed and put them on. She tucked the cream blouse in and looked in the mirror. She pulled the blouse out and debated which way looked better.

"Tuck it in. It shows off your figure better," Sam said, as he entered the room. He placed a cup of tea on top of her bureau.

"I don't know why I'm fussing. It's not like anyone is going to be focusing on my appearance." Cory tucked the blouse back in and picked up the matching suit jacket. "The last time I wore this jacket was when Nan died." She felt inside the pockets and pulled out some used tissues. "I guess I should make sure I have plenty of these." She placed the old tissues in the wicker bin. She remembered back to her grandmother's funeral. She'd cried so many tears that day. She'd been supportive and brave for her grandfather. She wasn't sure she would get through the day, but she'd made a resolution: no tears. Her grandfather wouldn't have wanted her to cry. She swallowed the lump in her throat and blinked back the tears.

"I've got some tissues, and you look nice. Arthur would have been very proud of you. I didn't make you any toast, because your mum said there would be breakfast at your grandfather's house." Sam put his tie on and checked his pockets for money. "We'll have to leave in about fifteen minutes. The traffic on the motorway will be busy this time of the morning. There's some mail for you downstairs. A few cards, I think."

"Thanks. I'll go and open them. Is everything sorted out at work?"

"I called in, and my schedule is clear until Monday. Brenda said she'd divert all my calls. I've put my phone on vibrate, just in case. I have a feeling the McPherson deal is going to go pear-shaped, and I did ask her to call should that happen. I'm sorry, Cory, I did try to clear the decks."

"No worries. The world doesn't stop because my granddad died," Cory said, the comment not aimed at Sam, but she knew she'd hurt him. "I'm sorry. That wasn't meant how it sounded. I *do* understand about work. I know this is a crucial time for you, and I appreciate how hard you worked this week so you could take the time off."

"I would do anything for him. He was like my own grandfather. I'm going to miss the old man. I'll meet you downstairs. I'm going to set the fax machine up on the computer."

FORTY MINUTES LATER, they turned into her grandfather's street. The house was in a cul-de-sac with about fifty semi-detached houses in it. Sam drove slowly round the huge oval shaped grass that was the center attraction. Cory had grown up playing on the field, commonly called "the green." It had been a safe place to play, as all the houses looked onto it. The close had only one entrance, which also served as the exit. They parked on the green, next to other family members' cars. The road in front of the house had been left clear for the hearse and other funeral cars. They walked up the driveway, greeting a few family members, and entered the house through the back door.

Cory walked into the kitchen area. Her mum was making breakfast and handing out juice. "Hello, Mum. Do you want me to do anything?"

Rita shook her head. "No, honey. Your granddad wanted everyone to have a good breakfast and a drink on him."

"But it's eight-thirty in the morning." Cory smiled. Only her grandfather would have everyone drinking alcohol.

"I have croissants, eggs, sausage, and bacon. Just help yourself. It's going to be a long morning, and the wake isn't until noon."

"Sam might have a bit, but my stomach doesn't feel too good. I'll just have some juice." She poured a glass of juice and walked out into the summerhouse, which was attached to the back of the kitchen. Her cousin, Sue, was there, looking out at the garden.

"It's the end of an era, I guess," Cory stated.

"It's hard to believe they're both gone. I keep thinking of all the years I've spent in this garden. I'll be forty next week. Can you believe it?" Sue sat in the patio chair.

"Forty. I forget there's a decade between us. I'll miss this house, too. It goes up for sale next month. Mum said Granddad wanted the money to be split among all his children. It's going to be strange to never come here again." Cory picked up one of the remembrance cards. The picture on the front was the one her mum had shown her earlier in the week. She turned it over, and her breath caught in her throat. There was her granddad, smiling back at her. It had been less than a week since she'd seen his smile. She closed her eyes and summoned up the strength she needed to quell the tears.

"The picture looks good, doesn't it?" Sue had tears in her eyes, too. "Where was it taken?"

"My wedding."

"God, time flies. I think the last time I saw you, we were here, but it was Nan's funeral. It seems we only ever meet at weddings and funerals."

"We both have busy schedules. How's London treating you?" Cory asked. Sue worked as an artist and designer in London.

"I'm moving back north. The job didn't work out for me, and Dad's been unwell. I think Mum might need me around a bit more. Mum and Dad have offered to put me up while I look for another job. How was your wedding? I'm sorry I missed it. I have to say, I never pictured you getting married. You never appeared the type."

"The wedding was good," Cory said. "What do you mean, you never expected me to marry?"

"I don't know; just a gut reaction. I remember you were always more into football and playing with the boys than romancing them. Still, that was a long time ago. Things change."

Cory didn't have an opportunity to continue the conversation, as Kerry walked into the summerhouse crying.

"Come on, dry the tears." Cory hugged her sister. She couldn't stop her own tears coming when she saw Kerry's anguished face.

"I wasn't crying until I saw the photo on the back of the card. I'm okay, really I am." Kerry wiped her eyes. "Mum seems to be handling things okay."

"That's because she has a mission. If she stops playing host, it'll hit her. Wait until later, when she's alone and has nothing to do." Cory passed Kerry an extra tissue and then added, "I hope Dad's prepared."

CORY MOVED FROM room to room. She managed to avoid her Uncle Keith. She had no intention of being trapped talking to the guy. Now was not a time to lose her temper. Her uncle seemed to know what buttons to push without trying. She glanced out of the window. Sam was leaning on his car talking to Pete, and Mike was talking to their father.

She continued to stare out the window, remembering the good times and the bad. Three decades had been spent in this house. Her heart sank when she saw the hearse enter the close. A man dressed in top hat and tails walked in front of the car. Cory saw her mother, three uncles, and two aunts on the front step. Her Aunt Eileen had flown in from Florida the previous day. Each sibling had a champagne glass in hand, and as the hearse stopped in front of the house, her Uncle Trevor released the champagne cork. He poured a small amount in each glass, and they clinked glasses and toasted their father. It had been something her granddad had done for her grandmother when she'd died, and now his children were carrying out his wishes.

Cory walked out onto the front garden and up to the hearse. She examined the simple floral display on the coffin. She stared in disbelief, unwilling to accept that her grandfather was lying in the box. They had been asked not to bring bouquets of flowers. Instead each child and grandchild had a red rose to place on the coffin.

The family walked to the funeral cars. Sam kissed Cory on the cheek. "I'll meet you there."

"Okay." The funeral cars would only take them to the crematorium. From there, they needed their own transport. Kerry got in first, and Cory followed. She looked at the seat opposite her and smiled at her younger cousin. No words were needed to convey their feelings. All Cory could feel was a tremendous ache in her heart and a pain in her throat. She closed her eyes and summoned up her happiest thoughts. Each one settled on Dylan.

Cory met Sam outside the crematorium. The tears began again, as Cory walked inside the building. She held Sam's hand as they walked down the center aisle. They sat in the second row of pews. Cory's eyes never left the coffin. The pain inside was ripping her apart, and the words from the song swam around inside her head. Her granddad was simply the best. She missed him so much.

Her Uncle Trevor began the eulogy. Cory began smiling, as her Uncle told story after story of her grandfather's life. Some of the stories she knew well, others were new to her. The clapping of hands brought Cory out of her thoughts. She focused on the words her uncle spoke.

"The one piece of advice Arthur had for all his kin was to follow your heart, as that turns into your dreams. He never regretted the life he gave up, because he found the one person who meant the world to him. They may have fought like cat and dog, and we all witnessed those fights, but deep down, they had a love that lasted fifty years. Arthur's last request was for you all to follow your hearts. So I'll end it here and pass it over to Mike. He's going to recall the memories that Arthur's many grandchildren have of him."

Cory wiped her eyes. Her brother began his speech. He looked nervous. Cory wanted to give him a hug. Her admiration for her brother grew with each utterance. He was no longer the little boy who had told tales on her. He was a man doing a sterling job to keep his emotions in check.

When Mike finished speaking, it was time for the vicar to say a few words. He invited the family to put their flowers on the casket. As her mother stood up, the tones of Frank Sinatra echoed through the room.

Cory watched her mum, dad, aunts, and uncles walk to the coffin. Each person placed a rose on the casket as the song filled the room. Every word meant something to Cory. *He did do everything his way.* She felt Kerry stand up next to her. She tried to follow, but her legs buckled. Sam caught her before she fell. He held her up.

She walked slowly toward the coffin and placed her flower on top of the other roses. She kissed the coffin. Words couldn't express how she felt. Cory had to finally say goodbye. Sam led her back to her seat and held her close. She watched her little cousin put a hand-drawn picture on top of the casket.

As the song finished, the coffin began to move away from the mourners and a pair of curtains closed after it. Cory shut her eyes. She didn't care who saw or heard, she couldn't stop the sobs. She couldn't fight the pain anymore.

The family gathered outside the crematorium. Hugs and kisses were swapped freely along with tissues. The sound of chatter and nose blowing filled the air. The wake was to be held at a nearby pub her grandfather had always liked. It was the pub where he'd had his first alcoholic drink as a young boy. Cory couldn't stand being near people. She needed her space. She let go of Sam's hand. "I just want to go and say hello to Nan and warn her to be good to Granddad."

"Do you want me to come?"

Cory shook her head. "I'd prefer to be alone, although I'm sure there'll be a few more people making their way down there, too."

She wandered down toward the tall, barren oak tree. Underneath the tree were some fresh flowers in a vase. She stood reflecting over the two past years. She missed her nan. She wondered how her granddad had survived the two years without her. He'd never looked at another woman, even though many women had tried to court the old man.

She turned and headed back the way she'd come, but instead of turning right, she continued walking straight ahead toward the rose garden. Here, the family had planted a rose in remembrance of her nan. It had her name and the date she'd died inscribed on a plaque in front of it. When she turned the final corner, she saw her mum and two aunts standing in front of the rose tree. She walked up and stood beside them.

Her Aunt Petunia hugged her. "How are you doing, Cory? He really did love you."

"Thanks. I'm holding up okay."

They stood reminiscing for a few minutes and then walked back up to the main entrance. As they walked up the hill, they passed the huge fishpond. Next to the pond, the red roses from the top of the coffin were laid out for people to see. Attached to each flower was a card. Cory read them, pausing to reflect on her own message.

```
Granddad,
You taught me all I know—thank you.
You will always be my hero.
I love you,
Cory
```

She stared at the words. One thought was going through her mind. *Follow your heart, Cory, follow your heart.* She looked up at the sky. *I will, Granddad, I promise.* With that, she walked toward the rest of the mourners.

DYLAN WATCHED THE clock. Earlier, her work had kept her occupied, but over the last hour, it had slowed down. She counted the minutes until her lunch break with Helen, who was picking her up. She kept herself busy surfing the web. She had settled on some British immigration sites. She looked up when the door to her office was opened.

"Yo, slowpoke, long time no see," Helen said.

"With the amount of time I've spent with you this week, people are going to start talking." Dylan slapped her hand on Helen's back.

"I'm starving. Where we going?"

"There's a '99' restaurant down the street. We might as well stay local."

"How goes the battle?"

"Nothing much going on. How about you?" Dylan asked, as they walked toward Helen's car.

"Jo is coming home tonight. Her last appointment got cancelled, and she managed to get a flight home. It feels like she's been gone forever. I've really missed her."

"I know. I've listened to you whine for the past few days, but I'm psyched for you, too."

After parking the car and waiting ten minutes for the lunchtime rush, they were seated in a booth next to the window.

"You never answered my question. How are things? Any news from the Wicked Witch of the East?"

"I forget how much you and Sarah hate each other until I hear comments like that. She's arranged for a realtor to see the house later today. No one could ever say she was slow at getting things organized."

"Wow, that's quick. What are you going to do once the house is sold?"

"I don't know. I haven't really given it much thought. Everything's happened so quickly. It depends on whether things develop between Cory and me. I could be moving to England, or she could come here."

"Would you really move? I don't like to think of you so far away — without friends or family. Selfishly, I like having you around, and I'd miss you if you went."

Dylan smiled in appreciation. "I'd miss you, too, even if you are a pain in my butt at hockey practice."

The waitress brought their drinks and waited while they read the menu. They ordered and resumed their conversation.

"Do you have any concrete plans?" Helen persisted.

"I did some web searching this morning. The good news is that Britain allows same-sex citizens to sponsor their partner into the country, and they have civil unions."

"Awesome, and we think those Brits are stuffy. They're way more progressive than our country when it comes to same-sex issues."

"Yeah, but the snag is we have to show we've lived together two years. That means getting into the country in the first place. I need to find a way to get us together for two years." Dylan sipped her strawberry milkshake.

"There's always the college option."

Dylan swallowed her milkshake too quickly and coughed several times to clear her airway. "No way. I barely managed to get my undergraduate degree. I'm definitely more a hands-on person than an academic."

"Relax. I didn't mean you. I meant Cory. You said she was a teacher. Couldn't she apply to a college here and get her master's?"

Dylan considered it. "That would certainly be a possibility, but it would cost a lot of money for her to do. What made you think of the college route?"

"I got my degree paid for through my graduate assistantship. I worked at the college as a trainer, and they paid for my classes. They also gave me enough money to contribute to the rent. It wasn't a lot, but I'm sure it would be enough if you had your salary, as well. I could look into it. They must accept foreign applications. I know we've had exchange students from Japan and England as undergraduates."

Dylan's eyes sparkled. "I never realized that's how you got through college. I assumed Jo paid for you."

"No. She wanted to. She thought I'd have more time to devote to studying, but I had my own reasons for taking the assistantship. I wanted to get some practical training in, have some monetary independence, and get out of the house. It was the best choice. I enjoyed it, and the college environment was fun and supportive."

Dylan paused while the waitress placed their food in front of them. She waited for Helen to ask for condiments, and then continued. "Sounds pretty good to me, I'm sold on the idea. All I can do now is hope Cory ends her marriage and is willing to be away from her family and friends for two years."

"When you say it like that, your future sounds pretty uncertain. I'll keep my fingers crossed."

"Can you cross your toes, too?" Dylan cut up her sandwich. "I do like the idea of the degree program. Could you check around at Waterbridge for me?"

"Sure. The graduate office is next to the athletic director's. I go past there on a daily basis. I'll do some digging around. I could pick up a catalog, if you want me to."

"That would be a good idea. I can send it to Cory and see what she thinks. Thanks, Helen, I'm feeling more positive about what could happen." Dylan took a bite of her sandwich and listened as Helen described her morning at work.

AFTER THE WAKE, Cory's family retraced their movements back to the crematorium to say one last goodbye. Her grandfather's ashes had been brought out in a large urn. The whole family was gathered under the same oak tree Cory had visited earlier. The weather had cleared up, making the somber event a little brighter. As each of her mother's siblings passed the urn, they scattered some of the ashes around the tree, while the grandchildren and Arthur's friends looked on. The ashes were scattered in the same pattern as her nan's had been two years before. At last, two souls were reunited. Cory felt a peace settle within her. She remembered Sue's comment. It was the end of an era.

ON THURSDAY EVENING, Cory was resting in her living room alone, except for Mungo. She stroked the cat's long fur. "I have to speak to Daddy, but I don't think it's the right time. Sometimes, I envy you. All you have to worry about is making it to the food bowl before Mary and Mitch, or finding a soft place to sleep." The cat purred in response. Cory looked around for her laptop. She hadn't checked her e-mail since Wednesday evening. She didn't see it, and then remembered she'd left it in the office. She stroked the cat for a few more minutes, and then decided that if Sam could check on his business, she could check her e-mail. She walked upstairs and into the office.

"Did the deal go through?" She asked, as she bent down beside the desk for her laptop.

"Yep, and to celebrate I've booked us into a hotel in the Lake District. I thought it would do you good to get away. You can clear your head, and we can do some rock climbing."

Cory looked at the website of the hotel he'd booked.

"What's wrong? Anybody would think I just told you some bad news."

Cory was panicked. She had no idea what to say. *Tell him now that it's over. The longer you wait, the harder it will be. A romantic weekend in the Lake District is not in your plans.* "I guess I'm just shocked. I thought you'd focus on other clients."

"The most important deal is complete. The rest can wait until Monday. I called Mike earlier to ask if we could borrow his climbing equipment. He asked if he could come up with us. The funeral took a lot out of him, and he needs a break."

"It sounds like it's already been planned, so I don't really have a choice. When are we leaving?" Cory's voice sounded hollow.

"I originally planned to go up tonight, but that would be a long trip after such a harrowing day. I thought we'd get up early and beat the Friday traffic. We can meet Clare and Mike on the M6 and have breakfast." Sam cleared the paperwork off his desk.

"What about Holly? Who's going to look after her?" Cory knew it was too late to back out.

"That was the best thing. The hotel accepts dogs, so Mike can bring Toby and we can take Holly. I've asked Craig to feed the cats, and he's okay with that. Everything's organized. All you need to do is pack and get some well-deserved sleep."

"I'll pack later. I'm going to check my e-mail and let people know how the funeral went." She retreated downstairs. She was disappointed, as she had hoped to spend some time chatting with Dylan over the weekend.

Her inbox was relatively empty, but she was cheered up when she saw a few e-mails from Dylan. The first was a card. Cory smiled when she saw the dancing Garfield before her. He was carrying a "thinking of you" placard. She opened the second e-mail.

```
Dylan Matthews
How are you doing?

Hi Cory,
    I wish I could have been with you today. I know
you must feel awful, but it does get better. I want
you right now to put your left hand on your right
shoulder. (DO IT!) Then put your right hand on your
left shoulder. Now, give yourself a big squeeze. I
wish I could be the one to hug you, take the hurt
away, and kiss it all better, but a cyber hug is all
I can offer.
    I began a countdown today. It's officially 40
days until you fly out, give or take a few days
either side. You are still planning to visit, aren't
you?
    Sarah has the realtor coming over tonight to
assess the house. She wants to move pretty quickly on
this, so I could be homeless soon. I thought I'd go
and live with my father, if the house sells. That
way, I can start saving money.
    Have to go do some work. I've basically clock-
watched the whole day.
    I wish I could have been there for you today.
Hugging you close to me.
D x
```

Chapter
Twenty-One

AT THE HOTEL on Friday afternoon, Cory and Sam agreed to unpack, change, and then meet Mike and Clare in the foyer ready for their first climb of the weekend. Cory put her weekend bag on the bed and placed her hands on her stomach. "I've got the worst cramps."

"Are you feeling sick?" Sam asked.

Cory counted the days on her hands. "Shit. I'm going to be miles away from any toilet, and I think I'm getting my fucking period."

"You always say that, and then it takes a week to arrive."

Cory ignored Sam's comment and walked into the bathroom, ready to prepare for the worst-case scenario.

THE FOURSOME SETTLED on a small, beginners' rock climb. Sam and Mike were both competent climbers. Clare and Cory had done some climbing, but Cory's fear of heights always held her back from tackling the more extreme climbs. The outcrop of rocks had a spectacular view and was mostly deserted. Cory wasn't surprised. The weather in March could be unpredictable, and many climbers preferred the comfort of indoor walls. Luckily, the weather was mild and dry. She felt quite comfortable in the clothes she was wearing. She changed her walking boots for her climbing shoes. They were a tight fit, and her feet protested mildly against being squeezed into such a cramped space. She listened as Sam and Mike discussed the route.

"I think we should top rope the climb and belay from the bottom," Mike said.

"Can we do it the other way around? I prefer the belay person to be at the top of the climb. I feel safer knowing the person at the top is holding the rope," Cory suggested. There was always a tiny fear in her mind that the rope would come loose from the object it was secured to, and she would fall. She looked up at the rocks. Although, it didn't look all that high, she knew it was.

"No, Cory. I agree with Mike. It gets lonely being the only person at the top," Sam said.

Cory watched Mike as he carefully free-climbed, clipping in the rope as he went. When he got to the top, he waved.

"Make sure you secure the rope," Cory shouted up.

Mike gave her the thumbs up. She knew she was being silly. Her brother was an experienced climber and had taken many groups out. She was in safe hands, but it didn't stop her from worrying. She waited patiently for Mike to tie the main rope and a safety rope around a boulder, and then he rappelled down the rock face.

"He's like a big kid when he's allowed to be," said Clare.

Cory took her eyes off Mike and nodded in agreement. "They both are. How are things going?"

"Yesterday was difficult for Mike. He spent so much time preparing his eulogy."

Clare sat down and leaned her back against the mossy rocks, and Cory did the same. "He did a great job. I was mad at first when Mum said Mike was doing it. I felt I should be the one to talk about Granddad. On reflection, I know Mike was the best person. I wouldn't have lasted two minutes on the podium. How's the house? Did you get those windows sorted out?"

"Things are good with the house, and Mike is happy with the progress. Thanks to Sam, we replaced the windows and the insurance company paid the difference, which helped."

"That's excellent news." Her brother had bought a run down, semi-detached house that had basically needed total rebuilding. He'd done much of it himself. On Cory and Sam's last visit, Sam had noticed the bay windows were caving in. On further investigation, they'd found the wood around them rotten. The rainwater had seeped through the old felt and onto the wood. Sam had told Mike and Clare that they needed to replace the felt and windows, or the whole front of the house would cave in. Mike had complained to the surveyors, who had missed this fault on their initial survey, and they'd been compensated.

"It is, and the house is definitely warmer with the new windows. Sam really saved our arses. We should be ready to add the extension in the summer."

"Speaking of warmer, the sunshine feels so nice. I may have to have forty winks, while the boys climb."

"I might join you. I'm exhausted, and a nap sounds good," Clare said.

CORY WOKE TO a voice yelling at her.

"Oy, sleeping beauties, do you want to climb?"

She opened one eyelid and glanced in the direction of the voice. Mike was waving the end of the rope at them. She turned her head to see Clare rubbing her eyes. "Wow, it's true what they say about country air. I zonked out completely. I guess it's time to stretch the muscles," Cory said.

They walked briskly to the bottom of the crag. The men had certainly been busy. Mike and Sam were wearing tops and shorts that had sweat patches all over them.

"Who's first?" Sam asked, as he slipped the rope into the belay bug.

"I'll go." Cory grabbed the other end of the rope and pulled it through the loop on her harness, tying a figure of eight knot.

"Taking in," Sam said, as he took in the slack.

Cory felt the tug on her harness. "That's me, Cory climbing." She called out the drill they had been taught in climbing classes. She put her hands and feet on the lower holds on the rock.

She felt her way up the cliff. There were some nice holds, and she started off with ease. As she reached the midway point, her heart was pounding, her arms were aching, and her legs were shaking—the buzz of climbing. She stopped on a small ledge to catch her breath. She looked up and saw the rope taut overhead. Then she looked down. She felt dizzy, and her stomach fluttered. She looked up again and focused on the tight rope. She imagined someone coming by with a knife and cutting the rope, sending her hurtling to her death. She clung to the wall. *Okay, just move your legs. Come on. We can do this. Look for a handhold. You're being stupid. Just climb.*

No matter how much self-talk she used, her body wouldn't move. She couldn't will her hands and feet to move. She was frozen.

"Sam, let me down," yelled Cory.

"Keep climbing. You can do this. You're tight on the rope. You're not coming down. This time you'll get to the top. You need to conquer your fear."

When she heard his statements, Cory began to cry. "Let me down. I can't go on. Please."

"No. You can do it." Sam held the rope tighter.

Mike looked at Cory clinging to the wall. "Maybe you should let her down. She looks shaky."

"She's fine. She does this every time, and at some point, she has to overcome what she's scared of. I know her. She just needs a little push now and then." Sam stood his ground with his brother-in-law. "Don't call my judgment into question."

"This isn't about you. This is about Cory," Mike said. "She looks petrified."

Cory stared down. She felt sick, and her stomach cramps intensified. She attempted to reach another handhold, but her arm muscles were weak. "Let me down. Now!" she screamed between sobs.

Clare came up behind Mike. "What's going on?" she whispered. "She needs to come down. What the fuck does he think he's doing?"

"Bring her down, mate." Mike put his hand on Sam's shoulder. "I don't know what's going on between you, but it doesn't take a genius to work out she's mad and scared as hell. She's not going to overcome her fear this way."

Sam looked up and saw Cory shaking. "Okay, hold onto the knot with two hands. I'm letting the rope out," he shouted up to her.

Cory blew out a slow, ragged breath and followed his instruction. She slowly walked down the crag. When her feet reached the ground, she gasped several times. Then she turned on Sam. "You, bastard. What the hell were you thinking?" She stopped yelling when he began laughing at her. "You have a lot to fucking learn. You are such a jerk at times." She elbowed past him and walked away.

"You arrogant son-of-a-bitch," she said over her shoulder as she stomped off. She couldn't believe the smug look she'd seen on Sam's face. She hated having her weaknesses exploited. She kicked a few stones in her path and sat on a rock. She looked back and saw them huddled together. She watched as Clare waved her finger at Sam and turned to walk her way. *He can't even come and do his own dirty work.*

"Is it safe to come near you? That's some language you spouted off back there." Clare sat next to Cory. "Are you okay?"

"I feel like an idiot. I don't know what comes over me. I like climbing, but I can't get past my fear." Cory took the tissue Clare passed her and blew her nose. "I'm sorry. Are you going to climb?"

"No. I'm not keen on climbing. I rarely go up. I was only going to climb today because you were doing it. I didn't want to look like a wimp. You just saved me from making my own scene. How about we take the dogs for a walk around the dale?"

TWO HOURS LATER, Cory and Clare met Sam and Mike at the car.

"We were just about to send out a search party for you two," Mike joked as he took Toby from Clare.

Cory opened the hatchback and let Holly jump into the trunk area. She closed the trunk and turned to walk to the passenger door. Sam prevented her from opening the door. "Are you feeling better?"

"I was never ill. I think the words you're looking for are 'I'm sorry.'"

"I was trying to help you get over your fear. How are you ever going to conquer it if you never try?"

Cory pushed him away. "When I decide to overcome my fears, you'll know. Most people wouldn't put the person they love through that much humiliation or fright. Now I know how you actually feel about me." She shot him an icy stare and got into the car.

THE FROSTY ATMOSPHERE continued when Sam and Cory arrived back at the hotel room. Cory locked herself in the bathroom and spent a good hour relaxing in a bubble bath, reading a novel.

They ate in a local pub. Luckily, there was plenty of entertainment, so Cory didn't have to speak much to Sam. After a fulfilling meal, Sam and Mike played pool while Clare and Cory listened to the local band.

When they returned to the hotel, Sam took the dog for a walk, and Cory went to bed. She heard the door open and listened as Sam walked around the bedroom. Holly climbed on the bed and settled on Cory's legs. It felt uncomfortable, but Cory didn't want to move. She didn't want Sam to know she wasn't asleep. The bathroom door closed, and Cory heard the sound of running water. She opened her eyes and called Holly further up the bed to cuddle her. She closed her eyes and fell asleep.

THE ROOM WAS cast with an early morning gloom. Holly let out a low growl, jumped off the bed, and prowled toward the bedroom door. Her swift exit from the bed disturbed Sam.

"Holly, cut that out. Come here." Sam clicked his fingers and Holly was at his side.

The growling and movement awakened Cory, too. She stretched out her body, and then curled up tightly, trying to remove the kinks in her back. It ached. She felt like she'd slept in the same position all night. Her hand touched the edge of the bed. She couldn't get any further away from Sam if she'd tried. There was a huge gap between them. Even in sleep, her body remembered how she felt. As if he had read her mind, she felt Sam rolling toward her. Before she had chance to move, his arm wrapped over her body. Forcefully, he pulled her toward him. She didn't want this. She didn't want his advances. No more excuses, this was the time to talk.

"Sam, this isn't working," Cory said.

"She's just unsettled, Cor. She'll be better tomorrow morning, when she's used to the surroundings."

Sam pulled Cory closer again, but she resisted. "I'm not talking about the bloody dog. I'm talking about us. It's not working."

Cory felt Sam's arms lose all rigidity, and she took her opportunity to move away. She turned to face him. Even in the faint light, she could see the muscles twitching as he gritted his teeth. She moved to switch the bedside lamp on and glanced at the clock. The light in the room was misleading. It had just turned seven thirty. She waited for Sam to respond.

"What do you mean, it's not working? I thought this weekend was what you wanted—a chance for us to be together. You've been nagging me for weeks to be more romantic." He rolled over, grabbed his sweatshirt off the floor, and put it on.

Cory was scared. The conversation she'd been dreading was here, and her nerve had disappeared. Fear, anxiety, and hurt rose and swirled in the pit of her stomach. "It's too little, too late. I'm not in love with you anymore."

"You don't love me?"

Cory saw Sam flinch. Cory knew she'd hurt him. "I didn't mean it like that. I do love you."

"But you just said you don't."

"I said I wasn't *in* love with you. I do love you, but it's not the same anymore. It's not what I want any longer." Cory was struggling to find the words to express her feelings. She'd thought of many ways to say how she felt, but now she couldn't remember any of them.

"I knew you weren't happy. I just thought it was because of your grandfather and the pressure of work. I thought this weekend could have been like a mini-honeymoon. I was planning on us taking a bigger one at Easter."

"We've barely spoken in six months. You seriously have no idea what's going on with us."

"So, tell me. What do you want?"

"I don't know."

"Bollocks. You've just said this isn't what you want. If I'm not what you want, then you must have some idea. How are you going to spend the rest of your life?"

Cory lowered her head. She ran her fingers through her hair. *What are you going to do with the rest of your life?* She had no idea. But she did know it wasn't going to be spent miserable. "I'm not happy, Sam. I haven't been for a while."

"Let's sort it out and work through the problems. I'm not going to lose my wife like my father lost my mother. I won't let you leave me."

"It's no use."

"That's it? You're giving up? You're not even going to try and save the marriage?"

Cory glared at him. "Don't turn this around and make it all my fault. I've tried talking to you. We go through the same conversations. I talk. I lose my temper. I tell you how I feel. You seem to listen, but you ignore what's said, and we return to how we were. It's a vicious circle, and it's killing me."

"Things haven't really been that bad. Granted, we've had some low points, but every couple has them. Women are supposed to whine and moan, and blokes are supposed to agree, and then forget."

"No. That's what you see on sitcoms, and how you perceive relationships. You don't know how many times I've cried myself to sleep, or cried on someone else's shoulder because I feel unloved."

"Are our problems common knowledge amongst your friends?"

"No, but I did need support. You weren't listening, and it was driving me crazy. I feel unloved, especially sexually."

"Is this about sex? If it is, I've told you a million times, it's not you, it's me. It doesn't mean I love you less."

"That's not how I feel. We haven't made love in such a long time."

"I've tried recently to get you interested, and you pull away. If you're not playing on that damn computer, you're working. You're the one who's been distant lately."

"I couldn't help it. I'd given up. There didn't seem any point in trying anymore. There are only so many times I can take rejection. A woman's conditioned from an early age that men want sex. In the media, men are portrayed as being able to screw anything. Imagine how I've felt, knowing that I must be so ugly and awful in bed that I couldn't even attract my own husband. It hurt. I hurt. I got tired of being told I was nagging you. It made me feel like you only had sex with me because I'd moaned, and then it lost the passion." Cory paused. She needed to calm down and collect her thoughts.

After a few moments of silence, and with no response from Sam, Cory continued. "I understand your family wasn't very affectionate, but I am. I need to know I'm cared for. I need to know I'm wanted. And God damn it, Sam, I need to know I'm loved." The tears rolled down Cory's face, more out of anger than sorrow. "I can't believe you noticed the distance between us and didn't say anything."

"You're serious about this, aren't you?"

"Yes."

"What are you going to do?"

Cory shrugged. "I don't know. I'm so confused at the moment. I'm disheartened with my life. I have no idea what's going on. My work no longer brings me the fulfillment it used to. Granddad dying has devastated me. Our marriage has fallen apart. I just wish I could take six months out of my life and escape—clear my head and find some direction."

"When did all this start getting too much for you? How long has this been going through your head? You should have talked to me."

"Like I said, I have talked to you. I feel like everything I ever wanted in life has changed." She knew it had. She'd known it as soon as she'd admitted to herself that she was attracted to Dylan—attracted to women. She should never have tried to please everyone, everyone except herself, that is. She knew what she wanted. She wanted Dylan. But now wasn't the time and place to say that. Sam needed to accept equal blame. They were both responsible for the break up of the marriage.

"But I love you, Cory. I do. I know you think I don't, but I do."

"I know you do. However, I need it all. I deserve a hundred percent of the puzzle, and the bits you can't give me are the largest sections. I need romance and passion. I want desire. I don't care if you think it's just made up in films. It's not. I know I can have that. It's not just sex. It's pure emotion. I want the mush. I want to do crazy things, just because I can. I want some independence. I want to be me."

"You seem to want an awful lot. What about me? What about what I want?"

"It's not about you anymore. The past six years have been about you. We've done things on your schedule, done them because you've wanted to do them."

"Bullshit. I've given you everything you've ever wanted. I bought the bigger house because you wanted it. I took you on holidays to places you wanted to go. I buy you anything you want because I know it makes you happy. Don't you dare tell me it's all about what I want."

Cory climbed off the bed. She needed to move about. Her anger made her gesticulations more active. She waved her arms in front of her. "That's just it, Sam. Those are materialistic things. I don't need them. Yes, they're nice, but money doesn't buy happiness. You know, I've realized that saying is true. I've been more alone these past few months than I've ever been in my entire life. I would have been happy with a slow dance in the lounge, or a spontaneous drive up in the hills to watch the sunrise." She debated whether to tell him exactly what was on her mind. *Might as well get it all out now — there might never be another time.* "And I was thinking about what you want. You want a wife who'll be by your side. Someone who will be quiet and agree with you. You need to be in control. You want a family, Sam. A family I can't give you."

"But you've always wanted to have children."

"I know, and I still do. However, I made a promise to myself that I'd never bring a child into this world if I couldn't guarantee it would have both parents together to love it. We're both from divorced families. I don't want that for our children."

"We can work on this, Cory. I'm ready to try for children."

"That's the problem. I was ready to start a family last year, but I gave you the time you needed. You never wanted children, you always said that. Now you've changed your mind, but so have I." She took a deep breath. As usual, she was doing most of the talking. She had so many things she wanted to say. But maybe some things were best left unsaid. "I want a break, time to get my head together."

"When did you decide all this?"

"I don't know. It gradually happened. At Christmas, I was miserable. New Year was awful. It was our fifth year anniversary, supposedly a time to make new promises and dreams, and we just seemed to be drifting."

"This all coincides with when you started playing on those damn Internet lists — meeting those new people."

"Those 'new people,' as you call them, are my friends. They have nothing to do with how I feel." Was she lying? She'd been feeling trapped and alone before she'd met members of the group — before she'd met Dylan. The openness of the group had helped her accept herself, accept who she was.

"Does this taking time out of your life include spending any time in America?"

The question caught Cory off guard. She didn't respond.

"I'm just trying to work out why suddenly our lives are being thrown into the air. Why you feel you need a break." Sam stood up and pulled on a pair of track pants as he spoke.

Cory shrugged her shoulders and looked down at her hands. She didn't know how to answer the question, and she couldn't think of a way to change the subject. She was saved from answering by a knock at their door. She looked at Sam.

"I'll go. You're in no state to answer the door."

Cory watched as Sam ran his fingers through his short hair. It didn't help his disheveled morning look. She took the opportunity to use the bathroom. She had felt her bladder pressing into her stomach while they'd been talking. She hadn't wanted to interrupt the discussions before she'd had her say. She washed her face and came out to find Sam putting his boots on.

"It was Mike. He's taking Toby for a walk along the trail. He wanted to know if I'd walked Holly yet. I should really take her."

Cory looked at Holly. She was waiting impatiently by the door, her tail wagging furiously. She'd been forgotten while they'd argued. "I know. She needs to go. Do you want me to come?"

"No. I need some time to think. Does Mike know anything?"

Cory shook her head. "I know you think I've told the world and his dog about us, but I haven't. The only people I've talked to are Angela and Dylan."

At the mention of Dylan's name, she saw his face blanch. Cory knew she shouldn't have said her name. "Go, before Holly leaves a puddle. We'll talk later, okay?"

Sam didn't respond. He picked up his coat and Holly's lead and was gone before Cory could say anything else to him.

Chapter
Twenty-Two

CORY SETTLED ONTO the sofa in her living room. She was glad to be home. When she awoke that morning, Sam had been out with the dog. Saturday night, he had propped up the hotel bar until the early hours, returning when she was asleep. She and Sam had put on a front and hidden their problems from Mike and Clare for the remainder of the weekend. The tension between Cory and Sam was exhausting.

Cory picked up the remote and turned on the television but she couldn't concentrate on the movie due to the intermittent loud noises coming from the bedrooms upstairs. When the banging began again, she went up to investigate.

Sam's side of the room had been stripped of the bedside table, shelves, and bureau. The holes in the wall, from the shelves, had been filled with spackle, and fresh paint covered the marks. The closet doors were open, and Sam's clothes had been removed. She left the room and went into the other room. Sam had rearranged the room to fit in the new furniture. He'd made the bed and put shelves on the wall. The television had been secured on a wall mount, and the bureau had his toiletries on it. She turned to walk away but collided with Sam, who was carrying magazines from the office. The magazines fell to the floor. Cory bent to help Sam pick them up. "You've been busy," Cory said.

"You made it clear we're over. I thought this was what you wanted."

"I would have moved out of the bedroom."

"It made sense for me to move out. I use this bathroom. Tomorrow, I'll call the estate agents and see if they'll come over to value the house. I've done a spreadsheet and split the household costs down the middle. I'm assuming you're staying in the house."

Cory stood up and handed her pile of magazines to Sam. "You didn't waste any time."

"I did a lot of thinking on the trip home. I'll let you know when the estate agents can come and view the house."

"Can we talk?"

"No. There's nothing left to say."

Cory went to what was now her bedroom. She closed the door and dropped onto the bed, dreading the next few weeks.

DYLAN SPORTED A bruise on her chin and a foul mood. The bruise was her fault; the mood was definitely due to Sarah. She'd already called Sarah three times and only gotten her voice-mail. She read the house appraisal form again and focused on the price Sarah had asked for the house. Dylan was furious. She placed a fourth call.

"Hello."

"Sarah, what the hell are you doing setting the price for the house so high? I thought we were going to take the average of the three assessments."

"I changed my mind. One guy said we could get three hundred thousand, and that's the price I want to ask. You do have the option of buying my share."

Dylan gritted her teeth, reining in her temper. "You know I can't raise that kind of money. Let's set the price a little lower and see what happens."

"No."

"Fine. Stick with the fucking price. Just make sure you pay your share of the mortgage." She heard the beeping of the call-waiting. "I have to go. Someone's on the other line." Dylan switched the call. "Hi."

"Hello, did you miss me?"

"Cory?"

"I hope so, otherwise I want to know how many other British women are calling you."

Dylan laughed. "I'm sorry. You caught me off guard. I wasn't expecting to hear from you. It's a much needed surprise. Where are you?"

"At home. We got back a few hours ago."

"How was the trip?"

"Worst holiday of my life."

"How so?"

"I talked to Sam yesterday. We're officially separated."

Dylan gasped. "No way! What happened? How are you? He didn't hurt you, did he?"

"Whoa. Slow down with the questions."

"Sorry. I'm a little shocked you said something to him so soon after your grandfather's funeral. I thought you'd leave it for a while." Dylan grabbed a spare sofa cushion and relaxed against the arm of the chair.

"I was a little surprised myself."

"Start at the beginning. I want to know everything."

"We had a shitty day Friday. He made me so mad."

"How?"

"We went climbing, and he wouldn't let me down when I got scared."

"Bastard. Did you get hurt?"

"No. More my pride got dented. Anyway, yesterday morning, I snapped, and it all came tumbling out."

"You told him everything."

"No. I didn't mention you."

"That was probably a wise thing. How did he take it?"

"Pretty good, actually—better than I expected. He's already moved out of the master bedroom, and we only got back a few hours ago."

"At least you've told him it's over. That's the hardest step. Now you can look to the future."

"I'm feeling very relieved, but scared shitless, too. It's an enormous step. I can't believe I've done it. Now, I'm looking forward to exploring ways to spend more time with you. How are things your end?"

Dylan sighed. "Where do I begin? Friday night, I waited over an hour for a realtor, who didn't show up. I then spent two hours chasing down Sarah. Boy, did I chew her a new butt hole."

"Why? It wasn't her fault."

"It was. She'd arranged the appointment, but forgot to pass on the message that he had cancelled. Then yesterday, three agents showed up."

"How did that go?"

"Like crap. She's priced the house so high, we'll never sell it. I've tried to talk her into lowering it, but she's not budging."

"That's good for you, isn't it? The longer she holds out, the longer you get to stay in the house."

"It's a double-edged sword. I get to stay, but the money I'd get from the sale would be real helpful right now. I'm struggling to pay my share of the mortgage and all the bills. Because she isn't here, she's refusing to help pay any utilities. I don't blame her. I wouldn't, if the shoe was on the other foot."

"True. Hopefully, she'll see sense. Did you play hockey last night?"

"Yeah. I might as well have stayed at home for all the good I was to the team."

"Why? You usually love going to hockey."

"I do, but I was so upset over the house situation that I defended the goal a little too well. I took my anger out on the defenseman and got a stick in my face. The referee called a penalty against me, and I cost my team an opportunity to score a winning goal. Other than that, I'm peachy keen."

"You don't sound okay. Did you do anything else?"

"Umm...I ate a frozen meal and watched some reruns of *Buffy the Vampire Slayer*."

"Your weekend sounds as interesting as mine."

"Sad, isn't it? I have to admit I'm lonely. I miss you."

"I miss you, too."

"I did spend time reading all our e-mails from the beginning." Dylan blushed when she spoke.

"You kept our e-mails?"

"Yeah. You never know. I might write a book one day," Dylan said.

"I was thinking about your visit. I want to run an idea or two past you. I know we only spent a week together and that you've only been a single woman for a day, but I don't feel like time is on our side."

"You're speaking rather cryptically for me. What exactly are you trying to tell me?"

Dylan spent the next twenty minutes filling Cory in on the details of a graduate assistantship. "I'm seeing Helen later and she's going to give me a catalog of courses. Can I send it to you?"

"Sure. It's worth a look."

"I did some calculations. If Sarah and I sell the house for a good profit, I could pay for your master's degree courses, with or without you getting the assistantship. We could get an apartment near the college."

"You've thought a lot about this, haven't you?"

"This is just one option."

"I know. It's just a lot to take in. Yesterday, I ended my marriage. Today, I have the chance to live in America. It's a lot to process."

"It is. I didn't mean to sound so forceful. I'm being a jerk. You've had a rough weekend."

"No. I appreciate you thinking about the future. I guess I never really thought about living outside the country and away from my family."

"Cory, this isn't our only option. We can explore the UK options, too. This is something for us to look into when you come over, if you're still interested...in me.?"

"Cut that crap out. You know I want to be with you. Do you know what hit me yesterday?"

"No, tell me."

"Promise you won't laugh."

"I promise."

"I was listening to the songs in the car. Most of the lyrics were about losing someone or being in love. I think I know now what it means to truly give up everything so you can be with the one you love. It's how I feel about you. However, the thought of leaving my family, my job, my home, and my friends is going to take some time to get used to."

"I know. I feel the same way. We'll figure something out." Dylan checked her watch. "Shit. I have to go. I wish we had more time to talk, but I offered to skate for another team tonight. They're down a player. If I'd known there'd be a chance to talk to you, I wouldn't have volunteered."

"Dylan, I haven't said this since you left. I...I love you."

Dylan held the phone to her forehead, relieved to hear the words. "I love you, too. I can't wait for Easter." She hung up and stared at the information sheets in front of her. She hadn't told Cory everything about the college application process. Dylan read some of the practice questions for the GRE exam and gulped. *Little by little. No need scaring the girl before she's agreed to apply.* Dylan looked back at the test. She read one of the sample vocabulary questions. *How in the hell would Cory know where to find a maar?*

Chapter
Twenty-Three

CORY RECEIVED THE package from Dylan. It had been sent to her school address to prevent Sam from intercepting it. In it was a Waterbridge brochure, a GRE study guide, practice test CD, and a note from Dylan.

```
Dear Cory,
    Here's the information I promised. I didn't tell
you there was an entrance exam because I didn't want
to freak you out. Don't be mad at me. For a brain
like you, I'm sure it'll be a snap.
    Call or e-mail me to let me know you got it. I'll
understand if you don't want to do this. The choice
is 100% yours.
I love you,
D
```

Cory reread the note and picked up the study guide. The news of an exam was added stress for Cory. Living in the house with Sam over the week had been a strain. The estate agents had surveyed the house and evaluated it at a decent price. Unfortunately, when they'd taken the mortgage out, they had taken a cash back to pay for extra furnishings and carpets. The mortgage tied them in for five years, with a hefty redemption fee if they sold the house. On hearing this, Sam had been reluctant to sell the house. He'd asked for time to search for other options.

Cory had yet to tell her family about the split. She had, however, informed Rachel about the separation and her feelings for Dylan. Rachel had been shocked, but supportive. Cory heard the knock on her door and looked up from the guide. "How was your afternoon?"

"Brutal. I hate Key Stage 2 tests. I'm tired of practicing for them. Is that parcel the one you were waiting for?"

"Yes. Dylan sent the college brochure, but neglected to tell me there was an entrance exam."

"No shit."

"Look at this study guide." Cory passed the thick practice book to Rachel. She watched as Rachel flipped through the English and maths sections.

"Bloody hell. How the hell are you going to pass this? I hate to say it, but it looks way too hard. Does Dylan know about your lack of maths skills?"

Cory shook her head. "No. She thinks I'm really smart." They reviewed some of the synonyms and antonyms page, and Cory pointed to one example. "I have no idea what the word 'defalcation' means, let alone the four choices they've offered as answers."

"You're going to have to make some bloody good guesses."

"Tell me about it. The third section of the quiz is an analytical section." Cory waited for Rachel to turn to the third section.

"You're good at these. They're similar to the questions we give on the eleven plus test," Rachel said.

"I know. It's my favorite section."

"Oh..."

"What's wrong?"

"It says here that this section isn't taken into account when the college processes the scores."

"Fuck. They're only going to take my English and maths scores." Frustrated, Cory ran her fingers through her hair. "How the hell am I going to pass?"

"Don't panic. I'll help you study. We'll take it one step at a time."

"You're talking like I should take the test."

"What do you have to lose? If you fail, you'll have to look at other options. If you don't take the test, you'll never know."

"True."

"When can you take the test?"

Cory opened the college brochure and took out the test application form. She read the information page, skimming until she found the test centers. She looked at the international section. "It says here that I can take it in Manchester or London. I'll have to check out the dates."

"I'd check with Dylan, too. Maybe you could take the test when you're there over Easter. That would give you a few weeks to study, and you'd still get your application in on time."

"That's a good idea. I'll ask her tonight."

"How are things at home? You'd tell me if things were too bad, wouldn't you? You know you can always stay with me if things get too rough."

Cory gave Rachel a side hug. "I promise I'll tell you. It's tough in the house. Sam has turned this whole separation into some kind of business deal. When he talks to me, it's like I'm a client. When we spoke Sunday evening, he had already divided up our assets and set a budget. As far as he's concerned, I'm a financial investor in the house."

"Ouch, that must hurt. Most men would be finding ways to romance the woman back. It doesn't sound like he's putting up much of a fight."

"I know. Deep down, I think I wanted him to at least fight for me. It would show that he cares. The way he looks at me scares me. I feel like he's my enemy. I know I have no right to expect anything from him, but I think I wanted him to try." She began to cry. "I feel such a shit. I know I've broken his heart, but I need to do what's right for me." Cory welcomed the hug as Rachel enveloped her. She rocked gently in her arms.

"Shush. Come on, you've been so brave. The hard part is nearly over. Don't think like that. You've given him so many chances to change. Even if he did beg you to come back, would you really change your mind?" Cory shook her head against Rachel's shoulder. "If he made all the promises in the world, how long do you think he'd keep them? A leopard can't change his spots. He's also a man. You told me the other day that you want to be with a woman."

"I know. I just feel so guilty."

"Why? You fell in love. It happens. You did the right thing, Cory. You didn't cheat."

Cory pulled slightly away from Rachel, but kept her arms around her. "I did, emotionally. I might not have made love with Dylan, but I cheated with my feelings."

"You're bound to feel guilty, but believe in yourself, and believe in Dylan. I wish I'd met her. She sounds wonderful." Rachel kissed the top of Cory's head. "I see a sparkle in your eye that hasn't been there in a long time."

THE HOUSE WAS quiet when Cory entered, but Sam's car was on the driveway. She looked up at the hook where Holly's lead usually hung. It was gone. She was grateful for a few minutes of relaxation. Her recent evenings had been filled with tension. She had taken to hiding out in her bedroom. She placed her box of schoolwork under the stairwell and went into the kitchen to switch on the kettle. While she waited for it to boil, she went into the lounge and booted up her laptop. She wanted to try out one of the mock GRE tests on the CD ROM. She put the study guide beside the laptop and went back into the kitchen. She heard the front door open and close. Moments later, Holly came bounding into the kitchen. Cory spent a few minutes fussing over the dog. She was rewarded with a sloppy lick. She picked up two mugs of tea and returned to the lounge. She stopped at the entrance when she saw Sam reading the study guide.

"Hi. I made you a cuppa." She passed the tea toward Sam.

He took it with one hand and held the guide with another. "What's this?"

"I think it's self-explanatory." Cory felt foolish. She hadn't wanted Sam to find out about her plans so soon.

"I know what it is. Why are you studying for it? It's got an American price tag on. No need to ask who sent it to you." He dropped the book back onto the table and stormed out of the room.

Cory sank onto the sofa. She knew she needed to read up on some of the math topics, but her mind was elsewhere. She connected to the Internet. As she was watching her e-mail download, a tiny beep sounded. She glanced down at the screen and saw the flashing messenger chat screen.

```
Dylan Matthews: I was excited to see you'd logged on.
How was work?
Cory Williams: It was okay. I missed Body Pump. I
wanted to look at the catalogue for college. I got
the study guide.
Dylan Matthews: Are you ok? You seem a little dis-
tant.
Cory Williams: You can always tell how I'm feeling.
How do you do that?
Dylan Matthews: Magic. And the fact you didn't greet
me like you usually do. What's wrong, honey? Are you
mad that I didn't tell you about the test?
Cory Williams: Not mad. A little disappointed, but I
understand why you didn't tell me. Sam just saw the
GRE guide. He's pissed, and I'm sure he's brewing for
an argument.
Dylan Matthews: It was only a matter of time.
Dylan Matthews: I'm sorry. I just read that comment,
and it sounded more casual than I meant it to be. I'm
worried about you. I feel useless. I should be there
supporting you.
Cory Williams: You do. You support me all the time. I
can feel it. And you're right, I do have to tell him
about my plans. I just don't have any concrete ones.
Dylan Matthews: What did you think of the exam?
Cory Williams: Tough. I don't know if I'll pass. How-
ever, if I don't try, we lose an option for the
future. I checked the test centers here, and they're
a bitch to get to. Rachel suggested I ask you to
check out test dates over there.
Dylan Matthews: Sure. I can go into Waterbridge and
see if you can take it while you're out here. If you
were interested, I was going to book a meeting for
you with someone in the graduate school. Helen said
you might need an interview. We could kill two birds
with one stone.
Cory Williams: Okay. How's work going?
Dylan Matthews: Not too bad. It's almost 1 p.m. I can
take lunch soon. What are your plans for tonight?
Cory Williams: I hadn't given it much thought. I get
the feeling Sam is about to explode, so I could be
talking to or avoiding him.
Dylan Matthews: Be careful, please.
Cory Williams: I promise. How is life your end? How's
```

```
Sarah?
Dylan Matthews: Being a pain in the ass. She's
obsessed with selling the house.
```

Cory could hear Sam banging around upstairs. She heard a loud crash.

```
Cory Williams: I have to go. From the noises
upstairs, I think Sam's reached boiling point. I want
to get off the computer. I don't want to wind him up
any more.
Dylan Matthews: Okay. Do me a favor. Take your laptop
and cell phone upstairs. That way, you can contact me
if things get bad. Promise me.
Cory Williams: I promise. I'll put the phone on
vibrate. We can talk later, if you want. Do you have
a game?
Dylan Matthews: No. There's a short practice tomor-
row. I was planning on doing my laundry and watching
a movie tonight.
Cory Williams: Have to go. I'll let you know what
happens later. Miss you.
Dylan Matthew: Be safe—miss you, too.
```

Cory carried her laptop upstairs. She placed her mobile phone in the pocket of her cargos. When she passed the office on her way back, Sam stepped out behind her.

"We need to talk."

Cory jumped at the voice. She held onto the stair banister. "Jesus. You scared the shit out of me." She moved down a few steps. The brusqueness in his tone frightened her. "Fine, I'll meet you in the lounge."

She put more distance between them by walking down the stairs quickly. Sam followed. Her heart was racing. She heard the patter of four paws on rug and relaxed a little. She was glad Holly would be near. She knew she'd be protected. They entered the lounge one after the other and sat on opposite sofas. An uncomfortable silence enveloped the room.

After what felt like an eternity, Sam spoke, "I want to know what's going on?"

"Pardon?"

"Come on, Cory, at least be honest with me."

"I have no idea what you're talking about. Honest about what?"

"You know. Don't fuck me around."

Cory caught the rise in his voice and saw the clench of his fist. "Calm down. I haven't developed extra-sensory perception. I'm not messing with you. You're going to have to be a little more specific."

"What's going on with you and Dylan?"

Cory shook her head. "Nothing," she lied.

"There must be. She calls most evenings. You haven't been the same since you met her."

"She's being a friend, offering me options."

"What options? I think I have a right to know what plans you're making. You asked for time out to think. But you haven't exactly talked about where you're going, where you're staying, and if you'll be working. As I see it, we have the house. If we sell it, we both lose money. However, you obviously have no intention of staying here."

"I might."

"I went online and checked out that study guide. It's for the GRE, and that's an entrance exam for American graduate courses. This leads me to believe you're not even staying in this country. All I'm asking for is a little bit of honesty."

Cory dropped her head, and took a few moments to compose herself. "I've thought a lot about my future and what I want. I know that I need to get away and evaluate my life. There are too many people here who want things from me. School takes so much effort, and I get more responsibilities every day. The pressure has been building this past year. I feel like I'm at breaking point. Mum will hound me non-stop when I tell her about us splitting up. She's not going to understand, and I don't want to explain my reasons. I don't want her in my private life. There's also Granddad's death. I need time to grieve properly."

"Cory, I know all that. I've watched you, and I know you've had more than your fair share of stress this year. You sound like you're thinking about moving away. Are you? To America?"

"Maybe."

"How the hell are you going to support yourself over there? I'm curious, as we have no savings."

"I know," Cory said, unsure whether to mention all her plans. "Dylan sent me some brochures about a college that offers graduate assistantships. If I applied and got accepted, I would work at the college, and they'd pay for my degree classes. I'd also have some money from a stipend. Dylan's offered to let me stay at her place, with minimal expenses."

Sam began to laugh. "Wow, that's very gracious of her. So, you're telling me that she's doing this out of the kindness of her heart? For Christ's sake, you only met her a couple of months ago. What's in it for her?"

"Friendship. Is that such a foreign concept to you?" Cory bit down on her lip. She could practically see the wheels turning in Sam's mind. She wished she could find the courage to admit her feelings for Dylan. She met his eyes, and was pierced with a stare that made her blood run cold.

"That's just it. I don't think this is about friendship. Let me tell you the way I view these plans of yours. I think this great change in your life is down to Dylan. What exactly is your relationship with her?"

"She's my friend." Fear overrode her honesty. As she saw Sam stand up, she backed further down the couch. He walked toward the lounge door, and she relaxed a little. *That was a close one. I might need to take Rachel up on her offer.* She tensed again when she saw him stop at the threshold. He turned to face her.

"I am only going to ask this question once, and I expect a truthful answer from you. In fact, if the past six years have meant anything to you, then I know I'll get an honest answer. Are you and Dylan more than friends?"

As she heard the words, Cory stomach churned. Her blood ran cold with panic. Unsure of what to say, she dropped her head into her hands and cried. She opened her mouth to speak, but nothing came out. She took a deep breath and tried again. She still had no words.

"I'm waiting. You have this one chance to be honest with me."

"We're...we're very good friends." She lifted her head to see if he believed her.

"Friends. Now, you're *sure* about that? I saw you in bed together. I watched her look at you. Cory, I've always admired your honesty, and I can tell when you're lying. If I meant anything to you, answer my bloody question. Are you and Dylan *just* friends?"

Cory used her sleeve to wipe at the tears. She gulped down her sobs. "We're...we're...more than friends."

"So you're lovers?"

"No. No, I swear on my grandfather's memory we're not. I wasn't lying, Sam. Not really." Cory looked down at the rug. "But, I do have feelings for her."

"You're gay? Bisexual?"

Cory curled her arms around her knees and hugged them to her. Her crying was out of control. "I don't know. I'm not sure what I am. All I know is I've hurt you, and I have no idea what my future holds. I'm scared." She closed her eyes and rocked herself. She felt arms come around her from behind. The last thing she'd expected was a hug from Sam. She moved her arms to his and held them close to her.

"Thank you for finally being honest with me."

"You're not mad?"

"I am. I'm so angry with you at the moment. When I heard you tell me you had feelings for her, I wanted to hit you, but then, I saw your face. I knew you didn't intentionally do this."

"I didn't, Sam, I swear."

"I believe you. I know you'd never swear on Arthur's memory if you didn't mean it."

Cory released her grasp on Sam. She heard him move away from the sofa. "How about I make a cup of tea, and we talk properly. I promise to try and listen."

"Okay. I'm going to use the bathroom. I need to wash my face."

CORY PICKED UP her mug and took a tentative sip. The sweet taste of tea felt so good against her raw throat. "It's true what they say, I guess."

"About what?" Sam asked.

"Tea. It really does help solve any problem," Cory said. She smiled at him. He was seated in his usual spot on the larger sofa. She had chosen to sit on the far side of the other sofa. His complete change of attitude had her off-balance. She wasn't sure if he had an ulterior plan.

"If you say so."

Cory tapped her feet on the carpet. She waited for Sam to ask more questions, but none came forth. Unable to stand the stares and silence, Cory spoke. "This is a little surreal. I'm not sure what you want to know. I'm a little scared to say anything."

"What are your real plans?"

"I don't have any set plans for the future. I'm going out to America at Easter. I'm hoping to check out the college and maybe take the GRE."

"Were you going to tell me about your trip, or were you just going to disappear?"

"I was going to tell you, but I wasn't sure how." Cory hadn't really thought about the practical side to her trip. "I was going to ask Dad or Mike to take me to the airport. I didn't use the bank account to pay for the ticket. It's my trip, so I used my credit card."

"I'll take you to the airport," Sam offered.

"Are you sure?"

"It'll save you having to explain to your parents why I'm not taking you. You know they're going to ask why you're going without me."

"That's easy. I get more holiday time than you."

"I know. But if I don't take you, they'll ask more questions. Have you spoken to your parents about us?"

Cory shook her head. "No. You asked me not to. I was actually grateful for the excuse not to have the conversation with them, especially Mum."

"Good. Can we keep it that way for a bit longer?" Sam asked

Cory finally met Sam's eyes and held them. She couldn't work out what was going on behind those eyes. He sounded all friendly, but there was something to the tone of his voice. "Okay. Can I ask why?"

"In one week, my world's gone from hunky-dory to complete disaster. I'm still trying to come to terms with the fact you ended it. Now, I have to deal with the truth you're leaving me for a woman."

Cory dropped her gaze to her tea mug. *I knew this would happen. I knew he'd lay the blame at my door.* She returned her attention to Sam. "I'm not leaving you for a woman," Cory said, frustration lacing her words. She noticed the spark in his eye.

"You've changed your mind."

Cory's heart sank. He just didn't get it. "No. I'm leaving you, but it isn't for Dylan. Leaving you *would* have happened at some point, and for all the reasons I told you last weekend. My feelings for Dylan just confirmed what I knew all along. You asked me earlier if I was gay. It's taken me almost a decade to answer that question, but now I know the answer. I am gay..." *I said the words. I can't fucking believe that the first person I come out to is my husband.* "But it's not the main reason for us breaking up. I was happy with you. I love you, but there isn't any passion or openness. Deep down, you must know that."

Cory waited for Sam to answer. She watched as he turned his attention to the sleek black cat that had jumped on his lap. He stroked Midge gently. Cory watched Sam display his affection to the animal. "Are you going to tell my parents about me?"

Sam shook his head. "I may appear to be accepting this, but it's tearing me apart. However, it's not my place to tell your parents — it's yours. I promise I will never tell them. You're my best friend, Cory. I'll try to support you as much as I can, but you're going to have to remember that this is difficult for me, too."

Cory heard the crack in his voice. She watched as he wiped at his eyes. "I'm so sorry. I hate myself for what I'm doing to you."

"Have you studied for this test? I thought you hated exams. Because of your anxiety, it took you four times to pass your driving test."

"I only got the guide today. I looked through it, but I don't stand a chance of passing it."

"You need to have more confidence in yourself."

"It's not that. The English section is a bitch, but the maths section is bloody awful. I haven't taken maths since I was sixteen. I don't even understand the formulas for the simplest equations. So I'm basically screwed." The tears began to well up again. Her one big chance to be with Dylan rested on her one big weakness in life: an exam. Not just any exam, but a math exam.

"I could help you."

"Seriously?" Cory was stunned. She'd never expected this from Sam. She didn't get it.

"I'm serious. I know what your maths is like. You have trouble balancing the bank account."

"Can we start tonight?"

"No. I was hoping we could catch a movie. The new Tom Cruise film is out. You're still into him, aren't you?"

"Yes," Cory said, "that sounds good. I need some time to get changed into comfier clothes." She got up and took Sam's empty mug out of his hand. She hoped Sam's attitude was a sign of things to come. She was beginning to think fate really did map out a person's life. Things definitely did appear to be looking up. She took the empty mugs into the kitchen, and then went upstairs to change. While she was there, she quickly wrote an e-mail to Dylan.

Cory Williams
You'll never believe what happened

 Hello Dylan,
    I just wanted to let you know things are very
good. I told Sam about the college, America, and my
feelings for you. He took it spookily well. He even
offered to tutor me and take me to the airport. We
both agreed we'd tell my parents in a month or two.
My mum can be very over-bearing. She put a lot of
pressure on us to get married. She'll be heartbroken
to hear we split up. I can't see her taking it quietly, and I'm not ready to have her ask me twenty
questions about what I'm going to do with my life.
It's not like I have any real answers to give her. I
thought I'd tell them when I return from visiting
you. I'll at least know more about the college
option.
    I'm still in shock about Sam's attitude. Can you
freakin' believe it? Anyway, he asked me to the movies, and we're heading out in five minutes. I'll let
you know what I think of the film.
    I miss you. I wish it were you I was going out
with tonight.
    Things are looking up.
Love you,
Cory x

Chapter
Twenty-Four

DYLAN READ THE e-mail again and banged her fist on the table. "She's going to the fucking movies with Sam," she said aloud. She stood up and paced her office. *He's helping her out. He's being supportive.* She sat back down and pressed the reply button.

```
Dylan Matthews
Friday Night

Hello,
    I was surprised to hear how well things went. I'm
happy for you, but I have to admit, the green-eyed
monster surfaced when I read that you'd gone to the
movies with him. I can't help it. I want to be the
one who spends time with you. Anyway, I am pleased
that he wants to help you study.
    I don't have any plans for the evening. I'm
exhausted. Work's been a bitch today. There were too
many end users messing up their computers and then
expecting me to perform miracles. I think I'll make
it an early night.
    I hope we get a chance to talk tomorrow. I'll
keep my fingers crossed that things go smoothly with
Sam. I'm still amazed he took the news so well. Tell
me all about what you said to him in your morning e-
mail. Thankfully, it's the end of my workday. I miss
you loads.
    Dylan
```

She gathered her jacket and knapsack, fumbling for her cell phone as it rang. The caller ID worsened her bad mood. "What?"

"Geez. Have you lost the ability to be civil at all?"

"Look, Sarah, you're lucky I even bothered to take your call. What do you want?"

"I was calling to ask if we could talk. Maybe go out for dinner?"

"What for?"

"We need to go over what repairs might need to be done to the house before it gets inspected."

"We just put it on the market."

"I know, but we could fix it up. We don't want someone to make an offer but then not be able to sell it because it failed inspection."

"Okay. I see your point. We did leave some of the outdoor mainte-nance for spring. I didn't have any great plans for tonight. How about we meet at the mall, grab something to eat from the food court, and then maybe go check out a movie?"

"I'd like that."

"I have to get back to work. I'll see you at six in the food court, and Sarah, no funny business. I'm not in the mood."

DYLAN ENTERED THE mall. It was a typical Friday night with lots of families and plenty of teenagers walking around the mall or eating dinner. She saw Sarah sitting at a small table for two. She walked over. "Hi. I'm sorry about earlier. My day went from bad to worse, and I took it out on you." Dylan felt the squeeze of Sarah's hand on her arm.

"I understand. We may have split up, but I hope you know you can always talk to me."

"Why the change in attitude? Last week, you wanted to kill me."

"I was hurt. Now, we have a common goal — selling the house."

"Good, because I have a few things to discuss with you. First, let's grab dinner."

Dylan headed toward the Mexican food counter, while Sarah opted for the jambalaya food bar. They returned to the table with their meals.

Dylan took a bite of her taco. "What do you think needs to be done to the house?"

"I think we should replace the wood by the back deck. It's begin-ning to rot, and I'm sure the inspectors will notice it, too. It shouldn't take more than a weekend or two to do it. My dad will pick up the wood for us, so that will keep the cost down. I can't think of too many things that would keep it from passing the inspection. We could tidy up the outside and clean the yard. You were never the gardener."

"True. Okay, we'll fix up the porch area and deck, and if you want to touch up the paintwork, I'll help." Dylan ripped the paper around her quesadilla and pulled it apart. "To be honest, I think we need to dis-cuss the price of the house."

"Can't we spend one evening together without arguing?"

"I'm not looking for an argument. You were the one who wanted to discuss the house."

"I know. It was an excuse to see you. I want us to try and mend some fences. Please, can we spend some time just chatting?"

"Sure, but we do need to discuss the price before the end of the evening." Dylan chewed on the soft tortilla bread. "What do you think about the Bruins? I think they have a real chance of making the playoffs if they keep playing the way they are." They ate their meals and caught up with family and sport news. After eating, they chose a movie to watch.

THREE HOURS LATER, Dylan and Sarah walked out of the movie theater.

"That was awesome. I'm full of energy now. I haven't laughed like that in ages. Can I interest you in a beer at the club?" Sarah offered. The only gay club in the area, The Twist & Turn bar, was situated opposite the theater.

"I don't think so. I'm tired."

"Please, just the one. Michelle said she was going there after work, and I don't want to wait on my own."

"Well, I don't want to meet your new girlfriend, either. Anyway, you wouldn't be on your own. You've propped the bar up so many times, they've probably written your name on one of the chairs."

"Come on, Dylan. I've really enjoyed your company tonight. We could talk about the house price."

"This isn't a ploy to get me into the bar, is it?"

"No. I promise."

"Okay, but just the one."

The club was beginning to get lively. Dylan ordered two bottles of Michelob and settled at a table with Sarah.

"I miss coming here," Dylan said.

"I miss coming here with you."

"Sarah, don't go there. I'm here for one beer and to get you to see reason. All I'm asking is for you to drop the house price by ten thousand, maybe even fifteen. We'll still make a good amount of money."

"I'll think about it."

Dylan waved at a few people she knew. She sat watching the crowd of people dancing. It killed the time, and she occasionally pointed something funny out to Sarah. She swallowed the last of her beer and stood to leave.

"Would you like one more? It's my round."

"I should go."

"Why? You said you didn't have any plans for the evening."

"Okay. But one more is my limit."

DYLAN FELT HER body moving, but she had no control over it. She listened to the beat of the song and swayed her arms above her head. She felt the sensation of hands roaming over her body. It felt wrong. Her head spun, and she tripped over her feet. She felt the arms tighten around her. She moved her feet clumsily to the rhythm. *1, 2, 3...1, 2, 3...1, 2, 3 – wave hands in the air. I can do this. I've got the beat.*

HELEN AND JO walked into the club.

"We haven't been here in ages. God, some things never change, it still smells the same," Jo said.

"I hear you. The smell of sweat, smoke, and a million perfumes. But it's the only gay bar in town so suck it up." Helen ordered the drinks.

"Babe, I thought you said Dylan and Sarah had split up."

Helen paid for the beers. "They have. I told you that's why I spent most of last week with her." Helen turned her attention to Jo. "Why?"

"Unless I'm mistaken, and I doubt it, isn't that Dylan and Sarah gyrating together?"

"Where?"

"By the speaker. Look where I'm pointing. I swear it's them."

"No way. I see it, but I don't believe it. The last time I spoke to Dylan she was ranting and raving about Sarah. Something's wrong. Honey, would you mind if I went to check on her?"

"Go."

DYLAN TURNED WHEN she felt another pair of hands on her body.

"I didn't know you were coming here tonight."

"Hel...Helen. I'm...d...da...dancing."

"I can see that. Do you want some water? Maybe, you should come and sit down for a minute. Catch your breath."

"Leave her alone. She doesn't need you. She's got me," said Sarah.

"How could you let her get like this?" Helen yelled, over the music. "How much has she had to drink? She's wasted. How did she get this way? What did you do to her?"

"I didn't do shit. In case you've forgotten, we're no longer an item. For your information, I turned up, and she was already like this. I'm just looking out for her."

"You're certainly keeping a *close* eye on her. Let her go. Jo and I will take her home."

"No. I'll do it. I have to pick something up from the house, anyway. It'll save me a trip tomorrow."

"Okay. You'll never get her to your car like this. I'll take this arm, and you grab the other. Dylan, we're going to take you out of here."

"No. I have to go potty. Don't want to leave." Dylan staggered and leaned heavily on Helen.

"I'll take you." Helen took a step toward the restroom. "Sarah, she doesn't need the both of us in there. Wait here. If I need your help, I'll come and get you." Helen had to shout to be heard above the music.

"Sure. It's probably your only chance to get your hands inside her pants."

"You, bitch. If she wasn't in such a state, I'd beat the shit out of you."

"Honey, ignore her. She's trying to goad you," Jo whispered in Helen's ear. "I'll help you with Dylan. I hope we get her to the bathroom in time." They covered the rest of the distance to the restroom.

"Thanks." Helen opened the restroom door.

"How'd she get like this?"

"I've no idea. She's going to have one hell of a hangover."

"I can see that. She's barely coherent. I've never seen her like this. It's so out of character."

"I know. She's going to be so embarrassed at the next game. I saw some players from other teams watching her."

After Dylan finished on the toilet, Jo and Helen walked her over to the basin. Jo wet some paper towels and wiped Dylan's face. "How's it going? Long time no see. What have you been doing to yourself?"

"Went dancing. Drank beer with Sarah. Feel...feel...sick," Dylan groaned, hanging her head over the sink.

Helen pulled a water bottle out of her pocket. She held it under Dylan's mouth. "Drink some of this. Please. Come on, Dylan, try for me."

Dylan took a few sips of water and then turned quickly. She rushed back to the toilet and heaved.

"She's going to regret this tomorrow morning," Jo said, after the second bout of vomiting.

"Tell me about it, and we've got a game tomorrow."

"She might not make that."

"I know. I'm more concerned about how she got this way. I'm worried something happened between Cory and her. I can't think of any other reason why she'd be here drinking. I mean, if she'd wanted to go dancing she could have called us."

"Didn't she come with Sarah?"

"Nope. Sarah said she met her here and that she was already like this. It doesn't add up. Do you think we should leave her in Sarah's hands?" Helen grabbed a few paper towels and held them out for Dylan.

Dylan held onto the wall and walked toward Helen. Her head hurt. Her stomach ached. She took the offered towels and wiped her mouth.

"She'll be fine. They looked like they made up. Ask her," Jo said.

Dylan let Helen support her against the wall. Her focus was blurred, and she had to squint several times to clear her vision.

"Hey buddy. How you feeling?" asked Helen.

"Like shit."

"Sarah's going to drive you home. Is that okay?" Helen placed her arm around Dylan's shoulders. "You smell like crap. Are you ready to go?"

"I love you, Helen," Dylan said, her voice muffled by her friend's shoulder. "I love Jo, too. I love Cory, best of all."

"I know. We love you, too. Do you want to go home with Sarah?"

Dylan nodded. "She's my friend, too. We made friends, and she danced with me."

Helen looked at Jo. "We'll let her go, but I'm checking on her first thing tomorrow." They all walked out of the bathroom toward Sarah.

"Took you long enough," Sarah snapped.

"She threw up. She's all yours."

"She always was," replied Sarah.

"Bitch!" Helen yelled and walked to the bar.

Chapter
Twenty-Five

CORY DIALED DYLAN'S home number.

"Hello?"

Cory didn't recognize the voice. Her heartbeat increased. It was just past seven in the morning, Dylan's time. "Who is this? Can I speak to Dylan?"

"No. It's Sarah. Dylan's still sleeping. I'll give her a message when she wakes up. It could be a while, though. We had a very busy night. Can I ask who's calling?"

Cory's stomach swirled. She held her hand over it. "It's Cory," she said, and then hung up. She ran to the bathroom.

DYLAN GROANED. THE ringing of the phone had woken her. She opened her eyes, but immediately closed them, blocking out the sunlight. She licked her lips. Her mouth was parched, like the Sahara—dry and rough. Fragments of the previous evening flashed in her head: the mall, the movie, the club, and Helen. *How the hell does Helen fit into this picture?* She moved slightly. She felt someone warm against her back—someone warm and naked. Adrenalin enabled her to sit up. "What the fuck." She turned and saw Sarah smiling at her.

"Good morning to you, too. You liked the 'f' word so much last night."

"Out!" Dylan pulled the bed sheet around her. She climbed off the bed and picked up their clothes, which were strewn over the bedroom floor. She threw them toward Sarah.

"It's hardly the time for modesty. I saw all of you, up close and personal last night. You do remember last night, don't you?"

Dylan trembled. Her headache hammered, and she could taste the remnants of vomit in her mouth. "I remember some of it...sort of. We went to the mall, watched a movie, and then went for a drink. From there, it gets fuzzy. Wait a minute, you got me drunk."

"You got yourself drunk. It's not like I held your mouth open and poured the beer down your throat. You were a very willing participant. Oh, before I go, Cory phoned a few minutes ago. I gave her your regards."

Dylan dropped to the floor, holding her sore head in her hands. "She called? You answered?" *What have I done?* "Go. Get the fuck out of my house."

"It's *our* house. I have as much right as you do to be here." Sarah gathered her clothing and left the bedroom.

Dylan curled into a ball. *I need to talk to Cory, but what do I say? What did I do?* She surveyed the room and her nakedness. All the evidence pointed to her worst fear. *Fuck, I slept with Sarah.*

CORY SAT BY the toilet, having thrown up her breakfast and lunch. The sound of Sarah's voice echoed around her head. *They had a busy night. What's that supposed to mean? Don't jump to conclusions. It could mean anything. Trust Dylan; ignore Sarah.* Cory stood up shakily and went to her bedroom. She changed into her gym gear and headed out. As she slammed the door shut, the shrill ring of the house phone sounded. Cory paused briefly on the doorstep but then continued to her car.

DYLAN ALTERNATED BETWEEN Cory's home number and her cell. Every time, she got voice-mail. She checked her e-mail. There were no current messages. She opened an earlier message.

```
Cory Williams
Good morning

Hi, D,
     Last night went well. We watched the new Mission
Impossible. It was good. Sam didn't talk too much,
but he didn't give me any attitude. It's made a huge
difference in the house. He was actually civil this
morning.
     I'm going to call you later—hopefully, not too
early for you. Sam's playing golf this lunchtime, so
I'll probably ring when he's out. We'll have more
privacy. The walls in this house are paper thin.
     I hope your evening in was good and you got some
well-deserved sleep.
Love, Cory
```

Dylan dialed Cory's number again. There was no answer. She went into the bathroom and turned on the shower. She stood in front of the mirror and checked her body for marks. Sarah had a habit of leaving scratch marks. Dylan was pleased to see none. She showered and dressed more slowly than usual. She walked into the kitchen and turned on the coffee machine. She looked up when she heard the door bell. "Come in. The door's open," she yelled, wincing as pain pierced her head. All she wanted to do was lie down and sleep some more.

"You're a sight for sore eyes. I never thought I'd see you walking this morning. Does your head hurt?" asked Helen.

"Like a bitch. How'd you know?"

"We were there," Jo replied, taking a seat at the breakfast bar. "We've been worried about you."

"Nice to see you, Jo. Was I that bad?" Dylan asked.

"Worse," Helen said, "but, at least, you got home okay. I gotta say, I had doubts about Sarah's intentions."

Dylan slumped into the seat next to Jo. "I'm not sure about that. I woke up next to her this morning...naked." She blushed.

"You didn't. No way," Helen said.

Dylan shrugged. "I'm not sure if anything happened, but I know I was naked. I don't have any recollection of last night past the third beer. I only went for one drink. The next thing I know, I woke up in bed with Sarah spooning me."

Jo patted Dylan on the back. "That doesn't mean anything."

"We were both naked. I can't believe I slept with Sarah. Cory'll never talk to me again."

"Calm down. Did Sarah actually say you'd done anything?" Helen asked. "To be honest, I don't think you could have managed it. You could barely stand on your own two feet after you threw up."

Dylan groaned. "Please tell me I at least managed to do that in the restroom."

Jo nodded. "Yeah, after we'd helped you to take a pee."

Dylan buried her head in her arms. "Kill me now."

"Dylan, you were wasted. I'd bet my last dollar you were sleeping like a baby by the time you left the parking lot. Sarah is just playing with you."

"I hope you're right. Not that Cory will ever believe this. It's just like you see in the movies or read in a book."

"What has Cory got to do with this? She's clear across the ocean. Unless you tell her, how's she going to find out?" Helen asked.

"She called this morning."

"And?" Helen prompted.

"And Sarah answered," Jo guessed.

Dylan nodded. "You got it. I was still unconscious. Cory's not taking my calls, so I have no idea what Sarah said. I do know the next time I see Sarah, I'm going to wring her neck. What I don't understand is how I got so drunk. I swear I only had three beers."

"What I don't understand is why you went out on your own," Helen said.

Dylan looked at Helen. Her right eyebrow rose questioningly.

"Why are you looking at me like that?" Helen asked.

"I didn't go on my own. I went with Sarah. I'd never be desperate enough to go to the club on my own."

Helen banged her hand on the table. Dylan glanced from Helen to Jo. She watched them making eye-contact with each other. "What am I missing? You two look like you're having some kind of secret conversation."

"When we asked Sarah last night how she'd let you get so shit-faced, she told us she'd found you that way. She didn't tell us she went to the club with you. So what happened? The last time I spoke to you, Sarah and you weren't speaking."

"We weren't, until yesterday. Sarah called me at work and wanted to talk about the house. We met, had dinner, and saw a movie. She asked me to the club. She said Michelle, her new girlfriend, was meeting her there. I only went because she said she'd discuss the price of the house with me."

"I don't think her girlfriend showed up. I didn't see anyone with Sarah last night. She left with you," Helen said.

"Who bought the drinks?" Jo asked.

"I got the first ones, and Sarah bought the second round. And I think she got the third ones, too. Yeah, I'd gone to the restroom, and when I got back, she had been to the bar. After that, everything gets fuzzy."

"Did you leave your drinks at any time?" asked Jo.

"No. Like I said, I was in the restroom when Sarah bought the third one. Why?"

"I think Sarah spiked your drink."

"It makes sense, Dylan. You were wasted last night. Three beers wouldn't make you that bad," Helen said.

Dylan clenched her fists. "You wait until I get hold of her. She'll wish she'd stayed away from me. I'm tempted to call Michelle and tell her exactly what her girlfriend was up to last night."

"I don't think she'd mind. I know someone who used to date Michelle. Apparently, as long as the person earns a decent salary and has a beating heart, she'll date them. I think Sarah's realized that she's not the apple of Michelle's eye. In fact, rumor has it that her eyes roam, almost on a daily basis. I tell you, there are no secrets in the gay world," Jo said.

"Speaking of no secrets. That reminds me, Dylan, you might want to wear your thick skin later. Half the Bears team saw your attempts at dancing last night. They'll probably give you a ration of shit during the game."

"Can things get any worse?"

IT WAS EARLY afternoon by the time Cory returned home. The weather was dismal and prevented her performing any tasks she had planned in the garden. She placed her gym bag in the hallway and noticed the flashing lights on her answering machine. There were three messages. She pressed play.

> Cory, it's Dylan. When you get this message could
> you call me?

Cory pressed the erase button. The next message began.

> Hi Cory, it's Dylan, again. Your e-mail said you
> would be around this morning. I was hoping we could
> talk.

Cory noted the stressed tone in Dylan's voice. She deleted the message and listened to the third.

> It's eight my time. Give me a call when you get
> this. Please.

Cory deleted it. Cory ran upstairs and picked up her mobile. In her haste to leave that morning, she'd left it on her bureau. She entered the security code and called the voice-mail service.

> Cory, it's Dylan. Give me a call when you get
> this. I love you.

> Cory, I'm worried about you. I know you spoke to
> Sarah. It's not what it sounds like. Trust me.

> Cory, I'm going nuts. Helen and Jo have filled me
> in, and I think Sarah set me up. Call me, and let me
> explain.

Cory deleted the messages and picked up the cordless phone.

"HELLO, DYLAN SPEAKING."

"It's me."

Dylan blew out a relieved breath. She walked into the kitchen for some privacy. Helen had left for the game, but Jo had stayed to keep an eye on her. "I'm so glad you called. I've been worried sick."

"So have I. I couldn't believe I spoke to Sarah this morning."

"What did she say?"

"She said you were sleeping and that you guys had been busy. She kind of implied something had happened between you. How did she end up at the house so early this morning?"

"She called me yesterday. She wanted to talk about the house. We went out for dinner and then to a movie. I figured if you and Sam could go out together, it wouldn't hurt for Sarah and me to do the same. Then she asked me to go for a beer."

"And?"

"I think she spiked my drinks, because the next thing I knew, I woke up this morning with her."

"You slept with her?"

"No...yes...I have no idea." Dylan began to cry. "I'm sorry. I swear I didn't plan any of this." She saw Jo signaling for the phone.

"Let me talk to her," Jo said.

"Hi, Cory, I'm Jo, Helen's partner. I just wanted to tell you that from what Helen and I saw last night, Dylan was drugged. She was barely conscious when she left the club. Sarah was so adamant about taking her home, we're sure nothing happened. Don't blame Dylan— Sarah's a psycho."

"Thanks, Jo. Can you put Dylan back on?"

Jo passed the phone back to Dylan. "Cory, trust me. Nothing happened."

"I know, Dylan. I trust you, and you don't owe me any explanations. It's not like I'm even your girlfriend. From what Jo says, you were in a pretty bad way. How are you feeling now?"

Dylan groaned. "Like a bulldozer is banging around inside my head. I made quite a fool of myself last night. If I ever show my face around there again, it'll be a miracle."

"Now I'm disappointed. I thought you were going to take me out to my first gay club."

Dylan smiled, the first heartfelt one of the day. "Since you asked so nicely, I could be persuaded. Thank you for understanding. I was so scared I'd lost you. As for you not being my girlfriend, I thought that was a given now that we're both single, or am I presuming too much?"

"You want to be my girlfriend, huh? It's definitely an offer I can't refuse."

"Thank God, we have all that settled. It sucks being so far away. I can't even give you a make-up hug or kiss."

"I know, but we'll be together soon."

Chapter
Twenty-Six

DYLAN PACED THROUGH the international arrival lounge. She checked each flight arrival screen as she passed it. When the status of Cory's plane changed to 'landed,' she fiddled with the bunch of roses in her hand and turned her attention to the arrival doors. After an agonizing thirty minutes, the doors opened, and the first wave of passengers came through. Dylan ran her fingers through her hair, straightened her shirt, and leaned against the railing.

Dylan saw Cory before Cory saw her. She waved, moved around the edge of the barrier and pulled Cory into a hug. "God, I've missed you so much. You smell awesome." She could feel Cory's arms tighten around her. She buried her head further into Cory's neck.

"Liar — I stink. Seven hours trapped in a canister does nothing for one's personal hygiene. You, on the other hand, smell freshly showered and look wonderful. Definitely a sight for sore eyes." Cory held Dylan at arms length. "Your hair's grown longer. It looks good."

"Thanks." Dylan blushed slightly under the minute examination. "These are for you. They're a little smashed. I got nervous waiting. How was the flight?" She handed Cory the flowers and hugged her again.

"Thanks for the flowers. As for the flight, it was long and boring, but necessary. I breezed through passport control, but we got held up in the baggage claim area. It took them ten minutes to get any luggage on the conveyor belt."

Dylan noted the bags under Cory's eyes and her attempt to stifle a yawn. "Did you get any sleep on the plane?"

Cory shook her head.

"Maybe you can take a nap in the truck on the way."

They headed for the exit. Dylan pointed Cory in the direction of her truck. She placed Cory's suitcase in the back of the truck and laughed when Cory headed for the driver's side of the car. "Whoa — slow down there. You've only been in America an hour and you're ready to drive?"

"Force of habit. I forget you guys are arse backwards. Nice truck. It suits you."

"Thanks. I'm guessing that was a compliment."

Cory grinned. "Yes it was. I just couldn't see you in a small car. Your body has a certain presence to it. I remember how cramped you were in my rust bucket."

"You're right about that." Dylan opened the passenger door. "This is your side, ma'am." As Cory moved to climb into the cab, Dylan placed her arms around Cory's waist and pulled her into a hug. Her lips tentatively sought Cory's. She deepened the kiss. Dylan remembered where they were, and slowly broke the kiss. "Welcome to America."

"What a welcome," Cory said. "That was a wonderful first kiss."

"There's more where that came from but you look exhausted."

Dylan successfully negotiated the traffic detours of the Big Dig, as the construction around Boston's Logan Airport was called by the locals. She smiled when she heard a gasp from Cory.

"Wow."

Dylan glanced at Cory. "It's pretty, isn't it?" She gestured toward the skyline of Boston.

"It's beautiful. The lights make it even more attractive, especially the neon blue on the clock tower. It kind of looks familiar."

"Ever watch Ally McBeal?"

"Yeah. I loved that show. Some of the women in it were hot. That should have clued me in to my sexuality, huh?"

"Maybe. Anyway the show was filmed in Boston. I think the clock is in the opening credits or was shown in some of the episodes."

As they drove over the bridge heading north out of the city, Dylan pointed out more sights.

"Dylan, I thought you lived south of Boston. Why are we heading north?"

"I wanted to surprise you. Helen recommended a lesbian-owned inn in New Hampshire. It caters specifically for women, no men are allowed. I wanted us to spend time together properly. We won't have to hide our relationship when we're together. I hope that's okay with you?"

"It's perfect. I'm glad you thought of everything. It's going to be great not having to think before I touch you, and I definitely want to touch you."

"I'm excited, too. However, it's too far to drive tonight, so I booked us a room at a motel just south of the New Hampshire state line."

"How many days are we staying at the inn?"

"I booked us in for three days. Then on Tuesday, we're heading into the New Hampshire White Mountains. My friends own a house, and no one is there this week. We'll be heading back to Massachusetts and my place on Saturday."

Cory yawned. "You're a dark horse. You kept all these plans a secret. Thank you for being so thoughtful."

"You're welcome. It's going to be a good hour until we reach the motel. You should close your eyes and get some rest."

"I will. I'm so tired."

Dylan could see, from the corner of her eye, Cory's head nodding.

She used her free hand to gently push Cory's head back against the seat. She didn't want her to have a crick in her neck when she woke up.

It was nearly ten-thirty by the time Dylan located the motel. There had been an accident on one of the roads, and she'd sat in traffic for a while. Dylan left Cory sleeping and went to check in. Dylan returned to the truck and opened the passenger door. She attempted to pick Cory up but couldn't get Cory out of the seat. Giving up, she nudged Cory. "We're here." Dylan helped Cory down from the cab. Their room was a short walk from the truck. "How're you feeling?"

"I'm exhausted. I can barely keep my eyes open."

Dylan opened the room door, motioning for Cory to go ahead of her. "Why don't you lie down? I'll get the bags. You're bound to be tired. Your body's on England time. It's nearly four in the morning over there."

Dylan retrieved the bags and then sat on the edge of the bed and watched Cory sleep. After a few minutes, she shook Cory gently. "I think you should get undressed."

"Can't wait to ravish me, huh?"

"You wish. Besides, some date you are. You were asleep within ten minutes of being in my company. Now I know how interesting I am."

"I'm sorry, D. I tried to stay awake but..."

Dylan placed her lips over Cory's, silencing her words. She kissed Cory tenderly, and then pulled away. "I was joking. Get changed. It's nearly eleven—way past your bedtime." She looked on, as Cory sat up and stretched her arms over her head.

"I feel bad."

"For what?"

"We haven't seen each other in weeks, and I fall asleep. It's hardly romantic."

Dylan reached out her arms and pulled Cory into a fierce hug. "Cory, relax. We haven't even had an official first date. All I want is to cuddle up to you and get the best night's sleep I've had in weeks. So, go and use the bathroom, and hurry back."

Dylan unpacked her overnight bag while she waited for Cory. She used the bathroom and got into bed beside Cory. She opened her arms and Cory cuddled up to her.

Cory kissed Dylan's cheek. "Thank you for understanding. I was nervous about this night. I wasn't sure what expectations you had."

Dylan sighed audibly. *Life doesn't get any better than this.* She could feel Cory's breath on her neck. "I don't have any expectations. I've dreamed about this moment a thousand times over the past few weeks, and it's perfect. I'm excited to show you around New Hampshire and Massachusetts, and I want you wide awake to enjoy the sights." She moved down the bed slightly so her head was level with Cory's. She kissed Cory. "Go to sleep. You're driving me crazy." Dylan rested her head against Cory's and held her body closer. In minutes, Cory's breathing evened out. Dylan shut her eyes. It didn't take long before she joined Cory in sleep.

CORY WOKE TO the pressure of her swollen bladder. She opened her eyes. The room was dark. Dylan's arms were wrapped possessively around her. She unfolded Dylan's arms gently and climbed out of bed. She picked up her digital watch and pressed the mode until she got the dual time zone button. It was two o'clock. She walked toward the bathroom and tripped over a bag. She landed noisily on the floor. "Ouch," she said, rubbing her legs.

"Are you okay?" Dylan asked. "You startled me."

"I'm sorry I woke you. Go back to sleep." Cory rubbed her ankle. "I tripped over a bag. I'm fine."

"No, it was my fault. I didn't think to clear stuff off the floor. Come back to bed. It's the middle of the night."

"I know. Usually, I sleep through the night, but nobody told my body. I'll be back in a jiffy."

Dylan shifted in the bed. She plumped her pillows, closed her eyes, and tried to summon up the dream she'd been in. The mattress dipped beside her and Cory's arm slid under her body. She smiled. *This is no dream. This is reality.* She turned and took Cory in her arms, receiving a kiss on the cheek. "Someone's not sleepy anymore, I see."

"It's seven in the morning according to my internal body clock. I make that time for a good morning kiss."

"Just a kiss?" Dylan returned Cory's kiss, with more passion. Her tongue lingered around the entrance to Cory's mouth. She waited for the invite before plunging her tongue into Cory's warm mouth. She tasted mint. *Someone brushed her teeth.* Small groans escaped her throat as she felt Cory's hands wander up her body. "Good morning," she murmured, huskily.

"I've missed you," Cory said.

Dylan gasped as Cory ran her fingers up her back. "I missed everything about you. In fact, it's about time I introduced myself to certain areas of your body," Dylan said. She placed her hands on either side of Cory's head and lifted it gently. She met Cory's gaze. She saw want and desire, and hoped Cory knew how she felt.

Dylan slowly pulled Cory's head toward her and relished the feel of soft lips on hers. Tingling sensations rippled through to her core. The kiss was tentative at first. She let Cory's mouth and tongue set the pace. She savored the moment. Dylan moved her hands to the back of Cory's head, pulling her even closer. She ran her tongue along the bottom lip, gently probing for entry. She deepened the kiss, exploring Cory's mouth with her tongue and ran it over her teeth. She pulled away and continued to lightly nibble on the soft lips. She looked into Cory's eyes, asking an unspoken question. Her response was a nod.

"Are you sure?" Dylan asked.

"More than I've ever wanted anything in my life. Has anyone told you, you talk too much?" Cory pulled her into another kiss.

They rolled onto their sides, their mouths never leaving one other. Small kisses turned into deeper, longer ones, and after Cory had explored every available area on Dylan's face, she began to move down her neck, eliciting moans of pleasure. She pressed on the long torso and rolled Dylan over. She straddled her and gazed down at the beauty.

Cory moved her hands over Dylan's t-shirt and stopped at the bottom edge of the shirt. "I want to feel your skin. May I?"

"Be my guest."

Slowly, Cory inched her hands under and began to retrace the path her hands had taken. Her eyes never left Dylan's. She paused as she pulled the shirt to Dylan's neck.

"Let me help you." Dylan raised her body slightly off the bed, allowing her shirt to be pulled off.

"I was hoping to be the one to seduce you."

"I like to surprise you once in a while." Cory's gaze never left Dylan's breasts. Her hands moved to the soft, fleshy mounds. She rubbed and rolled the nipples between her thumb and fingers. Her partner's moans pushed Cory to pull and squeeze harder. She lowered her mouth onto a succulent breast. She sucked slowly, listening to Dylan's breath catch. Sucking harder and licking around the now dimpled surface, she marveled at how her touch affected Dylan. She moved her attention to the other breast. She sucked the nipple into her mouth and then bit down gently.

Dylan's body was burning up, the fire between her legs was increasing, and she needed to free herself of the shorts she was wearing. She wanted skin on skin. Expertly, she flipped Cory over onto her back, reversing their positions. Then she pulled her into a sitting position and lifted the nightshirt over her head. Dylan paused in her movements to stare at how beautiful Cory was naked. Her breasts were pert; the nipples pink and very erect. Dylan bent to suckle on one of them, tasting her. It was intoxicating. She moved onto the other breast and slowly pushed Cory back down on the bed.

Dylan allowed Cory's hands to wander over her body. She moved her hands to lower her shorts and slipped them off. Then she turned her attention to Cory's underwear. She slid her body down and, taking the edge of the panties in her mouth, she edged them down Cory's body. As her head passed the tiny blonde curls, she smelled Cory's arousal. She paused and nuzzled her head in the curls, inhaling and kissing as she did so. She continued to kiss her way down the smooth legs. As she reached the tips of Cory's toes, she took the panties off and waved them. "Do you know how many dreams I've had of this moment?"

Cory shook her head. "No, but why don't you reenact them?"

Dylan chuckled. "Now there's an offer I'll never refuse." She retraced her kisses back up, pausing to tickle the back of Cory's knees. As she reached the strong muscular thighs, she stroked each one, which caused Cory to slightly open her legs and gave Dylan more soft, tender skin to caress. The insides of the legs were silky smooth and, as she kissed her way up, she could taste some of the wetness that had dripped there.

"You're so wet, and you taste so good," Dylan purred. She glanced up to see Cory gripping the bed sheet.

"You...you're...the...one...do...ing...it...to...me," Cory stuttered, as another sensitive spot was licked. "You make me so wet. Please touch me there, kiss me there, do anything there, before I explode," she gasped.

Not needing any further encouragement, Dylan lowered her head and moved even lower down the bed. She opened Cory's legs wider and paused before licking the center. It was like nectar, sweet, with a hint of salt. She licked all around the swollen area and then placed her tongue inside her lover. She felt Cory's hips push up and heard her groan with need.

"That feels wonderful."

Dylan alternated between licking in and out of Cory and moving her tongue over the swollen clitoris. Dylan could feel Cory swelling more and getting harder.

"Yes. Yes...oh God...oh God," Cory panted, "I'm coming. I'm coming. I'm coming."

Dylan continued to lick until she felt the pressure of Cory's legs against her head. Taking this as a signal to stop, she climbed slowly up Cory's body, kissing a trail, until she reached her lips. She kissed them gently and gazed into green eyes dilated with passion. "You okay?" Dylan asked. She kissed Cory slowly and then pulled away, waiting for a response.

"Hmmph," Cory said, "I'll be fine once I find my brain. I think it just vacated my head. Now I know what people are talking about when they say an orgasm can blow your head off. To use my favorite American saying, that was awesome—you were awesome. Thank you."

Cory stroked her hands slowly down Dylan's back. She kissed her, tasting and smelling her own arousal on Dylan's moist lips. She probed Dylan's mouth with her tongue and put her hand on the front of her new lover's muscled body. She traced the muscles of Dylan's stomach. She moved her hand lower, until she felt the slightly coarser curls. She paused. Tantalizingly, she ran her exploring fingers through them.

"You're killing me. Touch me, please."

Cory's fingers continued south until she felt the slick wetness. She dipped her fingers in it, and then slowly raised her index finger back up tasting Dylan's arousal. She moved her hand down again, wiping a finger through the moisture. She brought her wet finger to Dylan's lips.

"Taste yourself."

Cory placed her digit in Dylan's mouth, enjoying the sensation of Dylan's teeth and tongue against her finger. Then she placed her hand back down and slipped her fingers through the wet until she reached Dylan's vagina. She slipped her middle finger in and pulled it out unhurriedly. She replaced one finger with two, moving her fingers in and out, each time increasing the pressure and tempo. She could hear Dylan's breathing hitch, and at times, gasp for breath. Cory maneuvered her hand, allowing space for her thumb to place pressure on the engorged clitoris. Cory moved with her partner feeling the flesh around her fingers tightening. She increased the pressure on Dylan's hardened bud holding her tightly with her other arm, as Dylan's orgasm pulsed through her.

Cory kissed Dylan's face and lips. She left her fingers inside Dylan, feeling the vaginal muscles pulse against them — strong at first, and then lessening. Slowly, she removed her hand, and moved her leg up to replace her arm against Dylan's groin.

"I love you," Cory whispered in her partner's ear.

"I love you, too."

A FEW HOURS later, Cory lay in Dylan's arms, their legs tangled together.

"You okay?" Dylan murmured. Her body was exhausted, but her mind was stimulated.

"I'm fine, for the millionth time of answering." Cory nibbled the edge of Dylan's mouth. "I'm having a fantastic time. Can't you tell?"

Dylan raised an eyebrow and grinned wickedly. "At first I wasn't sure if the screams were from pain or from ecstasy, but from the way you grasped my hair and pleaded for God, I assumed you'd found religion." She watched as Cory blushed crimson and hid her head under the covers. "Hey, no hiding. I'm sorry. I was teasing. I didn't mean to embarrass you."

Cory lifted her head. "After what we just did together, I have no idea why I'm embarrassed. I guess old habits die hard. I'm not used to talking about sex. It was wonderful, D."

"I like it when you call me that. It sounds so loving when you say it." Dylan kissed Cory's fingers, only stopping when she heard a sniffle. She lifted up onto an elbow and looked at Cory's glistening eyes. "What's wrong? I didn't hurt you, did I?"

Cory shook her head. "No. I guess I'm overwhelmed and very tired."

Dylan turned onto her back and opened her arms. "Come here. I understand. The wait nearly killed me. I was so lonely, and I never thought this day would come. It feels so good to be with you. No one will ever separate us." Dylan felt Cory settle against her. She whispered soothing, loving words until Cory stopped crying and fell asleep.

Chapter
Twenty-Seven

CORY RUBBED HER rumbling stomach. "I'm starving. I thought we were going to stop for breakfast after we left the motel," she whined. "My internal clock thinks it's well past lunch time. Technically, I've missed breakfast and lunch." She turned her eyes away from the beautiful countryside outside the truck window and looked at Dylan. "Quit smiling at me. I swear, we could have driven to the tip of England and back by now."

"I'm not smiling at you. I'm smiling with you. I promise we'll stop at the next store or station. I would have stopped earlier, but you were quite happily snoring away."

"I don't snore. It's not my fault you wore me out." She caught Dylan's eye and pouted.

"Has anyone told you how cute you are when you sulk?" Dylan returned her gaze to the highway. "And it wasn't me who was awake at two this morning. Please tell me you're not going to be keeping British time the whole two weeks you're here."

"I hope not." Cory looked out the window again. "Are we still in Massachusetts?"

"No. I was going to wake you up when we crossed the state line into New Hampshire, but you were sound asleep. What do you think of the New England scenery, so far?"

"It's beautiful, quite breathtaking, although I've seen more alpine trees than I'll ever need to see in my life. How far away is the next hotel? You'd think there'd be a gas station or something out here."

"You must be blessed. I see the hallowed golden arches up ahead. Would you like a McDonald's breakfast?"

"I'll take anything that serves food and has a toilet."

When the truck stopped, Cory leaned across her seat toward Dylan and kissed her.

Dylan broke the kiss. "If you keep that up, we'll be making love right here, and your second night in America will be spent in jail for indecent exposure. Let's go get you something for that insatiable appetite of yours."

DYLAN CHECKED HER written instructions and took a sharp left, causing Cory to slide in her seat. "Sorry. I miscalculated the mileage. I think we're here."

"No worries. Good lord, it's spectacular. It looks like a picture postcard. I definitely need to get the camera out."

Dylan drove down the winding country road. As they turned the corner, a huge colonial house came into view. "Welcome to the Woodland Inn," said Dylan. She parked the truck.

Dylan handed Cory her suitcase while she carried the other bags. She led the way to the inn entrance. A stocky, older lady met them at the door. "Hello. One of you must be Dylan Matthews." She held her hand out.

Dylan placed a bag on the ground, and firmly shook the offered hand. "I'm Dylan, and this is Cory. You sure have a wonderful place here."

"I'm Kate. My partner, Judy, will be here later. I'm glad you like it. Let me give you a tour. Leave your bags here. They'll be safe."

Kate led them through the small dining area, past the kitchen, and into a living room. "Here's where some of the guests like to get together and watch TV or movies." She cast her arm toward a cabinet that was filled with videotapes and a few discs. "We have quite a collection."

They moved back to the middle of the room. Kate pointed to a door. "That's where the hot tub is. The rules are simple. Most couples spend an hour in there. You sign up on the door. Just remember to shower before entering, and no oils. It spoils the water."

"Okay," Dylan replied, catching Cory's eye.

"There's a CD player in there, in case you want to play your favorite music...or drown out any noises. Don't move the player. It's sitting where there's no danger of water getting in it."

"Cory, do you want to sign up for an afternoon dip?" Dylan whispered. Cory nodded enthusiastically.

"Young love. Ain't it grand?" Kate continued with the tour. She showed Cory and Dylan the pool area. "It's too cold to have the pool open this time of year, but the grills are available, and the weather has been pretty good. We have a few other couples taking advantage of the Easter specials." They continued walking around the front of the house and returned to where they had dropped their bags. "I'll show you to your room."

Dylan picked up Cory's suitcase and her own bag. She left Cory with the backpacks.

"My hero," Cory said in Dylan's ear, tapping Dylan on the ass as she passed.

They followed Kate up the stairs and down a short corridor. Kate opened a door. "It's the best room we have. I hope you enjoy your stay."

"Wow," Cory said as she walked past Kate into the spacious room.

Dylan shook Kate's hand. "Thanks for the tour and for choosing the room. It's beautiful." Dylan surveyed the room more intently. The most eye-catching feature was a huge four-poster bed, draped with lace curtains. She watched as Cory pulled the curtain open and ran her fingers over the bed spread.

"It's gorgeous, D."

"Yeah. The brochure doesn't do it justice." Dylan dropped the bags at the bottom of the bed and looked at the ornate, open fireplace. "I hope you know how to make a fire."

Cory shook her head. "Nope. The only fire I know how to make is a gas one. Turn the dial and press the knob."

Dylan laughed. "I hear ya. We'll have to find other ways to keep warm." She poked her head into the bathroom. "Whoa, Cory, come look at this."

Cory looked over Dylan's shoulder. "You've got to be kidding me. This is all ours?" The bathroom was huge. "I swear this shower could fit half a rugby team and still have room to move. I can't wait to try it out." Cory wrapped her arms around Dylan. "It's fantastic. Oh my God, are these floors heated?"

"It feels like it. I'm still blown away by the size of the shower. I think I could lie stretched out and not touch the sides."

Dylan examined the many little trinkets and accessories in the bathroom. As she picked up each one, she passed it to Cory. When she felt Cory's arms wrap around her waist, enveloping her in a bear hug, she put down the small antique soap dish she was holding.

"Thank you so much. This place must have cost you a fortune."

"I'd have paid ten times what it cost if it meant I could hold you in my arms. Plus, if we do go the college route, I may not be able to spoil you as much as I want. This is my way of thanking you for what you're thinking of doing for us. I wish I could save every moment on film so I could replay it when you're gone."

"I know. One day someone is going to design a virtual reality tool like they have on *Star Trek*. You could store up memories and replay them whenever you want." Cory squeezed Dylan one more time before releasing her. "I love you."

"I love you, too, more than I thought I could ever love anyone. Do you want to unpack?"

"Sure. I'm looking forward to this week together. It's a shame you have to go back to work when we return."

"I know. I wish I'd saved more vacation time."

"It's a pity you guys don't have Easter Monday off like we do in England. We'd have another day together."

"I know, but I'm leaving work at lunch time that day," Dylan said.

"How come? You're already taking Wednesday afternoon off for my college interview."

Dylan continued to put her clothes in the dresser. "Don't be mad, okay?"

"Now I'm nervous. Whenever someone prefaces a sentence with those words it's always something awful."

"It's not bad, but it's not good. I should have told you yesterday, but I chickened out. I wanted to spend a few days with you before you freaked out."

"I will flip out soon if you don't spit out what you need to tell me."

Dylan stopped folding her clothes and turned to take Cory's hand. "A letter came for you yesterday. The college has had a test cancellation."

"A cancellation? Does that mean I can take the test here?"

Dylan nodded.

"On Monday afternoon? That's why you're taking time off?"

Again, all Dylan could do was nod in response. She closed her eyes waiting for the fall out—for her little spitfire to explode.

"Oh," Cory squeaked. She sat on the edge of the bed.

*One...two...three...*Dylan opened her eyes and saw the shocked expression on Cory's round, pale face. "Yeah, I couldn't decide if I was pleased or pissed about it. I was excited we got a slot on the test schedule, but annoyed because it might ruin this week. Looking on the bright side, we'll know the results of the test before the interview. Are you okay?" Dylan knelt in front of Cory and wrapped her arms around Cory's waist, winding her fingers into the belt loops on Cory's jeans. She pulled Cory closer to her.

"I'm a little nervous. No, that's a lie, I'm a lot nervous. I brought the study book, so maybe when we reach your friends' place, we could go over a few things. I've been doing better. My average is about four hundred on each test, so I need to gain another fifty points on each part. I've been getting better at the analogies. Sam helped me with the maths section a lot." Cory patted Dylan's head. "Stop worrying. It's going to make for a crappy week if we both dwell on it."

Dylan watched as Cory went back to her unpacking. She turned to her own bag and took out some small wrapped packages. She unwrapped them and placed the candles around the room.

"You certainly have enough of them," Cory commented.

"Yeah. Helen said the exact same thing when I bought them the other day. I guess I got carried away." Dylan looked at the various candles and put a few back in her bag.

"Take those back out. I was teasing. I think they look awesome, and I can't wait to light them later. I have great plans for us. How about we go for a walk? I'll tell you exactly what I want to do to you."

CORY AND DYLAN walked through the woods behind the inn.

"I'm desperate to see a moose. There's so much wildlife out here that we don't have in England. I want to take a photo in to show my students."

"I'm not sure you'll see one. Don't get your hopes up. We probably stand a better chance if we go out after dusk." Dylan squeezed Cory's hand. After a few minutes of enjoying the scenery and the company, Dylan asked the question she'd been debating about. "How was Sam when you left him?"

"A little down. Besides helping me study, he hasn't spoken to me much. He dropped me off at the airport and asked me to call when I landed. Shit! I forgot until now."

Dylan watched as Cory ran her fingers through her cropped hair. She flipped open her cell phone. "Damn. There's no signal. If there's no signal nearer the house, I'll ask Kate if you can use their phone."

"Okay and thanks for asking about Sam. How's Sarah been?"

Dylan made a face. "I'm never sure how she'll be until she opens her mouth. She has been quite pleasant since the club incident."

"Probably because you could have reported her. It was reckless of her. It still pisses me off. She could have killed you. Who spikes someone's drink in this day and age?"

"I know. It bothered me for a while, but in her twisted mind, she thought she could win me back. I was angry with her, especially because when you spoke to her on the phone, she implied she and I had sex. Anyway, she admitted it was all a set-up. Now, I'm praying the house sells so we can move on."

"Have you had much interest in the house?"

"We had a couple look at the place yesterday, and they seemed to like it. I'm hopeful they'll make an offer. Since Sarah, Helen, and I did all the repairs to the deck and painted the outside, it's looking really sharp."

"What does Sarah think?"

Dylan shrugged. "She didn't say anything about the house. She was too busy ranting about your visit."

"But she knew I was coming."

"I know. She told me a few weeks ago that she was fine with it. Then she saw the letter from the college about the test date."

"How'd she see the letter?"

"She came over to pick up her mail, and I had stupidly left your letter next to hers. When she saw it was addressed to you at our place, she was madder than a hornet. She was pissed I had mail coming to the house for you. She threatened to do something if she found out you stayed at the house." Dylan stopped speaking when she saw the fear cross Cory's face. "I'm sure she's just shooting her mouth off. I'm sorry. I shouldn't have said anything."

"Don't apologize. It's not your fault Sarah is acting like a maniac. I feel safe with you around. We'll deal with Sarah together, okay?"

"Okay." Dylan lifted Cory's hand and kissed it. "Thanks for understanding and for going ahead with the test. I know it's been tough studying while you're teaching. I wish there was a way I could move to

England. Then you wouldn't have to take the stupid exam."

"We've both searched the Internet high and low. Realistically, the job market in England is saturated with computer-savvy people, many of them coming out of the European Union. You're third in line for any job offered behind the British and European candidates. Can we not discuss the test anymore? Let's not ruin our wonderful day."

"Deal." Dylan checked her watch. "It's nearly time for our turn in the spa. We should head back to the inn, and you can call Sam."

THE HOT TUB bubbled around Cory and Dylan. Dylan had put on the CD she had made especially for their reunion. She looked over at Cory, entwining her feet with Cory's. "How was Sam?"

"He seemed okay. I kept the conversation brief. I don't want to think about him. I want to enjoy this moment with you. I've never heard this song before. It's good."

"The lyrics sum up everything I've been feeling about you." Dylan moved her shoulders against the water jet, feeling the pressure relax a tight muscle.

"Who sings the song? It's spooky how closely the words suit our situation."

"The group's called Savage Garden. The song is entitled 'I Knew I Loved You Before I Met You.'"

"Very fitting. I keep trying to work out when I fell in love with you. It was way before you came to visit. It's strange, but I think you've always been in my life somehow...maybe in my dreams."

"Really? It would explain the connection we felt from the beginning. I'm convinced we're soul mates."

Cory pulled the cork out of the wine bottle Dylan had brought along. She poured a little wine into two glasses. She passed one to Dylan and held her own up. "Here's to the future."

"The future," Dylan replied, before taking a sip. She placed her glass on the wooden deck behind her. There was something she wanted to taste more than the wine. She pulled Cory toward her and kissed her soundly. She continued to kiss down the tender neck. When her head reached the water line, she lifted her lover up out of the water and settled her onto the convenient corner ledge of the tub. Gently, Dylan pushed Cory into a lying position, and continued her journey down the trim torso.

"I can't imagine what they had in mind when they put this shelf here."

When Dylan reached the edge of Cory's bikini bottoms, she kissed the softer skin firmly before removing the garment. She placed Cory's legs over her shoulders and supported their weight. "Now what delights do we have here?" Dylan ran her tongue through soft pubic hair. She could smell Cory's musky scent. Slowly, she dipped her tongue into the folds and tasted the wetness. She inserted her tongue when she felt Cory lift toward her. Dylan moved her tongue in and out, each time bringing Cory closer and closer to the edge. She felt Cory's hips buck when she touched her clitoris lightly.

"God, that feels good. Oh my god, don't stop. I'm coming."

A few seconds later, Dylan felt the spasms against her tongue. She pressed harder, sucking the juices as she pushed her partner farther over the edge.

"Stop, D. Please, you're killing me."

Dylan licked her lips and pulled Cory to a sitting position. "I aim to please." She helped Cory get back into the water, hugging her tightly. She released her hold.

"You're a pig, but a lovable one. I think I should put my bikini bottoms back on. We broke the spa rules. See?"

Dylan followed Cory's pointing finger and read the rules concerning patrons remaining clothed for hygiene purposes. "What can I say? I'm a rule-breaker."

Cory leaned over the edge of the tub and grabbed her bikini bottoms.

Dylan watched as Cory stood in the warm water. The bubbles were frothing against the muscles of her stomach. "I wonder how many times that's been done in here?"

"Gross."

Dylan grinned like a Cheshire cat when she saw Cory's disgusted expression.

"I'm sure chlorine kills all the germs, but just in case, I think we should continue this in our room." Dylan got out of the tub and wrapped a towel around her waist. She held out her hand to Cory. "Let me help you."

Dylan took the CD out of the player and picked up their wine bottle and empty glasses. She waited for Cory to towel her body and then Dylan led the way out of the room. She saw two younger women sitting on the couch, stifling their giggles. One of them caught Dylan's eye. "Nice CD you were playing in there."

Cory blushed, buried her face in her towel, and rushed past Dylan.

Dylan caught up with her. "What was all that about?"

"D, if they could hear our CD, think about what else they heard."

She pulled Cory into her chest and wrapped her arms around her. She cocked her head slightly and stared at Cory. "Don't let them bother you. I hope they enjoyed the show. I know I did. How about a shower?"

Cory followed Dylan into their room and into the shower. Her embarrassment soon disappeared when she saw Dylan's toned, naked body. All she wanted was Dylan. She pulled Dylan's head down to hers. The water splashed over their faces. The pressure of the shower water made it difficult to breathe. Cory slowly drew back, positioning her head away from the flow of the water, and stared into deep blue orbs. "I never thought kissing someone could be so erotic and so fulfilling. I could kiss you forever and never get tired of it."

Dylan wiped the water from her face and smiled. "I know exactly what you mean. We seem to fit together."

Cory reached down and picked up the soap and a washcloth. She lathered the soap onto the cloth and passed it to Dylan. "Would you mind washing my back?"

"With pleasure."

Cory relaxed as the foam moved over her tired muscles. "Mmm, that feels great. What a way to wash the chlorine from me." Cory groaned in pleasure as Dylan hit a particularly tight muscle. Cory moved her body under the washcloth as Dylan continued the soap massage. She could feel Dylan increasing the pressure slightly whenever she felt the knots under her fingers. Cory stopped Dylan's hand. She took the washcloth out of her hands and dropped it on the shower floor. She picked up the soap and grinned wickedly at Dylan.

"Why did you stop me? I was just warming up."

"I felt these body parts," Cory said, as she held each of Dylan's breasts in her hands. "I think they require some special attention and no extra equipment." She rubbed the soap over Dylan's erect nipples. She followed the trail with her hands, gently kneading and squeezing as they moved. She watched the rise and fall of Dylan's chest and heard the moans escape Dylan's lips.

Cory trailed the soap down Dylan's firm stomach and traced the outline of Dylan's defined abs. She knelt in front of Dylan's soapy stomach, glad when the water washed the foam away. Cory slipped her tongue into Dylan's navel, tickling as she licked. She lifted her face to see Dylan's sapphire eyes gleaming with desire. "You'd look awesome with a belly ring." She felt Dylan shudder.

"Never gonna happen, but don't let me stop you from fantasizing."

Cory lowered down on her haunches and paused. "I'm a little nervous. I've...I've never done this on a woman before."

Dylan placed her hands on Cory's head, tilting it upwards. "You don't have to. Come back up here."

"No. You've shown me twice how great it feels. I want to do this."

"Okay. Go with your instincts—just do what comes naturally."

Cory inhaled Dylan's arousal and parted the dark curls. She saw how swollen Dylan was, and the sight sent tingles to Cory's own center. Cory placed her tongue into the folds and moved her hands to the back of Dylan's thighs. She felt Dylan's legs shake slightly as she increased her tongue pressure and felt a shiver pass through Dylan's body.

"I think you lied. You're doing awesome."

The encouraging words urged Cory on. She licked and tasted Dylan, devouring the soft flesh, probing deeper and deeper with her fingers. She felt the quivers and spasms against her fingers and pulled Dylan closer to her. She breathed in deeply, savoring the smell.

Dylan placed her hands under Cory's arms and helped Cory to her feet. Cory kissed Dylan before wiping the water off her face.

"That was some seduction." Dylan placed her arms around Cory. "Thank you."

"You're welcome."

Chapter
Twenty-Eight

CORY BREATHED IN the fresh mountain air as they drove down the winding lanes. She was extremely tired, but satiated. The three days at the inn had been glorious. During the days, they had hiked the mountain trails. In the evenings, they had made love by the fire, after taking advantage of Judy's fire lighting services. She had averaged four hours sleep each night. Cory stared at the vast mountain ranges. "These mountains make British ones look like mole hills." She heard a groan and turned to Dylan. "You okay?" Cory placed a hand comfortingly on Dylan's knee.

Dylan shook her head and yawned. "No. If we don't stop soon, I'm going to fall asleep behind the wheel."

"Would you like me to drive?"

"Are you serious? I'd love to stretch my leg muscles."

"Sure," Cory replied more confidently than she felt. "The roads are pretty wide. There are no great intersections, so I should be okay. It'll be safer than you falling asleep and driving us over the edge. How far away are we, anyway?"

Dylan steered the truck into a rest area and stopped. "I think we're about half an hour away. For the last time, are you okay with this?"

"I promise. But no sleeping, as I have no idea where I'm going."

They traded seats. Cory pulled the seat forward and saw Dylan grinning. "Stop it. I can't help being this small." She heard a full-blown laugh when she hit her left hand against the door.

"The stick shift is on this side of your body." Dylan said, pointing to Cory's right side. "Are you sure about this?"

Cory frowned. "Sorry. I'm working on instinct. It's very hard to change a habit after so many years." She placed her foot on the clutch and consciously moved her right hand to the gear stick. It took a little bit of maneuvering, but she found first gear. She glanced up to check the rear view mirror. It wasn't where she expected it to be. Dylan waggled her finger to the right, and Cory checked the mirror and then looked over her shoulder. She pulled onto the road and tried for second gear. Changing through the gears, as she picked up speed, Cory felt her confidence growing. She glanced quickly to her right. Dylan was holding the edge of her seat in a death grip. "Are you nervous? Where's your faith?"

"I'm okay." Dylan looked at the speedometer. "Uhh, Cory, we don't drive that fast on these types of roads. We're not in England now. Try keeping it under fifty."

"Oops."

Cory drove steadily. Driving on the right wasn't too difficult. However, she listened carefully to Dylan when she had to take turns, especially the left hand ones. They entered a small town. She slowed down when Dylan instructed her to and pulled the truck up in front of a large house.

"This is it. It looks a little weather beaten, but it's a good solid house."

"How old is it?" Cory stretched her arms above her head and leaned over to peck Dylan on the cheek.

Dylan opened her door and climbed out. She stretched and then lifted the hard cover off the bed of the truck to retrieve their bags. "I'd say it was late eighteen hundreds. First thing we need to do is turn the water on." Dylan unlocked the door.

Cory followed Dylan into the house and looked around. The décor was late 70's style, and the furniture looked like it had seen better days. She followed Dylan on the tour.

"A friend owns this?"

"Four friends. I used to be an owner. When we bought it ten years ago. We had great plans, but as the years passed and my friends got married, their priorities changed."

"How come you're not an owner anymore?"

"I got bought out when I went to Germany. My friends and I come up for skiing in the winter and the lake activities in the summer. It's a little rough, but it serves its purpose. It's got a roof, four walls, and keeps the wind, rain, and snow out, so we have no complaints. Maybe one day, we'll all take a vacation together and give the whole house a good paint job. Which room would you like to sleep in?"

Cory shrugged. "I don't mind. You know the place better than I do. Wherever you're sleeping, I'm right beside you."

"Or on top of me," Dylan said. "For such a short woman, you sure like to spread out."

"Are you complaining?" Cory pretended to sulk.

"Quit making faces at me. You know I love sleeping with you in spite of the fact you're a bed hog. Do you want to help me turn the water on?" Dylan headed to a small door in the living room.

Cory followed her, admiring the way Dylan's jeans hung from her hips. They walked down old, rickety wooden stairs, and Cory shivered when she placed her hand through a large cobweb. The basement reminded her of the cellars she'd seen in horror movies. She moved closer to Dylan and placed a finger inside one of the back pockets on Dylan's jeans. Her eyes focused on the axe that was leaning against the wall. She pulled slightly on the pocket.

"What's up?"

"Nothing."

"Sure. You're just clinging to my butt because you love me. Fess up."

Cory looked at the tool table. A smaller wood axe was lying next to a piece of wood. Cory's mind ran riot. *We're out in the middle of nowhere. Rachel warned me I could be dating an axe murderer. Who really knows anybody they meet on the Internet. Now you're being stupid – you'd die for Dylan. That's just it – you could possibly be dying.*

Her fear took over her sensibility, and she froze to the spot.

"Babe?" Dylan clicked her fingers in front of Cory's face.

Cory snapped out of her daze and held onto Dylan's offered hand. She followed Dylan back up the stairs. She sat on the sofa and let Dylan hold her.

"Do you want to tell me what's wrong?"

Cory buried her head in Dylan's chest. "Too embarrassed," she said.

Dylan placed her fingers under Cory's chin and tilted it upwards. "Through our e-mails and telephone calls over the past few months, I think I know more about you than you do. Cory, I've seen every bit of you. Now, something happened to you down in that cellar, and I want to know what. Come on, nothing can be that bad."

Cory enjoyed the soft texture of Dylan's long-sleeved shirt. She snuggled deeper, breathing in Dylan's scent and a faint fragrance of washing powder. "It's silly. I saw the axes, and my mind flashed back to all the warnings I got off people when I said I was meeting an Internet friend. They said I could be meeting an axe murderer."

"You think I could be an axe murderer?"

"No. However, you hear all the Internet myths, and I'm a coward. I got scared. We're out in the middle of nowhere. I imagined someone breaking in and attacking me. The basement reminded me of a horror movie. The one where Kathy Bates played a psycho woman."

"*Misery.*"

"That's it. It's my over-active imagination again. I swear I get frightened of my own shadow."

"They're just wood axes. It's what we use in the winter to chop wood. You really are a town girl, huh? Nobody will hurt you. You're safe with me. I promise I won't hurt you."

"Dylan, I know you'd never hurt me, as crazy as I sound at times. Can...can anyone get in through the cellar?" Cory trembled as she spoke.

"No...yes...I mean, you can access it through the barn, but it's locked. This is a tiny town. Most people don't even bother locking their doors, but I will. I'll make sure we close every window and door before bed tonight. Okay?" She kissed Cory's head. "I didn't realize, honey."

"I'm a wimp. I always have been. I never go anywhere on my own in the dark. I never stay on my own in the house, if I can help it. I don't know why, but the dark really scares me. Always has. Thanks for not laughing at me. Sam always did."

Dylan hugged Cory. "Well, I'm not Sam, and I never want to see you as scared as I saw you downstairs. Let's go and unpack the bags." She yawned. "Then maybe we could just take a little nap."

"I like the idea of taking a nap. I'm knackered."

"Good. Then later, I thought we could take the truck and get some Chinese food from the restaurant a few miles away."

"Sounds like a plan." Cory stood up and took Dylan's hand. She let Dylan lead her toward the bedroom.

CORY WOKE TO a crashing sound. Disoriented, she grabbed to her side. There was no sign of Dylan. Fear gripped her, and her legs turned to jelly. "Dylan," she whispered. "Dylan, where are you?" There was no sound inside the house. She could hear the wind whistling and the rattling of branches on the side of the house. The rain that had begun earlier in the evening had turned into a storm.

"Dylan." Cory slipped her feet out of the bed and stood on unsteady legs. She shivered. The temperature had dropped significantly since she'd fallen asleep. She slid a t-shirt over her naked body and crept slowly to the door. She peeked into the darkness of the living room. Feeling braver, she moved slowly into the room. She could see a sliver of light coming from the cellar doorway. She retreated back into the bedroom.

"Dylan," she called a little louder. Her hand fell to the side of the door. She felt around and grabbed a large wooden stick. She closed her hand firmly around it and stepped back into the living room. As she walked toward the cellar door, she heard the steps creak. Fear rose in her throat. "Dylan," she whispered. No sound came back. She heard the squeak of the cellar door latch, and Cory lifted the bat above her head. Knees trembling, arms twitching, she waited as the door creaked open.

DYLAN GASPED AS she saw the shadow in front of her. When the light from the cellar caught the figure bearing down on her, she noticed the bat. She moved like lightning as the wooden object swung toward her. "Whoa! Stop! Jesus!" The bat hit her on the back. The blow wasn't as severe as she'd expected. Years of getting hit on the ice had toughened her up somewhat. "Cory? Is that you?"

Cory dropped the bat. She looked at the crumpled body. "Bloody hell, Dylan. You scared the shit out me."

"I scared you? You're the one swinging bats around." Dylan groaned as she stood up straighter. "It's a good thing you Brits don't know how to swing a baseball bat. Who the hell did you think was down there?"

Cory put her hands on Dylan's back. "Shit. I'm sorry. I was scared. I woke up to a banging. You weren't there. I saw the cellar light on and was petrified."

"Some might call you paranoid."

"God, I can't believe I hit you with the bat. The light blinded me for a moment."

Dylan touched her back. Cory laid her hand on Dylan's back where she was rubbing, but Dylan pushed her hand aside. "It's a little tender, but no damage was done. Come on back to bed." They returned to the bedroom.

"What were you doing down there?"

Dylan got back into bed. She wrapped her arms around Cory, cuddling her close. "The trees kept banging against the window, and they woke me up. I was cold and remembered we hadn't put any wood in the furnace. I figured it would only take me a few minutes. You were sleeping like a log. I didn't think you'd miss me. Hey, you're shaking." Dylan stroked Cory's back reassuringly.

"I'm cold and a little shocked."

Dylan, angry at herself, banged her head on her pillow, which caused the pain in her back to throb more. "No. I was stupid. I shouldn't have left you. I knew how you reacted this morning. I'm sorry, honey. You tired?"

Cory shook her head. "Not really. The power nap we had earlier seems to have recharged my batteries."

Dylan pressed the nightglow on her watch. "It's three o'clock." She moved her hand under the covers and traced a pattern across Cory's stomach. "Would you like a massage to sooth your beating heart?"

"My heart is beating because of what your hand is doing. You're a vixen, Dylan Matthews, and I love every bit of you."

Cory rolled on top of Dylan and kissed her. The kiss turned passionate, and soon Dylan was helping Cory peel her shirt off.

Chapter
Twenty-Nine

CORY LIFTED HER suitcase into the bed of the truck. "I can't believe this is the end of the first week. Time really does fly by when you're having fun." She hugged Dylan. "I had a lovely week here. It felt truly decadent to not have to think about anything but enjoying myself. Have I told you how much I love you?"

"Yes, and I love you, too. Now, go pose in front of the house, and I'll take the picture."

"You have to be in the photo, too. You're looking particularly sexy this morning." Dylan's long hair was loose over her shoulders. Cory had taken delight in brushing the ebony locks after their shower and had enjoyed running her fingers through the soft, shiny hair.

"Okay, but you're going to have to set the photo up. I have no idea how to set it up automatically."

Cory took the camera out of Dylan's hands and placed it on the hood of the truck. She looked through the viewfinder. "Okay, make room for a small one." She pressed the timer button and ran to stand next to Dylan. Dylan placed her arm around Cory's waist. Cory rested her head on Dylan's shoulder. She let out a contented sigh just as the camera took the picture.

"Don't move. I want to make sure we're both in the photo." Cory checked the LCD screen and showed the picture to Dylan. "Thank you."

"What for?"

"For making this week wonderful. I don't want to go home."

"No swear words allowed."

"But I didn't swear," protested Cory.

"Yes, you did. You said 'home.' That word is banned until next Friday evening."

"Agreed. Are we ready to hit the road?"

"Yes, and I expect to see some studying going on while I drive to my place."

"Yes, boss." Cory looked at the New Hampshire house one last time. She hoped they'd return one day. The week had been so relaxing. The weather had been tolerable after the storm, and they had even managed to catch some sun one of the days while they'd boated around the lake.

"Earth to Cory." Dylan started the truck and pulled onto the road-way. "Where did you go off to? You had a dreamy look on your face."

"I was storing the view of this house and hoping I'd see it again one day. This week has made me realize that I could live over here, if I was with you."

Cory stared out the window watching the last images of the village roll by. "What are we doing when we get to your place?" Cory swal-lowed hard, as she felt her ears popping. They were making their way down the mountain road. "Am I going to meet Helen and Jo this vaca-tion?"

Dylan changed gears and put her hand in the basket of junk she kept in between the seats. She picked out a packet of Lifesavers. "Want one?" Dylan offered the candy to Cory.

"Thanks. You read my mind."

Dylan popped one in her mouth. "I told Helen we might meet up. I wasn't sure how tired we'd be. It's up to you—your choice—a night in with me or one out with the girls."

Cory pondered the choice. "I'd like to meet them, not that I don't want to spend time with you. I do. But I also want to put faces to names." She felt Dylan's hand on her knee.

"I understand. We're going to have plenty of time together this weekend. On Sunday, I thought we could rest at home. I do have to go to an early morning hockey practice. We don't usually practice on Eas-ter Sunday, but, we're so close to the playoffs that the team took a vote and decided to take advantage of the holiday ice time and get together. The team we're playing on Monday is leading the league, and we're only a point behind them."

"I could come and watch you practice."

"You could, but I thought you might want to study with no distrac-tions. Helen and Jo offered to help you out. Helen's taken the test. She might be able to give you some advice, and Jo is good at math. We could invite them over for an Easter dinner."

"Sure. I haven't thought about the test since we left the inn. Now I'm nervous as hell." Cory opened the study guide. "I'm going to read the comprehension passages to you. We might as well go through the torture together."

DYLAN DROVE INTO her driveway and let out an audible sigh of relief. She was glad to be home after a long four-hour drive. She was also happy that Sarah's truck was nowhere to be seen. She gently shook Cory awake. "Hey, we're here."

Cory rubbed her eyes. "Huh?"

"We're here. This is my house." Dylan stroked the blonde wisps of hair off Cory's face. She looked adorable. "Come on, sleepyhead."

"I slept most of the way. You should have woken me. I was supposed to study. I'm sorry. I make a really lousy passenger. I think my mother used to take me out in the car when I was a baby to get me to sleep. It still works like a charm. I'm usually away with the fairies after the first mile or two."

Dylan climbed down from the truck. "Don't worry about it. It wasn't like you didn't warn me. Those comprehension passages almost put me to sleep, too. Plus, we haven't been sleeping much. Someone seems to keep waking up in the night and then needs physical activity to get back to sleep."

"I never hear you complaining."

"And you never will. All joking aside, you've had a stressful few weeks. Your grandfather died, you split up with your husband, and you've started your busiest time at work—not to mention jet lag. I know I was beat when I arrived home after the week in England with you. Give yourself a break."

Cory trailed Dylan up the path with her suitcase and backpack. The house was beautiful. It was a ranch style with a wooden porch and deck area. She liked the color of the paintwork. The inside of the house was just as quaint. Cory left her suitcase near Dylan's bag inside the front door. Dylan took her on a tour of the house. The first room on the left of the front door was the office. To the right of the door was a small living room/dining area. At the far end of the room was a huge, open kitchen with a breakfast bar. The bathroom and laundry room was off to the side of the kitchen. Cory walked behind Dylan into another room. It was a more spacious living room, which lacked furniture. They walked across the room to the bedrooms. She peered into the first bedroom which was empty, except for a shelf of Disney DVDs. The last room was the master bedroom. It was very plain and contained a queen size bed, bureau, and laundry basket.

Dylan put her backpack on the bed. "What do you think?"

"It's beautiful. I feel so bad you have to sell it. Is there no way you can afford to buy Sarah out?"

Dylan shook her head. "No. She wants a specific amount, and it's more than I can come up with. Anyway, I have my heart set on you coming over here for a few years. So, if we go ahead and do the college thing, I need to cut my overhead costs. Sorry about the lack of furniture. Sarah took most of it."

Cory put her arms around Dylan. "We have a bed and a sofa. That's good enough for me and the activities I might decide we'll do during my stay here. I'm starving. Do you have any food in the fridge?"

Dylan led her back to the kitchen. "There's not much in here. I have some frozen burgers and buns. I could rustle up some French fries to go with them."

"I'll take whatever you have." Cory sat at the breakfast bar. She tapped her fingers on the counter top. "You mentioned the other day that Sarah was angry about me staying here."

"She was. I was half expecting her to be waiting for us in the drive-way."

"She wouldn't do anything stupid, would she?"

Dylan shrugged. She placed the French fries on a baking tray and put them in the oven. "I hope not. We can stay at a hotel if you'll feel safer."

"No. I'm okay. You lived with Sarah for years. You know her better than I do. She was probably just mad."

Dylan put the burgers on the indoor grill. "I'm not sure what's going on in Sarah's mind anymore. I was thinking of putting another security lock on the door. I can't change the locks because she still owns half the house, but I can put deadbolts on the inside of the doors. That way, if she comes around while I'm at work, you'll know she's here. You wouldn't have to let her in. If she gets pissy with me, I'll tell her I beefed up the security because of burglaries in the area."

"I'll keep my fingers crossed that she doesn't come over."

"Keep those positive thoughts. Let's eat lunch, and then I'll call Helen and make plans."

DYLAN HELD CORY'S hand as they walked along Plymouth harbor front. "Are you nervous?"

"Yeah. How can you tell?"

"Your hands are sweaty. What are you worried about?"

Cory looked over the ocean. Small waves bounced over the rocks, and boats swayed against their moorings. The wind swept her hair slightly, chilling her body. She moved closer to Dylan. "I'm scared they won't like me."

"It doesn't matter what my friends think of you. I love you, and that's all that matters. Plus, what's not to like? You're pretty, you're smart, you have an awesome body, and you're great in bed."

"Thanks for the compliments, but I sincerely hope your friends don't know that latter point. I just don't want them to think you were better off with Sarah."

Dylan pointed toward the seafood restaurant. "I doubt it. Helen can't stand Sarah, and I don't think Jo ever felt real friendship for her."

Dylan opened the door and Cory entered the restaurant. The aroma of freshly baked bread greeted her. She looked around. "Are they here?"

Dylan waved at Helen. "They're over there in that booth."

Cory walked behind Dylan. She smiled in greeting. On Dylan's insistence, she slid into the booth opposite Helen and Jo. Dylan sat beside her.

Jo leaned over the table. "Hi, I'm Jo. It's good to meet you Cory. Dylan's told us a lot about you."

"It's nice to put a face to the voice."

"And this is Helen," Dylan said.

"Hello, Cory. I'm excited to meet the woman who has Dylan whipped."

Jo slapped Helen playfully. "Behave." Jo spoke to Cory, "You'll have to excuse these two. On their own, they're fine. When they get together, it's like having two kids constantly trying to embarrass each other."

"How was your week in the mountains?" asked Helen.

"Brilliant," replied Cory.

"Awesome. Let's order the meals, and we'll tell you all about it," Dylan said.

The menus were handed around, and they ordered their food. After the waitress moved away, Dylan told Helen and Jo about their stay at the inn. Cory began to relax as the conversation settled on common ground.

When the meals were delivered, Cory ate and watched the interactions between Dylan and her friends. She enjoyed the relaxed camaraderie between Dylan and Helen. "Dylan said you have your test on Monday. How's the studying been going?" Jo asked.

"I'm feeling more confident. Dylan told me you're good at maths. I was hoping you'd consider going over some algebra symbols with me tomorrow. There are a few I keep mixing up and some problems I have no idea how to solve."

"Maths? How cute is that?" Helen said.

Jo smiled. "Would you like to go over it tomorrow morning while these two are at hockey practice? It'll be a good excuse not to have to hang around a cold rink."

"Thanks, Jo. I forgot to ask on the phone earlier. Do you two have any plans for Easter dinner?" Dylan asked.

"No," Helen replied. "My mom and dad are vacationing in Florida. We thought about going to Jo's parents, but my work schedule is crazy, with spring training sessions."

"That's settled then. Dinner at our house after practice and studying."

"GOD, IT CAN'T be morning already," Dylan said.

Cory rolled onto her side and pulled the cover over their heads, blocking out the early morning sun. "I'm afraid so, love."

Dylan groaned. "But I just fell asleep."

"And whose fault was that?" Cory asked as she felt hands roam over her naked stomach.

"Yours." Dylan nibbled on Cory's ear. "Good morning, and happy Easter."

"Umm...happy Easter to you, too. I like waking up like this." Cory turned in Dylan's arms and gave her a short, tender kiss. "I have a present for you." Cory crawled to the end of the bed and reached over into her suitcase. She lifted out some sweaters and pulled out a box that held a chocolate Easter egg gift set and a card. She placed the gift in front of Dylan. "Here you go. An English tradition. I hope it's still in one piece."

Dylan opened the box and giggled. "*A Buffy the Vampire Slayer* Easter egg and mouse pad. Oh, and look, it's got Willow on it."

"Even I know Willow really has your heart," Cory joked.

"No. She's been bumped to second place since you came along."

Cory fiddled with the edge of the sheet as she watched Dylan slip her finger under the flap of the envelope and pull the card out. Her heart began to beat faster when Dylan opened the card and saw the poem.

"You wrote me a poem?"

"Yes. I had a lot of time on the plane. I wanted you to know how much you mean to me. I've never let anyone read my poems before."

"I'm honored. Thank you." Dylan read the poem.

You Are

You are my sunshine in the day,
My moonlight in the night,
The light that guides my way.
When you're near, it shines so bright.

You are the harbour for my love,
The saviour of my soul;
The hand that fits my glove,
The half that makes me whole.

You are the flame of my desire,
The fire in my chest;
Our love will never tire
From the heart within my breast.

You are the reason why I wake,
The cause of my sweet dream,
You are the river that's my lake,
My forever winding stream.

You are my laughter when I'm happy;
You wipe the tears when I despair;
You are the part that is the best of me;
You are the reason why I care.

You are the answer to my question,
The port for my love ship;
Your soul is my reflection,
Your essence forever on my lips.

Cory touched an errant tear that escaped Dylan's attempt to wipe her eyes. Cory rubbed the tear between her fingers, marveling at the emotion her words had stirred in Dylan. "Do you like it?"

"It's beautiful. I'm going to frame it and save it to show our grandkids." Dylan jumped off the bed and went to the closet. She grabbed a decorative paper bag. "Here you go." Cory opened the bag. She took out a fluffy Easter bunny. "He's cute. Does he have a name?"

"No. I thought you might like to name him."

Cory cuddled the stuffed animal. She could smell Dylan's faint fragrance on him. "I'm going to call him C.K., as he smells like you." Cory looked back in the bag and picked out a box of Lindtz chocolates. "I've heard these are delicious. Thank you. We should take some photos for our relationship scrapbook. I want to chronicle every holiday and special event." She leaned over and kissed Dylan. "Our first Easter together."

Dylan stroked Cory's cheek. "The first of many, I hope. I'm sorry it's not very traditional. I'm not one for church anymore. I might go and see my father later tonight. You'd be welcome to come along if you want to. Whether I go or not depends how late Helen and Jo hang out here."

Cory placed the gifts farther down the bed and stretched out against the flannel sheets. "What time is practice?"

"Too soon for my liking. I have to get up. I'll bring you a cup of tea. No point us both being up." Dylan climbed off the bed and walked out of the room.

"Have you no shame? Cover yourself up, or you'll frighten the neighbors," shouted Cory after her.

"If all my neighbors have got to do this morning is look at me, then good luck to them."

Dylan returned a few minutes later with a steaming mug of tea. "Are you sure you're going to be okay here on your own? I can stay if you want me to." Dylan pulled her track pants out of the closet.

"No, you missed practice this week already. I'm surprised they let you play if you don't practice."

"Usually, they don't. I told the coach about your visit. He's not stupid. He needs me out there. We're close to the playoffs, and he's not going to piss off one of his better players. He knows I don't abuse the system, and if I need to miss practice, there's a good reason. I'm not sure how many will be there this morning. Like I said, we took a vote, but some players might go to church instead."

"I'll be fine. I have your mobile number if I need you, and Jo will be here soon. She said she was going to drop Helen at the rink and come right over. I'm looking forward to getting all the juicy dirt about you."

Dylan crawled up the bed. "Babe, there is no dirt. You know everything there is to know about me."

Cory kissed Dylan's head. "I know I do. I was just teasing you. Now, go and do your stuff. Jo and I will tackle studying and hopefully, cook dinner, too." Cory kissed Dylan one more time, and then slapped her ass. "I love you."

"I love you, too—heart and soul."

CORY HEARD THE truck leave the driveway. She had breakfast and decided to go for a run. After dressing in her running gear, Cory picked up the house key and walked out of the front door. The weather was warmer than she'd expected. She began at a slow jog. Dylan's neighbors had decorated their yards and walkways for the holiday. Tiny chalked images of bunny paws were drawn down one neighbor's driveway, little plastic eggs dangled from various trees, cut out bunnies adorned lawns, and pastel pictures hung off fences. She picked up speed as she turned onto the main road.

After fifteen minutes, she'd worked up quite a sweat and estimated that she'd run about a mile-and-a-half. She turned back. The trip back felt better. The wind blew coolly over her warm skin. As she turned into Dylan's street, she noticed a black SUV on Dylan's driveway. She'd seen Jo's car the previous evening when they had said goodbye at the restaurant, so she knew it wasn't hers. Cory ran past the house and noticed the patio door was open. A chill tingled down her spine. *Sarah.* She continued to run, cursing herself for forgetting her mobile phone and for being a coward.

Cory turned onto the main road for a second time. She hadn't gone more than a few yards when she heard a horn honking. She looked up and saw Jo waving at her. She waved back.

"You're an early bird."

Cory slowed down and waited for Jo to pull into the side road. "I needed to go for a run to wake myself up," Cory said. "Now I'm being a big chicken and staying clear of the house. I think Sarah's there."

"Are you sure?"

"Does she drive a black Jeep?"

Jo nodded. "Did she see you?"

"I'm not sure. Do you think I should have gone in there?"

Jo opened the passenger door. "Climb in."

"I'm all sweaty."

"That's no problem. There's a towel in the back. Helen's usually soaked after hockey practice, so the car's used to it. I think you were very wise to steer clear of Sarah. She's been a little unpredictable lately."

Cory took the sheet from the backseat and placed it on the passenger seat and got in. Jo put a hand on Cory's shoulder and pushed her down. She felt Jo lean over her.

"Sarah's car is coming toward us. Stay low. My car's pretty new, so she won't recognize it, but I don't want her to see me."

After Sarah's car passed by, Jo released Cory. "Sorry about that. I kind of panicked. Okay, let's go see what little-miss-pissed-off has done to the house. For her sake, I hope she didn't do anything stupid."

Nothing appeared to be out of place on the exterior of the house. Cory untied her laces, slipped the key off, and opened the front door. She peered inside. Jo went to check the office while Cory went to the bedroom. Cory met Jo in the living room. "That's weird. I expected a mess or something." Cory glanced around the room as she spoke.

"Maybe she came by to check on things. She may not have realized you two were back."

"I suppose so, except my suitcase and bags are in the bedroom. I'm just pleased I decided to go for a run. I was thinking of taking a shower. Wouldn't that have been a freaky first meeting?"

"Yeah. I'm glad she had the good sense to leave. Why don't you go take a shower, and I'll look through the study guide so that we can get started on that when you're done."

Cory showered, dressed, and met Jo at the breakfast bar. She smiled at Jo, who was reading the test guide at the breakfast bar.

"You look better."

"Yeah, I feel better. I do appreciate the help."

"No problem. If it means we get to see your cute face around town and Dylan smile like she did last night, then I'll help any way I can."

Cory blushed at the compliment. "Thanks. It means a lot to know people are rooting for us."

Chapter
Thirty

Helen followed Dylan out of the rink. "Bitch alert."

"What?"

"Sarah's waiting by your truck. I'll go and get a coffee. She's always worse when I'm around."

Dylan patted Helen on the back. "Thanks. I'll try to make it quick." Dylan paused momentarily before she walked toward Sarah.

"I went to the house this morning," Sarah said, as Dylan approached.

Fear clutched at Dylan's heart. "And?"

"I see you ignored my warnings and moved her in."

Dylan ran a hand through her wet hair and rolled her eyes. "Did you see Cory? If you've hurt her in any way, I'll..."

Sarah interrupted. "I didn't do anything. I wanted to. I saw her things all over our bedroom, and I wanted to tear them up. But I didn't. How could you sleep with her in our bed?"

"I didn't sleep with her in our bed. You took our bed. Unless I'm mistaken, you're sleeping with Michelle in it. Seems like a double standard to me."

"Touché."

"Cut the sarcasm and tell me what you did."

"I've already told you. I didn't do anything." Sarah shook her head. "She wasn't there."

"What do you mean, Cory wasn't there?"

"I figured she was with you."

Dylan flicked open her cell phone and dialed home. The answering machine picked up. "Cory, it's Dylan, if you're there pick up."

"Hello."

"You're okay?" Dylan sighed in relief.

"Yes. Why wouldn't I be?"

"Sarah's here with me now. She said she visited the house, but you weren't there. I panicked."

"I went for a run. I saw Sarah's car, and then Jo arrived. What does Sarah want?"

Dylan moved a few steps away and turned her back to Sarah. "I have no idea. I'm so relieved to hear you're okay. I'm going to talk to

Sarah. I want to make sure she doesn't pull this crap all week. Helen and I will be back soon. I love you."

"I love you, too. Be careful."

Dylan snapped the phone shut.

"See? I told you she was okay," Sarah said.

Dylan turned around. "Sarah, this can't go on. I'm beginning to hate the sight of you. I'd hoped we could stay friends and get past the bitterness. It's not like I broke your heart."

"But you did," Sarah whined. "I miss you so much."

Dylan shook her head and snorted. "You have a funny way of showing it. You're so quick to tell me how much I've hurt you. How I screwed you over. But in reality, you dumped me and crawled into Michelle's bed before we'd even talked about it."

"You went to fucking England."

"I went away to try and clear my head. I didn't talk to Cory about my feelings until you told me it was over. I'll admit I was attracted to her. I knew I liked her, but I also had a commitment to you. You broke that commitment first. So cut the crap."

Sarah wiped her eyes. "I can't move on. I want us to be together, but you really love her, don't you?"

Dylan nodded.

"You never cared for me like this, did you?"

Dylan shook her head again. "Honestly, no. Look, I don't know what to do to help you get past this. I really want to salvage a friendship with you, but all you seem to want to do is make my life miserable."

"I don't mean to."

"We can't move forward unless we say goodbye to our past."

"I guess so."

"It does mean letting go of everything, including the house. I really thought we'd have an offer by now. Will you think about lowering the price one more time? It'll sell quicker. Maybe then we can build some bridges and become friends."

"Do you think we can? I've done some stupid things these past few weeks. I talked to Michelle last night. She told me I had to decide whether I was going to pine over you or move on. Despite everything, I want to make sure you're happy."

"I am." Dylan put her hand on Sarah's shoulder. "If you're really serious about me being happy, please don't come over to the house this week."

"Okay. I do want us to stay friends. I never want to see the hate in your eyes like I did when I first saw you today. Can we meet up soon?"

"Sure. How about next week? We'll talk about the house more."

"Call me."

"I will." Dylan hugged Sarah briefly and watched her go to her vehicle.

"Wow. That looked very civil," said Helen, walking up behind Dylan.

"I thought you were making yourself scarce." Dylan slid behind the steering wheel of her truck.

"I watched from across the street. I wanted to make sure you were all right. How'd it go?" Helen climbed in and closed the door.

"Better than I expected."

"Do you trust her?"

Dylan watched Sarah maneuver her car out of the parking space and then followed her out of the lot. "I think so. She seemed sincere. I guess only time will tell."

AFTER A HOME cooked meal and an evening of games, Dylan and Cory bid Helen and Jo goodbye and settled back onto the couch to watch television. Cory's unusually quiet demeanor caught Dylan's attention. "You okay?"

"Yes."

"I don't believe you." Dylan tickled Cory's rib cage, increasing the intensity when she heard Cory's giggles. "What's wrong? Are you worried about the test? I thought the studying went well today."

"Quit tickling me. I'll piss my pants. Please. I'll tell you all my worries."

Dylan halted her fingers' movement. "What's on your mind?"

"I feel stupid saying it."

"I'd never think that." Dylan rubbed Cory's arm. "Come on, a problem shared is a problem halved, or something like that. It's a good thing I'm not taking the English test tomorrow. Please tell me."

"I'm still worried about Sarah."

"Why? I told you she was fine. We parted on good terms at the rink today."

"I know. I'm being silly. However, she's been saying one thing and then doing another for weeks. This morning it scared me that she can come and go in the house. If I hadn't been running this morning, I'd have been in the shower. I just don't want my first meeting with her to be on my own. What if she flips out again? Tomorrow, you'll be going to work, and I'll be here alone."

"Sarah doesn't know that. For all she knows I've taken the week off, but I see your point. I'm going to put those locks on the door like we talked about. I think I have some bolts down in the basement."

"You have a cellar?"

Seeing the alarm in her Cory's eyes, Dylan bent down and kissed her head. "It's only accessible from outside and only goes halfway under the house. There's no way someone can get into the house from there." Dylan left the room.

On her return, Dylan affixed the bolt locks on to both entrance doors. "This should make us feel more secure. You're right. I shouldn't trust Sarah until she shows me she can be trusted more." Dylan glanced at the clock. "It's too late to visit my father now. I'll go and give him a call. We should make it an early night. Tomorrow's going to be a busy day." Dylan kissed Cory gently on the mouth and went into the kitchen.

Chapter
Thirty-One

DYLAN PULLED INTO the driveway and honked the horn. Cory, dressed in cargo pants and a tight white top, flew out of the side door. A light blue shirt hung loosely from her frame, billowing against the wind as she ran. Dylan's heart skipped a beat at the sight.

"Hey, gorgeous, did you miss me?" Dylan greeted Cory with an upper body hug over the center console. "I'm sorry. I ran late, and the freakin' traffic didn't help. Have you got everything?"

Cory checked her pockets. "Yeah, I have my passport and the letter they sent. How long will it take us to get there?"

"Not long. Fifteen minutes at most. Did I tell you how hard it was to get out of bed this morning? I wanted to stay and cuddle."

"I missed waking up next to you. You should have woken me."

"I thought about it, trust me, but I didn't think it was fair for both of us to get up at four thirty. I wanted to make sure you got enough sleep. I'm so proud of you for taking this test."

"I wish there wasn't so much riding on it. I don't have a great test record."

"Just do your best and we'll take it from there."

"I'll try," Cory said, meekly.

TWENTY MINUTES LATER, Dylan and Cory walked through the doors of the testing center. Dylan released Cory's hand and nudged her in the direction of the receptionist.

"Hello. I'm here to sit for the GRE." Cory rested her hands on the edge of the counter to try to steady her shaking legs. Her head was swimming with facts, and her heart was pounding.

The receptionist smiled at Cory. "I'll need the confirmation letter and a photo ID."

Cory's stomach contracted. She ran out of the reception area and into the ladies' restroom. She leaned over the toilet, waiting for her stomach to stop rebelling. After a few dry heaves, Cory was able to stand and walk to the sink. She wet her face and glanced up as the door opened.

"Cory," Dylan said, "we don't have to do this. We can walk away now and look at other options. There must be other ways for us to be together."

Cory wiped her face with a paper towel. "I'll be okay. This usually happens. I should've warned you. At least this time, I wasn't in a car."

"Why a car?"

"On my fourth driving test, I threw up during the practical test."

"Ouch."

Cory held onto Dylan's arm and looked up at her. "I know there might be other choices, but this is the easiest, quickest, and most practical one. I have nothing to lose. Once my brain conveys that message to my body, I'll be ready to go back in." Cory headed for the door.

"The receptionist said to tell you to take your time. You really worried us both when you ran out."

Cory paused at the door. "I'm sorry. I'm ready now. I promise."

Dylan walked over to Cory and gave her a hug. "I hate seeing you this nervous."

"There could be worse things I could be doing." Cory kissed Dylan's lips briefly. "I love you."

"Love you, too. I'll be here waiting for you."

Cory held Dylan's hand until she reached the receptionist. She handed her ID and letter to the woman.

"Ready?" the receptionist asked.

Cory swallowed, took a deep breath, and followed the woman through the double doors.

DYLAN STARED AT the large clock in the testing hallway. It had been three hours since Cory had gone in. She picked up her romance novel, only to place it unread minutes later beside her, just like she had done several times in the previous three hours. She couldn't relax enough to let the words sink in. She picked up her iPod and played a couple of the games. Frustrated, she switched to listen to songs, but rather than calm her, the taunting words irritated her. Her stomach rumbled, but she didn't want to leave the area in case Cory appeared. She began pacing again. It was the only action that she was able to accomplish.

Ten minutes later, the doors opened and a grim-faced Cory walked toward her. Dylan tried to smile encouragingly, but her heart sank. Helen had told them that the results would be posted on the computer screen at the end of the test. Dylan opened her arms and enveloped Cory in the biggest bear hug she could muster.

"I tried. I really tried," Cory whispered into Dylan's shoulder.

"It's okay. We'll work something out. I love you, and that's all that matters." Dylan squeezed Cory and made circles with her hands on Cory's back.

"It was hard. They gave me two maths tests. Can you believe it?"

Dylan pushed Cory slightly away and saw tears beginning to collect around the rims of her eyes. "Those bastards gave my girl two math tests," she joked.

Cory nodded and then rested her head back on Dylan's shoulder.

"Why did you get two math tests?"

"The proctor said that the test analysts throw in an extra test to rate performance on new subject areas. She said there's no way of knowing which test subject will be doubled or which one was the trial one. Of course, with my luck I didn't get two analytical sections. The analytical section was first, which relaxed me. I got six hundred points on that one. It's a pity they don't count that test."

"That was a good score. Let's get out of here. You must need some fresh air."

"Yes. I've got a killer headache. Anyway, the analytical section was followed by the first maths section, then the English, and last was another maths test. Thank God for National Curriculum Key Stage 2 percentages and data handling."

"How come?"

"A lot of the maths sections focused on mean, mode, median, and working out percentages. I teach my students those skills."

"What score did you get for the math test?" Dylan opened the door that lead onto the college courtyard.

"I got five hundred points on the math."

"That's good. Better than you did in the practice tests."

"I was surprised, as I didn't understand a lot of the algebra questions."

"How was the English section?"

"A bitch. I struggled on the vocabulary. I guessed a lot of them. However, the comprehensions were a little easier. I got four hundred and seventy on that test." Cory looked at Dylan.

Dylan leaped away from Cory like she had been electrocuted. "You freakin' did it! The passing score is only nine hundred. Fucking awesome!" Dylan jumped up and down waving her arms in excitement. She stopped bouncing when she saw Cory beaming from ear-to-ear.

"Gotcha. I know it was mean, and I shouldn't have let you think I failed, but after three hours, I needed some light relief." Cory stretched her back muscles and flexed her fingers. "I don't think I've concentrated so hard in my life."

"I should be mad as hell at you," Dylan said, pulling Cory into her arms. She lifted her into the air. "I'm so proud of you. You did it, babe. You fucking did it."

Cory tapped Dylan's nose. "Now, now, watch that language."

"I'm sorry, but there aren't any other words to describe how I feel." Tears brimmed in Dylan's eyes.

"Put me down. I need to stretch my legs. I hate to dampen the moment, but we still have the interview and application. I don't mean to rain on your parade, but I want to keep things in perspective."

Dylan wiped her tears away using a sleeve. "I know. I know. Still, it's good news." She checked her watch. "We have to move it. I'm supposed to be on the ice in an hour." She pulled Cory into a deep kiss. "You did it, babe. You've got the brains, and I'm about to show you my brawn. What a pair."

THE ICE ARENA was sparsely populated with spectators. Cory sat in the bleachers across from Dylan's team. She smiled at the woman who sat beside her and looked back at the ice as the teams warmed up. Dylan was by far the tallest player. "I've never been to an ice hockey game before. Are you a regular?" she asked the woman beside her.

"I've been a few times."

"Good. I was hoping you'd give me some pointers to the rules."

"I can try. You're not from America, are you?"

"That obvious, huh?"

"The accent kind of gives you away. It's very cute. Do you know someone on the team?"

Cory flushed a little. "Yeah. My...er...my girlfriend plays defense on the red and white team. She wears number thirteen." Cory pointed Dylan out.

"The red and white team is the Cardinals. Isn't her name Ryan or something like that?"

"Dylan," Cory informed her. "Do you know her?"

"I've heard of her."

"Really? That sounds intriguing." Cory didn't take her eyes from Dylan's form as she chatted.

"I know she's a strong player. I've also seen her at the Twist and Turn a few times, but you're not the girl I've seen her with."

"No. Dylan was involved with someone, but they split up recently." Cory felt uncomfortable discussing Dylan's relationships with a stranger. She focused on Dylan as she defended the goal area. Dylan seemed more intent on looking in her direction than following the puck. Cory saw the puck leave the blade of an offense player and shoot past Dylan, through the goalie's legs, and into the goal. Cory observed Dylan's anger at the goal, as she banged her stick on the ice and skated to her defense partner, Helen.

"I'm probably being way too nosy, but how long have you and Dylan been together?"

"Not long — a few weeks."

"Oh. You live in the States?"

Cory shook her head. "No. I'm just here for a visit."

"Really. Do you mind me asking how you two met?"

"Online. She came to visit me a few months ago, and we got on well." The buzzer blared to indicate the end of the period and Cory looked as Dylan gesticulated in her direction. She waved back and held her thumbs up. "I have no idea what she's trying to say with her mask on." She watched as Dylan skated to the bench and had what appeared to be an animated discussion with Helen.

THE SECOND PERIOD ended with the teams tied. Dylan sucked a mouthful of water from her bottle.

"Dylan, you have to calm down. You need to focus on the game." Helen wiped her brow.

"How the fuck can I concentrate when Sarah is up there talking to Cory?" Dylan turned her head in Cory's direction. *She's laughing for God's sake. She looks happy. Concentrate on your job and help your team. Cory's a big girl. She'll move away if Sarah gets nasty.*

"You can't do anything about it. Sarah promised she wouldn't mess with Cory. She's in a public place. Now, focus on the game. We need you. We can make up one goal, but not two. Don't blow our chances of getting to the playoffs. That last goal was your fault. You blocked Bernie's view. You're not paying attention to the game or to your position on the ice. Your head is constantly turned toward the stands. We need our best defender out there. Please." Helen flipped her mask down and skated to her starting position on the ice. Dylan followed suit.

THE CLOCK COUNTED down the last minute of ice time. Cory watched as Dylan skated with the puck from behind her own goal and down the ice. Dylan's stick lifted and connected with the puck in a blazing slap shot on net. Cory jumped up, cheering loudly. "Way to go, Matthews." She settled back into her seat.

"I have to go. It's been nice meeting you. It's always good when the team you're rooting for wins." The woman held her hand out to Cory.

Cory shook it firmly. "Thanks for explaining the game to me. Have a good evening." She turned her attention to Dylan's celebrations. Cory was relieved when the final buzzer sounded and the Cardinals skated off the ice the winners. She walked down to stand near the door to the entrance hall and waited for the players to come out from the locker room. She didn't have to wait long for Dylan.

"You okay?" Dylan asked, and then kissed Cory on the lips.

"Whoa. Now that's a greeting and a half." Cory pushed Dylan gently away from her. "What's wrong? You seem agitated. Your team won." She watched as Dylan's eyes surveyed the exit and the stands. "What's your problem?"

"Sarah." Dylan sighed.

"Is she here?" Cory turned her attention to the few spectators hanging around the edge of the ice. "Which one is she?"

"What do you mean, which one is she? You were sitting next to her.

What did she say to you?"

"Holy shit! That was Sarah? No way. She was so nice to me."

"Let's get out of here in case she's hanging around."

Cory held the doors open for Dylan and her large hockey bag. They walked out into the parking lot.

"I can't believe she came to the game. She has her nerve. I asked her not to come over."

"You asked her not to come to the house. You never mentioned the rink. It's all fitting together now. She did ask about our relationship."

"She did. What did you say?"

"Not much. She asked how we met and the basics. I wasn't about to tell a complete stranger our story, but it seemed rude not to answer the questions. The conversation kind of flowed the more I got into the game. Of course, now I know why you were so distracted at times."

Dylan opened the door of the truck for Cory. "Yeah. I was so worried about you. Helen gave me a good talking to. She pointed out that unless I left the ice and went to you, there was nothing else I could do. I felt helpless."

"Sarah left in good spirits and shook my hand. Maybe she got the answers she was looking for. Dylan, let it go. Hopefully, we won't have to deal with her again. I'm more pissed that I'll miss the championship game. I could get into hockey."

"Fingers crossed for Wednesday's interview. If that goes well, you'll be over in time to watch summer hockey."

Chapter
Thirty-Two

DYLAN SAT ON the sofa. She removed her shoes and rubbed her aching feet. "I bet you're glad that's over. I know I am."

"For sure. I was expecting a more in depth interview, like I had for my undergraduate degree, but it felt more like a chat. I was so pleased the Dean allowed you to come in with me."

"Me, too. Now you have some huge decisions to make."

Cory sat next to Dylan. "Dean Plinter definitely made it sound like the paperwork would be a formality."

"I know. I was really excited when he said you could participate in the non-certification teacher's route. What are your thoughts?"

"Ask me an easy one." Cory looked at Dylan. "I've enjoyed my time over here. I think I'm going to talk to my boss about taking an unpaid sabbatical from work. A few years back, a colleague took a year off to teach in another country. She then returned and used what she had learned to develop some of the social studies curriculum. With new disorders and syndromes being discovered here, America leads the way in knowledge of special needs students. I'm sure I can take time off to develop my skills in this area. At the end of the day, I'd have a job to return to when I complete my degree."

"Are you sure about this? You might want to take some time to think about it. It's a big step. I know when I spent time in Germany, I missed my mother so much, it hurt. Looking back, if I'd known my mother had so few years left on this earth, I'd have stayed here. I don't want you to have any regrets." Dylan put her arm around Cory's shoulder. "I'm a hundred percent behind any decision you make."

"I've thought about this for so many weeks. We all go through life thinking we've got an eternity. Nobody knows for sure how long their life is going to be. If I constantly worry about how long people are going to be around, I'll never do anything. My hero died, and I loved him so much. I dreaded Granddad dying, but for some reason, you came along just when I needed you. You filled the gap he left. I want to be with you. If I died tomorrow, I'd go happy."

"Well, I wouldn't be. I want you around for a very long time." Dylan kissed Cory's head, touching the fine, blonde hair lightly. "What about your parents? I've met your family, Cory. They adore you."

"They'll survive. I'm going to need time away. Mum is never going to come to terms with Sam and me splitting up. If I stay in England, she'll meddle. If you come over to be with me, she'll interfere. She'll never give us the time we need to build a relationship, and I don't think she'll accept our love."

"Do you think you'll ever tell them about me?"

"I hope so."

"I understand. I didn't say anything to my family until my mother asked me face-to-face. Take as long as you need, and when you're ready, I know you'll do the right thing."

"I hope so. Anyway, Mum and Dad have Mike and Kerry to look after them. For once in my life, I'm going to be selfish. I've done everything to please them—I even got married, and look where that got me. I have to please me. We also need time together without my family butting in. I know we get on great, but all relationships take work to iron out the kinks. Visiting on holidays is different from living together. I want that time with you."

"I want it with you, too."

"Ultimately, if I can't take a sabbatical and I have to give up my job, I know there will be plenty of other teaching jobs in England. There's a shortage of teachers. We're looking at me taking two years away from home."

Dylan relaxed back into the sofa, pulling Cory with her. "It's a huge step."

"This feels right, D. I feel so at peace. There's no test or interview to worry about. When I weigh up the options, it's an easy choice. One of us has to make a sacrifice. We want to be together, and this route is a win-win situation for me."

Dylan planted tiny kisses all over Cory's head. "I love the fact that you tell me how you feel. Sarah and I had lousy communication when it came to feelings and making decisions."

"I hear you. I'll miss Holly and the cats loads," Cory admitted. "Dylan, I want to be with you. I don't know how I'm going to get through the next few months without you around. I don't want to go home."

Dylan hugged Cory as hard as she could. "I don't want you to go. Just think, though, the next count down will be our last, hopefully. Dean Plinter said you could register for September's classes if you get the paperwork to him by the end of next week."

"I don't think I'll have too much of a problem doing that. I do need to find out how to get a transcript from my college. There must be an equivalent piece of paper."

"Good. Are you okay with going out with Helen and Jo tomorrow without me?"

"Yes. It beats hanging around here on my own. I miss you so much in the daytime. I wish you could come along."

"I'd love to be able to show you Provincetown and some of Cape Cod, but I have a meeting I can't get out of. You'll have a blast."

CORY SAT IN the back of the Highlander and enjoyed the scenery while listening to Helen and Jo tell about the history of the various towns they passed on the highway.

"It's going to take us a couple of hours to get to Provincetown. The views of the Cape Cod Canal from the bridge are awesome." As they approached a line of cars, Helen spoke again. "To help pass the time, we can see if we can find license plates from states other than Massachusetts."

"Is this what the traffic is like all the way down to Provincetown?" Cory asked.

"No. This is the back up from the rotary. Once we get around it, we'll be all set," Helen replied. She looked down at Jo's hand on her thigh.

"Are you okay? You keep holding your stomach. Do you want me to drive?" Jo asked.

"My stomach doesn't feel too good. I could do with a stop at the outlet mall so I can hit the can."

The view from the huge Sagamore Bridge that separated the Cape from mainland Massachusetts was breathtaking. Helen pulled into the mall parking lot. Cory took out her camera to take some shots of the bridge.

HELEN CAME OUT of the restroom and was pleased to see Jo following Cory into one of the stores. She took her cell phone off her belt and dialed Dylan's number. "How'd the job interview go?" Helen kept her eyes on the door of the store.

"It went awesome. They offered me the supervisor's job right then and there. I am so psyched."

"Congratulations. You must be relieved."

"I am. How's Cory?"

"She's good. Jo's doing some shopping therapy with her. I feigned an upset stomach, so they think I'm in the bathroom. When do you start the new job?"

"We're going to do some transitional training. I'll gradually take over supervising all the technicians."

"Did you get the rest of the week off?"

"Yeah. I explained about Cory staying, and he said I was going to have to work double shifts next week anyway to get to know the B shift technicians, so he gave me the days off now to make up for the overtime I'll be putting in then."

"Even better news, or our plan would have fallen flat on its face.

Where are you?" Helen maintained her vigilance on the mall corner.

"I'm at the house. I need to grab a few supplies, pack an overnight bag, and then I'll be on my way. I booked two hotel rooms with king beds earlier. They're going to be so surprised. Does Jo know?"

"No. I packed our gear in a black bag and put it in my hockey bag. There's Jo and Cory. I have to go. Call my cell when you hit P-Town. I'll let you know where we park. Drive carefully. It's a little busy on the roads." Helen hung up and joined Jo and Cory as they exited the store.

HELEN DROVE DOWN Commercial Street, Provincetown's main street. Cory watched the people milling around. It struck her as similar to a small fishing village she'd often visited in Cornwall. She saw many rainbow flags and same sex couples holding hands. "Is this the Key West of Massachusetts?"

Jo turned around to face her and grinned. "It's a good comparison. It's a very open and friendly place. This is nothing compared to the crowds that are here in the summer." She turned her attention back to Helen. "Babe, I told you we'd never find a parking spot on this street."

"Don't give me the I-told-you-so speech. It never hurts to try. We'll go down Bradford Street."

They parked in a large parking lot, a short walk away from the main shopping strip. Cory zipped her coat. The wind whipping off the ocean made the air feel ten degrees colder than it actually was. They meandered along the small streets, peering into quaint shop windows. She watched Helen and Jo as they walked hand-in-hand. She missed Dylan.

They ate in a little café. Helen checked her watch.

Jo nudged Helen. "You're acting weird. All morning you've been checking your phone or your watch. Do you have somewhere to be?"

"No."

"We're supposed to be enjoying ourselves. How's your tummy feeling?"

"Better. I'm sorry. I didn't realize I'd been checking my phone. I'm expecting a message from work about a meeting I couldn't make today. I promise I'll focus on you more."

"Can we go back to the clothes shop we passed on the way here? I saw a long-sleeve shirt that will look great on Dylan. I'd like your opinion," Cory said.

"Sure," Helen and Jo replied.

They returned to the store, and Cory picked up a blue shirt with rainbow colored cats walking over the chest. As they left the shop, Helen's phone buzzed. "What's up?" she said as she held it to her ear.

"I'm here. I dropped the truck off at the hotel. Where are you?" Dylan asked.

"I'm enjoying my day off. Jo and I are showing a friend the sights of

P-Town. We're just walking up Commercial Street. We're about to get the finest saltwater taffy in town. Thanks for letting me know about the meeting."

"Gotcha. You're sneaky when you have to be. I'll see you in five minutes. Take your time choosing the taffy."

"Have a good one." Helen looked at Jo and Cory. "The meeting went well. No problems. Cory, this store has the best taffy. You should buy some to take back to England."

Cory browsed the vast display of taffy flavors. She took a step to the side when she felt another customer enter her personal space.

Dylan moved closer to Cory. "Can I be of service to you, ma'am?"

Cory recognized the accent and the distinct scent she associated with Dylan. She spun around. "Dylan? How? When?"

Dylan hugged Cory and placed a kiss on Cory's open mouth. "Surprise? A nice one, I hope."

"The best. How'd you know where we were?" Cory moved out of Dylan's hug and glanced over at Helen and Jo. "Did you know about this?"

"I had no idea," Jo replied.

"I'm guilty of helping her out," Helen said.

"You had this planned all along, you little sneak, didn't you?" Cory nudged Dylan. "You and your little side kick. How'd you get more time off work?" She took a few moments to snap the image of Dylan to her memory. She was looking very alluring in her dark blue hip-hugging Levis that seemed to go on forever. They made her legs look long and lean. She had a white t-shirt, and a black leather jacket to match the black leather boots. "I know you had this planned because you didn't wear that to work this morning. You look awesome."

"Thanks. You don't look so bad yourself. Work wasn't a problem. I'll tell you later." Dylan held Cory's hand and walked over to Jo and Helen. She kissed Jo on the cheek and slapped Helen on the back. "You did good."

"Anything for you, buddy."

The afternoon passed more pleasurably for Cory with Dylan around. They strolled up and down Commercial Street, and Cory purchased gifts for her family and friends. As evening drew in, tired feet led them back to Jo's car.

Cory glanced back toward the main street. "It's really pretty here, D. I wish we had more time to see what it's like at night."

Dylan glanced at Helen and Jo, and then back to Cory. "Good, because I happen to have two room keys in my pocket."

"No way," Cory said.

Helen smiled broadly. "Jo, you're always teasing me that I can't keep a secret. Today, I think I showed you I can. Dylan and I planned this Sunday. We'd like to invite you two ladies to wine, dine, and spend the night with us here in Provincetown."

"Are you being serious?" Cory asked, turning to look into deep, blue eyes.

Dylan held a key out to Cory. "Yes. I didn't want to be away from you another minute. I wanted to celebrate the GRE success and my new job."

"Your new job? I'm confused," Cory said. "You're just full of surprises today."

"I'll tell you more about the job when we get to the room." She gave Helen and Jo their key. "We're staying at the Sailor's Inn. I dropped our bags off earlier. It's around the corner. Why don't we go and freshen up and then meet up for dinner?"

The inn was a small, family run hotel. Jo and Helen carried their bag up to their room. Dylan and Cory followed and continued down the narrow hallway to their own room.

"I can't believe you're here with me," Cory said, as she looked around the room. "This is a dream come true. I was so miserable this morning."

"Really? I thought you had a good time."

"I did, but I kept seeing couples holding hands and kissing. I was jealous. It made me miss you more." She opened her overnight bag. "You did a good job packing my bag. I like your choice of clothing." She pulled out a pair of black jeans and a tight fitting gray top. "Want to join me in the shower?"

"Sure. I want to show you how much I missed you this morning, too."

AN HOUR LATER, Dylan and Cory were walking hand-in-hand down Commercial Street. "Where are we going?"

"It's a surprise," Dylan said.

"But I thought we were meeting Jo and Helen for dinner."

"We are, but I want to do something first. They were enjoying their own private time together, if you catch my drift."

"I understand. Where did you say we were going?"

"You'll find out in a minute. Humor me, please."

They stopped outside a jewelry store. "Cory, I keep trying to live each day as it comes, but I get scared when I think about Saturday. I don't want to spend months away from you. I was thinking that we could each get one of our ears pierced. It'll be like a commitment to each other. We'll have the same ear done."

"I like that idea."

"We'll have to keep new earrings in and turn them three or four times a day. Every day when we touch the earring, we'll think of each other — not that I need anything to make me remember you. This will be our special time when we think of what we have to do to be together."

"It sounds romantic, D. It's not like I can wear a ring on my finger without getting asked questions. However, I'm a big girl's blouse when it comes to needles."

"A big girl's what?" Dylan laughed. "You definitely have some crazy sayings."

"It means I'm a wimp." Cory squeezed Dylan's hand. "But for you, babe, I'll do it."

"You sure?"

"Yep. I think it's a great idea. How about we have one done now, and then the other ear done when we return here together this summer?" Cory stood tall and kissed Dylan on the cheek. "Promise you'll hold my hand when they poke my ear."

"I promise."

Cory walked out of the store touching the new star-shaped stud in her right ear. Her ear was sore. She looked at Dylan's matching earring. "That didn't hurt half as much as I expected."

"No. He did a good job. We still have some time before we have to meet Helen and Jo. We could catch the sunset over the ocean."

The sea breeze caused Cory to shiver. Gallantly, Dylan wrapped her leather jacket across Cory's shoulder. "Thanks, babe."

"You're welcome."

"I mean for everything...for last week, for your support, and for the surprise today. It's been wonderful. I feel like I'm starring in the movies. You're showing me that dreams really can come true."

Cory stood in front of Dylan. She pulled Dylan's arms around her torso and gazed out over the ocean. She felt Dylan rest her chin on her shoulder and turned her own to kiss Dylan's cheek.

"I've decided that everything comes down to fate. Things definitely happen for a reason. Look at us, the way we met, the feelings we have for each other, the college acceptance, and my promotion, for instance. All our plans are coming together. I think it's the fates way of telling us we're meant to be together."

Cory sighed. "I hope you're right. I never want this feeling to end." She fiddled with the middle finger of her right hand. "I have a favor to ask." Cory lifted Dylan's left hand up. She slipped a small gold sovereign ring on Dylan's ring finger, "I know we just got our ears pierced, but I want to give you this. This ring was my graduation present off my granddad. It's the most precious thing I own, as it reminds me of how proud he was when I got my degree. I want you to wear it."

"No, Cory, I can't—it's yours. It means so much to you."

Cory placed her fingers to Dylan's lips, preventing Dylan from saying more. "That's exactly why I want you to look after it. It is my ring, and I'm going to come back for it. I know you'll treasure it. The next few months are going to be agony for both of us. I'm going to be counting down the months, waiting for the college to formally offer me a place, and tying up loose ends. You have to sell and pack up the house, begin a new job, and find us somewhere to live. It's at these low times that I want you to look at the ring and remember my commitment to you."

"I don't know what to say." Dylan touched the sovereign part of the ring.

"Say you'll look after it. It's the only jewelry my granddad gave me. I will be back to collect it...hopefully, very soon...to replace it one day with a ring of my own for you. Do you understand?"

Dylan nodded. "No one's ever trusted me so much or been prepared to give up everything for me. I know it's not going to be easy. There are still a few more obstacles for us to get over, but together, we can do it. We'll be together."

"Always and forever," whispered Cory. She closed her eyes and felt the arms around her tighten. The images from her dreams returned. They were the same arms, the same feelings. Her warrior was there, real and warm in her arms, and she knew they'd never be apart again.

THE END

ALSO BY J. Y. MORGAN
published by
Yellow Rose Books

Learning to Trust

Jace Xanthos, the director of a college Achievement Center has a new graduate assistant, Taryn Murphy. Both women cannot avoid spending time with each other, as they are part of an extended family. Both have their secrets and reasons not to trust, but when they find themselves opening up to each other, they realize their problems are very similar. Can a friendship develop between them or will their pasts haunt them forever?

ISBN 978-1-932300-59-8

FORTHCOMING TITLES
published by Yellow Rose Books

One Promise
by Lynne Norris

Theresa Parker, a carpenter, and her son Brian are struggling to find happiness and peace in their lives after Theresa's brother and sister-in-law are killed in a tragic accident then shortly thereafter, Theresa's partner ends their 5-year relationship.

Theresa contracts to build a house for Brian's first grade teacher, Madeline Geddes, who has moved to New Jersey to reclaim her life after breaking up with her partner. Theresa falls hard for Madeline but feels betrayed and hurt when Madelines ex-girlfriend arrives in town. Madeline must try to regain Theresa's trust. Can a child's simple understanding of love and friendship be what they need to bring them back together?

One Promise is a story of the heartache we suffer with life's painful twists and turns, the frailities of being human and the unparalleled joy that comes with letting love into our lives.

Available November 2007

The Heart's Strength
by Anna Furtado

In Book Two of the Briarcrest Chronicles Lydia and Catheine have become the caretakers of Briarcrest, and when a letter arrives from Catherine's old friend and former assistant, Sarah Pritchard, Catherine sets out on a journey that is both dangerous and embroiled in conflict.

When Catherine encounters an old friend in Willowglen, she forges a friendship with his daughter, Fiona, a tall, blue-eyed, raven-haired beauty. Fiona becomes an important ally when two churchmen from Spain set the town in turmoil claiming the authority of the Inquisition — with young Cate Pritchard at the center.

From their first meeting, Cate and Fiona are drawn to one another; however, Fiona refuses to act on her feelings out of loyalty and the oath she has given to Catherine. Cate, for her part, is uncertain about what to do with the new feelings she experiences for Fiona. And, one of the priest's has a deep, dark secret and an ulterior motive.

Finally, Lydia's arrival in Willowglen brings everything to a head and the women of Briarcrest, the Pritchards, and Fiona find themselves at the center of a terrible struggle — and each must dig deeply to find strength of heart amid the battle against the injustices they encounter. But will they all survive the ordeal?

Available November 2007

Family Values
by Vicki Stevenson

Devastated by the collapse of her long-term relationship, Alice Cruz decides to begin life anew. She moves to a small town, rents an apartment, and establishes a career in real estate. But when she tries to liquidate some of her investments for a down payment on a house, she discovers that she has been victimized by a con artist.

Local resident Tyler Sorensen has a track record of countless affairs without any emotional involvement. Known for her sexy good looks, easygoing kindness, and unique approach to problems, Tyler is asked by a mutual friend to figure out how Alice can recover her money.

While Tyler's elaborate plan progresses and members of her LGBT family work toward the solution, they discover that the con game involves more people and far higher stakes than they had imagined. As the family encounters unexpected obstacles, Tyler and Alice struggle with a growing emotional connection deeper than either woman has ever experienced.

ISBN 978-1-932300-89-5

Butch Girls Can Fix Anything
by Paula Offutt

Kelly Walker is known around town as the Fix-it Lady who can repair just about anything. That's true, except for the hole in her life left by the death of her lover, Anna. Her fix-it business provides the perfect hideout as she resolves other people's problems instead of focusing on her own shattered life.

Grace Owens, single mother, is determined to stand on her own two feet and make a fresh start for herself and her nine-year-old daughter, Lucy. Lucy has a goal of her own: she wants to master her math homework, and that is a hard task with a mother who doesn't understand division.

The three meet under a leaky kitchen ceiling. What each has to give, the others need. They must learn when to take risks and when to trust each other. Together, can they find the tools that will allow them to fix what most needs to be rebuilt?

ISBN 978-1-932300-74-1

OTHER YELLOW ROSE PUBLICATIONS

About the Author

J Y Morgan currently resides in beautiful New England with her partner and a growing menagerie of animals. She enjoys reading lesbian fiction, watching movies, pottering around in the garden, tinkering with computers, and generally hanging out with friends, both online and in real life.

VISIT US ONLINE AT

www.regalcrest.biz

At the Regal Crest Website You'll Find

- The latest news about forthcoming titles and new releases

- Our complete backlist of romance, mystery, thriller and adventure titles

- Information about your favorite authors

- Current bestsellers

Regal Crest titles are available from all progressive booksellers and online at StarCrossed Productions, (www.scp-inc.biz) and also at www.amazon.com, www.bamm.com, www.barnesandnoble.com, and many others.

Printed in the United States
85855LV00004B/35/A